ng but
orld.

Sally Spedding

Cold Remains

Sparkling Books

British Library Cataloguing in Publication Data. A catalogue record for this book is available from the British Library.

Cover image © istockphoto.com/ bradleym/ O_Slad

2.1

BIC code: FF
ISBN: 978-1-907230-28-8

Edited by Anna Alessi.

Printed in the United Kingdom by Short Run Press

For more information visit *www.sparklingbooks.com*

PRAISE FOR SALLY SPEDDING

"Her writing is so distinctly unique it will truly chill you to the bone."

Sally Meseg for *Dreamcatcher*

"Sally Spedding is a font of creepy stories, the kind of tales which wheedle their way back into your mind, hours maybe days and weeks later…"

Western Mail

"Spedding knows that before delivering the set-pieces it's essential to carefully build suspense through both unsettling incident and sense of locale – at both, she's unquestionably got what it takes."

Barry Forshaw, *Crime Time*

"Sally Spedding… has been credited with being a latter day Du Maurier…"

Crime Squad

"Sally Spedding is the mistress of her craft."

Welsh Books Council

SALLY SPEDDING was born in Wales and studied sculpture at Manchester and at St. Martin's, London. Having won an international short story competition, she began writing seriously and her work has won many awards including the H.E. Bates Short Story Prize and the Anne Tibble Award for Poetry. She is the author of five acclaimed crime mystery novels and a short story collection. Other short stories have regularly appeared in the Crime Writers Association anthologies. She is a full member of the CWA and Literature Wales for services to literature in Wales, and adjudicates national writing competitions. She finds both Wales and France complex and fascinating countries – full of unfinished business – and has a bolt-hole in the Pyrenees where most of her writing and dreaming is done.

www.sallyspedding.com

ALSO BY SALLY SPEDDING

Wringland
Cloven
A Night With No Stars
Prey Silence
Come and Be Killed
Strangers Waiting

To Hookers' Pen writers for their unfailing support;
and to Anna Alessi for lightening the darkness.

I am indebted to Emily Hinshelwood, a wonderful poet, for her time and expertise on technical matters. To the unique and inspiring village of Rhandirmwyn and to those who pointed the way.

Each heart has its graveyard, each household its dead,
And knells ring around us wherever we tread...

MARY T. LATHRAP, *Unfinished Lines*

PROLOGUE

Tuesday 24th December 1946 – 6.45 p.m.

Christmas Eve in Nantybai, Carmarthenshire, where the small knot of villagers who'd gathered to chat outside St. Barnabas' Church doors, hurry in to escape the fresh snowfall blowing westward from the Cambrian hills. The candlelight from within casts each crisp white crust on the tilting gravestones in an eerie light, and soon the organ begins its melancholy introduction – a tune that makes the young woman shiver even beneath her heavy winter clothes. For she knows all too well whose clever fingers play the keys, whose feet pump the pedals, yet she must be patient and wait for her lover to finish the last carol so they can escape together for a better life. A true and godly family life.

As she creeps from her shelter under the three Scots pines, and into the teeth of the weather, she knows in her heart she'll never again set eyes on this welcoming vestry or hear those same voices beyond it now raised in celebration of the Saviour's birth.

The snow lies deeper, less slippery by the track's side, and it's here she chooses to place her booted steps until she reaches the lead miners' cottages cwtched against the land behind. Her childhood haunt, with its nervous sheep, its stream hurtling towards the headwaters of the River Towy.

Mrs Jones, the church cleaner, is at home, she can tell. But no one else. For one brief moment, she's tempted to knock on her door and confess the daring plan to leave. But no. This miserable, now childless widow has too much of a gossip's tongue. And a gossip's tongue spells danger.

But danger's already here with the snap of a twig. Hot breath on her neck. All at once, without warning, two freezing, gloved hands are gripping her throat.

"You first, cariad, which, given your situation, is only fair..."

Her situation is not her fault.

She recognises the big man's voice, his unique smell, before a pungent whiff of gas makes her catch her breath, draw in too much of it as a cloth is pressed over her face. Now her head's spinning; her sturdy boots giving way on the sliding ice, but she must fight back. Not just for herself, for that new life kicking vigorously beneath her coat. "The Lord Jesus help me," she begs. "I adored you. Was trying to protect you, can't you see?"

But her words slide away like rain off the hillsides, and no-one is listening.

1

1.

Tuesday 31st March 2009 – 3.30 p.m.

Jason Robbins paused outside the doctor's surgery in Hounslow's Pinetree Road just long enough for a passing bus to spray his clean clothes with oily filth from the gutter. That was it. Time to move. He pushed the intercom button and, having given his name and appointment time to whoever's crackly voice had answered, was admitted into an empty, ochre-coloured waiting room where the smells of those who'd come and gone still hung in the stale air. Another pause, as he surveyed the dimpled, vinyl chairs, posters showing how condoms prevent AIDS and Chlamydia. How breastfeeding is best, and the sun, like booze and fags, an enemy to fear.

Right.

He chose the seat nearest a chipped coffee table, upon which lay a crumpled copy of *The Lady*. For want of something to do besides dwelling on his recent redundancy from Woolworth's, and his prat of a brother wanting him out of his flat by Friday, he picked it up and flicked through page after page of perfect recipes for this and that; perfect homes, jobs for nannies and a short story about a missing cat.

Great.

He was about to return the magazine to the table when something on page 15 caught his eye:

WANT TO WRITE A BEST SELLER?
Spend Easter at Heron House in Carmarthenshire's beautiful Upper Towy Valley, and be inspired by top fiction writer Monty Flynn. All modern comforts. Cordon bleu cooking and internet access. Young writers particularly welcome. Reasonable rates. Regret no wheelchair access.

There was a phone number but no website. He checked around the walls for CCTV surveillance, and seeing none, tore out the page and stuffed it in his jeans' back pocket. He'd never heard of Monty Flynn, nor ever been to Wales. And as for a computer, forget it. However, something had lit up in his head. A quivering little flame, but a flame nevertheless, so that when the tannoy over the door announced that Dr. Chatterji would see him now, he barely heard it.

3

***

"Citalopram, once a day, Mr Robbins. That'll help pick you up. And I'll see you again this time next month in case you experience any unpleasant side effects."

"What side effects?"

An impatient sigh followed as the perfectly groomed Indian doctor snatched the prescription from his printer, obviously keen to be off home. "Look, just try and take yourself away somewhere pleasant. Consider a new challenge. Make new contacts…" The rest of his advice was lost in the grind of rush-hour traffic just beyond his window; and Jason, still unhappy at the lack of a reply, hadn't felt it right to mention grieving.

He collected his pills at a nearby pharmacy and popped one in his mouth, letting its strange taste spread over his tongue as punishment for having let his life end up this way. For not having been there to save his best mate from being blown to bits by a roadside bomb in Basra. Yet as he stepped into the cool dark of the Gay Pheasant pub on his way back to his brother's flat, he could almost hear Archie egging him on. Not to waste what life he had left.

"Half a shandy," he said to the barman who looked like a younger version of his dead dad. The Doc had wagged a brown finger, saying no booze, but half a shandy wasn't exactly booze, was it? "And a packet of pork scratchings."

While the noisy world passed by, Jason studied the torn-out notice once again and, the longer he looked, an idea for a book bloomed into his mind. Gangland, that was it. London gangland. His brother, a financial adviser, had stories to tell about money launderers, fraudsters, the crap police who left the big fish untouched. Who'd even been known to join their ranks. He could sense the main characters already nudging their way into his consciousness, almost demanding he tell their story. But hey, get real, he told himself, finishing his drink and ordering another, what had his English teacher at the local grammar school said at the time?

Come on, remember…

"Too much imagination, Jason, and not enough skill. Writing's a craft you can't simply wave away as if it doesn't matter."

So, skill-less, with ambition crushed out of him by a man who'd probably only put words together for school reports, he'd holed up at the Job Centre for whatever paid work there was. Filling pies with slurry he wouldn't give to a dog, planting bulbs for the Council, until a sick leave cover at Woolworth's came up. But no good dwelling on it now. He'd soon have

4

enough redundancy pay to bribe his brother for ideas and to let him stay on at least until the 8th April. The day before the writing course was due to start.

"You look chipper," remarked the barman. "Got some skirt lined up for tonight, eh?"

I wish.

But that wasn't quite true. For his new project, he'd need space, a clear head.

"Yeah." He watched the shandy's foam slide back down inside his empty glass. He felt light-headed. Odd. "Time I shifted my butt."

***

The library was still open and, under the gaze of the middle-aged woman at the desk, whose breasts almost reached her waist, Jason filled in the registration form.

"What kind of books do you like reading?" she asked. "Dectective? Self-help?"

"Crime. Thrillers. The more gory the better."

She handed him a small laminated card covered by a bar code and pointed to a set of shelves next to where a line of nerds were bent over their computers. Here, the air smelt worse than in the doctor's, a mix of fart and feet, and for a moment he hesitated until the name Monty Flynn came to mind. He scoured the various spines whose authors' surnames ranged from D to H in perfect alphabetical order – but no Flynn. Perhaps he was so popular, his books were out on loan. Perhaps they'd been put back in a hurry and lay elsewhere. Just as he was about to give up, a black and grey book spine caught his attention:

Evil Eyes by Max Byers.

Having withdrawn the plastic-covered novel from the crowded shelf, he examined the hype on the back; the photograph of a spreading blob of blood on the front. And as for the author photo, half in shadow...

I like it.

A glance at the fly paper's busy withdrawal sheet was encouraging while a skim of the first page made him realise why. It wasn't until the librarian called out that the library was due to close, that he finally plonked the book down in front of her. "Do you have anything by a Monty Flynn?" he gave her his best smile. "I've been looking, but so far, no joy."

She tutted as she stamped the return date for *Evil Eyes* in two weeks' time.

"Please," he urged. "It's important."

She tapped out his request on her keypad, then shook her tightly permed head. "Not that I can see. But then this machine only goes back four years. We've been promised an upgrade when this recession's over but I'll believe it when I see it."

"He may write under a different name," Jason suggested. That seemed the most likely explanation.

"Many authors do. Especially women trying to appeal to male readers."

Jason knew that even hot-off-the-press books weren't in bookshops for long. That trying to get hold of Sheridan le Fanu when he'd been a horror fan, had been a pain in the arse. So the fact that this 'top fiction author' wasn't in Hounslow Library was probably no big deal.

Outside the building's cloying warmth, he paused to read some more, aware of his pulse on the run as a Russian thug called Gregor tipped his adversary over the side of a houseboat moored on the Thames at Deptford. Great stuff. On his way back to the shared flat in Gardiner Street, Jason stopped to savour more of the tight dialogue, the cool descriptions of the waterfront, and felt as if the main character – the unnamed narrator – was real enough to be walking alongside him.

***

He still had his own key, although only last night Colin had threatened to take it away. An over-the-top reaction to a carton of chicken tikka left on the new granite worktop and an empty loo roll in the cloakroom. At least the silver Merc wasn't yet parked nearby. Something to be grateful for.

Jason brewed up and popped another pill. He liked the buzz, the what-the-heck attitude he was feeling. And if his older bro was to turn up with more crap for him to listen to, he'd tell him where to stuff his flat. Italian-style wet room or not.

He took his mug of tea to the hall phone. That way he could see any arrivals through the patterned glass panel in the front door. He smoothed out the magazine cutting and, with Gregor's icy words haunting his brain, dialled Heron House's number. It seemed to ring for ever.

Come on...

He was about to replace the receiver when a woman's voice answered. Her Welsh accent so strong he could barely understand her.

"Jason Robbins here," he began. "I'm calling from London about the Write a Best Seller course..."

"I never heard of no course. You got the right number?"

"Yes. It's in the latest issue of *The Lady*. Underneath the advert."

An ominous pause followed.

6

"You're not gay, are you? We couldn't be doing with that round here."

Jason held the receiver away from his ear, tempted again to replace it. What had his old school motto been? Persevere. Archie would say the same.

"To whom am I speaking?"

"Mrs Davies. I clean up after everyone. Don't live here, mind."

That sounded like a boast.

"Who's your boss? Who's running this course?"

"Like I said, I don't know about no course, but Mr Flynn owns Heron House. Bought it last year. An Irishman if you please." She tutted. "Leave me your number and I'll get him to call you back. He's down the Fox and Feathers at the moment."

"Cheers."

Afterwards, feeling slightly unsettled, Jason drained his mug in one go, gathered up the cutting and took the white-carpeted stairs two at a time up to his box room overlooking the street. He sat in front of what had once been their mother's dressing table, and reopened *Evil Eyes* at page 10. So engrossed was he in the drowning man's efforts to save himself, that he didn't hear the silver saloon draw up outside, nor see the couple eating each other's faces while snaking their way up the steps towards the front door.

2.

Tuesday 31st March 2009 – 5.45 p.m.

Russian mafia villain, Gregor Vasilich, was delivering the *coup de grâce* to his drowning victim's head, when Jason heard the thud of Colin's front door closing. He tensed up. Was his bro back already, or had some yob mugged him and got his key?

Since losing his job, Jason's new one was to guard the flat while the money man was out. How demeaning was that? As if he'd nothing else going on. Clearly nothing as important as what went on in that swanky Clerkenwell office. The recession hadn't affected Colin at all. If anything, he was busier and richer than ever. But in the past month alone, there'd been a stabbing and two burglaries in Gardiner Street and Jason couldn't risk another. Then, not for the first time, it hit him like a wrecking ball that unless a bribe worked, he'd be out on that very street in three days' time.

Sod him.

Before he had time to peer between the vertical blinds to check if the new silver Merc was in its reserved parking slot, an all-too familiar voice rose up the stairwell. A mix of his own and his dad's. Less Estuary, more Sloane as the years had gone by.

"Jason? You up there again?"

A woman giggled. The Girlfriend, he thought, unable to actually use her name. Then the hall phone started ringing. He slapped down his library book to hover by the landing's banisters.

"Monty Flynn, you say? From Wales?" queried his brother in an incredulous tone.

"Sheepshagger," mocked Colin, whose grey work suit was way too tight. "They're all the bloody same."

"About a writing course?" Colin was speaking again. "No, I'm afraid you've made a mistake..."

"No, they haven't!" Jason had reached the hallway in two seconds, but Colin clung to the receiver. A sick smile twitching his lips.

"You mean, this call's for you?"

"So?" Jason felt his skin begin to burn. He blushed as easily as a tomato in the sun. "It's my business."

"Hey, I'm wetting myself," sneered The Girlfriend. "Jason, writing? Pull the other one."

He'd not been a warehouse operative for nothing. Colin's grasp on the

8

receiver soon gave way to his, and the disgruntled couple backed towards the kitchen door while he tried to compose himself. The receiver felt hot in Jason's hand. Its perforations almost clogged up with sweat. He wished now he'd topped up his mobile and used that instead. "Thanks for calling me back," he began once the caller had introduced himself as Monty Flynn. "Bit tricky here at the moment."

"Sounds like it. Why you need what we've got on offer."

"Your Mrs Davies didn't seem to know what I was talking about."

A pause.

"She wouldn't."

Jason coughed to fill another small pause. "I've just started reading *Evil Eyes*…"

"Max Byers, eh? I'm impressed."

"That's exactly how I want to write." Jason scowled at his eavesdroppers with such intensity, they finally retreated into the chrome and granite Heaven newly fitted last month. "Bringing real hard bastards to life. Having them slug it out. Plenty of action, death and blood. Yeah, death and blood."

"Mr Robbins – may I call you Jason?" The Irishman continued."This is what's flying off the shelves right now. Fast, gripping, pacy. So fast in fact the poor helpless reader needs something to grip on to. And remember, publishers do like a series."

Jason felt as if his heart would explode with all the possibilities. The sense of exhilaration beat running any day. And he was no mean runner.

"D'you take a good photo?" came out of the blue.

"My mum always said I did." That sounded pathetic, but the questions kept coming.

"You fit and active?"

"Yeah. Why?"

"Describe the pic of Max Byers."

"No trouble. Half in shadow. His eyes kind of glaring up at you. Evil eyes…"

"Exactly. You got good bones like him?"

Jason wondered where this was leading. "Sure."

Another pause. This time he could hear a young female voice in the background.

"Helen says to get yourself over here. I agree. I think we'd work well together. What say you?"

"Who's Helen?"

"Our cook. Prue Leith trained. Her rook pies are to die for."

9

Jason wasn't sure whether to laugh or register his disgust. The gloomy afternoon had become an early dusk. He shivered.

"Are you serious?"

"I am. It'll soon be rook-culling time up here. Mr Davies, my groundsman, is a right good shot. He bagged twenty in one hour yesterday."

Twenty?

"Send me the kind of mug shot we could use on a cover mock-up," Flynn went on. "Plus any personal details to make you stand out from the crowd."

Filling pies, filling shelves. I don't think so.

"What about my writing?" Jason ventured.

"OK. Get a title, first chapter and outline to me by the weekend. You on email? We'll get you a selling package going. Blurb, shout line, the works. You could be the next George Pelecanos."

"George who?"

"Never mind. But he's tops. One of the writers for The Wire."

"Cool."

Yes, the gritty serial had tempted him to watch, but his late shifts had clashed with every episode except one, and Colin hadn't let him use his TV's recording facility. "What about the actual words to choose when you're writing?" he ventured again. "Never mind getting them in the right order?"

A short, hearty laugh. "Son, I'm telling you, that's the easy bit."

"So when do I pay?"

"Twenty percent now, the balance on your last day. We take cheques but no credit cards. Sorry."

Odd, thought Jason, then dismissed it. "How many others have enrolled?"

"Three so far. One from Mull. The other two from Redditch. Thing is, people leave things until the last minute. Our maximum's eight, so everyone gets a good crack of the whip."

Jason tugged his chequebook out of his jeans' pocket. This was a momentous decision. He could feel it in every pore, every nerve ending. But his questions weren't over yet. "What sort of books do *you* write, Mr Flynn, and are they under your own name?"

A hesitation. A raspy intake of breath. "Let's just say I'm not exactly bosom pals with the Freemasonry right now. Both my books based on their rituals were withdrawn PDQ once I'd lifted the lid. Fictionally, of course, but my work was still seen as a threat to the status quo. My lawyer scooped enough damages from the publishers for me to buy this place. So some good came out of it all."

Jason felt as if a sudden shadow had engulfed him. A dense, cold shadow. His chequebook had just three cheques left. The Girlfriend was giggling, accompanied by clattering saucepans. Colin probably had his hand between her legs.

"I can tell you've a big drive, big talent, Jason," said Flynn suddenly. "Get over here and use it."

And with that, came Jason's promise of payment to be sent off first thing in the morning. All the while, imagined associations with that far-off place, began spinning faster and faster in his mind.

3.

Wednesday 1st April 2009 – 12.10 p.m.

In Heron House's gloomy kitchen, twenty-two-year-old Helen Myfanwy Jenkins used the heel of her hand to press down the pile of corned beef sandwiches that she'd just made, and immediately her mind hurtled back to her days and nights in Stanley Terrace, below Aberystwyth University's colonnaded presence. Seat of her dreams for three years where no money, and a lurking, unpaid loan, limited her diet to whatever she could place between two slices of cheap white sliced bread.

Then, such restrictions hadn't mattered. Art was her life; part of her soul, so as long as her pulse kept going, she wasn't that fussed about what ended up on her plate. Her friends, especially Heffy (Hefina) Morris existed on Marlboro Lights and Cadbury's Flakes. Others on pot, bought and sold at the Vulcan Arms every Friday night. There'd only been one crack-head in her year and he'd drowned after leaping from the pier the day the Degree shows opened. "My exhibition," Rhys Maddox had written on a note left on his bedsit's pillow. "Worth a Distinction, eh?"

As she wrapped the neat column in cling-film to keep it fresh for Mr Flynn's lunch when he got back from the pub, she wondered what that intense idealist would make of her now. Here in the middle of bloody nowhere, on pants pay, while her precious oils, acrylics and canvases had lain untouched for over a month. Having interviewed a girl from a nearby home for adults with learning difficulties, plus twelve other candidates, he'd offered her the job. She'd then naively flung her arms around his neck.

That had been a February morning of blue sky and scudding clouds – the kind no artist would get away with. And now look. Beyond the kitchen's two rattling sash windows, a gale rocked the budding crowns of oak and the dead chestnuts into a mad dance. If this storm kept on into the night, as they often did, the longest branches would reach over to knock against her wall. Bang, bang... Worse was when Mrs Davies – or 'Gwenno' as Mr Flynn more familiarly called her – hovered around like a stick insect, appearing from some shady corner, stroking the same old riding crop she always carried that tapered like a rodent's tail. Why Helen's preferred name for her was The Rat.

Another problem was the weather. Quite different from near the sea where she could take her sketching easel outside and make a preparatory watercolour, knowing that for the finished work, the light, the colours would remain unchanged. But in her heart she knew that while she continued here at the gloomy rabbit warren called Heron House, any creativity was hypothetical. Her materials would stay unused; her ideas unexplored. If she had to explain why, she would say because of a growing feeling of entrapment. Of not fitting in.

All at once, came the quiver of air behind her, and the sense that Mrs Davies' small, slate-coloured eyes were passing down her body from her hastily-gathered pony tail to her scuffed trainers.

"Mr Flynn's on his way," she announced, pointing her riding crop towards the door. "And the worse for wear again, by the looks of it. God help us is all I can say."

How she loved delivering bad news, thought Helen, not bothering to turn round. Especially the latest divorce or miscarriage. Even the vicar's recent speeding fine, or another's cancer. She was also first to deliver the morning post to Mr Flynn, and had probably steamed open what might be of interest. Once or twice, Helen's own mam had sent cards that had mysteriously gone astray, but this busy little woman had sworn blind she'd never seen them. Helen ignored her by transferring the sandwiches to a plate and adding a blue-iced cup cake – one of a batch she'd made yesterday.

"He'll be wanting something hot, not a picnic. And as for these writing courses he's starting..."

Helen blinked. Turned to face her. "What writing courses?"

She wished the woman wouldn't smile.

"Hasn't Mr Flynn told you? There's one on over Easter. Got you down here as *cordon bleu* trained." From her overall pocket, Gwenno's ringless left hand pulled out a crumpled flier, showing Heron House magically lit by rare sunlight; barely recognisable, in fact. The cleaner's tone soured. "Plenty of girls I know down the village can do a tidy roast. I've only to bend Mr Flynn's ear."

Cow.

"Your reputation may not matter much to you, Miss Jenkins," Gwenno went on, "but me and Mr Davies have worked hard here to preserve ours." She disappeared into the scullery, leaving Helen feeling her neck begin to burn; wondering why on earth Mr Flynn hadn't mentioned anything to *her* about writing courses.

"There must be some mistake," she told herself, needing to get to him before Gwenno did. What with a dodgy septic tank, a disused swimming pool thick with silt, and the draughts regularly putting out fires in the main reception rooms.

And then she recalled him speaking to a guy called Jason on the phone yesterday evening, while she'd been telling him about a length of down pipe blown adrift from the wall by her bedroom window. He'd not been the least bit bothered about that. Oh, no. It was Jason who'd made the big impression.

Having slammed the kitchen door behind her to create a satisfyingly loud bang, Helen cut across the big square hall-cum-reception room hung with old photographs of mid-Wales and its long-gone farming communities. She opened the front door on to the wind, that massive, lumpy hill the other side of the valley, and there, as The Rat had predicted, was her tall, slightly stooped employer spitting on his hands to slick down his wavy, greying hair. Using the iron boot-remover in the shape of a heron's head, he prised off his filthy Wellingtons while she bent down to pick up last year's dead leaves that had blown in. Big, soggy and clogged with dirt.

Helen was about to challenge him about Easter, but missed her chance.

"Worse than fuckin' Crosskelly, this," he muttered, carrying the boots into the tiled cloakroom, leaving her marooned in the lingering smell not of the usual whisky, but of outdoors. She saw how the heels of his mismatched socks were worn into holes. Normally, she'd have offered to fetch him new ones, but not now. "And to cap it all," he went on, "I've just seen some poor sheepdog mashed up below Golwg y Mwyn. Those forestry lorries drive too damn fast. One day, it'll be a kiddie."

Torn between sorrow for that needless carnage and bubbling resentment towards the man who now emerged pulling his old golfing jumper over his head, Helen merely said, "lunch is ready, Mr Flynn. The usual, I'm afraid."

"Your usual is what I like best. And for God's sake, stop calling me Mr Flynn. It's been a month now."

Helen took a deep breath. It was now or never. "Gwenno said you were starting some writers' courses here, with the first one happening over Easter? Is this true?"

"It is."

"How will I cope, then? It can't be sandwiches morning, noon and night, surely?" She made sure the crone wasn't around and lowered her voice. "She never stops pointing out my limitations."

Monty Flynn pulled his shirt's frayed cuffs below his jumper's sleeves, avoiding eye contact as she stuck to her guns. "I think I've a right to know if what she said is correct."

14

"Indeed, you have."

"And yesterday you spoke to someone called Jason. Is he coming here?"

"Indeed, he is."

"How many others?"

"Three so far. Though I've not yet said a word to anyone locally, in case any punters pull out and it all falls flat. I have my pride."

"And I have mine, Mr Flynn. You know that sardines on toast and boiled eggs are about my limit, yet you've put *'cordon bleu* cooking' on your flier. Gwenno showed me. And said I could lose my job if I didn't come up to scratch."

He glanced towards the kitchen. "I'll have to have serious words. I'll also pop into Llandovery this afternoon and get you an easy-to-follow cookbook. Need to collect my sleeping pills anyway. How about that?"

But another lie had come to mind. "You also told this Jason guy that 'Helen says you should get yourself over here.' In fact, I'd said no such thing."

He looked at her as though deciding if truth was a better investment.

It was.

"Sorry. But I've a lot on my mind at the moment. Not least that I need to make a go of these creative courses if... if I'm to hang on to Heron House."

"You mean the mortgage?"

"My dear Ms Leith. That's the least of it."

***

Ms Leith...

She'd not laughed. Instead, found a paper napkin used only once before, folded and curved it into an empty wine glass. She then unwrapped the cling-film, screwed it up into a tight, oily ball and threw it into a specially adapted milk churn that served as a waste bin.

She was still cross. Mr Flynn was as slippery as an eel. Probably had been since the day he was born, but that last remark of his still played on her mind. Was this perhaps why he'd not got rid of the Davies pair despite their incompetence? She'd never dared ask and now wasn't the time either. These writers would be paying good money. More than she could afford, even if she saved for a whole year. They'd have high hopes, just like she once had. They deserved a good deal. How would she like it if the boot was on the other foot?

And then, as she spotted The Rat creeping around inside the understairs cupboard, tried to recall meals her mam had put on the table before her da had left. Before she'd lost heart. Helen began jotting them down in the margin of last week's *Western Mail*. Cawl with mutton and pearl barley. Steak and kidney pie with ale and home-made puff pastry. Pork and prune casserole plus jacket spuds. She stopped writing. So far so good, but these scribes would expect at least a choice of puddings, when all she could think of was ice cream with a wafer stuck in it.

Damn.

Mr Flynn entered the kitchen and pulled out his usual chair at the head of the old oak table that had once belonged to some chapel or other. He seemed his usual, casual self. "Perfect," he said, upon seeing her architectural pile of bread and corned beef. Plus the cake. "As a reward, you're quite welcome to join my workshops, free, gratis and for nothing. Who knows, if you come up with a good, commercial story, we might be able to open doors. Get you in the best seller lists. What with your striking Celtic looks."

He took a bite of the topmost sandwich. A huge bite, in fact.

"You mean my red hair and freckles?"

"Very fetching indeed. I can see your cover photo already."

Helen excused herself. He was too full of the blarney. Perhaps why she'd accepted his job offer. But as for writing from imagination, she'd never been good at making things up. No, she thought, hefting her old, waxed coat over her shoulders. Her ideas came from what was there. Visible and real. Why she was going to see the one known as Aunty Betsan who lived in a small bungalow beneath the Nantymwyn lead mine's redundant workings. She couldn't rely upon Mr Flynn to deliver that promised cook book, so the elderly woman, well-known for her traditional Welsh cooking, was sure to help her out.

***

Helen glanced back at Heron House through the veil of rain, but didn't let its backdrop of rocking trees distract her from checking each of the windows in turn, including the three dormers nestling deep in the rampant ivy. And sure enough, there she was. The Rat and her cap of fine white hair, which when viewed from behind, revealed a pinkly glowing skull.

Two bullet-like eyes seemed to fix on her heart, to follow her out of the drive, along the rutted, muddy lane that soon gave way to spongy, mossy grass. Upwards then, towards Pen Cerrigmwyn with the wind on her back, Helen wondered how come she was so important to the woman, and when would Mr Flynn sort her out. She wondered too how long it would be before karting and 4X4 rallies would carve up this land the way both coal and lead mines once had. There'd been enough of that wanton vandalism near Aberystwyth. She stopped to survey an old ore hopper's rusted skeleton and other sad remains abandoned some seventy years before. Composing a possible painting in her mind.

Suddenly, in this wild, sullen world of the red kite and other airborne predators, she spotted something odd, out of place, just beneath the tallest spoil heap. Was it some large dog or wild creature escaped from the forestry? Hard to tell with rain now lashing her face. And then, using both hands as blinkers, she could see that whatever it was, had straightened up and now stood still as a post. But why there of all places? In such foul unforgiving weather?

4.

Friday 3rd April 2009 – 6.30 a.m.

Jason's bribe to his brother hadn't worked, so here he was, upstairs in the borrowed bedroom, getting ready to leave. He folded the last of his boxer shorts and added them to his dad's ancient suitcase. Alongside this, on his now stripped single bed, lay leftovers of a Woolworth life he never wanted to see again; takeover or no takeover. Four ballpoint pens, a red file crammed with hassling memos from his store manager, and a matching cap that had made him look like the village idiot. So there'd been an ex-employee in Dorchester who'd reopened the defunct shop as Wellworth's, but no way was he schlepping down there on the off-chance of a job. In fact, with that Easter week's course looming, job hunting was, for the time being, on the back burner. And God only knew when Monty Flynn would be getting his first chapter from him, never mind a mug shot.

He looked around what had been home for the past two months. His brother could have these crap souvenirs and the wonky swivel chair bought with the first bonus back in 1999; plus his framed Frith print of Bradwell-on-Sea where he and Colin had been brought up, and where their mum still lived in the clapperboard cottage within sight of the power station. He hoped both his brother's and The Girlfriend's consciences would ping when they saw them, but knew they wouldn't.

OK, he'd done well to find a bed after his landlady had defaulted on a buy-to-let mortgage. But he'd paid Colin the going rate, no favours asked. The mean sod could have let him stay on just one more week. Bribe or no bribe.

He closed the suitcase, giving each rusty lock a shove. Then, having checked in the mirror that his new, dark stubble was giving him the desired Max Byers look, lifted his leather jacket from the hook on the door and slotted *Evil Eyes* into his inside pocket. Combined with the drone of jets flying in and out of Heathrow, its story had kept him awake at night. But how could he return it to the library before reaching the end? He couldn't.

"Ciao," he muttered to himself as he crept along the thickly carpeted landing and left his brother's keys outside his bedroom door. Just to hear his and The Girlfriend's separate snores and to imagine their warm closeness, delivered a sudden and bottomless sense of loss. His dad, Archie, everything had gone.

Having hefted the remainder of his worldly goods downstairs and left two twenty-pound notes on the kitchen table, he hesitated for a few seconds, wondering where on earth could he go now?

**

He pulled up his jacket collar against the thickening drizzle, feeling the hardback's solid weight against his breastbone. He'd cheated and turned to its bleak ending which left open the possibility of a sequel. After that brief panic attack in Colin's hallway, this gave him some hope. His life too would go on. And just then, as an Eddie Stobart truck drew up alongside him at the lights and its driver gave him a thumbs up sign, he had an idea.

Never mind that the one public phone in Ali's Café was slimy with grease and the small booth itself was stickered with mug shots of various *'masseuses.'* Until he topped up his mobile, this would have to do. He pushed in a one pound coin and punched the number he now knew off by heart. Nothing ventured, he told himself as the ringing continued.

Don't sound too desperate...

"Yes?"

He took a punt. "Mrs Davies?"

"Who is it?"

"Mr Robbins. I spoke to you on Tuesday, remember? And Monty Flynn. I'm due to start the writing course on the 9th and was just wondering if..."

"Best you speak to him. Here he is now. Light sleeper he is, despite them pills. Drinks far too much of the whatjecallit, see; but will he listen?"

Jason hesitated, not only because of her lack of discretion. Maybe he should wait until later. He heard the Welsh woman pass on his name. Noticed a black guy in overalls come into the café and browse through the copy of *Metro* he himself had found on the table.

"Up with the lark, eh?" said the Irishman now on the line. Despite the woman's unflattering comments, he seemed as fresh as a daisy. "Is it about your first chapter?"

"No. And I'm sorry to call so early..." Jason's voice was almost lost to the espresso machine spitting out steam. "But I've a problem."

"A writer's prerequisite. The more the merrier. What problem?"

For a moment he wondered if the man was now on his own. His news wasn't public property. Not yet. He heard Mrs Davies being asked to start the washing machine and, having heard the faint slam of a nearby door, began his real-life story.

**

He should have been feeling relieved that thanks to the Irishman's empathy, he'd be spared flat hunting as a Department of Social Security case in the scummiest parts of London for the next week, but he wasn't. Scabbers were other people.

"There's always mum," a small voice persisted inside his head as he sat with a third mug of tea, watching the rain slew against the café's window and those people still with jobs to go to, leaning into it as if crossing the Mongolian plains. No way. Bad enough he'd had to rely on Colin for so long. Besides, Shirley Robbins had found herself another bed mate – not the first since his dad died after falling off scaffolding in Dalston. An ex-boxer, this one, wanting her all to himself.

Jason picked up the freebie rag for yet more sound bites on the recession and case studies of some of those affected, including a graduate in Media Studies who'd been one of hundreds queuing for one vacancy at KFC in Balham, to a pensioner whose nest egg had slipped down the pan. And then, on page 4 between news of a knife attack in Clapham and lane closures on the South Circular, was a paragraph headed:

WEALTHY EX-BUSINESSMAN
FOUND DEAD

A seventy-two-year-old man, iden-
tified as Charles Pitt-Rose, was found
by police last night, hanged in an
underground garage beneath his
mansion block apartment in Islington.
Anyone with information should
contact the Metropolitan Police at
their Tolpuddle St. station.

But why, with the café filling up and the busy din increasing all around him, did Jason feel as if someone had slipped an ice cube down his back?

"You done with that?" The same black guy was eyeing the paper.

"Not yet."

The stranger moved away, but not the sense of a dank, dark space and a lonely man maybe driven to the brink and beyond. Jason extracted *Evil Eyes* from his jacket. The victim, whom Vasilich had thrown in the water and shot, had been a Moscow gang member. Perhaps Charles Pitt-Rose had also been in deep trouble. Perhaps his death wasn't suicide after all. Whatever, stuff like this could be useful in his novel. Corruption and betrayal, ending with a car chase along Beachy Head.

Jason got up, checked his watch. That cold feeling still there, but excitement too.

He stepped outside into the hostile morning and passed the boarded-up Woolworth's without pausing on his way to Tesco Express to top up his phone, then on to the Tube. Suddenly, like a wraith, his brother's Merc glided by. Both Colin and The Girlfriend just shadows behind its tinted glass. Nevertheless, Jason waved, but to them he was invisible. A nobody. A failure. But not, he told himself, for long.

5

Friday 3rd April 2009 – 2 p.m.

Having heard the hall phone ring early, Helen had stopped in the middle of brushing her teeth to open her bedroom door and listen. That same Jason guy had been trying to cadge an extra week at Heron House. Bloody cheek, she'd thought, having herself been told in no uncertain terms that if any of her arty mates wanted to freeload here, then tough. They'd have to stay at the Fox and Feathers. Heffy, however, was the exception. Mr Flynn had liked the sound of her.

But why had The Rat still hung around, even though he'd ordered her into the laundry room? One day, when the pest had gone or died, she'd snitch on her big time. But right now, until a better job came along, she must cling to this one like a bluebottle to a fly strip.

"Mr Robbins will be arriving at 5.20 p.m. at Swansea station," Mr Flynn informed her later as he was getting ready for another stint at the pub. "I told him there'd be a car waiting, and afterwards, a nice three-course meal. Can we do that?" His eyes with their well-worn twinkle, weakened her defences as he pressed a crumpled twenty-pound note in her hand.

"We?"

"Come on, Helen. It's just a figure of speech. You know you're my main man round here. It's crucial we get things off to a good start. Our Londoner sounds like the kind of punter who'll spread the word. And right now, the word's what we need..."

***

For a start, her hair out of its pony tail scrunchie, for the first time in yonks, stuck out in all directions, refusing to lie flat against the nape of her neck. Secondly, her car, an aged Ignis with a dodgy tyre and even dodgier clutch, hadn't seen a vacuum cleaner since the day of her interview in February. Soil and dead leaves covered its once jolly mats, while a layer of stubborn green slime lined each of the windows.

At least it was a car, she told herself, still ratty at having to drive a round trip of eighty miles to include shopping *en route*. If Mr Robbins so much as mentioned the state of it, he could damned well leg it up-country on his own.

So preoccupied was she with overtaking those caravans and camper vans, that seemed to have sprouted on the roads overnight, she forgot altogether how two events had freaked her out recently. The first, on

Wednesday's walk to Aunty Betsan's bungalow up on Pen Cerrigmwyn, when she'd spotted what must have been the remains of that poor Collie dog Mr Flynn had mentioned. Bits of black and white fur lying in rain-thinned blood.

Next, a dark, motionless figure standing in front of the silent lead mine workings. She'd stayed there holding her breath for a few minutes until, as if she'd been dreaming, it faded away.

As for this strange experience, her boss didn't need to know everything, but Betsan Griffiths did. The neatly turned out spinster who'd claimed she'd once catered for local weddings and hotels in Llandovery and Llanddewi Brefi, had neither seen nor heard of any mysterious watcher. "Rain and wind, mind, can cause some right old tricks," she'd said, handing Helen four of her easiest recipes for main meals. "Mind you, some say that since that village was drowned under Llyn Brianne, there's been a few dead folk wandering about, looking for their homes. So she says."

"Who's she?"

"The cleaner over at your place."

"Gwenno?"

Instead of a nod, the woman had frowned. Something clearly bugging her. "I never call her that. She's done me too much harm. Her and her mouth. And she's not the only one."

"I'm sorry."

"You watch yourself."

"I will."

And then the back door had closed behind her, for the rods of rain to hit her skin and deliver, not for the first time, a gnawing sense of unease. What had Aunty Betsan meant by those strange remarks? What harm exactly? And who else had she meant?

***

"Can I help you, madam?" asked a large guy trapped inside a navy blue tabard at a Fforestfach store. "You seem lost."

"Parmesan," she said, suddenly realising why she was here. "And bay leaves. For a spag bol."

Once outside in the busy car park, she checked her watch. Ten minutes left for a rush-hour trip of six miles. She'd miscalculated the volume of traffic. So little passed by Heron House, that even the post van or forestry lorry was an event.

Her resentment at feeling used, mounted with every lurch and stop of her car. OK, so Mr Flynn had soon come clean about the writing courses.

23

But had he seriously been expecting her to rustle up the promised fare with no notice? Of course. That's how he operated. Impulse his middle name, with others – meaning her – picking up the pieces. Idris Davies, the groundsman, said the same on the rare occasions he'd communicated with her, but like his wife, he'd been at Heron House for years. So long in fact, that the oaks and dead chestnuts, the banks of rhododendrons and the bluebell trail, had become closer to him than any close relative. And, in his eyes, no-one, not even Mrs Davies, it seemed, matched up to them.

The wind was different here. Sharper, more gusty, coming off the sea. The rain too with no mountain barrier between these outskirts and the Bay. Helen switched on Radio 4, only to turn it off again. She'd given up listening to the news, but not so her mam up in Borth. An energetic primary school teacher, full of suggestions for what her only child with – in her eyes – a useless degree, should really be doing to 'ride the recession' as she'd put it. Undertaking had been top of her list of suggestions. 'Everyone has to die sometime. The one sure thing.'

So it was. But not just yet.

***

Once in Swansea, near the station, Helen parked her Ignis up on the kerb outside a greasy spoon café and switched off its grunting wipers. Her curiosity about the emergency arrival now outweighed her resentment at his nerve. Perhaps he was as old as Mr Flynn. Or older. Perhaps he had a shady past best kept hidden. As she tried opening her knackered umbrella against the wind, she realised with a churning pulse, she was soon about to find out.

Commuters. Swarms of them, striding, clack-clacking along the platform towards her like a dark, rough sea. Who was she looking for? There'd been no description asked for, or given. Just that Jason Robbins would be wearing a black leather jacket plus jeans, and carrying a battered suitcase.

And then she spotted it. Attached to a guy in yes, black leather and stone-washed denim who seemed paler than his travelling companions, with a more wary look in his eye. His gelled brown hair bristled from his head, and from the lobe of his left ear, glistened a small stud.

Not her sort at all.

However, she'd been trained to observe, to look hard at her subject, and saw that although that suitcase with its rusted steel corners, seemed medieval, the shoes weren't cheap. Nor the jacket that hung from a pair of broad shoulders. As he handed his ticket to the waiting inspector, she noticed there was no wedding ring. She also wondered what job he did to be able to take an extra week off. Why it was so important to come to Wales now, and whether or not he had a return ticket tucked away somewhere.

He glanced up, caught her eye, then walked past her, probably thinking that a representative of the grandly-named Heron House would at least look the part.

"Hi." She ran after him, pushing her wet hair off her face. Aware how naff she looked in the black suit not worn since her uncle's funeral three years ago. "Are you by any chance Jason Robbins?"

He stopped, turned to face her, that same wary expression giving way to a smile. "Are you Patsy Palmer?"

"Funny, not. I'm Helen Jenkins from Heron House." She held out her right hand like Mr Flynn had told her to do. "Welcome to wet and windy Wales. Or, as they say here, Croeso i Gymru."

6

Friday 3rd April 2009 – 6.25 p.m.

The motorway's commuter cars and delivery vans were soon replaced by muddy 4X4s and horse boxes, reminding Jason of rural Essex until he saw hills that almost appeared to be moving as rain clouds shifted overhead to reveal promising scraps of blue. He wound down his window to let cool air bathe his face. "Why Heron House?" he asked his less than talkative driver. "Do they breed herons there, or what?"

"They did," she replied, taking the road signed for Ammanford and Llandeilo off a big roundabout. "Some time in the seventies. Long after the lead mines had closed."

"Lead mines?" Monty Flynn hadn't mentioned anything about these when describing the surrounding landscape as being a second Garden of Eden. A wild, unspoilt refuge. Balm for the soul. However, it was easier to ask questions about their destination than having to explain to someone he didn't yet know why he was arriving a week early. As it was none of her business, he assumed Monty Flynn had kept his confidentiality.

Every time she hit a drain cover or pothole, his knees butted the glove box, his seatbelt tightened across his chest, and it was while stop-starting through Llandeilo's busy main street, that a rush of panic quickened his pulse. He shut his eyes and opened them in shock. For a split second, yet as if in slow motion, all the colours of shop fronts, traffic and passers-by seemed to morph into a uniformly dull brown colour; the pavements empty save for a few people moving around, dressed in clothes from what he guessed was the World War II era. This busy street had been replaced by a weird stillness, with just a few ancient Austin and Morris cars and a solitary pony and trap labouring up the hill in the opposite direction.

The Ignis was travelling on dirt, not tarmac, where scattered piles of droppings lay uncollected. The smell of wood smoke and manure met his nose.

"You OK?" asked Helen Jenkins, throwing him a glance.

"I'm not sure. Can you see something odd going on?"

"Where?"

"Outside. It's like... really strange. As if we're part of some old photograph."

"No, I can't."

He produced his mobile and turned its screen to face the now open window. "What are you doing?" Helen asked.

"Taking a video. You never know. For posterity."

Passers-by, wearing long black coats, noticed it and immediately shielded their faces.

Damn.

The screen remained blank. "It's not working. Look." He angled the phone towards her.

"I need to concentrate, OK?'

Just then, as he fiddled with Options and Film menus, the whole street scene reverted to its former bustle. "Bloody gizmos," he muttered. "They never work when you want them to."

"Just take a photo, then."

"Can't. It's too late. Everything's changed back."

He replaced his crap phone with *Evil Eyes*, still feeling unnerved. Could he really have imagined all that, or was it the pills? At least a book was reliable. Tangible. He found the page he'd been reading before sneaking another look at the grim last page.

"That looks like fun," she observed drily, before overtaking an open truck full of white goats.

"It is."

"Afraid we can't compete with that here. The worst we get is sheep rustling or some old codger in the backwoods doing it with his dogs."

Normally, he'd have laughed, but not now, despite the town's sudden return to its normal bustle. "Tell me more about these lead mines near Heron House," he said, to take his mind off it.

She sighed. "There were two. Nantybai near the church and the river Towy, and Nantymwyn higher up. They'd been around since Roman times. Apparently, both were closed in the late-1930s, putting hundreds of folk out of work. Why when war came many of the local men, including farmers, signed up."

"My best mate Archie did that. Jobless for a year, so he went for it. Kabul, if you please."

"What happened to him?"

"Don't really want to talk about it, if that's OK."

She shrugged. Put her foot down as the A40 opened out, and they continued in silence past large farms whose cattle slurry trailed across the road, splattering her windscreen. To the right, he saw beyond the grazed hills lay darker, sharper escarpments of what he guessed were part of the Brecon Beacons. He sat transfixed, comparing this naturally unfolding panorama with Hounslow. Yes, the Thames wasn't so far from its clogged-up streets, but here, between fields, the Towy flowed by without a single rowing fanatic or noisy cruise boat to break its reflection of passing clouds. Smooth, grassy banks lay on either side instead of overused pathways full of litter, dog shit and used syringes. Yet this was the very world that must feed the book he was about to start writing. A polluted, corrupt world, forever on the move.

"So why come to Heron House?" she quizzed, while they passed over an elaborate iron bridge into a town called Llandovery. That same River Towy now beneath them. He turned to her, but how to explain that his heart, which only yesterday had filled to bursting with ideas, was deflating like some kid's balloon. His main characters, Carl Spooner, a vicious pusher from Kennington and his sidekick, whose speciality was dousing his victims with petrol and watching them fry, were fading with every mile that passed.

He closed *Evil Eyes* and placed it on the floor between his feet. "To start a gangland thriller. Mr Flynn thought it was a cool idea and was keen to see a first chapter this weekend. Even checked I took a good pic for inside the back cover."

Suddenly, the Ignis lurched towards the nearside hedge. She quickly righted it, but not before he'd seen her expression.

"What's wrong with that?" he challenged. "What's wrong with him rooting for me? Best seller, he said, if you can see it through. And I bloody am."

Silence.

***

The road that apparently led towards Heron House, took her full attention, not only because of its narrowness, but also what else happened to be sharing it. A fox hunt in full swing, complete with huge, pale hounds veering from verge to verge, noses down. Small made-up girls on half-clipped ponies; horseboxes parked up nose to tail, plus a posse of quad bikes taking up what little space was left. Welcome to the countryside, he thought.

Half an hour later, with the commotion vanished up wet, stony tracks leading from the road, and a sign for Rhandirmwyn with its enticing-looking pub just a memory, gentle bends became the hairpin variety. Soft fields were now giant fir-clad peaks where small settlements nestled between their folds. More Alpine than anything thought Jason, aware of being sucked into a world as different as could be from the Essex marshes on which he'd grown up. Here a trickle of white smoke rising, there a black

28

swarm of birds cruising low over the land.

Rooks?

He glanced at Helen Jenkins' freckled face fixed on the way ahead. Her long pale eyelashes and her small nose weathered red on its bridge.

"So tell me about your rook pies," he said. "Mr Flynn was raving about them."

"Ha. He's a liar. I should have snatched the phone off him when you first called Heron House. He's also a lush. Big time. And as for the *cordon bleu* crap, forget it." She slowed down; her left indicator light flashing on and off while a bright blush burned on each cheek. "Look, I can easily turn round and take you back to Swansea. Trains to Paddington run till late. He'd understand. Whatever else, he's no fool."

Jason flicked off the switch, his stomach spinning like it had when he'd woken up in his brother's flat on his last morning there. "Just keep going."

"But you'll be paying good money. For what?" Indignation had lit up her blue-green eyes. Her chin stuck out. "You must be desperate. That's all I can say."

"Too right I am."

***

They didn't speak again until the unnamed turning became a cinder track pitted by water-filled holes and the uphill gradient levelled for half a mile to reveal a large, moss-covered roof and two tall, but unmatched chimneys.

"Here we are," she said, dropping into first gear despite the grumbling clutch. "Not exactly in the hub of things."

You could say that again.

Heron House, ten times the size of his mother's cottage, and clearly from a much earlier era, lay in its own leafy grounds beneath a dark swathe of a forestry plantation. Beyond this, the land rearing up against the sky, seemed shorn of grass, dotted with the odd windblown tree. Survivors, like he must be. He took in the house's three gabled upper windows jutting out like mean little eyes, then the heron-shaped weather vane, spinning on its perch. Next, his eye travelled down over the dense, dark ivy smothering most of the front wall, to the recessed front door whose steps lay strewn with dead leaves and other debris.

He'd missed the unusual gateposts.

"Who made those?" he finally pointed at the two stone pillars each supporting identical wrought-iron sculptures. Herons again. Beaks open, wings outspread as if for battle. Quite different from the weather vane. Their message seemed to be 'Keep out.'

29

"From melted-down cannons, so I heard."

Tentative connections began to form in his mind. Cannons and lead, rocks and caves. And when he glanced again at that same front door, almost hidden beyond its gloomy archway, he suddenly glimpsed three figures, again in sepia tones, who'd materialised from nowhere, standing below the steps. A family perhaps, made up of a woman who seemed to be pregnant, a stout man of indeterminate age, and in between them, a young, black-haired girl carrying a basket of cut roses. The two females wore what Jason recognised as traditional Welsh costume, while the man balanced a long fishing rod on his shoulder whose dangling hook bore what appeared to be a dead mouse.

Then, as quickly as the strange picture had appeared, it vanished.

What *is* it about this place? he asked himself as Helen Jenkins followed the curved driveway around an under-planted central island, where just one rose bush swayed back and forth in the wind. Perhaps he'd give his next dose of Citalopram a miss.

She pulled up next to a grey Volvo saloon in front of the first of three lock-up garages, which, like most of the house, were smothered in ivy. Broken branches and other detritus lay drifted against their tatty-looking doors. He watched her climb out. Neat butt, nice legs, he thought. Then reprimanded himself. He was here to write, not catch up on a non-existent love life, since Gina Colburn, who'd worked in the videos section of the Hounslow store, had dumped him last summer. "So this is Heron House," he said, dragging his venerable suitcase from the boot. "I've been on tenterhooks since I saw that advert."

"Where?"

He hesitated. Mrs Davies' reaction had been bad enough. "*The Lady.* What's wrong with that?"

Her laugh caught him unawares. Deeper than he'd expected. "You're kidding?"

"In the doctor's surgery it was. Perhaps your Mr Flynn was hoping to attract females rather than some geezer who's just lost his job and got nowhere to live."

Surprise wasn't the word for it.

"You?"

Just then, she turned towards the house as the front door opened, as if, it seemed, by itself.

7

Friday 3rd April 2009 – 8 p.m.

Gwenno Davies stood aside, almost reluctantly, to allow them both access to the cavernous reception hall where the log fire was busily spitting out green flames reflecting on the unfashionably papered walls. This time, her riding crop quivered in her right hand as she looked the new arrival up and down.

Jason stared back at her with undisguised puzzlement. One day, Helen promised herself, she'd make a painting of that woman's face and throw it into the fire to watch it burn, bit by bit. But that wouldn't be enough to shift someone who was clearly ensconced here for life. Part of the fabric were she and her husband. Like fag burns and other dodgy stains. At least the other old loony acknowledged her, despite the fact she couldn't converse in Welsh. At least he kept out of the way from dawn to dusk, pick-picking old leaves off whatever tree or bush he could reach, yet deliberately letting the swimming pool's contents grow thicker and blacker with them and any fallen ones as the months went by.

"Mr Flynn will be down now," snapped her enemy. "He said for you to wait."

Her little bit of power. Saddo.

"No worries," said Jason breezily. Although he'd turned down the chance of a lift back to Swansea, by the end of the evening, he could still change his mind.

Next came the soft, regular tread of suede on carpet. Thank God those legs now clad in dark blue trousers still seemed steady, and Monty Flynn's pock-marked skin not quite so pink as when he'd first arrived back from the pub. His odd socks, however, were still the same but the maroon velvet smoking jacket was new.

The moment he spotted Jason, his smile widened. The same smile that had brought her here too far inland from the sea country that she loved. He turned to her; his irregular teeth still on show. "I'm sure, Helen, that Mr Robbins could do with a nice strong cup of tea."

Mr Flynn laid a long-fingered hand on her shoulder. "Off you go."

Helen obeyed, picking up her bag, wondering if Jason, in her shoes, would be treated any differently.

Someone had got to the kitchen first, for the kettle was beginning to boil, letting out its usual thin scream. Then came The Rat's voice as she beat

Helen to the mugs. "I don't much care for that young man out there," she said. "Fit he is, that's for sure. I can tell by his eyes, see? The way he looked me up and down as if I was one of them killing ewes at the mart."

Killing ewes?

Helen flinched.

"If that's not proper manners, I don't know what is," the woman went on, now in full spate, while Helen appropriated the tea-bag tin and dropped a tea bag into one of the mugs. "And the Lord knows who else'll be turning up next Thursday. They could be criminals come for a nosey round, for all I know." Her deep sigh also delivered what Helen hoped was the start of a death rattle. "You being a girl on your own here – think about it. I know Mr Davies is of the same mind."

The sudden reference to that wrinkly in a filthy old boiler suit, made Helen add too much hot water. Her onlooker tutted while fetching milk from the fridge. Beyond the locked windows, dusk had deepened too suddenly. So had Helen's sense of claustrophobia.

"I went to see Aunty Betsan yesterday, for some decent recipes," she volunteered as casually as she could. A deliberate change of subject while putting her shopping in the fridge. She was up for a fight, if need be, adding, "so you won't be able to complain about my catering any more."

Immediately, the temperature inside the already cool room seemed to drop. The Rat set down the milk then pushed her forefinger's knobbly middle knuckle into Helen's breastbone. "How long is it you've bin here?"

"You should know. A month. Why?"

"And how often have you called on her?"

"Only twice." Which was the truth. "Why?"

"And has she bewitched you yet? Given you fresh-baked Welsh cakes as a parting gift? Tell me." The woman prodded even harder until Helen grabbed the finger and prised it away.

"Don't be ridiculous. Of course not."

"Well, let me tell you, my girl, she hides potions and poisons and uses them as punishment."

"Punishment? What for?"

Gwenno Davies drew closer, keeping her hands to herself, but her dry, thin lips almost brushed Helen's cheek. Meanwhile, laughter eked out from the reception area. Monty Flynn on top form, enjoying himself with his new recruit. Helen felt an all-too-familiar pang of jealousy.

"Why Betsan's suspicious of anyone who treads the path to her door. I should know. But I'm not alone thinking this. Oh, no. Not saying. Except

32

those who've had food there, or walked away with something she's made, come to no good," Gwenno said.

Helen tried to rekindle the image of the woman who'd been so eager to help. No way was this horrible accusation tying up. Instead, *"She's done me too much harm. Her and her mouth,"* came immediately to mind.

"Surely the police would have investigated her by now, if that had been true," Helen said.

"Oh, they have, but Betsan charms them, doesn't she? Nothing ever proved, see." The Rat backed away to listen in on the other conversation. "Travellers go on, eat other food from elsewhere. Think of it. How easy…"

"Stop!" Helen set the full mug on to a little plastic tray and added milk, sugar and a leftover cup cake. "This is crazy, and I'm fed up with all the gossip round here. Why can't everyone just get on with their lives? You'd think people would be grateful to live in an area like this. Ever been to Salford? My cousin took a job there last year. Knifed in the back, he was and lucky to survive."

"Ask Mr Davies if you don't believe me," she countered, deliberately closing the door so Helen trying to balance the little tray, couldn't pass through. "And you can be sure that when these so-called writers turn up, I'll be putting them straight."

"I'm sure you will. Now please open this thing. I've supper to get, as well you know."

Grudgingly, the woman obliged, letting tea be delivered to the Londoner now relaxed in one of the two deep-buttoned chairs by the fire. Mr Flynn's smile was in overdrive. "Helen, in case you don't know it, I swear to God you're looking at the next Max Byers. Jason's got this great idea for a début thriller." He enthusiastically slapped both arms of his chair. "It's got the lot. And he's just agreed to count me in when the squillions come rolling into his bank account. Just wish he'd sent me something to read beforehand."

Another pang of jealousy hit Helen's heart. The Irishman had never shown any interest in *her* preparatory sketches for paintings. She then told herself to get over it. What did it matter what he thought?

Meanwhile, the budding author's cheeks had reddened with excitement, and she felt mean to deny his moment in the sun. However, at uni, she'd spent three weeks learning about being a freelance. How a properly drawn-up contract between patron and client was considered paramount. Perhaps in private, she should warn Jason of the dangers of such a loose arrangement, especially after what he'd admitted in the car. Homeless and redundant, he was vulnerable. But was he also just plain unlucky?

"Well, I'd better get out of my funeral suit and start making that spag bol to celebrate," Helen said instead.

"Ah, the angel of Heron House has spoken," chuckled her boss. And as he did so, leant forwards to pick up the *Metro* that Jason had left on the coffee table between them. "Life in The Big Smoke, eh?" He skimmed through its well-thumbed pages. "You won't get me in any big city even if this place went up in flames and I was left standing in my pyjamas." Then all at once he stopped. Peered at the last-but-one page, his fingers stiffening as he did so.

"What's up?" Helen asked, used to his mood changes, but not this sudden. "Is it something you've just read?"

Without answering, Monty Flynn slapped the pages together, folded them tight and stuffed the bundle into his smoking-jacket pocket.

"I'm not to be disturbed. Understood?" he snapped, before springing from his armchair and striding towards the archway leading to the stairs.

8

Friday 3rd April 2009 – 8.15 p.m.

Having placed the heron-decorated fireguard in front of the dwindling fire, Jason carried his empty mug into the kitchen. Helen was busy tipping bright red mince into a frying pan; no sign of that strange old girl hanging around either, which made it easier for him to ask, "what's got into Monty Flynn, I wonder?"

"You tell me. You've obviously read that paper too, judging by the state of it."

"Is he connected to London in some way? Family, friends, etcetera?"

She paused before adding salt and pepper. The smell of the sizzling raw meat made him catch his breath. "Not that I know of."

"Or more specifically, Islington?"

Flushed and frowning, she refocussed on sealing the beef strands with the hot oil. "No. And why's it so important all of a sudden?"

"Charles Pitt-Rose – whoever he is – is dead. Found hanged, apparently." And in the next moment was aware of someone's shadow creeping along the adjoining scullery wall.

***

"Nosy old bat," muttered Helen ladling the Bolognaise sauce on top of his pasta and bringing it over. "She's always around. You watch her. And Idris her husband out there. They're seriously odd." She gestured towards the darkly waving trees beyond the window. "They live in, see. Up with the dawn and down at midnight. Mind you, there's an old Hillman Hunter in the second lock-up which she uses once a week. He never goes out, though. At least, not since I've been here."

She coiled some spaghetti strands around her fork without much enthusiasm, but he noticed she'd thoughtfully kept a portion aside for Monty Flynn in the old fashioned Aga. Not the flash dark blue version that Colin had recently installed, but cream and rust.

Colin.

His brother and his comfortable life now seemed so far away. Jason toyed with the idea to call him to say he'd arrived in one piece, but sod it. What did he owe him?

"She made out to me, she lived somewhere else," he said.

"She would."

In the pause that followed, he took the first tasty mouthful. "Great nosh," he said, licking the fork. For someone who'd confessed she could only make sandwiches, she'd rustled up a welcoming dinner.

"Thanks. But I can't lie. It was Aunty Betsan's recipe. She lives up by the old lead workings on Pen Cerrigmwyn. You'd love her. She's not far away. We must call in some time. She also makes the most amazing cakes."

Lead again...

Just then, before he could respond, Helen's face tensed up as she opened the fridge's freezer compartment, pulled out a big tub of vanilla ice cream and reached up to one of the store cupboards for a packet of wafers.

"Something wrong?"

"No, honestly. Sometimes I think too much about stuff." Helen scooped out a generous portion and dropped it into a pudding bowl, before forcing the wafer into its softening side. "There. And when you've eaten that, I'll show you your room."

***

She'd said 'we,' Jason reminded himself as he followed that same pert butt up the first flight of shallow stairs, yet hoped, ungratefully, she wouldn't be plotting a programme of things for them to do together. He had other plotting to do. For big bucks and a brighter future. Just to think of it brought that familiar adrenalin rush flood from his brain to his writing hand.

She stopped on the first, dark landing and he sensed she was still distracted. He let his dad's old suitcase rest on the worn carpet at his feet, also aware of the dead blackness beyond the bare, grimy window set into the side wall. Not since his Essex childhood had he experienced such an insidious pressure of the unknown, both inside and outside a building.

"The other writers will be sleeping just round that corner at the end." She flicked on a nearby switch, whereupon the few lights ranged along the faded, musty wallpaper, flickered into a dim life. "You're on the next floor. Mr Flynn thought a top room with a gable window would suit you better. That, after Hounslow, you'd enjoy its view."

"I'm honoured."

They took the next eight plain, wooden stairs into the attic area where an almost physical darkness cocooned him in its numbing embrace. He blinked twice to bring himself back to reality, which was more bare boards and a smell he couldn't quite identify.

"You've a little bathroom just further along," she added, switching on the single overhead bulb. "So no embarrassment there. Unless The Rat decides to share it with you or even some of the other writers when they show up. Please don't say anything to them beforehand. At least there was no mention of en suites."

"Too right. But where's your room, and Monty Flynn's?"

"My secret. But his is over the lock-ups, next floor down. More like a library, than a bedroom, he says. He's obsessed with books."

"So am I. Specially the one I brought with me."

"I saw it. Nice cover. Not."

"You wait till you see the one on my finished novel."

"Oh, and he's got a computer," she added as if ignoring the boast. "But I've never seen it."

"Any internet access for research, whatever? The advert said there was."

Instantly, her hand covered her mouth. In shock or amusement, he couldn't tell. "You're kidding. Here? Must be a typo. And as for TV, there's only the blizzard called S4C in the lounge. If you're lucky."

Damn.

Was that why no website had been given? And had Monty Flynn only watched *The Wire* on DVD? The scam word was growing bigger in Jason's mind. How would the other new arrivals react? Would the man really want to be had up for misrepresentation? Woolie's had been hot on that issue to the point of paranoia.

"Oh, and by the way, no-one's allowed in his study," his guide went on. "Not even The Rat – I mean Mrs Davies. No key either. I bet he's there now. Perhaps he'll say more about that news item in the *Metro* later. He snapped it up quickly enough, didn't he?"

Before Jason could reply, she'd moved on ahead and, having taken two Yale keys from her suit skirt pocket, unlocked a solid oak door, whose matching wooden plaque bore the hand-painted sign saying *MARGIAD.*

"Who's that?" he asked. "One of his kids who's left home?"

"No way. Mr Flynn's a professional bachelor." She stared up at it, letting her hand follow its shape. "Besides, it's a Welsh girl's name. Hey, this is really strange."

"Why?"

"I've never noticed it before."

***

Still preoccupied, Jason followed Helen into a long narrow room dominated, or rather choked by, a thick floral carpet. Big, blowsy roses connected to each other by twisted, thorny stems and a dominant border featuring them in miniature. Apart from a single bed covered by a floral duvet and unmatching pillows, there was an old-fashioned dressing table minus its mirror and beneath this, something that made him pause. A dark, body-shaped stain on the carpet, the colour of stale blood.

He bent down to sniff, and it was as if the foul, stilled breaths of previous dead incumbents suddenly clogged his nose.

"What the Hell's that?" He indicated the puzzling mark.

"God knows. Perhaps a spot of damp. This whole place needs ventilating." She pushed down the top half of the small sash window, and breathed in the soggy night air. "It's not been occupied at least since God knows when."

"I suppose that explains it."

That poky window would be his sole source of natural light tomorrow, and Jason moved towards it, willing dawn to come, only to be confronted by the lowering shape of some vast hill beyond the drive. Bigger than when he'd last seen it from Helen's car. So big, its summit was topped by clouds.

"You'll get a great view in the morning," she said, as if reading his thoughts. Dinas Hill, or Giant's Shoulder it's called. I don't think there's a Welsh version of that name. I must try and paint it one day."

That caught him by surprise.

"You're an artist?"

"Used to be." She handed him both keys, one labelled BATHROOM. "Trained at Aberystwyth. Anyway, breakfast's at eight, down in the kitchen. What do you normally have? Bacon or toast?"

Should he confess how depression had baldy affected his appetite until the spag bol had been placed in front of him? He didn't want pity. Hell, he could pay his way ten times over if need be.

"Both, if that's possible. I can give you extra."

She looked at him with those frank, sea-coloured eyes, and smiled. "My pleasure. But where on earth the other writers will go is anyone's guess. The dining room's full of old junk but Mr Flynn's been funny about shifting it. I daren't interfere." She gave the room what was to be a final glance, then left him to it.

Strange, he thought, lifting the suitcase on to a torn leather footstool. But something more than that was bothering him. Not just Heron House's antiquated decoration, or Mrs Davies and Helen Jenkins herself, who in unguarded moments, seemed more than ill at ease here. No, it was the fact that she as cook, hadn't been briefed about the writing course, but the old girl had. Why? And the more he dwelt on Monty Flynn's lack of common courtesy, the more puzzled he became.

Nine o'clock and, despite Dr Chatterji's warning, he was missing his evening bevvies. It was too early to hit the sack. Too late to wander around outside. Nothing for it but to sample the plumbing, pop an extra pill just in case, and reopen *Evil Eyes* at chapter 22.

***

His bathroom boasted one threadbare towel, a cracked wooden toilet seat that wobbled above a suspiciously stained bowl. Worse, the washbasin's hot water had emerged the colour of pee. Jason told himself to hang on until the course proper began. Once he'd penned the best first chapter ever, he'd put in for better accommodation. Monty Flynn surely wouldn't want to deny him. Timing was everything.

Back in his room, he was about to close his room's floral curtains to shut out the solid, black April night, when he heard a grating, raucous sound from behind him, making his blood freeze.

"Caw... caw... caw..." It went on, as something was scraping at the walls. Then whatever it was, brushed the top of his head.

A solid black shadow was roaming around the room, dipping down over that patch of soiled carpet, moving in ever smaller circles, coming in closer to him, skimming past his eyes. A bat maybe? He'd seen enough of them in his mum's cottage. But no. They were silent creatures. This wasn't. It was a bird with flapping feathered wings and a beak that ended in a strangely luminous area of white at its base.

Jesus.

It must have got in through the still-open window, but was making no effort to escape. He pulled a spare pair of jeans out of his suitcase and flapped at it, round and round until finally, with an almost threatening call, the intruder flew outside to vanish into the darkness.

He shivered as he slammed the window shut and drew the curtains tight together, aware of his thudding heart. He eyed the bed. It was suddenly tempting. Wider than the one he'd used at Colin's but without the same bounce, it was nevertheless somewhere to draw breath. To remind himself why he was here.

Having located the page in *Evil Eyes* that he'd been reading when Swansea station had appeared, he cast his mind back to that puzzling street scene in Llandeilo and those old-fashioned characters in front of Heron House. Were these the pills' side-effects Dr Chatterji had mentioned? He'd hardly been specific. If they were, why hadn't Hounslow also slipped into sepia mode? And what about the mysterious Margiad? In the morning, if Monty Flynn was in more conversational mode, he'd ask him who she was.

Suddenly, however, as he began devouring *Evil Eyes'* gripping climax on page 304, he noticed what seemed like a damp, cold breath on the back of his neck, before the book started to pull away from his fingers and the remaining pages turn backwards as if someone else, much stronger, more determined than he, didn't want him to read any more. "Gerroff!" he shouted, "this is mine!" He somehow managed to cling to its vinyl cover and slap the borrowed read shut, before flinging it hard across the room.

9.

Wednesday 2nd October 1946 – 4 p.m.

Lionel Hargreaves, fifty-three-year-old bachelor headmaster and sole teacher at Nantybai School, was counting out a set of dog-eared geography text books for the next day's lessons, when an urgent knocking on the classroom door disturbed him.

Because the wind was roaring through the Towy valley at full strength, he thought at first it might be a stray branch or a lightweight piece of machinery from a nearby farm, but no. Young Walter Jones from Brynawel, and habitual non-attender, wanted to speak to him. Now.

Lionel opened the door a fraction. "This is most inconvenient," he said. "I'm very busy."

"Please, sir. I've something to tell you."

He finally let the boy in, and pushed the schoolroom door shut behind him. He then returned to his desk. It wouldn't do for him to lift the lad's sodden cape from his shivering shoulders, nor to encourage any closer contact. Walls, especially these, had not only ears, but also tongues. He'd learnt that much since his appointment from Solihull just over a year ago.

"Sir," the skinny nine-year-old began, bursting with impatience; hopping from one leg to the other. "I was up Pen Cerrigmwyn picking spare wood for me mam's fire, when there was this great din, like a growling animal coming closer and closer up the forestry track behind me... honest to God I had to jump in the hedge and hide, else I'd have been run over."

"What kind of animal?" Lionel asked without much interest. "A wolf? A bull?" This really was a waste of his precious time.

"No, sir. More like one of them hungry lions out in Africa you once told us about. But it was a car. A big black one, sir, going as if the Devil was on its tail." As he spoke, his whole body began to tremble, whether from fear or being soaked to the bone, Lionel couldn't tell. Whatever the reason, he didn't much care. He'd worked hard all day, and simply wanted to get home before the weather worsened. Perhaps if this fatherless lad spent more time at school, he'd have been more sympathetic towards him.

His voice grew sterner than he intended. "And what would you like me to do about it? That's a public right of way although a poor enough one. Anyone can use it."

"This wasn't anyone, sir. I saw a young woman in the back, banging on the window. She was crying, sir. No, screaming. Like my mam when me da

41

got crushed by a tree."

Notes on that tragedy still lay in the class register. Not the first death in the plantation; nor, sadly, the last.

"Which girl?" said Lionel. "Come on, son. Spit it out. Can't you see I've things to do?"

Suddenly the boy's face lost its wild colour. His eyes stared ahead, motionless. His mouth too, stayed rigidly open like those on the marble angels in the church next door. To Lionel's horror, and before he could reach out, Walter Jones' legs buckled beneath him. He fell hard against the stone flags; his head of wet, dark hair, taking the weight of the impact.

"Holy Jesus!" Lionel knelt down next to him, desperate to hear a heartbeat, but already, an extraordinarily dark thread of blood was eking from the lad's left ear, trailing over the nearest slab and dropping into the first wide gap.

***

The funeral – a simple affair – was held the following Saturday at St. Barnabas' Church where Mrs Jones normally cleaned the pews and mended the hassocks. Today she sat dressed in shabby black, her sorrowful gaze fixed on the small, plain coffin placed before the altar.

Throughout the short service, Lionel was unable to shift her only son's terror-filled eyes from his mind. Remorse had devoured him like one of those tidal waves he'd recently witnessed off the Gower coast, and even now, as Walter's casket topped by nine pine cones, passed back along the nave, he couldn't bear to look at the widow's stricken face. When he offered her his deepest condolences, he was met with a look of pure hatred. But how could he tell her, or anyone else, the truth? That he could not have been more attentive to her son. Acted more quickly.

A much-respected doctor from Trecastle who'd been visiting his sister at the vicarage, had examined the dead boy and declared a fatal heart attack had led to the skull fracture, consistent with a sudden fall. The Carmarthen coroner supported his opinion, while the police, busy with a spate of sheep rustling, were still gleaning witness statements from the locals. Many, rather than admit ignorance, had let their overheated imaginations run amok as to what exactly had happened in the schoolroom.

Thus he, Lionel Alfred Hargreaves, who'd so far never put a foot wrong, was now the feared incomer. A malevolent cuckoo too big for the nest he'd been appointed to fill, because all other potential male candidates had either been maimed, shell-shocked or buried amongst hundreds of other war dead far away. If only the School Board had selected a woman for the headship, he thought. Perhaps she wouldn't have been in this situation. Walter had clearly wanted a father figure. And he'd let him down.

***

Arglwydd, arwain
trwy'r anialwch
Fi, bererin gwael ei wedd...

William Williams of Pantycelyn's closing hymn filled the church, and although the youthful organist played with fervour, Lionel's throat stayed closed, his endurance beginning to wane.

Once outside, in the sunny, autumnal afternoon, he stood apart from the rest of the congregation as the casket met the grave's gaping wound. However, such distance didn't prevent him hearing hostile mutterings from young and old alike, as ripe, red earth was thrown in. Even as he made his way along the narrow path to the gate, whispered oaths followed, not entirely lost to the wind.

"Walter was my best pal," ten-year-old Sion Beynon's unmistakeable voice reached his ears. "Now look what you done." The local shopkeeper's son rubbed away his tears with his sleeve. It was in that moment, with golden leaves drifting down from the ancient trees bordering the made-up road to Nantybai, that Lionel realised young Walter had sought no-one else's help to solve the mystery of the frantic girl in the car. Now he would make it his business to find out what had driven the boy to his door and why she might have cost him his life.

"Mr Hargreaves, are you alright?" came a male voice close behind him. "I noticed you earlier, and I'm shocked what folk here – who think they're good Christians – have said about you. It's bad enough how they've treated me, but today was inexcusable."

Lionel turned to see Robert Price the organist, a tall, good-looking man in his mid-twenties dressed in well-cut mourning black, clutching his music books. The rebel, who'd dared be a conchie during the war years and been punished for it too long by a diminished congregation and a bigoted vicar, joined him. Together they walked towards the crossroads."Thank you for your concern. But my conscience isn't yet clear enough for anyone's pity."

"I don't understand, sir."

A horde of rooks flew in ragged formation towards the church tower. Lionel wondered if they'd left their nests for good. A bad sign, so he'd heard.

"You will, you will. And now," he pulled his watch from under his waistcoat and glanced at the time. "If you'll excuse me..."

"I'm over at Troed y Rhiw should you ever need me," persisted his companion. "Don't forget. The youngsters round here think the world of you."

That hadn't been his impression.

Nevertheless, Lionel nodded his gratitude, and started on his way up the steep track to his right. At the halfway point, he took a deep and necessary breath. Despite the organist's kind words, his earlier resolve seemed to falter. Neither the beautiful, unfamiliar sun hovering over Dinas Hill, nor the sight of his welcoming chimney could drive away this sudden melancholy. For two pins he'd hand in a letter of resignation on Monday; pack his meagre belongings in his father's metal trunk, that had returned from the Somme without him, and leave this equally foreign hinterland once and for all.

But no. He'd made the newly-buried boy a promise. And the one thing his own father, whose name he'd been given, had said, "Always keep your promise, son. The one thing I learnt at the Front." But as Lionel crossed the dirt road, buoyed up by this memory of the hero who'd saved many lives on Vimy Ridge, he spotted a small, black-clad figure standing by his gate, carrying a long riding crop. Male or female, he couldn't say, yet with boots polished to the kind of shine rarely seen in these parts. And then he noticed their dainty heels, the immaculate riding habit accentuating a boyish frame. He wondered where her mount was, or if there wasn't one, did she normally go around dressed like that?

This stranger, whom he'd not noticed at the funeral, turned to him, pointing the tapering crop in his direction. Her pale face caught in the sun's rare glow. Her eyes hard as slate. "A warning, Mr Headmaster. For all our sakes, and yours, forget that foolish young boy ever came to see you. Do you understand?"

Lionel felt blood drain from his head, as he rested his weight on his stick. Her warning quite different from the graveside rebukes. This was another matter entirely.

"What foolish boy?"

"Walter Jones. I saw him going into your schoolroom."

"Why would he come to me? He never attends."

His adversary's gloved hand clasped his gatepost. He wanted to hit it away. Hit her away...

"Don't play games with me, Mr Hargreaves. I heard every lying word he said."

She must have opened the schoolroom door and listened like a fox in the night. Now he was boxed in and not cunning enough to escape. "I hardly think he was lying, Miss…?"

"Never you mind." She slapped the crop against his boundary wall, and before he could turn away, to walk down his path to Cwm Cottage, her other gloved hand reached down into her riding-jacket pocket.

The next few seconds passed as if he was encased in a slow-motion nightmare. The vivid kind he often experienced just before waking, where unwanted colours and sounds left him drained for the day ahead. The bombing raids over his widowed mother's house that he'd shared with her. The shrieks of children at play nearby.

The girl was holding a gun. Not the usual heavy-duty pistol used round here on vermin, but small, compact. Aimed all too steadily at his heart. "Remember what I've said," she fixed him with a stare, "or it won't just be your job you'll be losing."

"My job? What's that to do with anything?"

A short, mocking laugh. "I can say to the police and the coroner, if necessary, that while he was with you Walter Jones screamed for mercy. That I heard him quite distinctly as I was riding over to Cilycwm. It sounded as if you were doing him serious harm."

Lionel's empty stomach seemed to turn over, and bile began to work its way towards his throat.

"Who the Hell are you? Where are you from?"

A metallic click.

"I said, remember." And with that, the stranger backed away from him, gun still in place, before turning the corner out of sight. Her boot heels clack-clacked against the stones as she went.

With a trembling hand, Lionel turned his key in the front door lock, then suddenly stopped, listening hard. Thinking hard. If she'd heard a young lad in such distress, why not enquire at the time what was going on? Why pass on by? It didn't make sense. But something else did. Her threat. Could she actually be frightened? Didn't children behave in the same way when protecting their friends from deserved punishment? And the more he thought about her, and her tense little face, the more he realised she was little more than a child herself.

He let himself into the cottage's warm parlour, where the log fire behind its guard was still alive, wondering all the while who so desperately needed *her* protection? And why?

10.

Saturday 4th April 2009 – 9 a.m.

While the Welsh slate clock on the kitchen mantelpiece chimed nine annoying times, Helen finished setting breakfast for one and switched on the coffee maker. Her movements had noticeably slowed. Her body seemed to belong to someone much older. Lack of sleep, she thought, and excitement, because whatever her view on Jason Robbins scabbing an extra week off Mr Flynn for peanuts, there was something about him. An inner core of self-belief, perhaps. Plus his body wasn't bad either. All that physical stuff before he'd lost his warehouse job, had honed his thighs; the same for his lower arms. His hands too, were a nice shape, with squared-off nails. She was used to observing detail. Been trained to. As for the ear stud, she could soon get used to that.

"Hi, sorry I'm late."

So here he was. But nothing like yesterday when anticipation had shone in his eyes. She'd drawn and painted from enough models to recognise who was chilled out and who was burdened. He seemed to be definitely in the second category. "Is anything wrong?" she ventured, bringing over a full cafetière to the table, and the same mug he'd used for tea yesterday.

"Not sure. Perhaps I'm going mad."

"Tell me," she pressed, as he sat down and ran a hand through his now ungelled hair. "Is it a smell? You know, like the septic tank?"

"No."

"Or roses? Sickly sweet ones? I smelt them here when I first arrived. Talk about The White Lady in the Tower of London. Mr Flynn just laughed at me when I mentioned it, saying The Rat had probably discovered a new brand of air freshener."

"Nothing to do with any smell. Something much more weird." Jason's coffee stayed untouched while he recounted that strange bird's antics in his room, then the incident involving his library book. "And when I woke up, it was on the floor with whole pages torn out. I just don't get it."

"Nor me." She went over to the bread bin, pulled out a sliced wholemeal loaf and popped two pieces into the toaster. Her hand unsteady. Her mind on that top-floor room and how odd it had felt going in there for the first time. "Did the temperature seem to drop?"

He shook his head. "It felt warmer if anything. Especially near that stain."

Ugh...

"Toast?" she asked, before clicking the switch to ON. Better than dwelling on what he'd implied. Ghost stuff really scared her. The roses' stink had been bad enough. "One or two?"

"I'm OK, thanks. But he clearly wasn't. He pushed back his chair and stood up. "Is Monty Flynn around?"

How could she tell him that most days her boss rarely showed up till late morning and then it was off to the boozer. "He's usually in his office," she lied. "But like I said, that's *verboten*, even for The Rat."

"Is that *me* you're referring to?" shrilled an all-too-familiar voice from inside the walk-in larder. "Because if so, I'll be telling Mr Flynn right this minute. Then let's see what he has to say. I was here long before you forced yourself upon the world." She emerged brandishing not her usual riding crop, but a spray can of furniture polish and a wad of bright yellow dusters. Her crossover apron bearing a map of Wales was tied even more tightly over her mean little body. Helen noticed how Carmarthenshire lay folded in on itself around her waist.

"So what? That doesn't give you the right to snoop on everything I or Mr Flynn do," Helen said.

"I have *all* the right." She came close enough for Helen to see the pink veins in the whites of her angry eyes. Her bony forefinger wagging back and fore.

"What do you mean by that?" Helen challenged, hearing the cooked toast pop up.

"Cool it," whispered Jason. "Let's go."

"And you, young man," Gwenno Davies called after him, "if you've a whit of sense you'll take yourself back to where you came from. This girl will endanger you with her lies."

Helen saw him turn his back as the woman pushed past him out of the kitchen. A subtle move that drove him upwards in her estimation.

"I'm off," he said.

"Where?"

"Don't care. I need to think. Sort my head out."

***

"Bitch," Helen muttered after her enemy, who was creeping upstairs wiping off any possible finger marks from the oak banister as she went. Her patch of scalp glowing under the dusty chandelier. "No, Rat bitch." And to the Irishman hovering on the top step in his well-worn dressing gown who wouldn't say 'boo' to her, "I'm not sticking that woman much longer. Who could?"

Mr Flynn let Gwenno Davies pass, and from her lower position Helen saw a small smile of triumph stretch her uncharitable lips. She also noticed how her boss sucked at his right index finger.

"Did you hear me?" Helen's voice raised a notch to reach him. "Doesn't it matter what I think? Am I that invisible?"

But he slipped away without answering, back into his office-cum-bedroom over the lock-ups, and in that moment, Helen realised it wasn't just his sleeping tablets giving him that unhealthy pallor. She'd been when he'd picked up Jason's copy of *Metro* and read about that hanging in London.

Something was seriously wrong.

She took the shallow stairs two at a time and tiptoed along the first floor's narrow corridor before turning the tight corner at the far end to reach his door. Here she pressed her ear to its cold, old wood long enough to hear him on his landline phone asking Directory Enquiries for that Islington Police Station's number.

***

Helen didn't hang about, instead raced up to the attic floor and Jason's unlocked room where to her surprise, that *MARGIAD* sign on the door had gone. Likewise the dark stain she'd almost dared ask The Rat to clean. But more than any of this was the book that had inspired the Londoner to come here in the first place. It lay intact on his bedside table, not a page missing, and in perfect order. Had his story been made up? And if so, why?

This is crazy. In fact, more than crazy.

She glanced at his neatly made bed then out of the dormer window on to the persistent drizzle and that normally dominant hill opposite now just a harmless blur. Then something that made her heartbeat quicken again. Jason was standing in the gateway down below, beckoning her to join him.

She hesitated, ashamed at being so easily flattered. Yet no-one she'd so far met in Llandovery or on her one evening visit to the Fox and Feathers with Mr Flynn, had paid her any attention. No worries about her mam's one big fear all too loudly expressed when she'd landed the cooking job. "Don't for God's sake get embroiled with the peasants there. Wait until a man with proper work and a healthy bank balance comes along. Someone safe."

She should be so lucky.

And there was Jason Robbins gesturing to her as if stranded on some desert island. Another one down on his luck, but nevertheless, clinging to a big dream. Hers was to have her own place. New and clean, unlike Heron

House, complete with funky chairs and a big IKEA bed with drawers underneath.

She locked Jason's door just in case, and was about to go downstairs two at a time when she saw Mr Flynn waiting for her on the bottom step.

"I'll be away for the next couple of days," he said, before lowering his voice. "Keep an eye on the place, and if the Davieses prove tricky, just let it go. OK?"

What an odd thing to say.

Helen stared at his tense features. His crumpled dark grey suit she'd never seen him wear. Here was a man afraid. "Where are you going? Just in case."

"London. You've got my mobile number, but please, only in an emergency."

"There won't be any."

"Good. And don't give it to anyone else without my say-so."

"OK."

He suddenly gripped her nearest hand and she noticed a fresh plaster on that same right index finger he'd been sucking earlier. "Thanks for that, Helen. "Means a lot." He gave her the strangest look before snatching up a well-worn briefcase and fleeing away through the hall and out of the front door. Within seconds, he was revving up the Volvo then negotiating the central flowerbed on two wheels, spraying mud and gravel into the air as he went.

***

Having pulled up the hood of her waxed coat and zipped herself inside its slightly sticky warmth up to the chin, Helen checked that her limited set of house keys were safe in her pocket along with two snatched cup cakes, then joined Jason who stood eyes fixed on the grey saloon as it sped out of sight.

"I locked your room," she said.

"Damn. Forgot. Cheers."

"Now then, left or right?" she said as brightly as she could. Her employer's news could wait for the time being. Jason had been waiting for *her*, hadn't he?

"Talk about rushing off," he complained, still staring after the car. "Nearly ran me over."

"He ought to watch it." She then nudged his damp arm. "Listen, I've something to tell you. It'll freak you out."

"What?" But she could tell he wasn't really listening.

"Your library book's fine. If the weather wasn't so minging, I'd have brought it to show you."

That made him focus.

"*Evil Eyes* fine? How come? It was ripped to shreds when I last saw it."

"If you don't believe me, come and take a look."

"No thanks. I need fresh air." He duly upturned his face and drew in a great gulp of drizzle. "I can't get last night out of my head."

"Nor me. Left or right?" she repeated.

"Your call."

***

The mist that yesterday had made the massive hill almost invisible, now slipped away to reveal its shining greenness in awesome clarity against the sky. She could never reproduce that colour using manufactured paints. Viridian was too dark, too blue. Chrome green even mixed with gamboge, too dense. No, she'd have to search for some obscure plant dye, but right now, that wasn't exactly top of her agenda.

"Any graveyards round here?" Jason asked unexpectedly.

"Non-conformist church? Chapels? Take your pick. Why do you ask?"

"Who was Margiad?"

"I've said, I've no idea. Can't we just leave it?"

His answer was to follow the downhill track that his would-be tutor had just taken, his black jacket glistening on him like wet skin. His booted steps sure-footed. Suddenly, an M.I.A. track hit her ears. From where, she couldn't tell, until Jason paused, pressing a sleek, black mobile phone to his ear. Orange Rome. Very smart, but how come his caller had got a signal? He looked back at her, a deepening frown on his face as he listened. Whoever it was, didn't last long and, at the end, he seemed frozen stiff. "Remember me. Remember me," he repeated as if in some kind of trance. "What can that mean?"

"God knows. What was the number?"

He checked all the options.

"Zilch."

"Sex?"

"Hard to tell."

Helen's feeling of powerlessness turned her waxed coat into a prison. A hot, clinging one at that. She shook herself free of it letting the soft, spitting rain cool her face, her neck. She'd never had much patience with those who believe in the afterlife or the paranormal. Her mam had knocked those notions out of her young mind whenever she'd asked. Yet if something truly inexplicable did happen to her, she'd be off like a shot. As for her da,

50

the man with a secret life, hadn't he sometimes, like Mr Flynn, called her his angel?

Meanwhile Jason's call still bothered her. For a mobile to work, you either had to go two miles east or west from here, or to the very top of Heron House.

"It's not rocket science," Helen said. "You've got a help option, surely?"

But he was in another world. "Remember me. Remember me. I mean, who'd say that? My mother or her toyboy? My skinflint brother? My stores manager at Woolies? My dead mate Archie?"

She could tell by his frown he'd not meant to give so much away, but her encouragement nevertheless triggered his whole story and, by the time they'd reached an even more minor road off to the right, she realised why they both seemed to have more in common than she'd first imagined. How he was still grieving for the soldier, his best friend, probably buried in ten pieces.

***

Although dripped on by too many overhanging trees, they kept up the pace until an almost illegible sign for Nantybai appeared, together with a PERIGYL – DANGER OF DEATH warning sign about the lower lead mine's old workings. This came complete with the graphic silhouette of a dead man.

Helen knew from Mr Flynn that a once-lively hamlet had existed next to the church dedicated to St. Barnabas. Its hub, the old school, had long been demolished after a mysterious fire, while the mill, shop and smithy had died with their owners. All that remained were a few former lead mine workers' cottages, now holiday rentals or second homes. Way beyond her measly pay she'd realised, when one came up for sale last month. There was also the Red Kite campsite situated right next to the River Towy, and more than once, she'd been tempted to rent one of its static caravans and hike up to Heron House for work each morning. At least she'd have her own space, without The Rat listening outside her bedroom as she washed in its too-small washbasin.

Soon, at the lane's end, she and Jason were staring up at that same church whose rain-blackened slates and grey stone walls lent it a forbidding feel, as did the fact it stood marooned in a crowded but silent graveyard.

***

For some reason, it was here they parted company. He to the older area, she to the brightly adorned cremation markers and newer burials of mostly men. She glanced over to see Jason's head bobbing about amongst the

51

tilting headstones, and just then experienced a profound feeling their paths might do more than continue to cross.

"Hey! take a butcher's at this one." His voice came from behind the biggest memorial topped by a crouching angel who, despite seventy years of Welsh weather, seemed remarkably white. "Edmund Pitt-Rose QC and his wife, Joy. Dearly beloved and all that... I wonder if they're related to that poor sod who's just been found hanged in London."

Helen, in an effort to leave that suddenly cloying smell of roses lingering in the moist air, ran over to join him and stare at what was clearly a large family plot. "Who knows? But surely there aren't too many with that name around. Especially here. Unless, like the drovers they were passing through."

"See these dates? Joy died in 1937 and her husband almost thirty years later. Hardly passing through." He caught her eye. "Are you thinking what I'm thinking?"

"Yes. Islington. Where Mr Flynn was going earlier. To be honest, I thought he looked demented."

"Do the Davieses know he's gone?"

"Now that's a thought."

Despite their presence, an eerie stillness seemed to pervade the place. Helen slipped her arms into her coat sleeves, glad now of their warmth.

"Plot thickens." Jason knelt down on the wet, newly-mown grass, letting his fingers follow the stonemason's lettering. Their original gold leaf replaced by paint from a none-too-steady hand. The whole thing lovingly tended, obviously. "Joined for nine years until parted by death," he read, then looked up at her. "Had you heard of this surname before yesterday?"

"No. But looks like there's plenty of space for more."

***

"At this rate, I'll need to get myself a coat like yours." Jason stood up, shook out his sodden leather jacket and, shivering like a road drill in action, returned it to his back. "Mr Flynn might have warned me."

"Same here when I first arrived. The rainfall's ten times worse than in Aber. Nor did he say a word about who else was sharing his roof."

"You mean that married couple?"

Helen laughed then covered her mouth. Her mamgu had always said it was unlucky to laugh amongst the dead. "They're the barmy army, OK? I've been trying to tell you."

She then found herself looking at the grave of a Walter Jones who'd died in October 1946 aged nine. Only child of Eira and the late Iori. The sad remains of nine pine cones lay stuck to his pale granite slab. She wondered what had happened to him. If his mam was still alive.

Jason joined her. "Never mind my thriller, which isn't going anywhere, there's stuff happening here that needs an explanation. Fast. "Remember me," for a start. And the more I think about it, it was definitely a Welsh voice and female."

Again he fished out his mobile and tried RECALL without any luck. The same for SAVED MESSAGES and VOICEMAIL. All the while Helen watched him as if something between them had changed. She could have walked off. But no. She actually wanted to give him some small hope that he might perhaps fulfil Mr Flynn's expectations.

"There's something else I'd like you to see," she said. "Now this damned drizzle's stopped."

But Jason stayed put as if he wasn't finished. "I keep thinking of this boss of yours. Why such a big bee up his bum just now?"

She sighed. If he wanted to try his detective skills, it didn't have to involve her. "He never said. Just for me to keep an eye on the place and call him in case of emergency." She pushed back her coat sleeve to reveal her watch. "It's half ten already. I can't be out too long. Just in case." She moved away from the sorry plot towards a gap in the bordering hedge, but he soon caught up with her.

"There's something you're not telling me."

She frowned again. "OK. He basically said I mustn't upset the Davieses. Good, eh?"

"I don't get it. Why are they so special? Anyone would think they owned the place. Not him."

"Join the club."

They watched as a very elderly woman half-hidden under her umbrella, came through the small gateway carrying a flowerpot of something, and made her way to that same youngster's grave. She stood over it, as if completely unaware of anyone else.

"Look," he whispered. "I might not have written a single line of this book of mine, but I'm good at sniffing rats. Had to be in my job especially with all that Health and Safety crap dumped on us."

"There's one you've missed, then," she smiled, dug in her coat pocket and produced two of the same kind of cakes he'd had for tea yesterday. Their blue icing still unappetisingly Gothic.

"Cheers," he said, taking a bite. "Now, what was it I had to see?"

"Not far. I promise."

"Why not the lead workings down here, if you've got to get back?"

"The upper ones are far more interesting. Besides, I've had a thought. Once I've checked on Heron House, I could drive us to the pub. According to Mr Flynn, they do fab home-made chips."

At this, her companion's tired eyes sparked into life and, for the first time that day, she saw him smile. "And perhaps we can find out more about the intriguing Margiad."

"Right then. Wagons roll."

***

With a white, hiding mist lurking in hedgerow corners and among the neat, slate-roofed barns of a farm called Cysgod y Deri, they trekked along a muddy path churned up by so many sheep's feet and horses' hooves. With each step, Jason's boots made an embarrassing sucking sound. He whistled between his teeth probably to disguise it, but Helen was fixed on something far more serious.

"Pen Carregmwyn's to the right. See?" she said. "Pen means hill."

"Can't miss it. And are those Heron House's chimneys?"

"Correct."

They crossed Rhandirmwyn's main street – originally the turnpike road to Builth – and reached an overgrown junction with yet another weather-beaten fingerpost indicating a turning to the right.

"Up here," she encouraged, and soon, having reached a wide, grassy plateau, the valley view below made her catch her breath. That same farm and its outbuildings like so many tiny dice thrown onto green baize.

For at least a minute his gaze devoured the land and the sky before he turned to her. "Someone should paint this."

"I'm planning to," she said without thinking. And while he listened with what seemed genuine interest, she filled in the gaps of her so-far unsuccessful life.

"OK." He nudged her at the end. "You start on the painting tomorrow, and I'll start my thriller. Deal?"

She hesitated. This was not a realistic proposal. "Deal."

"Anyway, it'll give me an advantage before the other punters show up."

"Not competitive, then?" she grinned, suddenly becoming aware of a sickly, lanolin smell behind her. There, just a few steps away, in a hollow of foul water, lay the torn remains of a ewe and her lamb. Their spines interlocked. The bigger one resembling a long, brown Afro comb, the smaller version white and delicate. "Don't look," she said. "Nature's nasty." And next, as if from nowhere, came the roar of beating wings overhead. Rooks. Too many of them, blackening the sky.

"Move!" Jason grabbed her hand. His felt hot, solid. She found herself blushing.

"They're not interested in us," she said.

"Oh no? I'm not hanging around to find out. I'm an Essex boy, and those gulls out near Bradwell used to try and peck out my eyes whenever I walked to school."

She looked back on the black blur of feathers descending into the hollow, then rising again, beaks full. One even tugged at the poor lamb's spine and, having freed it, carried the trophy high over the forestry.

"Who lives over there?" Jason was pointing left to a neat bungalow nestling against a bank of cherry trees coming into blossom. A small white car parked outside.

"That's Golwg y Mwyn. Aunty Betsan's place. Must have been a cute cottage at one time, but the Welsh can never resist a new bungy. She's that brilliant cook I told you about. You'd not have had spag bol last night without her help."

"How come?"

"I cadged the recipe off her last Wednesday."

Odd what her host had said about The Rat and that despite her smile, she'd seemed ill at ease. Odder still that she, Helen Myfanwy Jenkins of No Fixed Relationship, should be here of all places, with a guy she hardly knew.

In silence, she and Jason sloshed upwards towards that dark kingdom of firs and pines she'd never dared go near on her own. Nantymwyn Forest. Big moolah for someone, she thought. She hated destruction of any kind, and to see these majestic specimens cut down to a uniform size, their sap weeping, trundling along the local roads, made her too want to weep.

"What's that racket?" Jason had stopped in his tracks. Head cocked.

"Only the sawyers hitting their logging targets. You wait till the trees fall. Sounds like thunder."

"So we're here just to listen to falling trees. Great."

Instead of replying, she led him up a steeper gradient to where not only the bare, ragged top of the hill was just steps away, but also where more than four hundred men had once toiled above and below ground for a miserly wage. The land had become boggy, studded with bristling, fan-like reeds. "This is the Nantymwyn site I was telling you about in the car," she said. "Terrible hard work it was, and dangerous. I've done some research into the living conditions of the men – women and kids too – who often came from miles away. Can you imagine what it must have been like here in the depths of winter?"

Jason nodded, staring at the all-too-visible industrial remains of what looked like an engine house guarding a dead tree, and nearby, a tall, two-tone chimney surrounded by silent, cropping sheep.

"There's no sign of the mine manager's house," Helen continued. "And talk was that several workers and those living nearby became seriously ill from the smelting. That graveyard's probably full of them."

"You mean lead poisoning?"

She nodded, thinking again of Heron House's two elderly occupants. "Never mind blood poisoning, it can cause mental illness severe enough for people to be institutionalised, hidden away by their families. Or worse. Apparently Caravaggio became really violent as a result of lead in his oil paints."

Jason had obviously never heard of that sensual painter's name.

"So no compensation, then?"

"I honestly can't say."

"You should have seen the Health and Safety freaks we had at Woolies. If it moved, disinfect it."

She smiled. "There were also lung troubles from the tailings."

"Hello?"

"Dangerous dust."

"And what the Hell is *that*?" He waved at a half overgrown cave-like opening set in the grass and surrounded by barbed wire and another danger notice.

"An adit. It leads to the Angred shaft."

"Adit? Never heard that word before. Do cavers and potholers come up here?"

Helen knew her second laugh was way too loud. Too out of place. He was staring at her as if she too was mad. "If you go down one of these, forget it. Make a will first. When Mr Flynn had a go, he said it was like descending to a watery Hell. Really shook him up, it did. He saw animal bones and God knows what else, so perhaps some predator had used that shaft as a kind of store."

"Wish I'd not asked," said Jason, clearly not joking.

Just then, a different object caught her eye. To the right of the opening stood the same eerie phenomenon she'd spotted three days ago. Black, motionless as before but now turned to face Dinas Hill opposite.

"Sssh," she hissed to Jason. "Look over there. Quick!"

He followed her pointing finger. "Why? It's just some old stone."

56

"No, it isn't. Can't you see? It's the figure of a man. Looks like he's in mourning clothes."

"If you say so." Jason sounded more than fed up. And, despite the cup cake, was probably starving.

"Is that the best you can do? I mean, this is freaky."

"Let's check it out, then. I can try taking a video again."

"No." She held him back with surprising force. "He's up here for a reason. He's obviously interested in this place and we mustn't interfere."

"With no coat? No umbrella? And if he *is* real, how come he's just appeared out of nowhere?"

"You're right." Yet she knew Jason was wrong. Could it be that whoever it was, had made a showing just for them, like for her on Wednesday? If so, why? "Let's just hang around a bit longer," she whispered. "All might be revealed."

Suddenly, before she could stop him, Jason cupped his hands round his mouth and hollered out "Yo there!"

Damn.

The effect of this din was immediate. The previously faceless figure turned their way. Despite Jason's closeness, Helen gasped in fear at that pallid, pained expression, and worse, as the young, brown-haired, pale man himself began to move. Towards them.

***

Jason began legging it down the forestry's waterlogged track. She could tell he was a good runner, not like some, all flailing arms and legs. "So you've seen him before?" he shouted at her.

"Yes. When I called in on Aunty Betsan. His suit's definitely from another era, and did you notice the black tie?"

"I'm thinking funeral too, if you must know." He speeded up, now slithering over wet stones and pieces of bark left by the lorries. The whine of saws had resumed, once more turning the whole scene into a kind of vegetative abattoir. "Christ, what is it with this place?" he complained. "I've come all the way from Hounslow to try and hit the big time, not deal with a load of ghosts."

Nevertheless, Helen couldn't forget the spectre's red-rimmed eyes. That open mouth set mutely in a cry. How, having reached out a hand as if to touch her, he'd merged with the drizzle.

"Why we're calling on Aunty Betsan," she said. "She swore blind to me that she'd not noticed anyone hanging around, but I think she was trying to protect me. Not give me any more worries."

"More worries?" He almost twisted his ankle and swore. "What d'you mean?"

"Nothing. But Mr Flynn said the same to me last Wednesday, about his mortgage being the least of his concerns. I can't help thinking he's in trouble. Perhaps there's no one else he can confide in. And do you blame him, given the alternatives there?"

"Look, you can't take on the sins of the world. He's a big boy. Not short of a bob from what I can see. Maybe he's gone to London to get some new deal, probably with Coutts. There's lots caught up in this slow-down now. Ex-bankers selling *Big Issue* under Waterloo Bridge, for a start."

He's right, she thought. Wasn't that the reason for the planned writing courses? And weren't there only four days to go until the first was due to begin? She then recalled something else.

"So why did she overhear him phoning Islington Police Station before he left?"

Jason didn't reply, as if he was too busy thinking up an answer.

***

As they approached the welcoming dwelling, Helen noticed that the poor dead ewe and lamb they'd seen earlier were now just tufts of sodden fleece. And for an instant she wondered how she'd react if she heard her mam had suddenly died.

"Wait," she said, as Jason reached the plateau first, where Golwg y Mwyn's inky blue slates and newly rendered walls glistened despite the grey light. "Betsan doesn't know you, and we don't want her scared, do we?"

"Thanks."

"I didn't mean it like that."

"Nice car," he said, admiring the immaculate white Modus aligned against the bungalow's front wall. "Bit impossible here without one."

Helen was too busy exploring the bungalow's four windows to reply. Three had their curtains open except those belonging to what she remembered was the lounge. Maybe the seventy-five-year-old was taking a nap in there.

Jason caught up, smelling of rain and wood sap. A smell she could get used to. "She's probably out the back in her herb garden. I'll take a look," she said. And, leaving him out the front, pushed open the unlocked side gate on to that same paved, weed-free path and glanced around at the beautifully tended plot that met her eyes.

No Betsan.

Helen made for the back door and found it unlocked, with no sign of any damage to either the Suffolk latch or the empty keyhole. "That's strange," she muttered to herself, finding it slightly ajar. "Betsan?" she called out. "It's me. Helen, from Heron House. Are you alright? I've brought a new friend to meet you. He really loved your spag bol recipe."

Silence, save for the distant call of birds and the rocking of Helen's heart.

11

Saturday 4th April 2009 – 11.30 a.m.

We don't want her scared, do we?

Even though Helen had tried to laugh that off, she'd made him look an idiot, and he'd been there, done that more times than most twenty-eight-year-olds, especially when grovelling to keep his Woolies' warehouse job.

"You ain't the only one affected," his boss, not far off his pension, had muttered as if he, Jason, had complained about some faulty piece of equipment, not goodbye to a monthly pay cheque and good managerial prospects. And now here he was clinging to his dream in a totally different world where, according to a *Wonderful Wales* brochure he'd skimmed through while waiting for his train at Paddington Station, myths and legends abounded. But nothing like that crazy, untraceable message on his phone, his shape-shifting library book and that body-shaped stain. Never mind the toffee-coloured time-slips…

He'd have to be extra focussed. Extra determined, otherwise, he'd be crawling back to TW4 with his tail between his legs, not having written a word. Which is why, when Helen called out to him from behind the cottage, he didn't answer.

"Quick! Something's wrong!" she yelled again, and during those next few seconds, while finally running in her direction, he knew that getting his best seller off the blocks would be a near-impossible task. That Monty Flynn who'd already plotted his route to fame, would soon be shifting his allegiance elsewhere.

***

He'd never seen a dead human being before. So waxen. So far away and so different from what he'd read in *Evil Eyes*. Unreal was how he'd describe it. The clean corpse, for a start. The peaceful pose. Betsan Griffiths sat propped up by cushions in a polished, wooden Captain's chair, as if she'd merely dozed off. The kitchen, too, seemed normal. Full of cookery books of all sizes and ages, with a table set for two and a simmering pan of lamb stew which, according to that *Wonderful Wales* brochure, the Welsh called 'cawl.'

The smell of it made his stomach lurch, so, using the nearby tea towel to cover his fingers, he switched off the cooker. His hands were trembling. Perhaps the early morning Citalopram was to blame. Perhaps not, but he'd already taken two more than prescribed.

Meanwhile, Helen was leaning over the dead woman, repeatedly and pointlessly checking the pulse in her neck. In her wrist. Smoothing her soft grey curls and, finally, tenderly closing her eyelids. Helen then turned to him, her own eyes shining with tears. "Poor old girl. She must have gone in her sleep. At least it seems she didn't suffer."

"You said the back door was unlocked?" Jason asked as if he'd not heard her.

"So?" She returned her attention to the dead woman, fiddling with her beige twin-set and the well-pressed rayon slacks, telling her how much she'd be missed, and to rest in peace.

"Best not to touch anything," he warned as gently as he could, careful not to let her see his less than manly lips quivering, "just in case."

"In case of what?"

"Either she opened this back door to someone she knew. Someone coming for lunch, or..."

"Rubbish! She was out in her garden. There's not a mark on her. Look."

"Wearing slippers? In this weather?"

Helen stood up as if defeated. He slipped a hand over her heaving shoulders, feeling her bones under her coat. "We should call the cops now," he said, pulling out his mobile, and was about to go for 999 when she stopped him. "Waste of time. Too many hills and trees. Let's check the landline phone."

"Where is it?"

Most people he knew kept theirs in the kitchen. But here, there was nothing.

"Try the lounge,"said Helen, but as soon as she'd clicked open another Suffolk latch, she gasped, gripping on to the door frame. "Oh my God, Jason. Look at this mess! Why would anyone do something so wicked? So destructive?"

"And vengeful, it seems." He stood right behind her, smelling her damp hair, taking in the chaos that had turned a once orderly room into a Council Tip. Thinking that maybe more than one perp had been involved. After all, Betsan Griffiths was hardly a lightweight if she'd been moved.

"She's done me too much harm. Her and her mouth," Helen repeated, picking up one smashed ornament after another. Elegant ladies posing, dancing; angels with outspread wings, children and dogs, you name it, but all with their heads broken off.

"Who said that?" Jason resisted the temptation to open the curtains. *Evil Eyes* had shown him a few tricks. Leave no trace, for a start.

"Betsan referring to The Rat. And I believe her. It's been bugging me ever since, especially how that crone stared after me when I set out for here on Wednesday afternoon." She examined the long, curly ears of a spaniel's severed head, taking care not to let its sharp, glazed edges cut her. "She also tried spreading rumours about Betsan, but I made it quite clear I wasn't interested."

"Rumours?"

"That her mam had bunked off, leaving her so suspicious that any stranger who'd eaten here or taken away something she'd made, came to no good. I don't know what her mam did, but that next bit's got to be a foul lie. Betsan liked people."

Helen picked up another decapitated head, this time belonging to a golden-haired boy. "These Ladro pieces were her pride and joy, but she'd no idea who'd inherit them after she was gone. Don't you think that's a peculiar thing to say? And something else," she repeated the dead woman's remark about Gwenno in full, but Jason was more concerned about a different kind of contamination.

"I've already said don't touch anything," he snapped. "Sorry, but there may be prints, and you don't want to be fingered, do you?"

"Course not. I'm scared."

Meanwhile, he was checking out the skirting board behind the newish-looking TV where only an empty hole remained. "No phone line," he said. "It's been pulled out. Might have guessed." He got to his feet, and extracted his mobile. "Worth another shot with 999. At least she'll be taken care of and the bungalow secured. Dammit," he snapped again, seeing that same rubbish message flash up. He was about to go outside and try a less sheltered spot, when he suddenly saw a yellowed corner of card poking out from under a carriage clock in the centre of the polished stone mantelpiece. This time, with his jacket cuff covering his thumb and forefinger, pulled it free.

NANTYBAI PRIMARY SCHOOL
MONDAY OCTOBER 7TH 1946
FIRST PRIZE IN THE GENERAL KNOWLEDGE TEST
is awarded to *BETSAN ANWEN GRIFFITHS of Golwg y Mwyn.*
Signed: Lionel A. Hargreaves BA Hons. Headmaster.

For a moment, he tried imagining the keen, young schoolgirl; what she might have looked like then, and how it had all come to such a sad end. He also wondered about that kitchen table set for two. For herself and another, or... Just then, he spotted fresh damage to the mantelpiece's edge. He called to Helen still staring at those two photographs. "This is what the figurines must have been bashed against. I just hope she wasn't made to watch." He turned to her. "We didn't see anyone arriving or leaving here, did we?"

"No. And don't tell me that ghost made his way over or I'll freak out."

It was then that Jason was aware of solid rain now hitting the roof. He felt hot. Short of air. He stumbled over the porcelain wreckage, back through the kitchen and the dead woman still tidily in place, out into the deluge where that same hill with its ragged top seemed to have swollen to twice its actual size and, if he wasn't quick, would implode under its own weight, engulfing everything.

He then realised he wasn't alone.

Helen...

"Get out!" he yelled back at her. "Hurry!"

But a mighty shotgun blast, like thunder above the rain, drove away his words and a rush of blackbirds from the nearby trees.

***

What lunatic was out shooting in this weather? Jason pulled out his phone again, protecting it with a free hand, remembering what Helen had said about lead smelting. How it had driven some local people mad. While water coursed down his neck, soaking his skin and his clothes under the expensive and useless leather jacket, he dialled 999. Surely, from where he stood by the car at the front of the cottage, he'd get a signal. But no.

He was just about to chuck the useless thing down on to the slippery grass when his wet ear picked up an all too familiar sound coming through its discreet perforations. A deep sigh like before, then that same haunting plea.

"Remember me... Please... I beg you... No-one else does and I'm so alone..."

Helen was standing at the gate, drenched and bewildered. He couldn't add to her woes. Not now. He shouted into his phone, "Who the Hell is this? Why pick on me?"

"Hell was my home... You will know. You will know..."

"Have you got through?" Helen shouted at him. "Please say yes."

However, as he shook his head, stuffing the phone back in his inside pocket, he heard a new noise. The heavy stomp of boots on loose stones behind him. He twisted round to see a short, well-built guy he guessed to be in his early seventies, dressed completely in black from his bushman's hat to his knee-high boots. A rifle lay strapped to his right shoulder, while his left supported a long pole to which the legs of some twenty fledglings – rooks, crows or ravens, he couldn't tell – had been attached by twists of wire. Each small, feathered body bore a clod of dark blood, and from the beak of the most recent target, hung a glistening red strand soon thinned by the rain. Each victim bore the same bare, whitish patch at the base of the beak as the one in his room last night.

Jason shivered. For the second time that day, his near-empty stomach turned over. As for the guy himself, there was something vaguely familiar about his unshaven face and pinprick eyes that made Jason stare too long. Could this be one of his unborn characters suddenly come to life, toothless and all? Or someone else entirely? Even an older version of that spook on the hill? Whatever. The grizzled stranger was lifting his rifle free of his body. "What you doin' up here?" he challenged in a thick local accent. "This is my patch, boyo. Understood?"

Jason's instinct was to say he'd got lost trying to find the campsite, but the rifle was way too handy for his liking. If he bunked off, Helen would be left in the cottage. In a kitchen still full of knives.

Sod it.

"We need help," he said.

"We?"

"My friend. She's up in that bungalow. Betsan Griffiths has been..."

The stranger's eyes switched away from him.

"Golwg y Mwyn?"

"Yes. I'm trying to get the police but can't get a signal."

At this, the bird-slayer began to run up the slope; his macabre cargo swaying from side to side as he went, while all Jason could think of was Helen catching sight of him first. "Wait!" he shouted after him, realising he didn't know the guy's name. "Wait!"

No joy.

Despite his own running skills, he was too slow and, as he neared the dead woman's little home, even the stinging rain couldn't disguise the frightened scream that filled his ears.

***

The slain birds lay in a line on the wet stone flags outside the back door. No way was Jason going to let any of them touch his boots.

From inside, came voices. His and hers.

"Sorry to give you a fright," the man was saying to Helen. "I do understand. But I don't understand *this*. What's happened to her?"

Helen looked more than relieved as Jason pushed his way in. The man, squatting in a pool of his own rainwater, was checking the old woman's pulse in her wrist.

"Too late for that, I'm afraid," Jason ventured, feeling that four people in that small space were definitely a crowd."We've tried."

"Betsan's been my nearest neighbour for years. I can't just stand by." The farmer glanced up. Offered his hand in greeting. "Gwilym Price, Cysgod y Deri it is, just below here. Buried my wife two years ago. Why I'm dressed like this. Mustn't forget, must we?"

Jason took it, noticing dried blood under the fingernails.

"I'm sorry."

"Cancer from the rain it was, see. Nuclear testing in the fifties, then Sellafield. Gets everyone in the end. 'Cept Betsan." The farmer straightened up. Used the soles of his boots to spread out the water on the stone floor, and in doing so, rubbed away any intruders' possible footprints. Jason didn't dare intervene. Not with that rifle in such close attendance. Nor did he quite believe him.

"Did you reach the police?" Helen asked, still on edge.

"Nope." Tempted for a moment to tell her about that same begging voice. A voice he now realised belonged to a young woman.

"I'll go," said Price. "They know me, see. I've caught 'em napping more times than Betsan here made hot dinners. "And what have they done about my best dog that got run over on Wednesday? Give you one guess." He lowered his head. "Bob and me won all the trials, we did. Local and national. He could round up a herd of bloody monkeys."

"So it *was* him I saw," said Helen. "What a horrible accident."

"That were no accident. Someone round here's got a grudge. A big grudge. Didn't run him over proper like. Oh no. Just his back end. He tried dragging himself back home..." His glistening eyes fixed on them both. "Can I trust you to stop here with my rooks?"

Jason nodded, his mind racing. Never mind the spooky stuff, was the man right? Was something pretty sick going on?

"Funny thing, I never saw her without her Jesus." Her neighbour rubbed his wet eyes with his dirty cuff. "So where is it?"

"Did she go to church?"

"Off and on. She wasn't that keen on non-conformism, but she was a good woman. A real good woman. Come the winter, if I'd not had the time to cook, she'd bring down a nice bowl of cawl and a home-made roll for me." Those small, moist eyes now fixed on the stove. "Looks like there's cawl here now. And," glancing at the formica table, where two lots of cutlery, glasses and side plates had been set out, "someone to share it with her."

Helen gasped.

"We never noticed that, did we? And it's a really obvious clue."

"The police," Jason reminded Gwilym Price, rather than acknowledge he'd been slack. Aware that the man just getting into his stride, had forgotten his offer to call them.

"No-one had a bad word to say about you," the rook-killer addressed his dead neighbour, stroking her hair. "Mind you, she wasn't short of a penny, what with all the cooking she done. Even the pub used her when their generator played up. And as for that campsite..." He turned his gaze on Betsan's dead body again, while Jason saw the second hand on his watch moving round too fast, and Helen tensing up. "I've seen enough death round here in my time, but not one so... so unmarked. There's no bruise, nothing."

"Poison?" Jason suggested, wondering if there might have been cash stored away somewhere. Making amends for his earlier slip-up.

The farmer shook his head. His hat still darkly in place. "Ever seen what that does to a body? She'd be soiled. Top and bottom. No, seems to me she was suffocated. Gently, mind, like they are in them hospices where my wife ended up. Can see it now. Grabbed from behind. Caught by surprise, and then perhaps a cushion. 'Cept there don't appear to be none. Only what she's sitting on."

"Maybe chloroform?" said Jason, recalling the vilest film he'd ever watched. "Ever seen *The Vanishing* where those young Dutch tourists...?"

"Don't!" Helen cried out. "That's enough!"

"And my guess is," Price continued, making for the door, "judging by the number of pigs I've dispatched in my time – and pigs is close to humans as you know – Betsan's only been gone an hour or so." He eyed the stove. "State of the cawl suggests the same. Cooker was switched on about then too."

"Maybe the table's set like this to be a red herring," said Helen, and Jason had to acknowledge she wasn't just a pretty face. A clever but fearful, pretty face.

"Hurry with that phone call, Mr Price," he said. "Whoever's responsible, may still be around. May want us out of the way, too."

***

On his way out, the farmer turned towards Helen. "By the way, Miss

Jenkins, how long is it you've been at the asylum?"

Her mouth fell open. "What?"

"Heron House."

"Why call it that?"

A short but loaded laugh followed.

Jason, aware of the stew's lingering smell, now something quite different, saw Helen's hand cover her nose as a sly brown stain spread down each leg of the deceased's rayon slacks and dribbled to the floor.

"Surely you don't need me to say. What with you, Miss Jenkins, working there and all. Those were Betsan's very own words."

12

Monday 7th October 1946 – 8 a.m.

Although the too-large black suit he'd worn for young Walter's funeral now hung in his wardrobe, Lionel decided to continue wearing its matching tie for the remainder of the week. Not only as a mark of respect, but also to remind himself of his mission. He'd spent too many sleepless hours imagining how blame would bring him an empty schoolroom, and now, having shaved and dressed, he glanced at his grandfather's old pocket watch.

Eight o'clock.

News on the wireless of the communist takeover of Bulgaria would have to wait. He was already late.

***

As Lionel opened his front door, the thick morning mist curled around his shoes, obliterating the sight but not the sound of shod hooves stopping by his gate. His pulse quickened as he recalled that unnerving encounter on Saturday, and just as he was about to slam the door shut, a muffled but familiar laugh, reached his ears.

Of course. What a fool I am. It's Carol.

"Only me, Mr Hargreaves," came her welcome voice. "I know I'm not usually this early, but everything'll take longer in this lot."

Carol Carr, young postwoman *extraordinaire,* leaned down from her saddle to hand him a substantial bundle of letters. "You're popular."

Not always...

He took the post aware of her fingers brushing against his. The combined smells of horse sweat and the damp morning assailing his nose. "You watch how you go," he said and meant it. "This fog'll be worse up by Nantymwyn."

"It's the oddest thing," as she patted her chestnut cob's neck. "But Lucky here hates going to Heron House. Every time, without fail, he digs his heels in outside the gates. Fair wears me out kicking him on, and more than once, I've had to dismount and walk up that drive myself."

How could he suggest she use a post van instead? During the war, Carol had come south from Shrewsbury to work in the Women's Timber Corps. He knew she loved being close to nature, whatever the weather, and had been sorry to leave at the end of last year. Even to lose her 'Lumberjill' nickname. No time now to dwell upon her strange remark or to tentatively ask her to call in some time next Sunday afternoon for a cup of tea. She had a job to do, and he likewise. Starting in half an hour's time.

"Don't give up here, Mr Hargreaves," she said out of the blue, before turning her mount round. "I've heard folks complain about what happened at your school last week. They're ignorant and cruel, and should know better."

Without giving him a chance to thank her, and having stuffed her curly brown hair back under her cap, she gathered up her reins and began to move off.

"By the way," he called after her, "you haven't by any chance noticed a large black car around here?"

"Why?"

He hesitated. Carol visited every door in the neighbourhood, often stopping to chat to those who'd not seen another living soul all week. But behind those doors lurked a multitude of mischievous tongues. Best to tell a lie.

"Last week during lunchtime, I took a walk up Pencarrig Hill and saw one travelling up the forestry road like a bat out of Hell. Nearly ran me over."

She thought for a moment while Lucky's front hoof struck the ground with impatience. "The only one I can think of belongs to Heron House. What make was it?"

Walter hadn't said...

"Not sure, but thank you anyway. I'm sorry to have kept you."

"No trouble." She raised a hand in farewell, kicked her mount on.

Heron House?

He'd never heard of it, neither had there ever been any children from there at school. He knew the class registers better than his own heart from as far back as before the Great War, when its doors had first opened. His curiosity about the demographics of this, a typical rural Welsh community through two major upheavals and the loss of coal and lead mining, had turned to astonishment upon discovering how many inhabitants had left for the New World and Patagonia. Most, evolved from the ancient Brythionic tribes, had chosen to leave their homeland that sustained only forestry, livestock farming and seasonal fishing. He'd also wondered how many had regretted their decision.

Now, he found himself following the cob's doleful hoof beats, even though the track became muddier and more slippery. "Who lives up there?" he called out after Carol. His voice thin in the choking mist. "I mean, at Heron House."

"Some big-wig judge, I think. Never met him though. Just the girl and boy who help out. Most of his mail's from Cardiff, mind; but I can't for the life of me remember his name. Double-barrelled, that's for sure."

"And the younger generation?"

"Too old for your school, if that's what you're thinking." She drove the cob forwards. "Got to move, Mr Hargreaves, or I'll never get round."

And so all trace of her faded, leaving him to imagine her sturdy figure rising and falling to the trot's regular beat.

***

As if arriving at Nantybai School without his carefully filled briefcase wasn't bad enough, half of Lionel's class of twenty were absent, with no explanation given. While he donned his Birmingham University gown before pinning up four posters showing the pyramids of the Nile and Tutankhamun's tomb on the wall next to the blackboard, those pupils who'd elected to attend, stared at him in a way he'd not experienced before. Ten pairs of accusing eyes kept up the punishment while he called the register. They'd brought the fog in with them. It clung to their damp clothes, their flattened hair.

Three boys, seven girls, most of whom had been at Walter's funeral and, when the last name had been called, Lionel Hargreaves made a decision. He was about to rely on a hunch as slender as the vaporous air now dispersing over the desks.

"Instead of learning about Hiroshima or the massacre at Oradour sur Glâne, which took place in France just four days after the Allied landings, we're staying much closer to home. In fact," he replaced the tin of drawing pins in his desk drawer, "I want to find out just how clever and observant you all are."

The surly stares vanished just like that cold, white cloak that had descended on the whole area overnight.

"How'll ye do that?" asked Dai Meat's son, Aled; deliberately omitting the word 'sir.'

"By a little general knowledge." He glanced from one child to another. Most were, like Walter, small for their age. All except Aled who had access to plenty of protein without a ration book's permission. "Now then, have you each a piece of paper and a pen? The answer should be yes. If not, come up to my desk. Oh, and at the end, there'll be a prize," he added, without

70

thinking what or how... A paper kite perhaps? Or a set of coloured pencils conjured from nowhere?

The scramble that followed took him by surprise, and not for the first time, he remarked to himself how easily people are bribed. Even the young. Especially it seemed, the young. When all were ready, keenly watching his lips, he withdrew his watch and, for maximum visibility, laid it on his blotter. He mustn't jump straight in. Rather, try a more circuitous route to the answers he wanted. "You have four minutes per question. Number one," he began. "How many working farms are there within a ten-mile radius of The Fox and Feathers?"

"Why?" Aled again withholding the word 'sir.'

Lionel didn't reply. The other nine pupils were thinking hard. Thanks to his efforts, all could at least write legibly. Better in English than Welsh which was more the language of the hearth and, if the current 'Welsh Not' continued, doomed to stay there. Also, all, unlike some of their older relations poisoned by the lead fumes, were thankfully *compos mentis*.

While they wrote, he stared at Walter Jones' empty desk and then at the floor where he'd fallen. All trace of his blood had been cleaned away, making the next question more necessary. "Now then, name all the big houses within that same ten-mile radius."

"Poshies and Saesnegs," piped up Alys Humphreys whom he knew had been abandoned as an infant and taken in by the smith and his wife just two doors away.

Her neighbour, Betsan Griffiths, an unusually fair-haired twelve-year-old, glanced up at Lionel as if expecting a reprimand for even breathing the same air as Alys. But a reprimand could wait. Too many words were already flowing on to paper, especially from this same blonde pupil whose father had perished on Normandy's Juno Beach. Whose final letter home sent in May 1944, hadn't arrived until last Monday. "Time's up. Question three is transport. How many different pony and traps have you seen since summer ended?"

"This is stupid," hissed the orphan. "What do we need to know that for?"

"A prize." Aled now busier than the rest.

"Question four," Lionel continued. "How many camouflaged trucks are still being used by the Home Guard?"

"My tadci's one of them, sir," boasted Kyffin Morgan, the lad nearest to Walter's desk, and his best friend. "Did you know he's being kept on till Christmas, just in case? You seen his pillbox down by the Towy?"

"No, I haven't."

"Or the barbed wire he won't let anyone touch?"

Lionel shook his head. To him, all this smacked of paranoia. Not the only dark side to this otherwise lovely part of the world. "And finally," he returned to the job in hand, and the most important question of all. "Number five, everyone. Wait for it. How many big black cars?"

***

Once the small class had trooped off home to lunch, he scoured their answers, aware of his late father's less than positive opinion of him peck-pecking at his mind. Supposing there was chatter in their homes about big houses and luxury cars? Supposing someone other than friendly Carol Carr would soon be knocking on his door? The girl with the gun came to mind.

Before also leaving the schoolhouse, Lionel placed all but one of the answers into the smouldering fire, where the addition of paper made the flames turn blue and reach up the chimney. With not a moment to lose and the fireguard securely in place, he locked the door behind him. Freed from his gown and, with gloves on and coat collar pulled up over his ears, he followed the track away from his cottage, up towards Cerrigmwyn Hill. Each step bringing a tangible sense of foreboding.

13.

Saturday 4th April 2009 – 1.30 p.m.

Helen had never seen anyone eat so fast, not even Mr Flynn after most of a morning spent in this very place. Jason had used fingers too, when a knife and fork would not only have been more civilised, but might also have demonstrated that after all the touching and hand-holding up on the hill, she wasn't invisible.

He gobbled up the last of his chips and washed them down with a half pint of real ale that Judy Withers, the publican's dolled-up partner, had suggested he try.

"I thought you were feeling queasy," Helen said ungenerously. She'd barely touched her scampi. When she'd broken the first bread-crumbed shell, the colour and smoothness of what lay inside, had so reminded her of Aunty Betsan's dead flesh, that she preferred to pick at her lettuce leaf instead.

"I was." He wiped his mouth with the edge of his sweatshirt sleeve and, with the first unwelcome pangs of a period pain, she realised how different from women men really were. Less guilt for a start.

"What did you make of that Gwilym Price referring to Heron House as an asylum?" she began, as a couple wearing damp Barbours entered the room, with a brown Labrador in tow.

"We've been through all that. Probably jealous. I mean, if he has to resort to killing poor rooks for a living."

Indeed, they *had* been through all that, while struggling down through the torrent from Golwg y Mwyn – now a crime scene – to this warm haven. But Helen wasn't so sure about Jason's too-slick answer, and resolved to speak some more to the farmer. Sooner rather than later. "I wonder if he didn't have a thing for Betsan, though," she ventured. "And not just for her cawl. Even though she was quite a bit older. Just the way he touched her. Did you notice? He didn't hang about getting the cops and the ambulance either."

"But did you see his face when the Fuzz did show up? If looks could kill."

Obviously still hungry, Jason was studying the laminated menu's dessert section. "He wouldn't be top of my list for a party."

He gestured to the blonde at the bar and, having checked that Helen didn't want anything else to eat, ordered himself profiteroles. "Mind you, his suffocation theory was interesting. Might nick that idea for my thriller."

"At least the fat cop didn't dismiss it."

"Mr Halitosis?"

She nodded. Being grilled at the bungalow by DC Rhydian Prydderch plus his equally large sidekick Sergeant Rees for half an hour had been no joke, and she'd been almost glad to get back to Heron House to check if her boss had perhaps made contact. If the roof was still in one piece. Only when The Rat had waylaid them both with a barrage of questions, did Helen suspect the woman knew nothing of Mr Flynn's last-minute plans or of Betsan Griffiths' death. OK, she'd told herself. The nutter could catch up at three o'clock. Officially.

"You two feeling a bit better now after your ordeal?" Judy Withers enquired over the heads of her latest customers both knocking back a double G&T apiece.

"Yep, thanks," smiled Jason, while Helen tried to stem the small surge of jealousy that made her wish the bubbly blonde with the glossy lip plumper had work to do in the kitchen.

No such luck. She was bringing over his profiteroles. A lumpy mountain of chocolate and cream. Her perfume in close-up was way too strong. *Poison*. Heffy's favourite, and, a fleeting memory of the two of them running along Aberystwyth's promenade in the blustery west wind, made Helen's eyes sting all over again.

"She were a real pet, were Miss Griffiths," the woman said. "Let's just hope it were natural, if you get my meaning."

"So do we." Jason's annoying smile still lurked at the corners of his mouth as he attacked the mounds of choux pastry. "There are several possibilities as to what happened."

"Can't think who'd want to do her in. No-one from Rhandirmwyn, that's for sure. I expect the police will soon be here picking our brains. Let's hope we can help get a result." She walked away on her strappy, heeled sandals. Panty line visible beneath her tight skirt.

"You mean, get yourself in the papers," muttered Helen under her breath, signalling to Jason she wanted to leave. He however, seemed rooted to his seat, staring after her. "How long have you both been running this place?" he asked before draining the last drop of his beer.

"Almost two years now." The blonde began wiping over the bar and polishing the mirror behind it. Her reflected mouth doing the talking. Her kohl-rimmed eyes on his. "So any folks we've not yet met, we've certainly heard of them."

Helen felt her hackles rise. How could these people possibly know what lay hidden in Heron House's shadows? She pushed her loaded plate to the middle of the table as Jason began speaking again. "So have you heard of anyone called Margiad? Possibly connected to Heron House."

"Not me. But my Doug might know. Sounds an old-fashioned name to me."

Jason looked disappointed.

"And speaking of Heron House," the woman now caught Helen's eye and turned to face her. "Where's that gorgeous Mr Flynn of yours? Never usually gives us a miss."

A second shot of jealousy hit Helen's heart. Her interrogator must have remembered their one visit here together. May have fancied him.

"London," said Jason before Helen could fob her off. "Maybe to do with some businessman there who's just been found hanged. A Charles Pitt-Rose."

"Thanks, you." Helen landed a kick to his left shin. He let out a yelp and stood up. His already rosy cheeks burning bright. A small blob of cream on his chin. "We agreed not to spread this around."

"You OK?" Judy Withers looked concerned.

"I'll have to be," he replied, making for the door, while Helen pulled her waxed coat off the back of her chair. Unrepentant, she too needed space to think. To rebuild the wall she kept around herself. To guard what little remained for her paintings yet to be born.

"Now then, that name rings a bell." The blonde announced all of a sudden.

Helen started. Saw her lift up the bar flap and come over again. "The moment your boyfriend said it, I knew."

Meanwhile the 'boyfriend' had placed himself outside the window, staring in, while Helen's pulse rate quickened.

"Used to live where you are. So Mr Price said."

"At Heron House?" Helen asked.

"That's the one. With two of those special places where herons breed."

"Heronries?"

A nod. "All killed, they were. Pulled to pieces, so he said."

Asylum...

Helen watched Jason disappear from view up the road. "That's terrible. Who did it?"

"No-one seems to know. I think at one point, Mr Flynn planned to restock till he began exploring other ideas that could make him some dough."

"You mean writers' courses?"

The other woman seemed surprised. "He's not mentioned them. Mind you, a nice little earner for us if that did happen. Our new menu's really taken off."

Helen was tempted to sit down again. That dull, monthly ache had intensified. She needed a paracetamol and a hot water bottle, but DC Prydderch was coming to the house at three o'clock, and she had to be there before The Rat nibbled at him first. "There are some Pitt-Roses buried in the churchyard," Helen said."Edmund and his wife Joy." She then added their death dates. "Were they from Heron House as well, I wonder?"

"Not sure. But we heard it were empty a good while before Mr Flynn came along. At least, sort of empty."

"What do you mean?"

Just then however, a troupe of hungry campers, Helen assumed were from the Towy's riverside site, converged on the bar, bringing the wet afternoon in with them. Helen managed to pay, pocket her change then slip out behind them, too deep in thought to notice she was being watched. In fact, more than watched. Followed.

***

Helen caught up with Jason at the top of the track that led to Heron House. "How's your leg? I didn't mean to kick it, you know. It's girl stuff, OK? Otherwise known as The Curse…"

Suddenly he stopped. Faced her with beer still on his breath. He placed both hands on her shoulders with such a weight, she tried to free herself.

"Look, I've gone through quite a bit recently. Do you understand? Do you?" His voice sounded different in ways she couldn't explain. "And now I've a book to write. Why I've come back here. Or have you forgotten?"

"Come *back* here?" she repeated. "I don't get it."

He let go to produce his wallet and extract two twenty-pound notes which he stuffed into her coat pocket. "Petrol and pub grub, so I don't owe you anything. And by the way, I got through to Orange. They've no record of either of those calls I had. Not a sausage."

She handed him back his money.

"You had more than one call?"

"Yep. Two. The second was an hour ago up at Betsan's place. I didn't want to freak you out." He moved on, lengthening his stride, and that same sense of loss she'd felt, when following Rhys Maddox's coffin at his funeral, enveloped her.

"According to that blonde bombshell in the pub, a Charles Pitt-Rose *did* live here," she called after him. "What d'you make of that?" But he was too far away; his black-jacketed figure soon lost amongst the wall of still-bare trees that seemed to guard the old, neglected swimming pool.

She then heard him and another man speaking, but couldn't make out who. Time to return indoors. Period pain or no period pain, there was important work to do.

**

With the cop's visit only fifteen minutes away, Helen wasted no time and, having checked as best she could that no-one had tailed her indoors, ran up to the first floor with the weight of her wet coat slowing her down. She continued to run along the narrow, unlit corridor until she turned the nasty little corner where Mr Flynn's office-cum-bedroom was situated over the lock-ups.

Her head throbbed like a beating drum. Her mouth dry as dust while she tried to compose herself, listening harder than ever for the slightest sound of her adversary, The Rat; mentally preparing herself for lock-picking. Last autumn, there'd been a cop drama on her mam's TV, where a banished husband returning to the family home, used his Visa card and a ballpoint spring on the property's more vulnerable side door. She'd watched closely, little realising how soon she'd be aping this actor's every move.

However, none of this trick was necessary, for the door handle was already turning sweetly in her hand; the widening gap revealing her boss' sanctuary inch by alarming inch. She could only think that his being in such a rush that morning could explain this carelessness.

She closed his door behind her and tiptoed towards a substantial oak desk – the battered variety that's often left for firewood at the end of a country auction. On it, in surprising orderliness, stood a computer showing a Mountains-of-Mourne screensaver; a collection of pens and felt tips, plus a framed black and white photo of some leggy boy fishing from a boat. She guessed it was him by his gap-toothed smile, but not his hair, thick, wavy, almost white, blowing in the wind.

But where was his supposed library? His own published books? Unless hidden behind a false wall, there wasn't one hardback or paperback to be seen. And what about a possible internet connection? No time to check. She had to focus on the desk's six drawers, each bearing an empty keyhole and unidentifiable smells. It did cross her mind that perhaps The Rat had got here first and helped herself, but no. She soon found quantities of clear plastic wallets that slithered around in her hot hands. A quick perusal showed they contained a copy of her own contract and other stuff including handwritten notes on property law, particularly landlords' and lessees' rights. Because of the murky light, she had to carry these over to the small sash window at the front. Unlike Jason's identical window, its frayed cords had broken, but there was no time to speculate why Mr Flynn hadn't done a repair. Her own rapid breathing filled her ears as she passed his unmade bed whose mattress showed not the usual imprint of a sleeping body, but of turbulence.

At last.

The marginally better light revealed a stapled collection of papers headed HERON HOUSE. At the same time, her dull groin ache began to bite. Her throbbing head to return with a vengeance.

And what was this leaping at her from the page?

RENTAL AGREEMENT FOR HERON HOUSE.
Date: 12/2/07
BETWEEN MR. CHARLES PITT-ROSE,
owner, of 3, Sandhurst Mansion, Thornhill Avenue, Islington.
London N4 8TJ
AND MR. MONTGOMERY FLYNN
formerly of 10, Burnside Villas, Crosskelly. N.Ireland.

There were other shocks too, not least that someone much stronger was suddenly behind her, pinning her sore stomach against the window sill. One hand over her mouth, the other, pulling the pages from her hand. A man whose reek of sweat and cheap aftershave made her gag.

Only when the blue and yellow chequered police Range Rover swerved into the drive, did her assailant draw back and run from the room, but not before she'd registered his approximate age, the bald head, scruffy clothes and huge, muddy trainers. A complete stranger, who could, without this timely interruption, have probably killed her.

14.

Saturday 4th April 2009 – 2.50 p.m.

When Jason had left Hounslow, the municipal plane trees had been bursting into leaf, while the line of cherry blossom along Pinetree Road created a pale pink haze that went some way to soften the façades of its shops and offices. Here, however, at Heron House, it seemed the chestnut trees' twisted old branches would never bud. Instead, they hung dripping over, what must have once been a handsome swimming pool, like so many malevolent, grasping arms, host to a colony of rooks whom he felt were keeping him under observation. He tried to identify the one who'd so brazenly commandeered his room last night, but none – as far as he could tell – had quite the same vivid white patch beneath the beak.

From his vantage point at the top of the overgrown bank, he then watched Idris Davies in his baggy boiler suit, wield a huge besom – bigger than anything Woolies had stocked – sweep every single dead leaf into that rectangle of black slime. With every small disturbance, it gave off an equally pungent whiff of organic decay as the nearby septic tank. The man must have lost all his sense of smell.

Whether or not the real ale was making him set caution aside, Jason called out to him. "Why are you doing that? It needs emptying, not filling in any more."

But the gardener was either stone deaf or ignoring him deliberately, and Jason who'd endured enough of that kind of rudeness from his ex-manager, felt his blood heat up. He also noticed the guy's unshaven neck. The way his lips moved as he brushed, allowing a wet, pink tongue to pop in and out.

"Hi? Mr Davies?" he tried again. Louder this time, but in a more reasonable tone. "I'm Jason Robbins."

The guy angled his head towards him like some old turtle eyeing him up and down. "Who?"

Jason repeated his name, adding, "I'm a writer."

"Writer? What you doin' here, then?"

"There'll be more of us come Friday. Why I'm concerned about the state of this pool, and the septic tank. That it over there?" He pointed to the rusted, raised lid set in a hollow below the overgrown bank.

"What's them to you?"

"To be honest, they stink."

A pause, during which the old man's body language took a turn for the worse. But Archie Tait wouldn't have run. Nor the private investigator hero in his thriller, whom he'd now named Dan Carver.

"That's your opinion," snarled the gardener. "Mine is that wino's got no business letting strangers in. Bad enough he hired that tart in the kitchen when my Gwenno could have made food much better."

That tart?

Jason felt his cheeks seriously burn. This was well out of order, but the old man had started sweeping again, deliberately directing wet debris up on to Jason's boots.

He'd paid a deposit for the course and good money for the time being. He wasn't up for being humiliated. "I'll pass your slander on to Miss Jenkins. See what she thinks."

The obsessive sweeper turned his back, and Jason felt his warmed-up blood was now a cold snake uncoiling itself around his internal organs.

"Where's the witness?" His adversary gestured towards the dead trees. "Them rooks there? I don't think so." He moved away, swinging his broom defiantly from side to side, muttering stuff Jason couldn't quite hear. He noticed how the birds left their branches and, like some huge black flower, cast a mysterious, moving shadow over the whole scene.

"The Fuzz is coming at three o'clock," Jason shouted after the man, his cheeks now red hot. "Wanting to know who topped Betsan Griffiths. Might be best to show your face." Jason almost said 'ugly mug' instead,' but restrained himself.

Idris Davies turned again to face him, jabbing two angry fingers in the air.

***

Naff off yourself.

Still angry and half-tempted to run after the prick, Jason slithered down the rest of the bank towards what had once been an expensively tiled poolside terrace, wide enough for any number of tables and chairs. And the more his eyes roamed from its moss-encrusted pattern to the rusted side-bars of invisible steps into what had once been water, other, more shadowy shapes began to materialise. He blinked twice to clear his vision, aware of a cold, rogue breeze stroking his skin as these shadows became solid, moving. However, unlike those three mysterious figures he'd seen on his arrival at Heron House, this quartet were all men of Colin's age or thereabouts, kitted out in morning suits and cummerbunds that strained over their well-fed stomachs.

They grouped and regrouped as if in slow motion with easy familiarity, drinking from glasses of vivid, red wine. The only colour, made all the more startling in the monochrome silence.

Was this some after-dinner gathering with the women still indoors? Or the kind of secret meeting Monty Flynn said he'd dealt with in his books? Too late, Jason realised he'd forgotten to breathe and, having taken a sudden, deep gulp of the tainted air, hiccuped far too loudly. The phone, ready in video mode, fell to the ground.

When Jason straightened up, the four guys who'd stopped their mute conversation were appraising him in such a way, that although that nippy breeze had eased, he had to steady himself with the help of a handy branch. It was as if those eyes – four icy knives – had suddenly pierced his heart.

***

Still shaken, still dwelling on Idris Davies, and the strange swimming pool gathering, Jason heard wheels rattling the gravel on the drive behind him. He turned to see that same chequered Range Rover he'd spotted at Golyg y Mwyn, complete with DC Prydderch looking fed up.

Join the club, he thought, not only because Helen's recent kick had drawn blood on his shin, but his planned best seller featuring Dan Carver was receding from his brain by the second.

"You did tell the Davieses I'd be here?" the cop said through his open window. A whiff of cheese and pickle wafted Jason's way. "Can't stop long, see. We've an incident down the town."

So much for his promised thorough investigation, thought Jason. Whereas Dan Carver, a man of principles, would leave no stone unturned in his quest for justice. "I did, just five minutes ago," Jason said, "but he buggered off. As for his wife, when have I had a chance to see her?"

The corpulent cop, perhaps anticipating a complaint, softened his tone.

"And Miss Jenkins, your partner? She around?"

"I've already explained to you. She's not my partner. I left her near the pub. We'd had what you might call an altercation." He liked that word, but not its reality. He wondered again where she was.

The Range Rover churned on past him, whereupon its driver climbed out, engine running. His bloodshot eyes glanced around until he pointed in the direction of the bare chestnuts. "Who's that over there?"

Jason followed the fat forefinger to where a skinhead wearing jeans and a dark blue top was vaulting over an old stile and running up the hill beyond.

"God knows. Never seen him before. But the gardener might have."

The cop pulled his two-way from its holder around his sizeable girth and spoke in Welsh to whoever had answered. The five words Jason recognised were "Heron House, suspicious," and "Idris Davies."

Prydderch ended the call and checked his watch. Had the Fuzz really somewhere to go that was more important than this? Jason urged himself to keep thinking like Dan Carver to make him even more real in his mind. Suspicious of everything and everyone. No holds barred.

"Was Betsan killed?" Jason asked.

"It's beginning to look that way."

Jason loped off in the direction of the stile, but soon realised that the effort was a waste of breath. Neither the running guy nor Idris Davies was anywhere to be seen. And what the Hell was Helen doing?

All he had for his trouble was waterlogged boots and a throbbing head. Back at the house, the cop was waiting for him, black briefcase in hand, unimpressed. The Range Rover's engine now turned off.

"We should try and catch him," Jason panted. "He could appear again. Nick stuff, whatever."

"We will. Any stranger round here soon gets noticed and people talk. My God, how they talk." DC Prydderch indicated the house's porch. "Who's that woman standing there?"

"Gwenno. Mrs Davies. The gardener's wife. Got some pretty weird habits, too."

A flicker of interest showed in those unhealthy eyes. "Such as?"

"I reckon you'll soon be seeing for yourself."

***

But no. Gone was the dowdy skirt and shoes, the apron and that weird riding crop. In their place, a neat, grey dress with prim white collar. Matching heels too, and pearly pink lipstick, applied in a hurry it would seem, spreading beyond her thin, dry mouth. Ignoring Jason, she curtsied and held out her hand to the uniform busy scraping his shoes on the iron heron.

Jason saw her smile, then cottoned on. She must be on the pull. She also must have somehow known this cop was coming.

"I'm so very, very sorry to hear about Miss Griffiths," she pre-empted the visitor. "A lovely, lovely woman. Whoever would want to kill her? I do hope to goodness she didn't suffer, that's all I can say."

She did me harm. Her and her mouth.

"How come you've heard about it?" quizzed the Fuzz.

A tiny pause which he didn't seem to notice.

"My Idris was up the hill, see. Saw your blue and yellow car coming away from her bungalow. Then he met Gwilym Price. Likes to blab does that one. What living alone does to you."

"*We* never saw Mr Davies, nor anyone else," Jason countered, and was rewarded by a look of pure venom. "We – meaning myself and Miss Jenkins – were both at her home for quite a while."

"Is there somewhere we can sit?" asked the visitor, snapping open his briefcase and pulling out a red file that reminded Jason too vividly of his last job. "With your husband too?"

Those flirty eyes immediately hardened. "Why him? I can help you much better. Anyway," Gwenno spat, "where's that Miss Jenkins?"

That tart.

"I've already spoken to her, and I'm sure she'll be along shortly." Prydderch's look matched hers. "Mrs Davies, may I remind you, this is a murder investigation."

That 'm' word and all its implications made Jason shudder. Gwenno, however, seemed to relish it.

"How was she murdered?" The old woman persisted.

"I'm not at liberty to say. But we must start by collecting statements from everyone who happened to be in the vicinity of Golwg y Mwyn this morning. Give your Idris a shout, eh? And while we're at it, have you noticed a man in his early forties hanging around this house and grounds?"

He added the guy's description and all the while, the cleaner's piercing little eyes fixed on Jason, who was miffed *he'd* not provided the details considering he'd done all the running. Now his beery head was paying for it.

Gwenno shook her white curls. "Honest to God, sir; I can't think who that might be. Now then," she smiled at DC Prydderch again, "I'll bring some tea through."

"No time for that, ta," said the visitor as he and Jason followed her into the reception hall where a log fire was beginning to fade, making little difference to the big room's overall chill.

Once seated, the cop reopened his briefcase and lifted out a thick notebook. The kind Jason had ready for his thriller's notes. "Where's Mr Flynn?" he asked no-one in particular, as if to test the water.

The old woman seemed genuinely confused. "Isn't he back from the Fox and Feathers yet? That's where he is most mornings."

"He never went there," said a younger, female voice from the stairs beyond the hall. "He's gone to London, and I've just had some thug upstairs attack me."

Helen.

Pale yet defiant. Oddly beautiful, even in her damp Barbour.

"That's an extremely serious allegation, Miss Jenkins," the Fuzz snapped, clearly unsettled.

Jason immediately went over to stand next to her. "Are you OK?" he whispered.

"Sort of. No thanks to him over there."

"I thought you'd gone back down the pub."

"Well, you thought wrong." She was now staring in disbelief at the lipsticked cleaner whose hands were gripping the fabric of her dress. Then Helen turned to the detective constable, at the same time, lifting up her jumper to reveal a reddened strip of skin just above her navel. "Did this myself, did I?"

Jesus.

"Do I have to call Llandovery?" Jason had put on his Dan Carver voice.

It worked.

DC Prydderch reddened before turning to the old couple. "Best if you wait here. You too, Mr Robbins."

"But..."

"The less distraction the better. We've statements to write then I got to get back, remember? Now then, young lady, show me exactly where this supposed incident happened."

***

Fifteen minutes later, Jason, under instruction from DC Prydderch to find the missing gardener, returned to Heron House with Idris Davies plus his clogged-up besom, stop-starting in front of him. The man was obviously reluctant to see anyone, never mind the Fuzz. He'd been urinating by a former pig pen up near the far fence when Jason had found him. Not a pretty sight.

"DC Prydderch's in a rush," Jason explained to Davies. "Won't take long. Besides, we're all in this together."

"All in what?"

"Murder."

"Speak for yourself." The gardener turned that reptilian eye on him again. They'd almost reached the porch. Time was running out.

"Did you happen to see Gwilym Price today?" Jason pressed his casual button. Under-used of late.

"Should I have done?"

"Or a bald-headed guy running away from the house?"

84

"When?"

"Just after I'd seen you."

"After you insulted me, more like."

Jason let it go. The man, like his wife, was a downright liar, but he wouldn't be counting on PC Plod to pursue it. Nor move his bulk to check for footprints by that stile before they got messed up by wildlife, or even this man himself if he'd something to hide.

As he held the front door open for the gardener and his broom to go in first, he told himself that if Betsan Griffith's puzzling death was ever to be solved, he'd do it. And then, as if a black rose had suddenly bloomed in his mind, he remembered the name Margiad.

***

"Ah, Mr Idris Davies, I believe. We don't have much time, but we need your help." DC Prydderch waved the surly looking man towards the one vacant armchair and passed both him and Jason a blue Lottery biro and statement form apiece. Gwenno glared at her husband as if his being indoors was a crime in itself, while Helen, drawing a small picture of Betsan sitting upright in her Captain's chair, was still avoiding Jason's eyes. He wondered what else she'd said about her recent ordeal. Obviously not enough to divert the Fuzz from Miss Griffiths. Being dead was the only way to get attention, it seemed.

"Accuracy, remember?" the Fuzz with bad breath reminded everyone. "Accurate movements. Accurate times. To fabricate, or leave out crucial information is a criminal offence."

With his first sentence down in black and white, Jason's words seemed to fly from the one decent Woolies' ballpoint he'd kept. In fact, he had a job to keep to the facts and not exaggerate. 'This isn't your book,' he'd warned himself. 'Stick to the facts.'

Suddenly, Idris Davies crumpled up his sheet and threw it on the fire whereupon a twisted, green flame spasmed into life. "Can't read nor write, see," said the man whose grizzled head seemed even smaller than ever for his body. "Never bin to school. My sister here neither. Too busy working, we was." He pointed to the woman whose paper also lay untouched. Whose shocked surprise was a picture. She tried to leave her seat, but the Fuzz, sitting alongside her on a worn settee, restrained her. He handed Jason and Helen a spare sheet each.

And then the penny dropped.

Sister? Jesus.

Helen stared from one Davies to the other. "But I thought..."

"He means wife," barked the cleaner. "Too much fresh air it is. Affects the brain. His brain. I keep telling him, mind."

Meanwhile Idris Davies had lowered his head, muttering, while the cop drummed his fingers on the top of his file. "Are you married or not?"

"Never," insisted the gardener. "She made a mistake, didn't she? Likes to call herself Mrs for some reason, but it's not true. 'Sides, if we was a couple, where's her ring?"

At this, the old woman seemed to stiffen, except for her right hand fiddling with that empty wedding finger. Jason could imagine the air between them in private would be not just blue but navy blue. "Where *were* you married, then?" he asked her as if he really cared. "Locally or outside the area?"

"Can we please move on?" the Fuzz cut in. "Perhaps you, Mr Robbins, could write down what Mr Davies says; and you, Miss Jenkins, do likewise for Ms Davies. I want dates and places of birth. Relationship to one another and the deceased; current residence and lastly, but vitally, where you were between 5 a.m. and 11 a.m. this morning. Also, if you've any thoughts on who Miss Griffiths might have been expecting for lunch." He glanced at his watch then the cleaner. "You go first. And by the way, please remember, this is a legal document. Mr Price of Troed y Rhiw has already been very helpful."

A lie. The farmer had given him short shrift.

"What about my boss?" asked Helen. "He was in his dressing gown till nine."

"Mr Flynn will need to call into Llandovery police station immediately upon his return. By the way, has anyone any news of him?"

"He's OK," said Helen almost too quickly. "I can give you his mobile number afterwards."

"Diolch."

Again the cleaner tried to stand. A look of disbelief tightening her bitter face.

"She never said he'd gone to London. I mean, how come it's incomers knowing more than us?"

"Ask Mr Flynn," said Helen. "And by the way, I'm as Welsh as you are."

The cop coughed. "Now, Ms Davies, and please speak clearly so Miss Jenkins can understand."

"*Mrs*, if you don't mind."

As Jason watched her begin, he resisted asking how long they'd lived at the house in case she'd volunteer it. She didn't, and the minutes ticked by until both bland accounts had been signed by two wobbly initials apiece. Idris Davies claimed he'd woken at 7 a.m. and not left the grounds at all after that. He'd seen Gwilym Price passing by with his rooks mid-morning when the farmer had given him the sad news about Betsan. As for her having any living relatives in the region, the answer had been an emphatic no. In unison. Something about the Davieses' manner was more defiance than denial. "Were you both here at Heron House a long time before Monty Flynn bought it?" Jason finally ventured.

"Not relevant at this stage, Mr Robbins," the Fuzz manoeuvred himself out of the settee to gather in the four statements. His bulk blocked out the meagre light from the front window as he locked the statement file in his case and snapped it shut. "Go on for ever, otherwise."

"Quite right," added Gwenno. "None of his business."

"Just one thing, while everyone's together," persisted Jason. "Have any of you heard of someone called Margiad? She may have lived here. Even died here. The reason I'm asking is I saw a sign bearing her name, outside my room door. Then it vanished. Other things happened last night, too. Things you wouldn't believe." He felt his cheeks colouring up as he spoke. Aware of Helen looking at him in a way he couldn't fathom.

The mantelpiece clock chimed half past three.

He wished he'd never asked the question, nor volunteered the rest. It had just happened, almost without his control, and at the end he felt as if he'd stepped into his own grave to be buried alive by silence.

***

Half an hour had passed. The cloakroom sanctuary reeked not only of discarded coats, macs and mud-encrusted boots, but bad drains. Jason stood wedged against the old-fashioned washbasin while Helen sat on the toilet lid, head in hands. They'd not only accompanied the lumbering Fuzz back to his wheels during which he'd promised to find her attacker, but trekked up to that old stile again to search for clues. Now, free of the Davieses' hostile stares on their return, it was catch-up time. To discover what had turned the girl in front of him into a living ghost. But she beat him to it. "Weirder and weirder, don't you think? Hard to know who to believe."

"That Fuzz certainly didn't want me digging up stuff on the so-called brother and sister. And didn't you think the earth around that stile had been conveniently raked over?"

"Possibly." As if she was dwelling on something else.

"Describe this guy who put the frighteners on you," Jason whispered.

"Tallish, strong, bald. Cheap jeans and serious b.o..."

"Dark blue top?"

She nodded.

"Got to be the same guy I saw. Is this what you told Prydderch upstairs?"

"Yes. And there's to be a chopper search of the area by four o'clock."

"In half an hour? I'll believe that when I see it."

She looked up at him. Her eyes misted by tears. "To be honest, Jason, I've never really felt at home here. Now I'm frightened."

In certain films he'd seen, now would be the moment to step forward and get physical. "You've got me," he reassured her instead, but needn't have bothered. As before, she wasn't listening. Something had indeed changed. Heron House was neither a safe workplace for her, nor the inspiring retreat he'd hoped for. In less than twenty-four hours, it had become somewhere to retreat from. Yet why had she been targeted like that in her own space? It didn't add up. He took a chance.

"You weren't in your room, were you?"

The look Helen gave him said it all.

"You can tell me."

She lowered her voice. "I was in Mr Flynn's office. Its door was unlocked. I found stuff he'd hidden away in a Private and Personal box file. Can't you see? I had to find out what's really going on here. Why he dashed off like that."

There was clearly more to Helen Jenkins than met the eye.

"You didn't leave any prints?"

"No. I pulled my jumper's sleeves down over my hands."

"Wool can leave fibres," he warned.

"For God's sake..."

"Go on. Did you get a result?" The dampness from their own and those long-abandoned outdoor clothes brought that same sense of claustrophobia he'd felt at Betsan Griffiths' place. He could still be back in London before the pubs got dodgy. Find a bed somewhere to tide him over.

"You'd never guess. For a start, Mr Flynn doesn't own Heron House. Only rents it." She stood up. Put her mouth to his ear at which his pulse immediately speeded up. "Charles Pitt-Rose is the landlord. He also lived in Islington. I've seen letters. Receipts, proof."

"Jesus. For how much rent?"

Cracks in the Irishman's edifice widening by the hour.

"Wait. There's more. Apparently, he's also been bribing Mr Flynn to keep the Davieses on here. Those two creatures come with the territory. Nonnegotiable. Can you credit it?"

"With difficulty. Were they referred to as being married?"

"No. I only saw their names." Helen had spotted herself in the plain mirror behind him, and grimaced. "I warned you they were bonkers. And something else. It was Gwilym Price who told Judy Withers that Charles once lived here."

Another reason to meet up with the old farmer again, thought Jason, realising just how secretive the Irishman had been.

"So what'll happen now this Charles Pitt-Rose is dead?" He was aware of a tightening in his chest. The Armitage Shanks' cold porcelain in the small of his back growing colder.

"God knows. But I was just hunting for any sign of a will, things like that, when this creep appeared telling me to mind my own effing business or else."

"Had you seen him before? Think."

"No."

"Must have known his way round, though."

"That's what I thought. And I wonder who else has access to this place?"

Jason was trying to shove black thoughts to the limbo area of his brain.

"Did this Judy person mention any Margiad?"

She shook her head. Her wet hair at the front had begun to curl.

"The silence here couldn't have been any more deafening when I did."

"At least you tried."

"Either she's off-limits for some reason, or no-one has the faintest idea."

Just then came a rubbing sound followed by a sharp thud against the bottom of the door.

"Ssshh. Listen!" he hissed.

Somebody was repeatedly pushing against the wood.

"Who's in there?" came Gwenno Davies' nasty little voice.

"Only us," Jason turned the key and stepped back for her to survey the scene. "Helen's feeling sick."

But instead of sympathy, anger curdled the whites of her hard little eyes. "She'll be more than sick if she keeps on the way she is. Keeps upsetting things. Mark my words."

15

Wednesday 9th October 1946 – 12.45 p.m.

Lionel Hargreaves should have changed into his walking boots. Mistake number one. The second was taking what he assumed to be a short-cut up by the Post Office where lunchtime meant no-one was there to answer his pressing questions. Here, the stubborn mist drew him into its cold, dense embrace, and he soon found himself sliding down into a waterlogged gulley, suddenly meeting a roughly-trimmed hawthorn hedge on the other side.

"Ouch!" A trickle of blood reached the corner of his mouth, and another his chin. He managed to pull himself clear, but almost slipped again.

"Hello, sir," came a young lad's voice from behind him while a hand pulled at his coat. "I got you safe. This way. Steady, sir..."

Once Lionel had reached *terra firma*, he wiped his wounds with a handkerchief, immediately spoiling it. He looked with puzzlement at his young helper. "That was most kind of you. It's Gwilym, isn't it?"

"Yes, Gwilym Price, sir. Cysgod y Deri it is. Too busy seeing to me mam to get to school, in case you've been wondering."

He had, and now recalled the string of noughts by the boy's name in the class register. How promising this curly-haired lad had once seemed at the start of last year's autumn term. How Bryn George the Truant Officer, or 'Whipper-in' as he was known, had been turned away whenever he'd called at his home. At least Gwilym had a good heart, thought Lionel. Something no conventional education could guarantee.

"Well, I hope we see something of you soon. You've a good brain, lad. A pity to waste it."

"Where ye goin,' sir?" asked the boy as if he'd not heard a word.

"Just a walk, to think about things before lessons start again."

"What things, sir? You don't need to be out in this weather to think. Besides, Old Peris Morgan's on guard duty up by the forest. And we all know he's got a screw loose."

Lionel remembered Morgan's grandson's remarks about him in class. How proud he'd seemed.

"Got a gun and a rifle, he has," volunteered his helpmate. "To keep out the Boche."

Lionel hesitated. He'd wasted too much time already. But dead Walter's tearful face came once more to mind. "I'd heard about the heronries up at

Heron House," he said. "Thought I'd take a look. I've been a bird lover since I was a child."

"Not this way, sir. You'll most likely get shot. Follow me."

***

The fog had folded itself away, leaving a windless afternoon with a sky as flat and grey as his cottage walls. Lionel let the truant find a track he never knew existed, past a redundant concrete tower he assumed had been used for storing lime; then uphill, at least on stones rather than churned-up dirt.

"Not far, sir," panted his young companion, before pointing to a white single-story bothy, whose tin roof was home to a row of fat, black rooks. "That's Golwg y Mwyn. Betsan Griffiths lives there. Tidy she is. You must teach her. Should've brought my rifle. Mam likes rook pie."

Lionel could think of nothing worse and wondered if his helpful quiz winner was inside having lunch, perhaps wishing like him that the dreary afternoon was over. His thoughts drifted to relighting his sitting-room fire and placing Mahler's 9th symphony on the new gramophone's turntable. To him, this work played by the City of Birmingham Symphony Orchestra summed up Europe after war, and never left him dry-eyed. Not only for the fallen, but the young growing up in its shadow.

Just as his leg muscles began to complain, Gwilym plucked at his coat sleeve. "It's here, sir. Heron House. See how huge it is."

Indeed it was. But not only that, observed Lionel, shivering despite his thick, winter coat. The word 'disturbing' came to mind. Each window seemed too mean for its ivy-clad walls and both chimneys too tall. Then, all at once, the curtains in the top right-hand gabled window were suddenly pulled together by unseen hands. Why now? And why in such a panic?

"See them posh cars, sir?" Gwilym interrupted his thoughts, pointing to the right-hand side of the house. "They must have cost a few bob."

So, Betsan had been right.

But to Lionel, those three, sleek, black saloons parked almost out of sight, reminded him more of hearses rather than conveyances for the living. And could one of these be the same that Walter Jones had seen near the forestry that day? If so, where was the mud from such a trip? All sets of tyres seemed immaculate. As did the shining bodywork. "Listen!" he said suddenly. "Can you hear that strange noise?"

The lad cocked his damp, unruly head. "Them's rooks, sir. That's their call. Godless, my da used to say."

"I'd like to believe you, Gwilym. But please, listen again."

91

"Can't, sir. Mam's waiting. Needs her food, see. But if you want them heronries, they're round the back. By there..." He pointed left towards a plantation of mainly deciduous trees, most already bare of leaves but not birds. "Don't go near The Drop, mind. It's bad." Then, before the boy could be stopped, he'd turned on his heels and run off.

Lionel shivered again as he continued to focus on that intriguing curtained window, tempted to advance further up what was obviously a newly-gravelled drive, and explore what Betsan had described in her test.

All at once, from behind, a hand fell on his shoulder. Its weight made turning round impossible. His pulse took on a different beat.

"Your name, squire?" The unseen man's accent was unusual for a native of this strongly Welsh area. English public school and Oxbridge seemed more likely. Cultured, yet menacing. Could this be the judge that both Carol and Betsan had mentioned? Could this be Edmund Pitt-Rose?

"Be so good as to remove your hand," said Lionel. "I'm no criminal. I'm merely out for a walk."

"Then have the courtesy to remove your shoes from my drive."

Lionel backed away, and in doing so, turned to see up close, his adversary's prematurely jowled cheeks, the veined, pale brown eyes; the formal suit and a tie bearing a heron-shaped gold pin. A once handsome man, he thought. Also, judging by his bulky midriff in an age of austerity, one who enjoyed the pleasures of life.

"Your name, squire?" the man repeated the question in an even more imperious manner. "I'm waiting."

"Who I am, is none of your business and if you persist in intimidating me, I'll report you to the police."

A short, sour laugh followed. "You won't get very far with that, so let me save you the trouble. Most of them are in my pockets, with no desire to climb out."

Then came that same haunting sound again, creeping from that house through the chilly, damp air. Louder now. Definitely female, Lionel thought. And not just crying, more a prolonged wail that made the rooks spread their wings and heave themselves from their chimney perches into the dull sky as the front door opened. A short, thin creature, no more than fourteen or fifteen, dressed in black save for a white apron, gestured for the man to come in. Could this be that same young woman who'd appeared in riding clothes threatening him after Walter's funeral? Her features were certainly sharp enough. Her eyes possessed that same hard brightness. If she recognised him, she didn't show it.

"You trespass round here again, squire," the suited man prodded his shoulder, "I'll get my lad to give you the kind of send off you're unlikely to forget." He almost swaggered off towards the house without glancing back.

Most of them are in my pockets, and have no desire to climb out.

What an odd thing to say, if he really was a judge. Odder still, his lack of response to what had clearly been human shrieks. Lionel turned away from the curtained window, the air of secrecy and gloom that he felt from just being there, and realised he'd forgotten to ask the bully to confirm his name.

With a less than steady tread, and the added burden of guilt that he'd not had time to investigate those baleful cries, he took the downwards track back towards Nantybai, all the while listening out for the sound of a car engine. A big car engine, eager to mow him down.

***

1.30 p.m.

Lionel was late. More than late. By fifteen minutes in fact and, hearing the din coming from the playground, ran back to school to find a fight in full swing. Girls against boys – a feature of most play times and hard to eradicate. This time, because his quiz winner wasn't there, they were one less.

"What's wrong with your face, sir?" asked Aled. "You been in a fight, too?"

To reply that he'd stumbled into a hedge would have cost his credibility dear, yet invention wasn't his forte. "Of course not," he panted. "Some dog jumped up at me out of the blue."

The children dropped their fists to listen. "Must have been a stray, judging by its condition." Lionel drew his whistle out of his coat pocket. A whistle that had seen action at Ypres. His short, shrill blast always did the trick. "Five seconds to get to your desks," he said. "One... two..."

"*You* were late, sir," Kyffin Morgan reminded him on his way in. "I'm telling my da."

Without replying or removing his coat, Lionel ushered the unruly little mob into the schoolroom where that ailing fire was now completely spent.

"Where's Betsan?" he asked, arriving at her name in the register. "Was she unwell?"

"No sir," piped up Aled. "It bothered her to win."

***

With conflicting images and emotions crowding his brain, Lionel trudged home after school, still wearing wet shoes and hiding a heavy heart.

93

Tonight, instead of Mahler, he'd play something light on the gramophone to block out the echo of what he'd heard at Heron House, and the weight of that hostile hand on his shoulder. So, the witty Franz Léhar it would be.

By six o'clock, with the *Land of Smiles* finished, and a piece of ham plus half a small swede boiling on top of the stove, he drew the curtains across and poured himself a glass of sherry. Despite the welcome sweetness on his tongue, he knew he'd have to see his apparently unhappy pupil before tomorrow. Her home wasn't so far from Heron House. Kill two birds with one stone, he told himself, settling back into what had once been his father's favourite chair and waiting for dinner to cook. Just then came a tapping on his front window, followed by a deep Welsh voice.

"Mr Hargreaves? You there?"

For a moment, he couldn't move. Didn't wish to move, until the tapping became knuckle on glass to match the shouting. "Peris Morgan, it is. Heard you went up to Heron House today. Well, sir, I got things to tell you, if you value your life."

Ignore him. Remember Gwilym's description?

"And by the way, sir," the stranger persisted, "our Kyffin thinks you're a right good teacher. Too good to lose, say I."

At that last, unsettling compliment, Lionel set down his glass, turned the stove to low before parting the curtains inch by inch. Dusk wasn't too far advanced for him to see a man at least in his seventies, so protected against the cold by a greatcoat and wide-brimmed hat, he could barely make out his face. "I have to warn you before it's too late. Part of my job, Homeland Security it is, and I take it very seriously."

"I can see that," Lionel muttered crossly to himself. However, it wasn't the promise of more news, but the look of real fear on the old warrior's face, that made him unbolt the door and invite the man in.

16.

Saturday 4th April 2009 – 8 p.m.

"She'll be more than sick if she keeps on the way she is. Keeps upsetting things..." Helen imitated that friendly forecast as she and Jason sneaked past the dining room where The Rat was angrily polishing the best cutlery. "Charming."

"Don't keep torturing yourself. She's not worth it," Jason said.

He was following her upstairs to the first floor only to discover that someone had locked Mr Flynn's room and scrubbed the corridor carpet outside it. The bleached patch on its floral pattern and the nostril-fluttering scent were surely proof the old cleaner was responsible. Had she also a full set of keys after all? If so, who else but she had tried to cover up the stranger's intrusion?

"You were right about those Davieses after all," Helen said, keeping a lookout while Jason explored the worn woollen pile on his hands and knees. She tried not to focus on the way his taut thigh muscles pushed against the backs of his jeans as he moved from spot to spot. "The brother and sister bit may just be the start. God, I wish I'd been able to spend longer in that study, but there *was* something I've not told anybody."

"What?" Jason looked up at Helen.

"That bald guy didn't just try to stop me looking around, he was... you know..."

Heffy would have had no problem describing his arousal. The pumping motion of his hips against hers, the heavy breathing... Just thinking of it, made Helen's period pain re-announce itself. It was getting worse.

"All the more reason to find the bastard."

He finally stood up, brushing carpet fibres off his knees. "We can try this study again via the window."

"Are you serious?" she asked.

"Not half. A broken sash is very handy."

She then shook her head. "I ought to be rustling something decent up for supper, or The Rat will snitch that I've not earned my pittance."

To reassure her, he patted her shoulder. "Bacon and egg would be great, if you've got them. But I'm well used to seeing to myself. Had to, or else I'd have faded away."

"Like that strange man in black up the hill?" She looked him up and down. "I don't think so."

Just to see those fried eggs' phlegm-like whites in the frying pan, turned her grumbling yet aching stomach. However, Helen persevered with their cooking until Jason's plate was full. She then tackled the washing up while he finished his meal overseen by a creepily solicitous Gwenno Davies so obviously trying to win him over after the earlier surprises. But how that smiling mask changed when Helen brought him over a mug of coffee. Not that he noticed, being too absorbed in his library book.

"Don't rush him," The Rat snapped at her. "Can't you see he's busy reading?"

At that, Helen cast aside her apron and went upstairs to her own room where the first thing she did once inside was turn the key in the lock behind her.

And soon here he was, wanting to come in. She hesitated, weighing up the pros and cons of him invading her space. He'd not exactly told The Rat to bog off; besides, his stunts in the pub still rankled. But with Mr Flynn away, he was all she'd got. And who was to say that pervert who'd already manhandled her wouldn't re-appear?

"Helen?" he said again. "Please..."

She unlocked the door. Jason stood with a sheepish look on his face, holding two wine glasses in one hand and half a full bottle of Sicilian red in the other, left over from yesterday's spag bol. The omens weren't good. Nevertheless, she could do with a drink.

"Nice pad, except for the view," he observed, scanning the dark, swaying trees beyond the window then the room's pale pink walls, a 1970s' paper lampshade too big for the room and the newish but useless TV with its digi-box. "Can we swop?" He looked as though he meant it.

"I'd consider it if you'd not been flirting."

"Hello?"

"With The Rat. I don't like you even smiling at her, if that's OK. Gives her the wrong impression and makes things harder for me."

"She's old enough to be my Grannie."

Helen eyed the door. "I don't care."

"Fair enough."

They then sat on opposite sides of the bed while he unscrewed the bottle top, poured out her share and handed it over. "To the fibbing Mr Flynn, that he soon gets back here." And when his glass was also full, "To Betsan. That we find her killer."

"We?" The wine was cool on her tongue. This bottle wasn't going to last long, she thought.

"You don't think that uniformed porker's going to deliver, do you?"

Helen shook her head. He was right again. Even though this room hadn't been the yob's scene of crime, DC Prydderch's evidence-gathering technique had been risible. For a start, he'd neither been able to bend down to check for footprints, nor ask any meaningful questions. And as for mentioning a proper forensic examination... But did she really want that? No. Her lie could get her into trouble and in a recession a good reference was like gold dust.

"Hey, who's this?" Jason stretched out a free hand towards the bedside table to pick up the photo of her mam – a singleton all over again – then one of Heffy. Her usual stunning self, making everyone else at the BA Degree ceremony seem ten years older. And poorer. He read the names on the back of each before replacing it. "You look just like her." he said, and Helen blushed, flattered.

"Who? Heffy?"

"Your mum."

Great.

Then she remembered something from Mr Flynn's office. Took another gulp of wine. "Apparently, The Rat collars the post the moment it arrives. Mr Flynn wrote a memo to himself to tackle her about it, but he won't. Even though he suspects her of keeping stuff back. Seems he has to put up with her agenda. But why?"

"*Their* agenda, you mean. The delightful brother, don't forget. It was like pulling teeth getting him to meet the Fuzz."

"You did seem pretty pissed off," she said.

"I was. Like you say, makes you wonder why they're so special. I mean, look at them." He got to his feet to peer at a small framed print of St. Peter's crucifixion that had pride of place on the wall behind her single bed.

"The original fresco's by Michaelangelo," she said. "Sixteenth century."

He seemed impressed. She watched him crane towards each sorrowful detail, waiting for him to ask why, out of all the art available, she'd picked this for such an important position.

He did ask.

"It was already here when I moved in. Hidden away in that wardrobe." She indicated a large walnut affair dominating the opposite wall. "And I couldn't be bothered banging in a new nail when one was already in place."

"Why not put something up of yours?"

"Maybe soon."

Jason returned to the print. A grimace spoiling his otherwise OK mouth. "This is hideous. What a way to go."

"Apparently St. Peter didn't feel worthy of being crucified in the same way as Jesus. Besides, to crucify someone upside down was actually more compassionate. The victims suffocated instead."

He touched St. Peter's eyes. "Well, he doesn't seem to be appreciating it much." He turned to her. "Dare I bring this kind of punishment into my book? Hey, think of it. Gross."

"Up to you."

Silence, as the former breeze now a vigorous wind, batted the nearest chestnut trees' bare branches against the window's glass, and a low moaning sound entered the room through an unrepaired crack above the sill. Jason tilted up the picture frame's lower edge as if looking for something.

"What are you doing?" She was aware of her mother's eyes following her every move.

"Just playing detective. I've got mine sorted now, by the way. Dan Carver. Ex-DI from Sunderland. A misfit and poker addict but straight as a die. What do you think?"

Helen stared at him. How could he be so unfocussed when so much had happened? "Please can we leave it?" she said.

"You mean my hero?"

"The picture." She wished she had the courage to phone or text Mr Flynn to update him and find out more of his deal with his landlord. "All I can think of is what'll happen if Charles Pitt-Rose really is dead. If you want to play detective, why not find out why the Davieses are so important they must be kept on here? Did he leave a will? And why did Betsan refer to Heron House as the asylum?"

"There's a name on the back here," he announced, still fixed on his own agenda. "Margiad, would you believe? And a date. October 1st 1946. Was it a present, or had she bought it herself I wonder? And could she have once lived here?"

But Helen's train of thought had already taken her way beyond this room; this house of too many shadows and the choking hills. Like a runner fleeing some evil force whose breath was burning her heels, she must make the break. But where to go? Not back to her mam – that wouldn't last a week. They were just too different. To Cardiff and some dump in Bute Town, or even a hostel in Penge? She shivered just to think of it and then, like a sly ray of sunshine, recalled what her Final Year tutor had said about her work at the Degree ceremony where she'd picked up one of only three Distinctions. "Never mind the Brit Art pack, Helen. With your Gothic take on landscape – especially the Welsh landscape – you could be the next Edward Hopper."

As if.

She finished her wine and glanced over to that old lightweight picnic table, home to an array of paintbrushes including squirrel hair, pony hair and the more robust synthetics best for laying in big areas of paint. Then to a roll of cotton duck canvas tied with sparkly pink ribbon, which Heffy had bought her as a leaving present, defying her to use it. As did a folded-up easel and two already stretched blanks, primed and waiting. Tomorrow she'd dust off her best mahogany palette, assemble the easel and set out her oils and acrylics from hot to cool to zinc white. In readiness.

"The writing on the back of this matches that plaque on my room door." Jason carried the framed print closer to the paper-shaded light bulb. "It's a pretty weird picture to have in a bedroom."

"This may not always have been a bedroom," said Helen, testing that the cap on a tube of Hooker's Green wasn't too tight. It was one of her favourite colours, and should she start painting again, ideal for forestry and those shadowed, lower slopes.

"That's a point. Was there anything about her in Monty Flynn's den?"

"Nothing I could see. I'm sorry but I was more interested in The Rat and its brother."

Her voice sounded thin, bloodless. She suddenly wanted her space to herself again. To sort out her head. Make some decisions.

***

An hour later, with Jason back in his room to read some more and catch an early night, Helen slung her pink suede rucksack over her blue, hooded fleece and slipped outside into the windy darkness. Her right hand lay clamped over her mobile inside her pocket, as if it was her lifeline, even though she only had nine pounds left in credit and there'd be no reception for a few miles at least. No way was she going that far. Not after that bald pervert had pressed his sweaty body against hers.

With loose strands of hair whipping her left cheek, she made her way past the three lock-ups to a clearing which in daylight gave a view of the Doethie Valley and its pretty, tumbling stream far below. Too late to worry that the house's main security light at the front hadn't come on, or that suddenly she felt a different fear slow her heart and her feet. Just as she was about to access Mr Flynn's number, another came up on screen. Heffy.

Dammit.

Two rings of Rihanna's *'Umbrella'* and a voice not heard since Christmas, filled her ear. "That you, Hellraiser?" said her best friend. "I don't believe it. You still gotta pulse?"

Normally, Helen would have laughed. "Just about. Where are you? Still in the lap of luxury at Bates' Motel?"

A pause. Helen knew something was up, but seconds and money were ticking away.

"Not for long. The crusts are splitting just like yours did. It's pants, to be honest."

Heffy's parents owned and ran one of the biggest and priciest hotels in Aberystwyth's town centre. *Boutique,* she called it. All glass and chrome, plasma screens and Egyptian cotton sheets with a thread count in treble figures.

"I'm sorry, Hef. Try and hang on in there. Perhaps it's just a blip." Yet in her heart she knew that staying together for life was the hardest thing. People change just like the landscape through different seasons. Besides, as her da had argued with her mam before she'd kicked him out, humans aren't biologically programmed to last the course. They needed variety. Different experiences. In short, monogamy was an unnatural state of affairs.

"You too," Heffy broke in, now sounding much further away. "Why not come up tomorrow for a few days? You could have a king-size all to yourself. I'm sure Mr Sex-on-Legs can spare you."

Not funny, and the faintest whiff of fag smoke made her turn round. "I'll see what I can do. Trouble is..."

"Yes?"

"Some pretty funny stuff's happening here. I've got to be careful."

"All the more reason to chill out. Oh, come on. Catch-up time, eh?"

Helen peered at the invisible wildness around her. It seemed as if the whole place was at war with the wind. Perhaps a trip up to Ceredigion would do her good. After all, the other writers weren't due here for a while. She might even start that painting for her mam.

"Are you sure?"

"You know me."

She did, but there was Mr Flynn as well as Jason to consider. Annoying though he was, the newcomer was different from the needy, self-regarding guys she'd known at Uni. He'd paid his deposit, even though money was tight. He had a book to write, and he needed to get off those happy pills.

"You've pulled, haven't you?" her friend probed. "Come on, you can tell

Aunty Heffy."

The trouble was, she couldn't; and way overhead as the biggest, blackest cloud parted to reveal a single, throbbing star, it was time to be straight.

"I'll call you back tomorrow. Promise."

"You said that last Boxing Day."

"There's been a murder. I've been groped. I'm trying to cope. OK?"

The line went dead. The force of air slapped her hood up against the back of her head. That earlier fear had solidified. Supposing that ghostly figure from up Pen Cerrigmwyn should reappear, or that skinhead whose erection had jutted against her buttocks. "Come on, Mr Flynn, come on..." she pleaded to the phone, having seen his number up.

"Yes?"

It was him, but not him.

"Helen Jenkins here. I don't mean to distur..."

"I said only phone in case of an emergency."

She flinched inwardly. "This comes pretty close. Have the Llandovery police been in touch with you yet? Jason and me found Betsan Griffiths dead in her bungalow this morning. All her ornaments smashed up..."

Silence, save for the creak of nearby branches. The rush of more debris by the lock-ups. She wondered where exactly her boss might be. Whether inside or out was hard to tell. "Mr Flynn. Are you OK?

"I used to be."

Was he in tears? This man who could charm grease from the bottom of a chip pan? Who'd charmed her and Jason into being here? It sounded like it. But why, and what could she do? "Look, I don't want my credits to run out," she said, then heard him swear under his breath. "Thing is," she went on, "you left Heron House in a hurry this morning, and I had to warn you, that's all."

"Thank you, and I'm truly sorry to hear about the dear woman, and your own frightening experience. But warn me about what?"

"DC Prydderch wanted your mobile number, and I gave it. Do you mind?"

Pause.

"So I'm a suspect? Good God."

"Of course not."

"Ever my reliable Helen."

Was this irony or something else entirely? She heard him sniff, blow his nose. "Now I need you more than ever," he said.

"Are you upset as well because Charles Pitt-Rose is dead? I'm only guessing."

A strange, short laugh. "You're not stupid, are you?"

She gulped. "I put two and two together. That's all."

£8.20 left in credits.

It was now or never, she told herself as a sudden sliver of moon lit up the top of The Giant's Shoulder. "You rent off him, don't you? And the Davies couple have to be kept on here or else. Why?"

In the longer silence that followed, she sensed her meagre job slipping away.

"Who told you those downright lies?"

Quick, think...

"Someone I met by chance in Somerfields, the minute I mentioned where I worked. They also said Idris Davies and Gwenno were mad."

A deep sigh insinuated itself into her ear. Come on, give us more blarney, she said to herself as he began to speak.

"Helen, my treasure. My right-hand person. If I'd listened to such gossip three years ago when I bought – yes bought – the place from Mr Pitt-Rose, I'd never have crossed the Irish Sea."

Liar...

"So why are they there, despite everything?"

"Both are utterly benign, believe me. I know Gwenno's tongue can be as sharp as a fish knife, and she's sometimes upset you..."

Sometimes?

"But they keep out of my way. What a writer and a thinker needs. Peace and quiet, as our visitors on Friday will discover."

"Are they brother and sister, or married?"

"Labels, labels... To me, they've always been close. Looking out for each other. What an odd question."

"Nothing's as odd as they are. I don't think you've told me the full story."

"I will. I swear on St. Patrick's heart."

"So why dash off to London? Why say you need me more than ever? What for? And which guy was it who managed to get into your house to scare me? Who knew his way around?"

"Hang on, hang on, you don't unders..."

"And why," she interrupted, seeing her phone credits shrink even further, "didn't you tell the beloved Gwenno where you were going?"

Her questions were caught by the wind and blown away high into the brooding sky and, while she hung on for an answer, was suddenly aware she wasn't alone. A trace of cheap perfume reached her nose. A hard hand in the small of her back was pushing her, forcing her forwards on the slippery, rough grass towards the boundary's unfenced edge, below which, she knew the Doethie Valley waited like an open throat.

17.

Saturday 4th April 2009 – 9 p.m.

Jason knew he wouldn't sleep that night, not just because the mighty blast hitting his room window threatened to break the glass, or that Dan Carver and the gangland perps who'd begun to sprout in his mind, like that cress he'd once grown in a margarine tub as a kid, were being shoved aside by stuff he couldn't ignore. No, it was dreading that body-shaped stain on the carpet reappearing fibre by fibre, or another stray rook behaving as if his room was its territory. Worse, *Evil Eyes* again being torn from his very hands.

He sat himself down at the dressing table with that same book now weirdly intact; safely to one side, and a so-far unused refill pad in front of him. Its lined bulk had felt immediately inviting when he'd added it to his shopping basket an aeon ago. However, instead of plotting his main character's life history up north until setting up as a flatfoot in Hoxton, he wrote *OPERATION ROOK* on the pad's cover. Fact, not fiction. Truth, not guesswork about everything he'd so far discovered about this strange place. His thriller could wait until Tuesday, giving him a few clear days before the other writers arrived.

Having finished his *ACTION PLAN* list, he began searching for a suitable hiding place. Having his own key to the door meant nothing. Heron House was a snake pit. Even Helen, it seemed, wasn't safe.

On impulse, having stuffed the writing pad under the mean arched space beneath his wardrobe, he locked his door, crept along the unlit corridor and down the faintly creaking stairs to the next floor. Helen's door was locked. No reply to his knocking either.

Something was wrong and he wasn't hanging about to find out what.

***

The sudden rush of air hit him first as the heavy front door swung open, rattling the trinkets on the reception hall's mantelpiece, scattering ash from the dead fire. Then Gwenno Davies, her white hair wild around her head, her once neat dress torn, smeared by grass stains, burst into the room.

"Out of my way," she pushed past him. Her earlier chat and obsequious attention long gone. "You and that little witch shouldn't be here. And d'you know what?" She jabbed his shoulder. "There'll be no writers coming. You'll see."

Jason gulped. "What d'you mean, no writers?"

"Like I said."

Mad bird...

"So where's Helen?"

"Pushed me over, she did. Out there. I was only looking for her. How's that for gratitude? Vicious little madam, I'm telling you." She pointed at a torn flap of fabric hanging by her hip. "Anyway, this is evidence that she's not right in the head. Drugs it is, see. I know her sort."

And before Jason could turn round and follow her, she'd reached the kitchen and slammed its door shut behind her.

Shit.

Should he track the woman down and squeeze that skinny throat for an answer, or focus on finding Helen?

A no-brainer, but then he realised he'd left his boots in his room. Too late to go back. He'd have to try the cloakroom for a replacement pair.

***

"There'll be no writers coming. You'll see."

Was this no more than a spiteful wish on her part or the truth? Whatever, it stayed in his mind as once outside in the teeth of the wind, he ran first towards the stinking pool, shouting out Helen's name. Then to the left. The stiff borrowed boots proving way too big; their laces trapped underfoot with every step. He wondered whose they were.

"Helen? You OK?" he yelled twice.

The gale answered by almost ripping his jacket from his body. His ears from his head. Christ, where on earth was she? One press of his thumb on his phone's keypad and up came her number. A spark of hope. But when he pressed the little green icon to ring it, got nothing.

He tried again, his heart slowing down. Was it the wind hitting the perforations and rebounding back, or that strange breathing like before, this time without the words?

Just then, came the faint sound of gravel being disturbed. Any number of possibilities occurred to him from hungry fox to the skinhead who'd legged it over the stile. He was about to crouch down behind some large and prickly shrub, when a brightening torch beam turned the rough ground yellow, followed by a familiar smell.

Stale blood.

"Didn't mean to scare you," came a gruff Welsh voice, and the more Jason stared above that probing beam into the crazy darkness, the more he recognised Gwilym Price. As before, a rifle jutted from his left shoulder, his bushman's hat was secured around his head and under his chin by a length of rag. "Been concerned about you and the girl since this morning," he added. "Thought I'd just come by. See how you were, like. Always take myself off end of the day anyway. Helps me sleep, it does."

Normally, in daylight with Helen safe and sound, Jason would have thanked him. But right now, he just needed to know she was safe. "Helen's gone God knows where," he said. "Must have left the house without me noticing. And that Gwenno Davies has just accused her of assault."

The farmer whistled through his absent teeth. "Well, don't believe a word of what that woman says. Them two's been known for a long time. Get my meaning?"

"On Wednesday afternoon, apparently, Miss Griffiths told Helen that Gwenno's mouth had done her harm."

"I can believe it. Jealous of her schooling, I expect. Betsan was bright, to be sure. Went on to College in Swansea and all. Became a qualified chef."

"Did she use your birds to make rook pies? Does Helen?"

"Who said?" asked Gwilym.

"Monty Flynn."

"Bloody liar. Only starving miners and other poor folk like my mam ate them. Free food when times was hard."

The following silence didn't last long.

"So what will you do with all those you shot?" Jason queried.

"Bury 'em of course. Bad omens, see. Some say it's just folklore, but I know otherwise. When they all leave their nests together, that's the time to kill. Stops a curse, see?"

"On who?"

"Whoever's owner or tenant of the land."

A pause, filled by the wind driven upwards from the valley on their left. A stinging cold blast biting Jason's ears. "Did you know the Davieses were brother and sister, not a married couple?" Jason said.

The guy's torch beam moved away.

"Let's help you find your girl, eh? We can talk some more as we go. She's either in these grounds somewhere, or over near The Drop."

"What the Hell's that?"

"Follow me."

They took it in turns to holler out her name, but as before, only air replied. Moments later, the farmer suddenly held Jason back. "Any further, son, and you won't see morning. You think there'd be a fence here. Health and safety for a start. But not at Heron House. Not at the asylum."

That word again.

106

Jason shivered.

"Had a visit from the Council last year," the man went on. "Was told to fence off my septic tank and pump house, if you please. And find eight hundred quid to get the spring water tested. Stuff the EU, say I. If my mam and da could see what our men died for in both wars, they'd be leaving their graves, never mind turning in them."

But before the man finished, Jason's brain clicked into gear. Helen's car. *Of course.* It hadn't been out the front or by the lock-ups. He was losing it big time. Just twenty-seven hours in this place had messed up his head. "Her Suzuki's gone," he said, retracing his steps.

"Well I never saw no car on my way up. Unless she took the short cut." His companion trained his torch's beam towards the house. "My Nissan's not far. Can take a look round with me if you like."

"Thanks. But she might be heading for London to see her boss."

"How'll she get there this time of night?" Gwilym Price pulled his hat further down over his face as the moaning wind powered towards them, bringing with it more of that stale-blood smell from the morning. "And why?"

"I'm afraid that's private. At least for the moment."

The farmer glanced at him. "Boyfriend trouble, then?"

"No. At least I don't think so. Look, I hardly know her."

Silence.

"We could try Llandovery Station," the older man volunteered again. "Check if her car's there. Call into the cop shop if you like. No love lost between them and me, mind. But tough."

***

Jason relegated Dan Carver and his imminent abduction on page 3 to the back of his mind. Helen was missing, and he had the chance of wheels. So why the hesitation? Who really was this rook-killing guy? This owner of a dog possibly killed on purpose? More to the point, why after just one minute was he, a total stranger, opening the green 4X4's passenger side door and settling in its comfortable seat and belting up? Because he had to trust the man. End of story. Helen was out there somewhere and possibly in danger.

***

For a farmer, the 4X4's interior was pretty neat, with no sign of blood, fur or feathers. Nothing would be as valeted and dust-free as Colin's Merc, nevertheless it was a damned sight cleaner than Helen's. A pile of empty wooden crates in the back section crashed together as his driver took the

107

bends way too fast, but this was his road. Probably known it for years. Nevertheless, Jason was still glad to see the Fox and Feathers' welcome glow light up the way ahead and he asked if they could stop. "Helen and I had lunch there earlier," he explained, hoping her little red car was parked in the unlit lane alongside. "Perhaps she went back."

However, it didn't take long to realise that Helen was neither part of the rugby club nor the group of local quilt-makers having a last drink. The same blonde behind the bar, who was all smiles, hadn't seen her since the afternoon.

Back in the Nissan, neither man spoke as one unrecognisable road kill after another passed under its chassis. Not so a perfectly whole dead badger whose big, padded paw stuck up as if in defiance. Gwilym Price tried to skew the car around it, but missed. Jason heard the faint sound of crushing bone beneath the wheels before the boxes rattled together again and his seatbelt tightened under his heart.

"Did my best, poor sod. But you wait till I catch who ran over my Bob." The farmer then turned to Jason. "Did that Detective Constable Prydderch ever make it to Heron House?" In any other situation, the way he said Detective Constable would have been funny.

"He did. And Idris Davies swore he saw you up by Miss Griffiths' this morning. Is that true?"

"When exactly?" The farmer frowned, giving a stiff wave to an even older man leading a goat along the grass verge.

"After Helen and I had left there."

"There's another liar. I never saw him," Gwilym said.

"That's how he knew she was dead. So he says."

Again the Nissan lurched again to one side, this time to avoid a large pothole brimming with water. The driver's face set hard, while the road gradually widened between more closely grouped cottages and smallholdings. Jason peered out yet again, hoping to catch a glimpse of a red Ignis. Instead, saw armies of small, lighted windows. Lives dwarfed by those vast, lumpy hills on either side. He was beginning to miss Hounslow already. Even his pint-sized bedroom in Colin's house that overlooked a bus stop and busy pavements.

He was also missing Helen.

"Idris Davies certainly didn't want to see the Fuzz," Jason added.

"Doesn't surprise me, mind. Not clapped eyes on him for years since I first started at Nantybai school. Not that either of them ever attended. Too busy with each other, so it was said. Get my meaning?"

Jason stared at him.

"Incest?"

"I'm not saying. Talk was, mind, and you won't believe this; he got his sister pregnant. My late wife Carol had to help with the birth. Heard all this screaming while she was delivering milk up there. Day of our local show it was. July 3rd 1967. Plenty of gossip, mind. You can imagine. Small place like this."

Jason felt more than cold. "Boy or girl?"

"A boy, Llyr. A right dosser, he was. Friggin' useless. But worse than that, to be honest. Worked for me once after he'd left the special school in Cilycwm and the wife was still alive. Never again. Didn't like his ways, see." He glanced at Jason. "Nor did she."

"Why?"

"Cruel he was. Caught him at it, taking too long to kill the pigs. Laughing, he was, as he cut their throats. Said if that method was good enough for Jews and Muslims, it was good enough for him. Liked to hear them squeal, he did. Gave him a real buzz. I reckon he ran over me Bob on Wednesday. He'd have enjoyed doing that."

"The Davieses told DC Prydderch they had no living relatives in the area."

"I know better," Gwilym said.

Jason shivered. His jacket that had cost him two months' pay, felt more like ice than leather as the road passed between settlements and houses. Street lights too, and a bridge through which he saw the beginnings of Llandovery. "Where's he holed up now?"

"No idea. Moved away east, some said, but not before nicking some old Forestry Commission truck."

"Can you describe him?"

"Going back years, mind." The driver paused to give Jason another glance. "Same height as you, but more thick-set."

"And his hair?"

"Bald as a coot. Since the day he was born."

***

By the time they reached the small, deserted railway station Jason trusted Gwilym Price enough to fill him in about the escaping stranger witnessed by both himself and the fat cop. The same guy most likely to have accosted and threatened Helen in Monty Flynn's study.

"Who knows? May be keen to come back. After all," the driver added, pulling into an unlit car park and circling its perimeter, "he was born here.

P'raps he's got rights."

"To what?" Jason pressed his nose against the window glass, looking for two cars. A grey Volvo and a red Suzuki Ignis.

"Heron House, of course. After all, them two idiots have been kept on there since the year dot. There may even be something in writing."

He'd obviously not yet heard about Charles Pitt-Rose, but as before, Jason held back. Let him talk.

"When my Carol was the postwoman, she sensed there was something odd about the place. How secretive its occupants were. How, despite almost daily visits, she rarely saw a soul."

"We should tell the cops about this son of theirs. If it *was* him on the loose, there could still be DNA traces in the house. Did you see any police chopper around any time after four o'clock?"

"Don't make me laugh."

And before Jason could also ask about anyone called Margiad, or that mysterious spectre lurking by the old lead mine, he spotted the boot of a red hatch tucked back from the station's main building. Although the two security lights weren't at full strength, he knew immediately whose it was.

***

The wind drove an empty crisp packet against Jason's forehead as he climbed out of the Nissan and ran towards the Ignis. "Door's open," he shouted, before trying the others. All locked, including the boot.

"Everything looks normal to me." The farmer who'd joined him, used his torch's beam to scan the interior. Yes, the same debris lay on the floor, and various shopping lists littered the top of the dashboard, but nothing suggested anything other than carelessness.

However, Helen wasn't careless.

"She'd never leave her car unlocked." Jason's voice was lost even before it left his mouth. "She gave me a lift from Swansea to Heron House yesterday, and when we arrived, I saw how she checked and rechecked that all its doors and the boot were secure."

"In a hurry, perhaps?" suggested the other man, feeling the bonnet with a bare hand. "Whatjecall's still warm."

It was too. But instead of bringing a comforting sensation, Jason sensed only danger. "In a hurry for a non-existent train?" he challenged. "For a National Express bus that passes through twenty miles away? I don't think so." But why did no-good Llyr Davies come to mind again? The skinhead from the asylum. "Where's the cop shop here?" he asked. Gwilym Price pointed towards a road leading to the left, opposite the station, signed for

Builth Wells. "Not far, it is. Bound to be someone in there in the warm, twiddling their thumbs."

***

Gwilym was right. And once inside its reception area blinking defensively against the too-bright strip-light, Jason off loaded his growing fears about Helen to the Desk Sergeant, Edward Rees. A man with expressionless, weather-beaten features.

"And while we're at it," added his companion, "I'd like to know why no chopper came over Pen Cerrigmwyn this afternoon as promised, and who deliberately killed my prize-winning sheepdog. My best friend."

Sergeant Edward Rees squared up to him. Jason noticed his smooth, neat hands at odds with his face. "We had an important incident in town. Didn't DC Prydderch mention it?"

"Yes," said Jason, wondering how the Hell someone with advanced rigor mortis was sitting on a good incremental wage and a gold-plated pension. "But there'll be a far bigger one if someone round here doesn't get off their butt. And soon."

Jason, like Gwilym, was too angry to notice the strange expression on the Sergeant's face. His pretty hand hovering over his phone.

18.

Saturday 4th April 2009 – 11 p.m.

She shouldn't be running after Mr Flynn like this, Helen told herself. But what choice had there been? For a start, he had freaked her out and then The Rat had tried pushing her into The Drop. She was sure of that. The memory of those strong wiry arms grappling with her shoulders, pushing her inch by inch towards that black hidden valley, had come to the fore. How that bony hip had connected with hers with an almost superhuman power.

Originally, she'd planned to drive herself to Islington, but her petrol gauge was already on red before she could reach the only garage still open on the Brecon road out of town. The station car park had come just in time. So had the guy in a black beanie and matching duffle coat who'd introduced himself as Ethan Woods, a family man who didn't normally offer people lifts in his van at night. Especially young lone women.

Now, with his wheels swinging on to the M4 – the same route she'd taken with Jason only yesterday – she realised that in her rush to take up the timely offer of a lift, all the way to central London, she'd left her driver's door unlocked. Too late now to get back to Llandovery.

Shit.

"You OK?" asked the man next to her, passing over a warm bag of Everton mints. She didn't take one. Instead said, "I should have locked my car. I never forget to do that."

His laugh was a surprise. Different in every way from Jason's. Not that he'd done much of that since arriving at Heron House. "Plenty of folk'll be there come morning. And it was hardly Piccadilly Circus when we left."

She couldn't argue with that, but still she fretted as they roared along in the middle lane and the eerie glow of Port Talbot's steel works, invaded the van's cab. She then noticed an empty tax disc on her side of the windscreen. Wondered if he was insured.

"You don't sound very Welsh," she observed, to break the silence.

"I'm not, but I am back and forth to your rainy country twice a week. Tregaron way mostly." He crunched like a horse on his mint and slowed down. "Them poshies down in Surrey like the taste of fresh lamb off the hills. Pays me to keep going."

The way he said 'fresh lamb,' made her edge surreptitiously towards the window where regular bursts of spray shut out the blackness beyond. She was not only bone tired, with that same groin ache becoming a deep nagging pain, but also too knackered to call Jason. But she must phone her mam first, though.

She pulled her phone from her grass-stained fleece pocket. £4 left, while a welcoming sign for SERVICES 1 MILE came and went. For a second, her driver glanced at her phone, then back to the road ahead. His beanie now covered his eyebrows.

"Can we stop there so I can top this up?" she asked, clicking on the green glow of her mother's land line number.

"Say please."

She glanced at him in surprise. "Please."

He tapped the fuel gauge with a leather-gloved finger. "Next one'll do. Got to shift. This lot's to be in the shops first thing."

Really? To her, even frozen lamb still possessed a nauseatingly sweet smell, so why wasn't it on his clothes, in the used, heated air? OK, so she'd been too stressed to notice or question what he might or might not have been carrying when his muddy van pulled up alongside her dead car and made the offer she couldn't refuse. But the more she thought about it, the more she remembered the open area behind them being empty.

The guy glanced at her again. This time for longer, then had to brake sharpish behind a coach, his wipers on full speed, sloughing off the brown spray.

Damn.

Eluned Jenkins was either out or too fast asleep to hear her phone ring. "Be in touch tomorrow," said Helen, once BT's automated voice had finished, and the bright, busy lights of Sarn Park Services became night. "And don't worry."

"Who were you calling?" he asked.

"My mam. Why?" Normally she'd have told him to mind his own business, but she'd cadged a lift, hadn't she? Once again, she was beholden. But not for long. When her paintings started selling and she'd got her own place, she wouldn't be in this situation ever again.

£3.50 left.

"Why would she be worried?" the man persisted. "I don't get it."

His tone had sharpened. But right now, she needed him more than he needed her. "I always say that to her. Whatever."

"My kids don't."

"Perhaps you give them more space."

Just then, her Nokia juddered in her hand. Jason's number came up,

113

beating her to it. She held her breath as he came through. Too loud, on the move as well, it seemed. "I've been trying to get hold of you…"

"I'm OK. But my car's not. It's in Llandovery station car park. The driver's door unlocked. Can you please try and make it secure?"

"Sorted, no worries. Just been to the Fuzz there. Mr Price gave me a lift. Look, you can't just take off in the middle of the night. Was it because of Gwenno?"

The Fuzz word had been too loud. She lowered her own voice to barely above a whisper. "No. Though she did her best to push me down into that valley. It was something Mr Flynn said that made me leave. Tell you later."

"Tell me *now*."

"I can't. Look, Jason," she was whispering now, "you shouldn't have done that. I mean go to the police. This is *my* business."

Now Ethan Woods was leaning towards her, his beanie clear of his bright red ears, while that same mix of sweat and stale aftershave, she'd smelt that morning at Heron House, hit her nose.

"So where the Hell are you?" Jason wasn't giving up.

"Got a lift to London."

"Anyone you know?"

"Erm… No."

"Helen, you're crazy. I'm coming to find you…"

"You can't."

And that was it.

The driver suddenly switched on his radio. Amy Winehouse plus strings. Helen reached out to turn down the volume, but that black leather hand pushed hers away.

"He let you have it," the guy observed as if he'd not done anything. "Not cricket to speak to the fairer sex like that."

So he'd heard that much…

"Jason, eh?"

"No. James, actually."

"Could've sworn you'd said Jason, which just so happens to be my youngest's name.

It was then, despite the van's warm, cosy cab, she felt her skin ice up. Jason had called her crazy. It had hurt, but he was right. This guy had sniffed a lie like an owl sniffs meat. "What's with the Fuzz?" He eyed her in a way that made her grip her phone even harder. "That didn't sound very helpful."

"Look, Mr Woods, my period's come on. I need to sort it. I really don't want to spoil your seat."

"Next stop, eh? Like I said. Anyway," he shot her another glance, a slight smile on his chapped lips, "I'm used to blood."

One of her failings, she knew, was her inability to suss out character. Hadn't it taken her a full month to realise Mr Flynn was a fully paid up member of the Chameleon Club? Gwenno Davies too? Nice as pie at first, yes. Just like with Jason, until the dark stuff seeped through. Why, to her painting tutor's disappointment, she'd never tackled the portrait. Hers would have been too superficial to show any truth. Not that there was much to read in Ethan Woods' face. Just his round, blue eyes, chapped lips and fox-coloured stubble.

SERVICES 28 MILES.

Don't panic, she told herself. He's just a bloke. The ones she'd known, including her da, rarely said the right thing, especially to do with female stuff. But Jason was different, and she wished now she'd not been so arsy with him.

Over the Severn Bridge with the last of Wales and Saturday slipping by to the throb of Bob Marley's 'Exodus' and that sudden surge of blood down below that meant the next Services would probably come too late.

***

"I'm on my way to Islington. Wait for me." Helen whispered in reply to Mr Flynn's standard voicemail instructions, having checked neither adjacent cubicle in the Ladies loos at Leigh Delamere Services was occupied. She stuffed her own phone into her rucksack, willing him to soon pick up her message. But perhaps he too was asleep, exhausted.

With a night-time sanitary pad that felt more like a small house between her legs, she opened the heavy fire door bit by bit on to the too-bright BP Shop. She blinked, then spotted her driver's sturdy back as he stood by the till paying cash for his diesel and a giant Mars bar.

So far, she'd only seen him up close and seated. Now, while a sudden rush of blood left her body, those broad, slightly stooped shoulders, the thick neck and the way he moved towards the exit, brought everything back. So he'd added a donkey jacket and covered his shaved head. But he'd missed one important detail. Her eyes followed his thick-soled, white trainers as they unexpectedly turned from the exit and began walking towards the door she was holding.

No...

She let it close without a sound and shut herself in the furthest of the six cubicles. Voices now. His and someone else's. A woman.

115

Bastard.

"It's a ginger," he explained. "Pony tail, blue fleece with hood, jeans, pink rucksack. May be in trouble. Mentioned her period starting and looked pretty pale. Reckon you should take a look."

Helen held her breath while shivering with too much fear to bother about him calling her a ginger. Her rucksack felt too heavy on her back. Her blood, inside and out, way too hot. She thought of her room back at Heron House with all her painting gear waiting to be used, mam, Jason, whom she was missing already, and Mr Flynn, for whom she'd taken such a stupid risk.

"No joy so far," said the woman clicking open next door's cubicle. "But I'll keep looking."

No you won't.

Helen charged from her hiding place, causing the woman in the navy trouser suit to lose her balance while she yanked open the door into the shop and, head down, pushed through the queue who temporarily barred her way, and headed for the door. Someone stuck out a leg and she almost fell, but was upright again, weaving her way between the newspaper and magazine displays.

"C'mere bitch!" yelled Mr Beanie behind her. "Before it's too late."

The glass automatic doors parted then closed behind her. She'd just a few seconds to hide again. To recoup. Around the back of the shop, illuminated by the glare from a small barred window, stood four giant wheelie bins. She snatched up the first three mucky lids in turn, only to recoil from the stench of rotting waste piled high inside. Number four seemed different. Drier, and not so full. She plunged in a hand and felt paper and more paper.

Thank you, God...

She threw in her rucksack and, gripping the bin's front edge with both hands, up she went and dropped down onto an unstable bed of mainly cardboard. She then closed the lid over her as quietly as she could.

Only her breathing was audible now, and the sudden, unexpected rip of parcel tape against her boots. Her pursuer's threats seemed to be drifting away in another direction, but she couldn't be sure if he was now on his own or not. Even changing his mind. She was taking no chances. The luminous hands on her watch showed half past midnight, and she was just about to check her phone's credits to call 999, when, like a bolt of electricity in that dark, airless box, it began to ring from inside her rucksack.

No...

Would he hear it? Even someone else putting rubbish out?

116

Her rucksack lay below her in the farthest corner, and only by stretching out a foot to reach its straps, could she reel it in. But as the ringing continued, she had the strongest feeling that if she answered, she'd be toast. The tosser calling himself Ethan Woods had stared at her little screen, hadn't he? Number highlighted and remembered. Perhaps he had a special memory gift. Mild autism. Unless her driver had been in her room before visiting Mr Flynn's study.

That stray thought, and another of him foraging in her knicker drawer, made her blood turn to ice.

"NEW CALL... NEW CALL... NUMBER WITHHELD."

Wait...

And then the invitation to leave a message after the tone. When it came, the debris under her boots seemed to collapse, taking her deeper into the polyurethane coffin's dead musty air.

19.

Sunday 5th April 2009 – 12.30 a.m.

That bruising wind, that had accompanied Jason and Gwilym to Llandovery, was now an unearthly stillness where nothing stirred. During the journey back, instead of quizzing his driver more about Heron House and its history, Jason fought sleep by staring out at the familiar landmarks and the dead badger now little more than a sorry heap. Its entrails straggled glistening into the road.

***

"I should have asked the Fuzz about Llyr Davies," Jason said, as Gwilym Price hauled up the handbrake outside Heron House.

"Don't you worry, son," said the farmer. "It'll all come out in the wash. To me, that Sergeant seemed more clued up than Prydderch. And as for Miss Jenkins, she's got an old head on young shoulders. She'll be alright. And her car."

"Glad you think so. Wish I could believe it," said Jason.

Gwilym Price then handed over a battered business card. "I'm only a stone's throw away, remember?"

"Cheers." And with a lungful of thick, oily diesel, Jason ran half-blind with tiredness over the gravel past the circular flower bed and its solitary rose, towards the front porch. Encouraged by a light from indoors glowing through the door's two frosted glass panels, he rang the bell.

After five long minutes, Idris and Gwenno Davies appeared with besom and crop at the ready. She, swamped by a camel-coloured dressing gown, with hair a mess and lipstick smudged up her cheeks, looked like some red light district's favourite granny. He, equally dishevelled, wore pyjamas that seemed to belong to another age and to someone else. Why did sex come to mind? And the gruesome thought of them at it, made Jason miss her first question.

"I said, what time of night is this?" her pink mouth jerked as she spoke. "We'll be telling Mr Flynn when he's back. That's for sure." She eyed his feet. "And the fact you've stolen his boots."

"Thief," added the gardener as if she'd suddenly empowered him. "And the sooner you go back to where you come from, the better."

"Hounslow," she spat out the word. "Coon country."

"Excuse me," Jason kept a lid on his anger, "I'd like to get to my room. The room I've paid for."

The pyjamas stood aside to let him pass. "You're not welcome here. Nor that slapper either."

"You've already made that quite clear," Jason crossed the gloomy reception hall, full of strange, penumbral shadows, cobwebs and dust strands hanging low enough to brush his forehead. "So put another record on, eh?"

"Where is the little madam?" the sister called out, looking out over his shoulder.

"You tell me. You tried to kill her."

"Slander, Mr Robbins, is a serious offence. And we've friends who'd help get you in trouble, haven't we, Idris?"

"Indeed we have."

Jason wasn't going to waste his breath at this stage. He ditched the stinking boots and, despite his legs feeling like two lead weights, took the stairs three at a time to check Helen's room was still locked. It was. He then made for his own. All he could think of was her out there, with some stranger – or more than one. Christ, he shouldn't have let her go. Easy to say that now, when he'd not even noticed she'd left Heron House.

Once inside his fusty, over-decorated room, he pulled down the sash window's upper portion and felt the dying wind on his face. Reception for his phone was sure to be better up here than at ground level or in the Nissan where he'd last tried to contact her. No such luck. He was just about to chuck the useless piece of junk across the room, when that other voice he recognised immediately, swirled into his ear. He faced the black, still night with its hidden hills and impenetrable forests; the secrets and lies of the dead and the living. His heart churning.

"For God's sake, who are you? What do you want?"

"I have come and I have gone. Suffered and been punished, but no more. It is time... It is time..."

And was that some bird he could hear calling out in the background, or something else? A kitten, perhaps? Some other young animal?

"Time? What for? I don't understand..." That cold, damp air from outside filled Jason's mouth, stroked his skin. His hand shook on the phone that suddenly seemed heavier, like a lead weight.

"You saw them by our swimming pool, didn't you?" That same young woman's voice continued after taking a deep, grating breath. "Those foul, arrogant men who used me for too long. I was there with you. Couldn't you feel it, deep in your soul?"

"Yes," he lied, just to get rid of her.

"So, Mr Robbins, please open your writing book and pick up your red pen. That way, you'll remember me and what I had to do to survive."

***

Mr Robbins...

How weird was that? And about his red pen. But what stuck in his knackered brain like a maggot, wasn't only her tortured message but 'our' swimming pool. Not 'the' or 'their' – Jason rubbed his eyes, trying to revisit that tiled terrace with its black-suited men and their blood-red wine. Had whoever just spoken to him, in that faintly threatening way, belonged here at some point? But how? When?

Dammit.

All Jason wanted to do was sleep, so that in a few hours' time, he'd have the energy to check again on Helen and get the Fuzz properly involved. So far, Sergeant Rees had arranged for her car to be secured, but seen no need to dust it for prints. "Probably met up with a friend," he'd opined. "Someone she knew." But something in Helen's voice had told Jason otherwise and, as he crept downstairs to use the landline phone in the reception hall, realised that her finding a handy lift at that time of night in that small, snoring town, had been like snow in July.

999.

"Police," he said to the automaton who answered. "My friend Helen Jenkins who's a cook at Heron House in Rhandirmwyn is on her way to London by road and could be in danger."

"Which road?"

He only knew of the M4 and said so.

"What vehicle?"

"God knows."

"We need far more precise information than this. Where in London exactly?"

"Some mansion block or other in Islington." Neither the *Metro* newspaper nor Helen herself had given any more detail than that. "I believe a Charles Pitt-Rose was living there."

"Was?"

"He's been found hanged."

"And your friend's age?"

"Say twenty-three."

After what seemed like a lifetime and a million questions later, Jason was connected to Dyfed Powys Police in Carmarthen where a DC Jane Harris

120

took down what details he had. Also both his and Helen's mobile numbers. "If she's on pay-as-you-go, there may not be a trace. But we'll try. I was told Islington…"

"That's right, and I've a hunch she may be seeing her boss, Monty Flynn, there. Charles Pitt-Rose was his landlord. He did once live at Heron House. Has any news of his death reached you here?"

"Not so far. And I'm very sorry to hear it. Do you have this Mr Flynn's mobile number?"

"No."

So the deal was that Helen must reply to him first.

Here goes…

Her ring tone was alive alright, but for some reason, she wasn't picking up.

"C'mon… c'mon…" he urged her, but whenever had life ever gone to plan? He stared at his receiver, wondering if texting Helen would suffice, when he was suddenly aware of a shadowy movement by the door to the stairs.

"What's going on?" Jason called out, only to see a naked Idris Davies and his besom advancing with the speed of someone half his age. All old muscle and menace, his crinkled cock and purple balls swinging as he moved. Jason slapped the phone down and bent to pick up a pair of brass fire tongs. "Where's Llyr, your son?" he shouted. "And don't tell me you haven't got one. He's been here, hasn't he? Attacked Miss Jenkins, and the rest. And don't think I'm not onto it. The police as well."

Jason's pulse was high jumping in his wrists and his neck, as he slapped down the receiver and waited for the kill. Instead, to his surprise, the besom slipped from the man's grasp and without making any effort to retrieve it, Idris turned on his heels and ran back the way he'd come. His shrivelled buttocks wobbling with each stride, his strange fearful cry diminishing as he ran off into the house's dark, mysterious heart.

***

Back in his claustrophobic room, Jason locked his door, took a few deep breaths before closing his window and lying down by the wardrobe to access his refill pad. His hands probed the shallow wooden arch from left to right, back and fore, until with a sick ache in his gut, he knew he was wasting his time. *OPERATION ROOK* had vanished.

Shit.

Ignoring the faintly cloying smell of roses that suddenly seemed to reach his nose and swill around his boiling head, he was soon hurtling down to the next floor, groping his way along the papered walls and their tilting pictures, until he reached his destination.

The cohabiting brother and sister. A sliver of light showed beneath their door. The faint hum of voices. Time for action.

Bang, bang, bang and a kick for good measure. He felt good.

"Open up!"

Almost immediately, three bolts were drawn back. Three turns of a key, then a gap wide enough to allow the thick smell of sex to eke out and for two crazed eyes to meet his. The gardener again, still starkers.

"No, Idris!" came a shriek from behind him. "Leave it." There's enough trouble as it is."

"I'm no coward. I'll sort the runt out," Idris said.

But Jason pushed the door further open to see something he'd rather forget. Gwenno Davies in the huge bed, holding its silky brown duvet up to her chin. But it was the bright blonde wig perched on her head that made him start. Then the fluffy handcuffs and the riding crop…

Asylum.

"Who's been in my room and nicked my notepad?" Jason yelled. "You or that lovely son of yours?"

The gardener backed away, but not her. "I'll call the police!" she hissed. "Then you'll have a record. No more jobs for you, Saes. That'll teach you to put your nose where it's not wanted. And another thing…"

Jason let her rant on while he sussed out what he could of the room. Classy curtains and carpet; no expense spared, it seemed. But it was the bed and its padded champagne-coloured headboard that dominated even the pale wood dressing table and matching double wardrobe. Against the door hung what appeared to be a woman's black riding habit from much earlier days. Closer to, he also spotted a mobile phone on the nearest bedside table. A sleek little silver number. And something else that made him catch his breath. He'd never seen an actual dildo before, but what else could the thing be? Creamy white and surely too thick, with a distinct kink halfway along its shaft.

But Jason had to get back on track. And soon. "What did you do to Miss Jenkins to make her leave like that?" he challenged the old woman. "Try to strangle her? Push her out of the way? Well, let me tell you couple of psychos, I'm sticking here till she's found safe and well. OK?"

With that, and not unexpectedly, the door was slammed in his face; the bolts slid back into place. The key viciously turned.

Tempted to retrieve the besom and chuck it in the pool, Jason reminded

122

himself to stick to what mattered and, right now, Monty Flynn's study was tops. In total darkness, with his own boots in hand to silence his journey across rugs and creaking floorboards, he reached the front door and with the tiniest of clicks, set the latch.

Once outside in the night's oppressive stillness, and too close to the front wall to activate the security light, he groped his way along the thick ivy until his hand connected with the front lounge's stone windowsill. Ten paces later, came the lock-ups with the ivy still conveniently in place.

He tucked his boots out of sight and, having tested his weight on the cold damp foliage, began to climb. So far so good, and within seconds, as a scrap of acid moonlight poked through the clouds, his fingers found what they were looking for: a moss-covered windowsill.

***

The lower portion of the sash window, although broken, moved sweetly upwards at an angle, enough for him to wedge it open with clumps of ivy. Next, he curled himself over the sill into a large, oblong room divided into sleeping and working areas. A desk and filing cabinet stood to the right, with a single bed, armchair and open wardrobe to the left. A noticeable smell of drink and fags lingered in the air. But where were all the books Monty Flynn was supposed to own? Helen had been right about that. In fact, where was anything?

Jason paused, ready if necessary to hide in the darkest corner, out of the moonlight's glow. This was how Helen must have felt. A nervous trespasser. He gave himself five minutes to find what he was looking for. Hadn't Gregor Vasilich boasted on page 83 of *Evil Eyes*, that 'knowledge is power?' However, as Jason directed the pale green light from his phone on to the oak desk and its many drawers, he realised someone – or perhaps more than one – had got there first. Not even a paper clip remained. The computer and framed photographs that Helen had also mentioned, had gone. But why?

Just then the phone light suddenly died. He clicked it on again to see the filing cabinet, too, had been emptied. And then, without warning, his Orange Rome phone began to vibrate in his hand.

20.

Wednesday 9th October 1946 – 4.30 p.m.

Having relieved his unexpected visitor of his sodden reeking hat and coat, and suggested the rifle stay in the lobby, Lionel hefted a pine log on to his fire and indicated the second of two armchairs whose green upholstery and walnut feet, almost matched the one belonging to his late father.

As a result of the bombings in his native city, the chaos of death and destruction, he'd grown to crave order. A simplicity of material things that allowed his mind to burrow whichever way an idea took it. But nothing could have prepared him for what was about to come from Peris Morgan's mouth.

The old soldier, with an inch of whisky now in his glass sat bolt upright as if in bed, enduring a bad dream or some long-ago memory from days spent at the Front during the Great War. It was then Lionel noticed that his left eye stayed still, more opaque than its partner. Was it real or artificial, he wondered. Yet despite this and other privations, the man still felt driven to serve the land of his birth. He also had a few questions to answer.

"So what makes you think I've been up to Heron House?" Lionel began.

"Not sayin', sir."

"Was it young Gwilym Price?"

The stranger hung his head, which Lionel took to mean 'yes.' "You've things to tell me about it," Lionel reminded him, lowering himself into his own chair with pen and a small notebook at the ready. Thirty-three years of teaching had shown it was best to write things down rather than rely on an over-burdened memory.

"I have, sir." The old man eyed the pad. "But be sure to burn your paper afterwards. D'you understand, sir?"

As if in anticipation, the flames caressing the base of the log, sprang into life, leaping halfway up the chimney, releasing the sappy smell that would normally soothe Lionel into a doze. But not now. This time he was tense. On alert. He'd rarely seen a man so fearful since he'd left Birmingham's mean, ravaged streets.

"Someone should set fire to that damned Heron House, too." Peris Morgan took a mouthful of whisky as if to fortify himself, and licked his cracked lips before continuing. "What they do up there is shameful. More what you'd find down Cardiff docks or Soho, not here among decent, clean-livin' folk." He paused, drawing in his slightly wheezy breath, while

124

outside, beyond the still-open curtains, the grey dusk had become an impenetrable black. He got up to shut it out, aware both his hands were trembling. His usually reliable legs more those of someone more elderly.

"You'd think bein' judges and all, they'd know about what was proper and what wasn't."

So Carol hadn't been mistaken.

"Judges? How many?"

"Three at least. Top of the heap and rich as Croesus, so I've heard. Come up country for fun and games. But," he wagged a knobbly forefinger in Lionel's direction. "Not what you and I'd call fun and games. I've heard the screams, the yellin,' the cracking of whips. 'Specially the cracking of whips. You wouldn't believe it. But what did Constable Prydderch say when I told him? Live and let live. That there was no law against festivities."

"Festivities?" Lionel also wrote that down, unsure what to divulge about Walter's visit to the school and what he himself had witnessed up by the Nantymwyn lead mine. This Home Guard veteran was still a stranger, after all.

"Sir, I say orgies."

Holy Jesus...

The word came as a shock, but couldn't completely erase the memory of how in civilian life, Lionel's own father had been taken to court by a wealthy but dissatisfied customer with a cunning barrister, and lost most of his savings in costs. Why he'd joined up and why, in his last letter home, he'd warned his only son to steer clear of 'those black, Godless beetles who'll suck you dry.'

Having recovered from Peris Morgan's shock announcement, Lionel had to ask the vital question: "So who exactly lives at Heron House?"

His visitor set down his glass and wiped his mouth with his jacket cuff. A brown leather affair, creased by years of wear and weather. "I never saw no wife myself, but to my da, she was a real beauty. Joy was her name. A Cardiff girl. Died giving birth a while back now. Buried in St. Barnabas' Church, she is. The grave's very well cared for. Always has been. Must have cost an arm and a leg, mind, a plot like that."

"This baby?"

"A son it was. Charles, as I recall. Never saw him either, mind. Must be the same age as our Kyffin."

"Well, he certainly doesn't attend my school," said Lionel, almost adding that the cries he'd heard at Heron House weren't those of a young boy. "Never has done."

"Talk is he's in some posh place down Dorset way. Can't be sure, mind." He glanced at Lionel. "Don't understand it, to be honest. But there you go. With what's supposedly going on at home, best he's not around."

"Who's his father?"

The old soldier eyed his whisky glass. Drew his jacket closer over his stained woollen shirt, even though the log in the grate was fully alight, giving off more of the scented smell of pine.

"I'm assuming Edmund Pitt-Rose. Why I've come calling. Heart o' stone he has, and God help you if you find yourself up in front of him in court like some poor devils I know. Treated worse than the salmon in his keep-net." His voice dropped to a whisper. "Sion Beynon's uncle over in Salem for a start. Stole some sheep. Got ten years and hanged himself in Swansea jail the next month."

"Who else lives there?" persisted Lionel, who often had to refocus his charges at school. He'd never known youngsters chatter so much as the Welsh – often delightfully so – but one had planned a lesson to get through.

"I glimpsed a young woman wearing a black dress and white apron. Hard little face, and even harder eyes. Couldn't have been more than sixteen."

"Gwenno Davies. Stuck-up little piece, given her situation." Peris drained his glass and replaced it on the side table rather too sharply. Whether deliberately or not, Lionel couldn't decide. Normally at this time of day, Lionel'd fetch his pipe and, with three practised pushes of his thumb, fill it with his favourite brand of tobacco. But there'd be no pipe now. He was aware of a slow but inexorable unravelling. The way the mist undresses the hills after a damp night.

The man opposite was in his stride. Lionel topped up Peris Morgan's empty glass. Whatever it took to loosen that tongue even further.

"Her and her older brother Idris are – you know – touched up here." His visitor tapped the side of his forehead with a finger missing its top knuckle. "All the lead smelting that went on, see. Specially down here in Nantybai. Mind you, they wasn't the only ones. Oh, no. My daughter had terrible nightmares for years. Would take herself off sleepwalking. Once, we found her wading along the Towy. No clothes on, mind."

Lionel had heard of such cases on his travels, also during the three school Governors' meetings he'd attended since his appointment. How the mines' owners had insisted that conditions for workers and community safety had always been a priority. But he wasn't here to fill his head with the world's

126

stories, troubling though they were. He needed some answers.

"This so-called judge said he'd set his lad on me. Would that be Idris Davies?"

A nod. "Evil little ferret. Keep out of his way, if I were you."

A serious warning coming from an armed man big as a shed. But Lionel hadn't finished. "Have you ever seen his sister wearing a riding habit. Polished boots, all very pukka?"

At this, Morgan smiled a ragged smile. "Oh yes, and I can tell you about her little Welsh costume, too. Talk about butter wouldn't melt. Till she starts speaking, that is. And as for her riding crop, can you guess what that's made of?"

Lionel was caught by surprise.

"Leather?"

"Thought you'd say that, sir. No, it's a bull's dick, dried and stretched. So Dai Meat said. A friend of his over in Hereford made it for her. She's never without it. You see, her and Idris are the Cerberus, guarding Hell's gates."

Lionel was too startled by news of the crop and Peris Morgan's unlikely show of erudition to jot anything down, while all the while, the picture of Heron House was growing more bizarre by the minute.

Lionel then made a decision. The time had come to share his own fear. "She threatened me with a gun after Walter Jones' funeral on Saturday," he said. "I was quite shaken up, just like today during my lunch hour."

"I'm not surprised. Only fifteen, mind, but she's the spy, the lookout, while tending the grave and all. More than once I've been tempted to take a pot shot. Vermin those two are, sir. Vermin, and that's a compliment."

When he'd finished, Peris Morgan raised himself from his chair and moved towards the window, patting Lionel's shoulder as he went. "You're a good man, Mr Hargreaves. Although you're no Welsh speaker, you've done a lot in your first year in Rhandirmwyn. But if I were you – and unlike me, you've many more days to live and nights to sleep – I'd get yourself back to the Midlands. More people, see; where you wouldn't stand out like you do here. You'd be safe."

Lionel stared at the fire, then his notebook's jottings. No, he told himself. These aren't going in the flames. Nor am I leaving. "So whose screams did I hear coming from the house?" he persisted. "There must be someone else up there. What are you keeping from me?"

A pause followed, as long and dark as the Severn Railway Tunnel where too many workmen had perished.

"If I tell you, sir, you must swear never to breathe a word. Even when you've gone. Let me hear it."

Lionel swallowed hard as if a stone had lodged in his throat. "I swear."

"There's a young woman. Just two years older than Gwenno. The daughter. Spit of her mother she is, if what my da said was true. I've only caught sight of her the once. Hair as black as a rook's wing. Eyes as dark as any coal could be."

"Please go on," Lionel urged him as he might a shy pupil. His heartbeat quickening.

"She's the one they all come to see. Those... those..." Here Peris Morgan faltered. His voice beginning to break up, as his listener watched the once lively log suddenly give up the ghost and lie on its ashes like some old charred relic.

The same girl as young Walter had seen?

"Has she any friends from the village?"

"Her? No, sir. She's more like a prisoner. All I can say."

With a shiver, Lionel recalled what Betsan Griffiths had written down to win his prize. How she was apparently unhappy at winning. Now he knew why, but Peris Morgan was speaking again. "There *is* one friend, sir, if you can call him that. The conchie. Talk is, he's been sniffing around her. My wife saw them together by the old adit up Pen Cerrigmwyn. Kissing they were."

"The organist from St. Barnabas?"

"Yes, sir. A fool for love. But sure as there's breath in my body, his dainty little feet won't be pumping those pedals for long. And hard as it might sound, I wouldn't care. In my book, cowards like him don't deserve to live."

"That's rather harsh, Mr Morgan. It seems he's suffered enough already."

"Pah!"

The last of the Home Guard snatched his hat and coat from the peg in the lobby. "Tell that to those poor lads who never saw their loved ones again."

The silent night soon claimed him and the quickening tread of his boots on the stony track, while Lionel shivered again in the still, damp air. Having checked his fire was well and truly dead, he picked up his torch and his beloved tweed overcoat then closed his front door behind him.

There'd be no relaxing tonight. Not with three important visits to make, and while he picked his way over to Troed y Rhiw, realised with a jolt, he'd forgotten to ask the worthy but misguided bigot the unfortunate young woman's name.

128

Just then, as he reached his gate, he was aware of his visitor retracing his steps. Peris Morgan, smelling of whisky was close enough to send a tremor of apprehension through Lionel's body. "Something I just remembered," Peris Morgan began. "Them judges at Heron House what I was telling you about. Heard a whisper they call themselves The Order, though God knows what that means. Might just be gossip, mind."

"That's a strange name," Lionel said, half to himself, immediately thinking of Masons. Besides, Betsan hadn't mentioned anything about that.

"I'll leave you now. Just you watch yourself, sir."

"I will."

Yet the moment the other man had gone, Lionel drew his coat tighter around his body and let his lit torch roam for a few moments around the surrounding dusky bushes and trees that had suddenly acquired an air of menace and danger.

21.

Sunday 5th April 2009 – 6 a.m.

'There'll be no hiding place. So don't get cocky. And if you squeal to anyone else, you'll end up in bin bags where no-one'll find you. Got it, bitch?'

That message left on Helen's phone was from someone definitely male, definitely Woods, but more of a Welsh intonation than in the cab. Perhaps he'd also lied about living in Surrey, and the rest. She had thought of nothing else since, and yet, as a dirty grey light seeped under the slightly wedged-open lid into her squalid quarters, she realised from her watch showing 6 a.m. she must have slept.

What the Hell's that?

Had war suddenly broken out in the middle of Wiltshire? A grumbling roll of wheels and men shouting were drawing closer. She pushed up the bin's lid a bit further to see what was going on.

Damn.

A vast refuse lorry, complete with churning drum and a bad smell, was backing up while a fluorescent yellow guy was already investigating the first bin in the row.

Stay calm. Get a grip.

She must wait for the inevitable. To get out and run would only arouse suspicion and might bring the willing Trouser Suit on her case. Besides, if that threat *had* been left by Ethan Woods, he probably wasn't far away and at least she'd have company.

Here goes...

Suddenly more daylight appeared and the peak of a red baseball cap followed by two startled eyes stared down at Helen. The hydraulics' din drowned the man's surprised shouts.

"I can explain," she croaked, aware of her period surging southwards. "I'd nowhere else to go. This bloke was chasing me."

"You Welsh?"

"What's that got to do with it?"

"All Taffies are bonkers." Nevertheless, two filthy gloved hands reached down towards her. "Up you come before you get shredded."

Her knees wouldn't straighten, nor her elbows. She was as stiff as her ancient mamgu, still clinging to life in her Care Home up in Machynlleth. The bin man called for help, and as the rotting rubbish stench filled her nose, two more hands pulled her clear and helped her along to a wooden

130

bench conveniently placed near the Travel Lodge's main entrance.

"Thank you," was all Helen could say. Her eyes beginning to sting.

"Got to get back," explained the one in the baseball cap. "We're on short time as it is. Fuckin' stingy council."

With the men gone, big fat tears fell on to her precious rucksack, until an inner voice told her all wasn't lost. She'd got her Visa card, hadn't she? And a working phone that only needed a top-up.

"Come on," she sniffed. "With a bit of luck, I could be with Mr Flynn in a few hours."

***

No sign of the Trouser Suit or the white van and its driver. Something else to be grateful for. With less stiffness now, Helen returned to the shop and its welcome loo, where a basinful of hot water and a nice-smelling hand wash made her feel ready to face the day.

Ten minutes later, with her phone topped up, she dialled the taxi firm's number given to her by the Asian guy at the till. She was warned that the bill could exceed a hundred pounds. "Sod it," she told herself. At least she'd be safer than here. At least Mr Flynn might put her in the picture.

She waited by the counter until the shopkeeper had finished stacking a new delivery of cigarettes, then she said, "that man with the black beanie. Did he ever come back in here after I gave him the slip?"

"Not to my knowledge. I'm often in the storeroom. But," he indicated a small TV positioned discreetly near the till angled away from prying eyes, "he'll be on this if he did."

"CCTV?"

"Sure. Remind me of the time."

She tried thinking back through the blur of her recent nightmare. "Must have been half past midnight."

"OK." He flicked a switch and swivelled the screen round until its monochrome duplicate of the shop itself and surroundings came up on the screen.

"And he had this van. White it was," she explained. "Newish, judging by the state of it."

But no lamb...

"Take a look, but be quick," said the guy. "We're getting busy again."

And sure enough, the grainy sequences showed the odd motorist and biker filling up at the pumps, until he swiftly swivelled the screen away from new customers queuing up to pay. "All quiet," he said once the shop was empty again, letting her look until suddenly, she spotted a shadowy, but nevertheless familiar figure running between the vacant pumps and round the corner where she'd been hiding.

"That's him." Helen's finger stabbed the screen. "Look!"

"12.38," the clock says. Off to the Travel Lodge by the looks of things. There's nothing else out the back apart from our rubbish bay."

Her period pain kicked in again as the film ended and a new one began, showing Ethan Woods in his beanie and duffle coat pushing open the hotel's outer door and not coming out again. So he could have seen her on that bench. Could still be there, with his van tucked out of sight.

"Seen enough?" The guy was clearly busy with yet more boxes of stock arriving.

"I have, thanks." She then noticed the Cosicab taxi draw up alongside the shop's front window. Its driver, a smart middle-aged woman wearing a maroon dress. "If he comes in here and starts asking about me, say you don't know anything. Please."

"I'll warn my brother. My shift ends in ten minutes."

His promise followed her outside where the silver Mondeo's rear passenger door was already open.

"Your firm said they'd take Visa," Helen said, keeping a lookout for the black beanie.

"That's fine. You want Islington, right?"

"Right."

***

No chat. No radio, or inquisitive glances. Just a professional called Maureen doing her job, cruising along the damp tarmac between the other Sunday morning early birds like her, a long journey to make. No sign of that white van either, and after signs for Swindon came and went, Helen gave up looking and closed her eyes...

Her mam's favourite scene of a sunny autumn day – with blues and greens of sky and water contrasting with the reds, oranges and browns of leaves about to fall, came into view. But gradually, the planned sky had become earth-coloured, dome-shaped. Nothing like the intended vista from Dan y Bryn, her mam's chalet bungalow. And the more she tried to retrieve her original idea, the more the pressure on her brush increased until stroke by stroke, colours that had mysteriously appeared on her palette were in place.

This was no seascape or landscape. She was staring at a face. But not only that. A beautiful, screaming face...

The taxi driver was eyeing her through her rear-view mirror. "Shall I pull

132

over? Do you need to get out for a minute?"

To Helen, the voice seemed to come from far, far away, while beyond the car's windows a bleak, grey world sped by. She simply said, "can you please turn the heater up? I'm freezing."

The woman frowned. "Will do. But it's already near max."

How could it be? With skin that felt shrunken over her bones? Fingertips numb, cheesy-pale? Even the inside of her mouth was like an ice-box; the nerves in her teeth dancing to a hurting tune. And all the while, the vision of that terrible, tortured face filled her mind.

***

More traffic now near the eastern end of the M4, and the Mondeo slowed down alongside a solitary, static wind turbine whose white blades almost blended with the lightening sky. Normally, Helen would be envisaging this same aberration repeated hundreds of times on every beautiful Welsh hill and wondering yet again what she could do to stop it. But not now, with survival top of her agenda.

Suddenly, Rhandirmwyn's stifling beauty seemed like two massive hands gripping her throat until she couldn't breathe. Those terrified eyes she'd seen on that canvas, boring into the far reaches of her mind.

"I'll stop if you like." Maureen's concern made her drop down another gear. "Just say when."

"I'm fine, thanks," Helen wheezed. "I just need to get to Mr Flynn."

"Flynn, you say?" quizzed the driver, negotiating a big roundabout signed for Hammersmith and routes south. "Is he Irish?"

"Yes. Apparently he's written two novels."

"I'm impressed."

"About the Freemasons."

"I love anything like that. Conspiracy theories, alien encounters. Dan Brown meets David Icke, I suppose. Odd I've not heard of him."

"I think the books were withdrawn early on. Their publishers had cold feet. So he said."

Maureen didn't reply.

***

At last Helen stepped out on to the damp, uneven pavement and waved the Mondeo away. Not for the first time did she feel suddenly stranded and alone, missing Jason.

"There'll be no hiding place. So don't get cocky. And if you squeal to anyone else, you'll end up in bin bags where no-one'll find you. Got it, bitch?"

She scoured her surroundings, listening hard for that van's distinctive engine, and then, just as she was about to phone Jason and her mam again, heard a man's voice calling out to her. First of all, she looked upwards at Sandhurst Mansion; but there on her right, three cars along the nearby kerb, was the familiar grey Volvo and its driver with a not-so-familiar expression in his eyes. Mr Flynn himself. Or rather, what seemed to be a dishevelled, older version. He looked worse than she did.

Having unfolded himself from his seat and, with his driver's door still open, Mr Flynn walked towards her, arms spread wide. That same sticking plaster attached to his right index finger. "I've been worried stiff about you, Helen Myfanwy Jenkins. How the Hell did you know I was here?"

"That *Metro* notice gave me a useful start, then my cab driver took a guess."

The hug that followed this lie took her by surprise, taking the air from her lungs until he spotted her taxi indicating to rejoin the traffic. "What did that cost? Please, I can't let you pay."

"Mr Flynn, I'd actually prefer it if you told me the truth."

He rolled his eyes. A stray cloud covering the pale sun cast his face in shadow.

"Not again, Helen. You've already given me the third degree."

"Some weirdo attacked me at Heron House yesterday, and then late last night must have followed me to Llandovery where I was dumb enough to cadge a lift from him. Ethan Woods he called himself. I recognised the same trainers. How he had the same build and smell... Is that his real name? Do you know of him?"

"No, I'm sorry. You just have to be so careful these days. And as for Heron House, the Davieses are supposed to be on guard." Her boss inclined his face towards her. In close up, his normally wavy hair was a greasy mess. "Why no mention of this when you left your message?"

Helen inwardly counted to three to calm herself down. He was wrong-footing her. The sod.

"Do the police know?" Mr Flynn asked.

"Yes. DC Prydderch went looking for clues, but he's rubbish. Shall I tell you about this freak's vile threat to me? Shall I? It's still in my phone. There'll be no hiding place..." she began, hearing her voice tremble. When she'd finished, she noticed how those same eyes had closed. That mouth a tight unmoving line.

***

She followed him towards the apartment block, unsettled by this sudden change of mood. Reminding herself from now on to watch and listen. To not give too much away because with every passing second, the man now in front of her was becoming more of a stranger.

A police cordon had been stretched across the entrance to what she assumed was the underground garage. The sight of it adding to a growing sense of danger. Nevertheless, she kept her distance, even when her boss introduced himself and shook hands with a short, anxious-looking Philippina dressed in a belted camel coat already waiting by the gateless path. He then turned to Helen. "Mrs Pachela used to clean for Mr Pitt-Rose. And this is Helen Jenkins, my cook at Heron House." He gestured for Helen to come closer, but she held back. Something about this obviously pre-arranged encounter felt very wrong indeed.

"You know what I've come for," he returned to Mrs Pachela whose red-rimmed eyes were welling up. "Keys, as agreed."

His wallet was already out and open, revealing a wad of new notes inside.

"I'm sorry, sir," said the woman. "They won't be ready until four o'clock. I did try..."

Disappointment slackened his shoulders. "Not good enough," he tutted while shoving the wallet back in its place. The sun slid out from behind another hanging cloud, revealing the cleaner's perspiring olive skin.

"Four on the dot it is," he barked and, judging by her expression, didn't need to add 'or else.'

"On my heart, sir."

"Good." But there was no smile.

"Fifteen years I worked for Mr Charles after he moved from Fulham." Mrs Pachela added, sniffing into a paper tissue. "I can't believe what's happened here. It must be the work of the Devil."

"Did he have any lady friends?" Helen ventured, despite her boss' impatience to be off. "Or boyfriends?"

But the upset woman didn't have a chance to reply because the Irishman had taken Helen's arm and forcefully steered her away up the street. "Out of order, Helen. Remember. It's me who asks the questions."

As they reached the Volvo, Helen, still smarting from his rough handling, found herself studying a not-so distant phone booth whose glass sides reflected the surrounding chaos. And the longer she looked, the more she realised who the thick-set, shadowy figure inside may be.

22.

Sunday 5th April 2009 – 7.30 a.m.

Colin's late-night call had caught Jason by surprise, interrupting a dream where he and Helen had been strolling hand in hand along some empty unfamiliar beach. His normally predictable brother had urged him back to Hounslow.

"Why? What's up?" Jason had said.

"She's dumped me, right?"

"The Girlfriend?"

"Fancies her boss instead. Has done all along, apparently. Look, it's pretty weird here on my own."

Not as weird as here.

Jason had known what was coming next and jumped in.

"I can't. Sorry, mate," he'd said. "I really am."

"C'mon, Jaz. You can have my room. Borrow the Merc whenever."

Jaz? Colin hadn't called him that since they'd been kids at school together. Before one got lucky and the other not.

He'd watched raindrops racing down the pane. He'd not gloated, knowing what being ditched was like, but no way would he take the bait. He was needed here. Helen needed him, never mind the dead Betsan Griffiths and the demanding invisible enigma with as yet no name.

"So that's it?" Colin again, sounding half the guy he'd been last Friday.

"'Fraid so, but thanks anyway. Hope you get something sorted."

***

Jason reached out to the bedside table and, like last night, took his Orange handset over to the window, beyond which the ugly lump of Dinas Hill seemed to have grown in every way. He dialled DC Jane Harris, then prayed this time she'd pick up and stay on board. She did. "I'm calling about Miss Jenkins again," he began. "She may have reached London, but I need to be sure."

"I should have a result some time this evening," DC Harris said.

"Evening?" She might as well have said next year.

"Mr Robbins, traces normally take two or three days. I'll do my best."

He thanked her then rang Helen.

"Yes?" came a man's voice. Irish. "Who's that?"

Jason heard his own sigh of relief. "Monty Flynn?"

"I think so. Just about. You want Helen?"

136

I did in my dream.

"Yes, please," said Jason. "I've been worried sick."

"She's fine. She's with me. I'll pass you over."

Archie Tait had sworn he'd been 'fine' too, with both legs off and half his face. The word should be banned. Then, at last, Helen was speaking. "I've been to Hell and back if you must know," she said, barely audible. "I managed to do a bunk from that lift of mine at the Leigh Delamere Services near Swindon. A white Ford Transit van it was, with no tax disc." She then described the driver who'd briefly tried the Travel Lodge. Even down to his stubble and black leather gloves.

"Dark blue top? Like the one you'd seen..."

"I couldn't tell." Then she repeated the man's threat.

Never had Jason felt so helpless.

"Are you OK?"

She let out a brief grim laugh.

"Where's this freak now?"

"God knows. I had to hide in a wheelie bin all night. But I now know his trainers were the same as that skinhead wore yesterday in Mr Flynn's study."

Jason realised then that should anything happen to her, the life he'd so determinedly envisaged for himself would crack open. "Listen," he said, as a posse of ragged rooks fanned out from the roof of the house and diminished like sooty specks against the pale sky. "This is important. I'm putting two and two together, right? According to Gwilym Price, the Davieses had a son, Llyr. Early forties by now. No hair since birth. Nasty bit of work. Used to race around in some green truck he nicked from the Forestry Commission. The cops know about him, too. He's got form..."

All he could hear was the murmur of traffic.

She's gone.

"Helen? You there?"

"Stop it!" she snapped. "I don't want to hear any more."

"Who picked you up in Llandovery? Tell me."

Another pause. Would she or wouldn't she cut him off?

"Ethan Woods, so he said. Brings Welsh lamb to butchers in Surrey, but I swear his van was empty."

"He could have killed you."

"I coped, didn't I? I'm here now and I don't need a minder, thank you. I *am* twenty-two."

Now came another voice in the background. The guy who'd so far not made much effort at being Monty Flynn. "Was he a skinhead beneath that beanie?" Jason pressed on. "Did he have a Welsh accent? Is there anything else you'd recognise?"

She wasn't bothering to answer, and Jason's neck was beginning to burn as it always did when he faced a brick wall. Time was also against him. She was too far away. "Look, I don't want you getting hurt. That's all."

Another pause. Then Helen again.

"Look, we're back on Tuesday. Meanwhile, there's loads to sort here, like looking round Charles Pitt-Rose's flat."

"Why? It must still be a crime scene. And the garage."

"Mr Flynn wants to find out more about the Davieses."

Jason felt that inhospitable morning touch his still-warm skin. Thoughts of danger and death refusing to budge. "Well, tell him this. Someone's totally cleared out his study. I checked in there late last night. He needs to know."

"You're kidding?"

"I am not."

Pause.

"Don't tell the police," she sounded breathless. "You mustn't. He'll deal with it."

"That's an odd thing to say."

"I know him. Right?" But she didn't sound very convincing.

"I can get a train. Be with you by five o'clock. Just give me the address."

"No." Then she dropped her voice right down. "Mr Flynn wants you to stay at Heron House. He's scared, OK? He's just confessed the whole writers thing was a lie. It's not happening."

"What?"

Clever Gwenno...

Yet he felt as if a cold black shadow had crept from the corner of the bedroom to envelop him, suck air from his lungs while the floor beneath his feet began to shift. His more pressing dream of writing his thriller, slipping away...

"He wanted witnesses, and me and you seemed the best of the bunch," she continued.

"Witnesses? What for?" Now his heart was slowing down.

"Just do as he says. You told me you liked solving problems, so please be there. For me as well. And could you check my room's still locked?"

But Jason's mind was elsewhere.

"Hello?" Helen said.

"Course I will."

So *that's* why no other bedrooms had been set aside for paying visitors and that grotty black swimming pool not smartened up. He'd been stung.

"One thing," he said. " Are you on pay-as-you-go with Nokia?"

"Why? Are you checking up on me? Don't you trust me and Mr Flynn?"

"Do *you*?"

***

The morning was coming alive with the peck-pecking of more rooks on the mossy roof above him; an early chainsaw screaming up in the forest, and all the while, snatches of one of Jason's favourite videos sneaked into his mind. *The Whicker Man*, where the unsuspecting cop had been lured to some wacky Scottish island to investigate a non-existent crime. He'd found the ending unwatchable. The whole premise profoundly disturbing and here he was, not acting, but for real, in a similar Land of the Zombies. Had brother and sister put the Irishman under pressure not to have anyone else here? If so, why? Why too had Charles Pitt-Rose died?

Suddenly, helplessness and shame replaced the fear to still his whole body. Helplessness because normally by now he'd be down in the reception hall tearing through Yellow Pages for a cab to take him to Swansea. Shame because he'd not told Helen he thought he loved her.

Just then, the tinny beat of *Paper Planes* broke into his regrets. By some miracle DC Harris had got through. She'd bust a gut to get a trace off Helen's phone, but no joy, at least he was able to say he'd spoken to both her and her boss.

"That's good."

And then came DC Harris' news that made Jason prop himself against the old dressing table. "My colleague DC Prydderych at Llandovery wanted to tell you himself but he's on his way to an accident on the M4 near Binfield, just east of Reading. A white van it is, rolled off the hard shoulder some time after midnight. No sign of the driver, mind, but he must be somewhere."

Ethan Woods?

"Two things lead us to believe he could be a Llyr Davies from Beulah who picked up your friend Miss Jenkins late last night from Llandovery station."

"Beulah?" He remembered that name from the tourist guide. "That's not so far from here."

"Exactly. He rents a room in the village. We're trying to trace its absent owner."

Deep in his gut, Jason knew this was getting too close to home.

"Interestingly, that same van's tyre tracks exactly match those by Heron

139

House's grounds," she went on.

"And near Golwg y Mwyn?" His pronunciation of the bungalow's name wasn't perfect, but she understood.

"Yes. There'd been a U-turn nearby. Rain usefully softens the ground."

"So *that's* how he'd got away from that stile."

"Quite possibly. And secondly, a receipt from the Fforestfach Tesco store for 4.40 p.m. on Friday 2nd April, with Miss Jenkins' name written on the back, was discovered deep inside the passenger side cubby hole. To me – and not because I'm also a woman – for her to have hidden it, showed great presence of mind."

A small, but fierce glow of pride seemed to swell Jason's heart. "I'd say that's typical. Have you spoken to her?"

"Just now, yes. She's fine. I advised her and Mr Flynn to be vigilant. You as well, Mr Robbins. Although, judging by what we know of this Llyr character, he goes to earth, often for ages. But we have a DNA sample from a source in that cab, and it's being matched now with that from a cold case going back five years."

He took a punt. "From when he worked for Mr Price?"

"Sorry. I can't say."

The gigantic Dinas Hill had suddenly morphed into a sick shade of green while that detective's attractive voice continued. "Sergeant Rees will be calling on you late morning to see Mr Llyr Davies' parents," she added. "I'd be grateful if his visit could be kept a surprise."

"Sure."

"And we know what Idris said to DC Prydderch about them being brother and sister, but remember, the old boy gets easily confused. They both do."

Jason shook his head. Why would Gwilym Price lie about the Davieses?

"There must be certificates somewhere," he said. "Proof they're married. Proof this Llyr really is Idris' son."

"We're looking. Meanwhile, just do as I ask. And may I add politely, that this matter is none of your business."

Silence, in which Jason wondered what Dan Carver would say now.

"Can I ask when Miss Griffiths' post-mortem's being carried out?"

A slight pause.

"Tuedsay afternoon. Oh, and another reminder. Mr Flynn will need to fill in his statement as soon he's back from London."

***

Jason got dressed without bothering to wash. Something he'd never done even in that crowded Penge squat when he'd first moved to London. But he couldn't risk meeting the siblings from Hell or he'd probably have killed them. Now, like his almost vanished hero Dan Carver, he had to be prepared. Be on alert.

The house felt too quiet. Too full of secrets brushing by him, filling the gloomy corridor as he headed for the windowless bathroom. By the time he'd zipped up his jeans, any indecision about what to do next had been replaced by a strategy. At least until Tuesday. Go on the charm offensive, he told himself. Butter up the Odd Squad, draw them out. Discover, if he could, who'd cleared out the study, and how come his *OPERATION ROOK* notepad was still missing. Finally, with a bit of luck, find out more about the son.

***

The kitchen didn't feel right without Helen. Even less so with the diminutive figure of Gwenno Davies silhouetted against the one window, scrubbing out the kitchen's Belfast sink that was twice as big as Colin's trendy version.

"Bore da," Jason smiled, even though she still kept her back to him. Even though it nearly choked him to say it. "Sorry I disturbed you both last night. Anxiety, that's what it was. After you'd said there'd be no writing courses, I guess I panicked."

But would even she believe such a rubbish excuse? He wouldn't be hanging around to find out. With the coffee machine empty and cold, he picked up the half-full electric kettle and switched it on. Spooned instant coffee and three sugars into a mug while the rain outside still fell on the sodden trees and she kept up the scrubbing – her pale, bony elbows pushing in and out like some featherless battery chicken trying to get off the ground. "Yer a bag of lies, Mr Robbins. Just like our useless sandwich maker. And like I said, we'll be telling Mr Flynn about your invasion of our privacy in our bedroom. Because that's what it was."

On the word 'privacy,' she turned towards him. Her appearance the same as when he'd first clapped eyes on her. White hair in disarray. No make-up, the crossover apron in place and her scuffed black boots firmly placed on the stone flags. No sign of that weird riding crop. However, there was something different about her eyes. The direction of their gaze for a start. Their almost brazen focus. On his fly.

Oh my God...

141

He repositioned himself to press against the worktop as he poured boiling water into his mug. The aim now to grab a few biscuits from the nearby tin and hotfoot back to his room. But before he could do any of these things, she was there, next to him. One wet hand clenched over his like a dead weight. While the other...

"I'll tell you everything, Mr Robbins. That's what you want, isn't it? Everything?"

That free hand was now on his zip. Tugging it against the denim fabric, moving it downwards. He felt dizzy, hot. Unable to break away. Coffee steam burning his nostrils. Before he knew it, she was in there. Shit. She was in there, inside his boxer shorts, stroking away, sliding her fist up and down, up and down his unplanned erection. She knew what to do alright. Christ, she knew what to do...

"There's a nice big boy you are," she cooed as she worked him, "and getting bigger. I could tell by the shape of yer nose, first time I saw you. Now then, Jason, what's really bothering you. Why are you staying on here when there's no need?"

On his foreskin now. Easing it back and pressing an expert finger into the little eye beneath, making him gasp. There was too much blood down there. Too heavy, with nowhere to go except out in the open and out of her hand...

Kneeling now, she took him in her crinkly mouth, back and fore, back and fore... "Ask, ask," she murmured, suddenly pulling away, prolonging the moment of release. Jason glanced down, about to close his eyes and fall over an edge he'd never had any intention of visiting, when he saw not the face of an old dried woman, but someone young and eager, whose large dark eyes rested on his. Whose soft, plump mouth expertly returned to the business. "I'll tell you everything about being in Hell," she said, as a different darker room complete with that crucifixion print and a distinct smell of roses had suddenly enveloped them. "I'm Margiad Pitt-Rose who lived here too long. Who's been trying to make you listen. So are you ready to listen?"

"Yes. Yes. Yessss..."

23.

Sunday 5th April 2009 – 9 a.m.

After a Detective Constable Jane Harris had phoned Helen, to check if she was OK, there'd been no time for her to tell her boss how stressed Jason had sounded. No time either to call Heron House to say sorry to him, when he'd only tried his best. In order for herself and Mr Flynn to return to Rhandirmwyn on Tuesday as promised, there was a revised agenda to keep. All Mrs Pachela's fault.

However, Helen now knew from two respected sources that the creep who'd assaulted her at Heron House, and given her the lift, had been the Daviesies' son. As for the Irishman, his name should surely be Monty Con Merchant Flynn.

***

Tolpuddle Street police Station was still more than a mile away in the heaviest traffic Helen'd ever seen. A deep tide of steel and glass jerking along in first gear between every impediment under the sun.

Tension still crackled between them like a summer storm. Flynn'd been annoyed that she'd given DC Prydderch his mobile number, and angry that the Philippina had let him down.

"Stupid cow," Mr Flynn muttered. "Bloody foreigners. And why are you staring at me?"

"I'm not. Just wondering what's the matter with your finger?"

"Nicked it on something in the boot, that's all."

"Best give it some air."

"Not *this* air. Fucking dump," the Irishman then swore again as the congestion zone announced itself. With deeper frown lines and an untrimmed shadow around his mouth, he looked ten years older and, although he seemed tense as a violin string, she had to speak out. Break her resolutions. Again.

"If I'd known the Daviesies had a son, do you think I'd have gone with him last night or anyone remotely like him? If you had told me half the stuff you should have."

He turned as sharply as an eagle after prey.

"Where did that nonsense come from? There is no son. End of story." He crashed the gears. Was suddenly driving too fast.

She mustn't cry. Not now. Her job was to keep her eyes and ears open. For her and Jason's sakes.

"As for that wretched couple, I've had to pretend everything's normal, can't you see? But they want a fight. A reason to..." he said overtaking a cyclist too quickly and getting a V-sign in reply.

You called them benign not so long ago…

"Go on," Helen said.

"Do I really need to spell it out?"

"Yes."

"Get rid of me. Mince me up. Burn me, bury me alive, whatever. I was never meant to be on their precious patch in the first place. Oh, no. And once I've seen the deceased's solicitor later on, you'll realise why."

"She's done me too much harm. Her and her mouth."

"Could they have killed Betsan, do you think?"

He crashed the gears. The noise of it was hideous.

"Wouldn't rule it out."

"I want to tell you what Jason and me found at her bungalow yesterday morning."

"Later, please. I shouldn't speak ill of the dead, Helen, but Charles Pitt-Rose – lying toad he was – insisted the Davies pair to be 'harmless' and 'devoted.' His exact words as I signed away my first three months' rent on the dotted line. If it weren't so tragic, I'd be splitting my sides laughing."

Helen couldn't envisage that, as another break in the murky cloud allowed a pale patch of sunlight to catch the end of his nose.

"And get this," he was now in second gear, "after that three months was up, he was paying *me*. Hush money, it's called." He glanced at her, as if testing her reaction. "I should have said no. Bejesus, I should have told him where to stuff it."

"He must have been desperate not to rock the boat."

"That he was."

And then another thought crossed her mind. If he found out she'd been snooping in his study, her P45 would be getting its first airing. "So why not simply leave?" she asked him, to push that unwelcome thought away.

"I would have done when the poisoning started. Remember my nosebleeds? Lasted for hours."

She felt more than cold, and not just because the sun had disappeared. Everything was slotting into place. How the doctor had called round barely a week after she'd been at Heron House to ensure the Warfarin powder was left nowhere near breakfast cereals or dried milk in the pantry.

"And the welcome notes they both left for me. You never saw those." Mr

Flynn added with a sarcastic smile.

"No. But I don't understand. When DC Prydderch turned up about Betsan yesterday afternoon, Jason and I had to write their statements for them. Idris Davies said neither he nor Gwenno could write."

A dismissive snort caught her by surprise. "Don't you believe it. Lying eejits."

"Did you keep those notes as proof?"

A shake of that dishevelled head. "They beat me to it."

"Perhaps DC Prydderch could catch them out."

"Come on, Miss Jenkins. You've been there long enough. Charles Pitt-Rose knew full well about those two. They're as deep and devious as the Liffey. You wait. Wouldn't surprise me if they had him topped as well."

"Is that why you wanted me and Jason as witnesses?"

His nearest hand left the wheel to clasp hers till it hurt. Really hurt.

"Just don't judge me, Helen. That would break my heart. Promise?"

"OK." Yet his clammy grip had left several red marks.

"May Mother Mary bless you," he said.

But she hadn't finished.

"Idris let slip he and Gwenno were siblings."

Mr Flynn turned her way. *"What?"*

"You can imagine how she reacted to that. More like an angry rat."

The Irishman crossed himself, muttering something under his breath before braking at yet another set of temporary lights. Islington was now grinding to a halt.

"To Hell with the lot of them." He hit his wheel twice. "Him and all. Mr Fucking Pitts-Whatshisname."

"He's dead," she said.

Silence.

"It's not my place to say this," Helen ventured, "but if you make out you hated him too much, the cops might think you killed him."

"Me string up a twenty-three stoner? I don't think so." He suddenly turned to her. "Do you trust Mrs Pachela to get the keys?"

She shrugged.

"I don't know any more."

"What's that supposed to mean?"

"Nothing."

"It's vital I check out the flat before leaving London." He looked at her again in a way that made her realise their relationship had altered. Trust was a word fading fast. "I need more information on the Davieses for a start. And that's in all our interests."

She didn't like the way he patted her right thigh. Stroked the same hand he'd marked earlier. She withdrew it, nudging further away from him as he finally took a left into Tolpuddle Street. Here, some way down from the Metropolitan Police HQ, a lucky parking place for one whole hour materialised as if by magic.

"This all sounds like the thriller Jason was planning to write," Helen said. His disappointment had affected her too.

"No need to rub it in. My misleading him is for me to sort." Mr Flynn switched off the ignition. "I'm sure he'll understand my predicament. And when we're in this Holy of Holies, please leave the chat to me. I've already spoken to one of the cops here on the phone. A retard called Purvis."

Helen couldn't keep the fresh hurt from her mind as his rant continued.

"They're all bent as corkscrews," he went on. "All thumb-squeezing, nipple-tweaking Masons, and don't forget it." He pulled a crumpled black tie out of his glove box, and added it to his open-necked shirt. Smoothed down his hair and both eyebrows.

"I'd better stop here, then," she said. He turned to her, eyelids flickering as if with exhaustion.

"I've achieved nothing since I got here yesterday. One obstacle after the other. I was on the point of giving up when you phoned. You're my right-hand man, remember?"

Now was the time to capitalise.

"So, who was Margiad?" Helen asked. "Or I'm not moving. She's been haunting us." Just to say that, made her period pain worse. Her skin to turn cold again.

"Us?" Her boss stared at the busy pavement.

"Me and Jason. He'll fill you in. There've been really weird things happening in his room, for a start. And she's been phoning him on his mobile several times where there's been no normal reception, begging him to remember her. But no number's ever come up."

"Impossible."

"Ask him. Then there's me smelling sickly-sweet roses when there aren't any, and while I was dreaming away in the cab this morning, up comes a young woman's screaming face on my canvas when I was actually imagining painting a landscape for my mam. All this apart from the man in black who waits by the old adit up Pen Cerrigmwyn."

Mr Flynn finally glanced her way. His eyes boring into her soul as he spoke. "Helen, I've always felt I could speak frankly to you. Now don't take this the wrong way, but would you like me to contact your mother? Or a doctor friend of mine in Llandovery? Perhaps he can prescribe something…"

Don't react. Stick to your guns.

"You were going to tell me about Margiad."

Helen noticed the pulse in his neck. The subtle tightening of his fists.

"I've never heard of her so there's nothing *to* tell. Now, for your own and Jason's well-being, I'd be careful. You don't want to be accused of taking illegal substances, do you? Not with the jobs market being so tight. And remember, in this cop shop we're going to, I'm doing the talking. Yes?"

She nodded, trying to conceal her fury.

"And as for your mishap last night, don't mention it. We'll leave that to the local cops, OK?"

Mishap?

"Why?" she asked.

"Just do as I say."

***

Helen hadn't been inside a police station since some old biker had caught up with her walking home from youth club to give his penis an airing. A purple thing that he'd waggled with both hands. Later that day, she'd been the centre of attention in a busy world of uniforms keen to catch him before another kiddie was traumatised. But here in this cool reception area with its unmanned front desk, it was as if she and the Irishman were invisible. Where were the yobs and muggers? Rapists and arsonists? Was everyone busy dealing with a catastrophe?

Still bottling up her anger, she and the Irishman trekked around in search of human life apart from those on the many Sapphire safety posters depicting lone women in scary urban car parks, on streets and the Tube. How to deter burglars and prevent credit card theft. Nothing for anyone like her holed up in the hills with a pair of lunatics. Or here in London, playing with fire.

Suddenly, her phone rang. Eluned Jenkins' number flashed up. Helen hesitated. Yes, she'd wanted to hear her mam in the van last night, but now was different. Guilt with a capital G took over and, as her boss was turned the other way, she made for the exit.

"My timetable's been altered yet again," her mam complained. Then added, "you're not alright, are you? I can tell from the message you left me."

"I'm fine. In London on business with Mr Flynn. We're back in Wales on

Tuesday. I'll call you then."

"What business? He's not, you know… sharing some hotel room with you?"

Always her first thought.

"Oh, mam. He's old." And, in a forgiving mode said, "By the way, I'll try and get up to Aber on Thursday for your birthday. Should have a nice surprise for you."

"You're not pregnant?" she asked as two strapping black guys in overcoats pushed past Helen and through the swing doors. "Can't blame me for asking. Hefina's at least six months gone. Did you know? Talk of the town, she is. Now there's a loose sort."

So *that's* why Heffy had wanted to see her. But why no mention of it during their Boxing Day chat? But then, hadn't she been the same about Jason yesterday?

Having brushed a sudden sense of longing away, Helen bristled at her mam's judgemental tone. The efficient, armour-plated primary school teacher who'd not said a word about the parents' split. That being rather too near the bone.

"Like I said, I'll be there Thursday."

Then came something else entirely. "You'll never guess. Talk about a small world," her mam went on. "I went to this St. David's Day charity event in town. Help the Aged it was, seeing as it comes to us all. And when I told this old girl – something Powell I think – that you'd landed a job at Heron House, she let slip she'd lived there, too. Started to get tearful so I wasn't going to push it."

Helen watched the world go by as that dark-bricked ivy-clad prison with its three pointy gables and the black heron weather vane slid into her mind.

"When was she at the house?" Helen asked.

"No idea, but she's ninety-two, would you believe it? A governess, so she said. Maths and science her main subjects. Fancy that. Nancy's the name. That's it. I remember now. No wedding ring, mind, but a tidy outfit from the Stroke Association shop. Fair play."

"Living in Aber?"

"Sheltered housing it is, near the fire station. Fallen on hard times it seemed. She's not local, you can tell by her accent. We exchanged addresses but perhaps you could say hello when you're up here."

Helen's period kicked in again. She winced. Wished she was fifty and in the menopause.

***

Detective Chief Inspector Jobiah was clearly in a rush, but having checked both hers and her boss' IDs, and reasons for being there, switched on the laptop he'd brought in with him. He confirmed the general details of what he and his team had discovered in the dead businessman's garage then, with restrained civility, addressed the Irishman.

"On the phone yesterday morning, my colleague DC Purvis let slip to you that Mr Pitt-Rose's death was suspicious. He was out of order. So far we've had no reason to change our view that a well-prepared suicide is the most likely cause. However, a painful and protracted one at that." His tone sharpened. "My man felt pressured by your questions. Your assumptions that another party might have been involved. I admit one could assume the deceased had an interest in homosexuality, but so far there's no real evidence."

Helen stared at Mr Flynn, bristling like an angry terrier. "I was merely trying to establish what had happened to a man I liked. Got on well with and never crossed swords which, I'm sure you'll agree, is rare between landlord and tenant," Mr Flynn said.

The word 'tenant' was like a bone dug up and brought to light.

"Indeed," said the cop.

Helen also sensed the tension ratchet up in this too-small room with its dismal, energy-saving bulb and she longed for the one barred window to be flung wide open. The clash of rutting stags came to mind. A familiar sound in early autumn in the forests around Llangurig.

"So I reiterate, this appears to be a tragedy of Mr Pitt-Rose's own choosing, and if you have any useful information as to why, we'd be glad to hear it," DCI Jobiah said.

Mr Flynn's cheeks had turned bright pink. He'd met his match. Was he actually climbing down? Yes. The coward.

"From my regular dealings with the deceased for the past three years, I admit I had noticed a gradual personality change. I'd argue that for several reasons, owning Heron House weighed on his mind, and being such a distant landlord must have been doubly tricky," Mr Flynn said.

"So where were you last Thursday afternoon from, say, 14.00 hours onwards?"

Her boss' chilling glance caught her on the hop.

Do it. Fool him...

"With me," Helen returned the glance. "In your study, remember? Later on, I made you a plate of cold beef sandwiches for supper. That's what I do, see. Sandwiches."

Jobiah allowed a smile to creep along his mouth. "Can anyone else vouch for you, sir?"

"If it's suicide, why ask me this?"

"As I'm sure you know, sir; there are suicides and suicides."

"Mr Flynn wouldn't help anyone to die," she insisted. "He'd more likely give his own life to save them."

"Thank you, Helen." Her boss' left hand rested on her knee but she managed to wriggle away.

"Quite some cook you have, sir." The Detective Chief Inspector was scrolling down his screen before checking his watch. He knew how to keep you on the boil, she thought, wanting to be out of there fast. "I wish our nanny at home was as loyal. However, another witness to your being at Heron House would help. Is anyone else living there?" He looked up expectantly from one to the other.

"Yes, Idris Davies," said Mr Flynn. "Gardener, and younger sister, Gwenno, who's the cleaner."

"Well there's a coincidence. We happen to be co-ordinating data on a certain forty-one-year-old Llyr Davies missing from the M4 near Reading after an accident there first thing this morning. He may be heading for London. Any relation, I wonder?"

Mr Flynn's cheeks had turned a peculiar colour. Helen knew that the close, stuffy room wasn't the reason.

"Most of Wales is made up of Davies, Evans, or Williams."

"He *could* be their son," Helen said spontaneously, not looking at Mr Flynn at all. "I saw Gwenno Davies' stretch marks once, when she was walking around naked on the top floor."

Her boss' pursed lips had almost disappeared.

"Brother and sister, you say?" Jobiah began typing as if news of incest was a daily occurrence. "We'll check that out."

Fear pricked at Helen's skin as another question came her way. This cop hadn't needed her story at all. "Son or not," Jobiah began, "did DC Harris tell you he's got form? How you, Miss Jenkins, had a lucky escape?" He smiled at her again. "Leaving your receipt in the van could be very useful evidence indeed."

Damn…

Mr Flynn's left shoe connected with her leg. It hurt.

"Look, Detective Chief Inspector," he said, "just find this Ethan Woods and bang him up. Then I'll go along with the suicide theory. When's the post-mortem, by the way?"

"Wednesday. And I don't do bribery."

"What about the Inquest?"

The DCI paused. "Undecided. But *intra mura's* a possibility."

The Irishman seemed to freeze in his chair. "Holy Mary. Why's that?" Another short pause. The big guy was stalling.

"We're talking of perceived risk." He switched off his laptop, closed the lid and stood up. "Now, if you'll excuse me, I have to go."

Although he held open the door for them to leave, he hadn't finished. "By the way, and, just as a formality, we'd like a swab from you both for our temporary records only. Prints too. Won't take long. And please, Mr Flynn, leave us your landline phone number so we can call these Davieses for confirmation of your status."

Her employer bristled again. "DC Prydderch's already got my mobile number, thanks to Miss Jenkins here."

"I said landline." The cop held out a remarkably long brown hand, but only Helen shook it, while her boss hung back. She expected him to fight, but no. It was as if too many ill winds had demolished his fake sails.

"I'd like to see Mr Pitt-Rose's body," Flynn said.

At this, the DCI's tone darkened. "And Llandovery would like a statement from you, regarding a Betsan Griffiths the moment you arrive back in Wales. Not my remit, you understand, but I did say I'd pass it on."

The Irishman's pallor intensified. He paused to check his pockets and retie a shoelace. While he did so, Helen whispered to the senior policeman what Gwilym and DC Harris had told Jason about Llyr Davies. How his birth certificate was being searched for.

DCI Jobiah frowned. "You should have said."

"I couldn't."

"And something else," Jobiah gave her a knowing look. "A Maureen Chivers of Cosicabs has just made contact to say you'd hired her from Leigh Delamere Services at 0600 hours this morning. She's been worried about you."

Helen saw her boss straighten up and stare at her. Her blood cooled.

"I'm sorry, she must have mistaken me for someone else."

But Jobiah wasn't buying that. "I'm here all weekend, Miss Jenkins," he said. "Call any time if you want to talk."

***

The senior cop gave Helen's arm an encouraging squeeze before escorting them both towards the lab where they were to have the spit scooped out of their mouths. Little did he know, or been allowed to know. The net around

151

her was imperceptibly closing and, afterwards, while trailing in her boss' slipstream of rage out into the capital's Sunday morning, she couldn't see any way of escape. Her shin still stung every time she put her weight on that leg. His sudden violence had unnerved her, and here he was again. Filling her head with his crap.

"I warned you about the Met. Terrorists would be treated better than us. What about *our* human rights? Do you realise in an hour's time we'll be on a national database of felons, perverts the lot."

"I don't understand."

"You wouldn't," he said.

Thanks.

"Your obsequiousness was quite unnecessary," Mr Flynn said.

"I only shook his hand because I'm a well-brought-up Welsh girl."

"And *I* tried not to look. As for that smile he flashed at you..."

"Some appreciation for my alibi would be good," she said.

He didn't slow down.

"Thank you."

Bastard.

"So why couldn't I tell him about my nightmare with Llyr Davies? Why am I less important than that waster? It doesn't make sense."

Her boss increased his pace. Lengthened the distance between them, so he couldn't hear.

"Perceived risk, eh?" said the Irishman once she'd caught up with him, as if nothing was amiss. "Plot thickens. I've only heard of closed inquests for deaths of national significance. Something stinks."

"Ask the solicitor," Helen said.

"Mmm. A long shot, but if her office is in her house, she might be willing to see me today. Better than hanging about till Monday."

"Why not phone first?" Helen said, thinking how a Sunday meeting might well cost him double. Good.

"You're a genius," he smarmed.

More of the blarney.

"No, Mr Flynn. That's you."

***

Dee Salomon had said yes, but only for fifteen minutes maximum as she had a choir practice at half past three. While bells on some nearby church pealed out ten o'clock, they rejoined the Volvo. More sun now, warming her face, making her tired eyes close up. Helen just wanted to stop; to feel its unfamiliar caress for a while longer, but Mr Flynn was already disabling the car alarm. It was then that a rush of panic seemed to also disable her heart. She suddenly needed Jason's reassuring presence alongside. The smell of his leather jacket. The way he sometimes looked at her, as if she was the only girl left in the world.

"Mr Flynn, I'm scared," she called out in a voice she barely recognised. "After what that Detective Chief Inspector implied about Charles Pitt-Rose's connections, please don't take us into any more danger. I think we should leave it all alone."

The Irishman glanced over to her. Still pale. His eyes oddly blank.

"My dear, indefatigable Miss Jenkins, I regret to tell you, it's too late."

Too late? What could he mean? And then, with a deep shiver, she remembered that man in the phone booth near Sandhurst Mansion. Wondered where he was now.

24.

Sunday 5th April 2009 – 10.10 a.m.

For a good half hour, Jason let the shower's unreliable flow provide some relief from that moment of total madness. How could he stay on here now? Writers or no writers? He'd let the old bird touch him up, bring him off, and yet... yet... That hadn't been quite true, had it? She'd not been the only one.

He turned the dial to maximum, kept his eyes tight shut, pretending, he was back in Colin's all-white wet room; remembering his brother's call. What would he say if he knew? It didn't bear thinking about.

Finally, he stepped out of the shabby cubicle and, having grabbed the grey threadbare towel, used it to further punish his body, especially down there, until everything hurt. But still he didn't feel clean. Instead, marked as if by some malign presence. Or, rather, a malign, manipulating presence.

Red, sore and befuddled, he ran back to his room, clutching his clothes. Here he pulled his dad's empty, battered suitcase from under the bed. Never mind OPERATION ROOK or his deposit cheque. They were history. The thing was now, to get out; preferably without bumping into She Of The Nifty Fingers.

Breathless, he hauled the case to the door and lifted it down the next two flights of stairs to the unlit reception hall and its dead fire. He was alone. So far, so good. He'd be back in London by the evening and could meet up with Helen. Persuade her to leave Heron House, just like him, and then, back in Hounslow, he'd go for any kind of work he could. Shelf stacking, street sweeping, whatever. And start his book. Dan Carver, like himself, had been suppressed for too long. His feet and socks felt damp inside his boots; his shirt and sweatshirt rucked up under his jacket. A mess, in other words. Inside and out. But better a mess free of this snare, than trapped within it.

Shit.

The front door was not only bolted, but locked.

Don't panic.

And then, from inside his jacket came that familiar ring tone. He was on it, backing into the cloakroom as he did so, forgetting about the suitcase. He pressed the phone's cold casing next to his ear, thinking Helen, even though her number hadn't shown up. Just the blank, green screen.

"I've something to tell you," he hissed. "I'm getting out of Heron House. Just wait for me. I'll be there."

"You can't! I need you. Remember me, Jason. I'm not letting you go. Not now. Not ever..."

Jason?

Freaky or what? That wasn't Helen, but that same needy voice, harder, sharper than before, like a razor cutting into his head. "Didn't you enjoy what you let me do yesterday? Say yes... yesss for me, just like you did then."

No...

"Margiad, please leave me alone. That was a crazy mistake."

"What you think doesn't matter. Nor will leaving, because *I* won't leave you alone until you've helped me. It's *my* story you'll be writing, not yours. There's no-one else who can do it. I've waited so long. Me and my..." Here, the voice faded, only to rise up again like a surfer's wave. "Just promise you'll free us. Promise me..."

Us?

"I can't."

"Then I won't say why you're really there."

***

He rammed the phone deep inside his jeans' back pocket alongside the battered cutting from *The Lady* that had started this. Out of sight, but not out of mind. This unseen creature was clinging like a limpet. Besides, supposing Margiad's so-called story he had to tell was a bag of lies? How would he know? And what had she meant by 'us' and then that last strange threat?

'He wanted witnesses, and me and you seemed the best of the bunch.'

He pushed his way out of the cloakroom only to find Gwenno Davies sitting on his suitcase, smiling in triumph, while both hands and their painted nails rhythmically stroked the length of the riding crop lying across her lap. "And where do you think you're going, Mr Robbins?" she challenged him. "Not leaving us, are you? Not now."

"Get off my property, and let me out of here. Or else."

"Or else what?"

"I'll phone the police." It sounded pathetic, like he was a kid all over again in the school playground, up against someone more cunning. More determined. He knew what might shift her, though. Not for nothing had he learnt poker during tea breaks at Woolies.

Don't show your hand.

Hadn't Betsan Griffiths complained about her harmful mouth? And this woman she'd clearly feared, had almost pushed Helen into The Drop.

Ammo for later, he told himself.

"I can actually save you the bother," she said, getting up with surprising agility and depositing her toy on his suitcase. "There's one of them here already. Why, I'm about to welcome him in."

***

Sergeant Edward Rees had indeed arrived, complete with the same muddy Range Rover parked just beyond the one window.

The old woman primped her hair and from her apron pocket produced her bunch of keys. All types, all sizes. She dangled them provocatively under Jason's nose.

Don't lose it.

One false move and he'd land up in the same boat as her elusive son. Being fingered. That thought led to another as the front door bell's melancholy chime kicked in. She could claim Jason had made her commit an indecent act and, with several recent stories of elderly women raped in care homes lurking in the media, she'd have the upper hand. No, rephrase that, he told himself, feeling sick. But then, what was worse? That, or revealing how a septuagenarian and a ghost had brought him off?

***

"We're a bit slow off the mark this morning, Sergeant." The cleaner put on the same sickly-sweet voice she'd used while busy with Jason's fly. "All this drizzle it is, see. If we'd had some nice sunshine to wake us up, you'd be seeing quite a different situation."

"What's sunshine when it's at home?" Sergeant Rees, complete with hair hosting droplets of rain, chose to stand next to her. But none of this mattered. What did, was Helen.

"Can I fetch you a tea, coffee?" Gwenno wheedled. "Or whatever else you fancy?"

"Great. Tea, ta." His gaze flicked from her disappearing form to the suitcase and the crop. But Jason got in first.

"Any news of her son?" he asked. "Been picked up yet?"

"Nothing so far." The cop eyed the suitcase again. "Those yours?"

"Only the case. I'm off back to London. Things aren't working out here, that's all. No-one's fault. I need to see for myself that Miss Jenkins is OK." Helen would have kicked him again for that lie, and rightly so.

"Playing hard to get, is she?" The Sergeant's man-to-man wink didn't work. He'd already witnessed Jason's anxiety about her and her unlocked car. It wasn't worth an answer.

"You wanted to see both Mr and Miss Davies about their son," Jason

156

reminded him.

"So I did."

"*Mrs* Davies to you," shouted Gwenno, but Jason hadn't finished.

"And perhaps to ask how come his van's tyres match those prints up by the stile, not far from Miss Griffiths' bungalow, and why he's been making his presence felt, like some long-lost termite."

"Shut that filthy mouth of yours before I... I..."

"Just one more," Jason persevered. "Won't take long. Why would Idris Davies lie about seeing Gwilym Price passing by with his rooks, and getting news of Betsan's death from him, if it wasn't for protection?"

At this, the old girl slammed down the tray she'd been carrying from the kitchen, picked up the heavy teapot and advanced towards him. With each enraged step, Jason saw his future at risk of slipping away. But just then, he didn't care. "And what did you mean by threatening me with friends who could get me into trouble?"

"That's enough, Mr Robbins." The Sergeant, unexpectedly quick, placed himself between the two of them, cupping the teapot in his soft hands. Took the heat. Positioned it out of play in the cold grate and escorted her to the nearest chair. "Calm yourself down, Gwenno. We don't want to be calling the Cottage Hospital, do we now?"

"Who does this Saes think he is? I want to hear him say sorry."

"No." Jason was on a reckless roll, forgetting how much he had to lose. "Isn't it odd too, that your Llyr's started putting in an appearance now that Charles Pitt-Rose is dead?"

"What?"

In slow motion, she slumped from her seat to the floor, her legs and arms sticking out in four directions. What little light there was, seemed to suddenly fade as if that black, gaping cave of a fireplace had begun to spread beyond its old-fashioned tiled surround, and turn the already gloomy hall into the inside of a tomb. And inside that tomb lay a stricken figure whose black suspenders pulled at her stocking tops, puckering the bands of pale dry flesh beyond.

***

"Up you get." The cop knelt beside Gwenno Davies, trying to move her to a more decorous sitting position. "Gently does it." But she resisted, keeping her eyes tight shut.

"Shall I call an ambulance?" Jason felt his stomach on the move. This was more than he'd planned for. Her condition looked serious, but why such a

157

drastic reaction to his news? OK, Monty Flynn had been paid to keep her and her brother on. Helen had learnt that much. Was it fear of possibly being turfed out into a whole new world, or something else altogether? Not for the first time did he wonder who now inherited this miserable pile. Perhaps Helen and the Irishman would let him know before they got back.

But hey, there was his dad's ancient suitcase, packed and ready to go. What was he waiting for? The longer he stayed, the bigger the risk of Llyr Davies spilling to the cops that Helen had been in Monty Flynn's study. Next step, she'd be suspected of clearing it out. There was also the risk of him being done for indecent exposure.

He shivered as small noises erupted from Gwenno Davies' throat. Small, scared noises. The cop glanced up at him. "Best you'd not mentioned the death, son," he said.

"Sorry," Jason lied, objecting to such familiarity. "I assumed she already knew about Mr Pitt-Rose. I wonder if Idris does."

"You leave him alone," she mumbled, raising herself on to both elbows with the help of the cop. His muscled buttocks below the edge of his jacket presented a terrifying sight.

"Could you pour her a cup of tea?" he suggested. "Plenty of sugar."

While Jason fiddled with the dainty cup and saucer and a pair of stiff sugar tongs, Sergeant Rees managed to lift Gwenno Davies back into her chair. "Does Mr Davies carry a mobile phone or some way I could contact him?"

"No. And there's no signal round here neither." Came rather too quickly. "Says they rot the brain, he does. Anyway, why all these questions? I thought you'd come about Miss Griffiths. Like your friend DC Prydderch."

She waved the tea away, but not before Jason noticed her hand shaking. Her bottom lip, too.

"It's about your son, Llyr," said the Fuzz, shooting Jason a glance. "We're wondering if you knew his whereabouts last night?"

Her fingers gripped the arms of her chair. "What about him? He's dead too? That it?"

"No, and not in any serious trouble either, but it would help if..."

"Not in any serious trouble?" Her voice grew shrill as a gull's. Eyes sharper, harder. "But oh, he's *given* it. Since the day he ruined my womb. He knows what we both think. No love lost despite what he might say."

Jason stared at her, unable to connect this outburst with her earlier remarks when Helen had complained about him. Precious time was slipping away. His detachment from Heron House and its incumbents

158

growing stronger with every second. Yes, he'd promised Betsan he'd fight her corner and find her killer, but things had changed.

This old woman with too many secrets was either mad or bad or both. Also scared. "What do you think'll happen now?" She focussed on the navy blue giant who'd helped himself to a sugar lump and was dissolving it in his mouth. "Why am I so nervous? Why can't me nor Idris sleep at nights?"

"Tell me, Gwenno," Jason said.

"Because Heron House might now be ours. And Mr Flynn, who's protected us from our own flesh and blood, might leave."

25.

Sunday 5th April 2009 – 12.15 p.m.

Half an hour to spare, and to Helen's relief, The Coffee Bean Café, just a couple of streets away from D. H. Salomon & Co in Camden, had an immaculate loo. Although she'd lost way too much blood, the fresh pad from the dispenser and fragrant hand cream helped make her feel more up to the challenge of keeping tabs on the wily Irishman and learning the real truth behind his busy agenda.

The café's whole ambience, unlike its counterparts in Aberystwyth, was slick and efficient. Mr Flynn was clearly still as tense as when he'd ignored the affable proprietor and bagged the one spare table which looked out on to a trendily paved street just off Primrose Hill. Here, he scoured their surroundings with the watchful eye of some animal in the wild. Was he, too, on Black Beanie watch? If so, on her behalf or some other reason?

She couldn't tell, and dared not ask. Instead, sat opposite him and noticed how sunlight caught the ends of his chaotic hair. Cast his bad skin in an even more unflattering light. Here was a man who'd toyed too much with her emotions and, despite his touchy-feely ways, his often syrupy tongue, had treated her with callous disregard. His recent threat when she'd asked about Margiad had been one threat too many, and represented the end of the road. She too could act and lie. And now rehearsals were over.

She was also aware of how, although this area was less busy than Islington, cranes of impossible height and reach, still loomed high above the rows of fine, pastel-coloured buildings whose Doric columned porches and Georgian-style windows, reminded her of parts of Aberaeron. But there any similarities ended, for these were mostly occupied by accountants, insurers and the like, and instead of the smell of the sea, a sly pervasive dust hung in the air.

She felt scruffy and looked it, not that Mr Flynn seemed to have noticed. She stared out at the weekend strollers decked out in the latest gear. Young women her age in thigh-length boots, sporting Vuitton and Gucci handbags. Some pushed giant-sized buggies, others were draped around men who could easily have stepped out of Hello! Ogling the celebs was one of her weekly sins which only made her situation in Heron House seem risible.

Mr Flynn placed their order then cracked each of his finger bones in turn.

So he was preoccupied. Tough. He'd not been assaulted, lied to and insulted. He could damned well pay for her.

"Not only did Jason see a guy who might be Llyr Davies..." she began, but was cut short.

"There is *no* Llyr Davies. Understood? That's the end of it."

"He was hanging around Heron House yesterday before he picked me up," Helen raised her voice. "And I swear this morning he was in a phone booth not far away from us in Thornhill Road."

The Irishman cracked his left thumb joint, making her start. Reminding her of an abattoir she'd seen on TV when the poor beasts had fallen and not got up.

"Remember what I said about a doctor?" he said.

That's nice.

Just then, their coffees and buttered toast arrived. He spooned extra sugar into his coffee cup, drained it and poured himself another. The thug off-limits for the moment.

Helen glanced at her toast without much appetite while a toddler, dressed against the chilly morning, looked in and waved at her. Normally, she'd have waved back, but when she didn't, the child moved off, visibly disappointed. Mr Flynn took a big bite of his toast. Melted butter glossing his lips.

Her da was always more communicative when eating. She had nothing to lose.

"What was the name of Heron House's owner?"

"Why?"

"Just curious."

Don't hold your breath.

"Edmund Pitt-Rose. A fine judge, so I've heard."

She recalled that pristine plot in St. Barnabas' Church graveyard. The name of his wife, Joy. The repainted gold leaf inlays. And Jason. How he'd eyed her over the tops of the memorials.

"A busy man, by all accounts. Worked away most of the time."

"Is that why there was a governess?"

Another disconcerting look. A small shake of his uncombed head.

"First I've heard of one."

She nibbled some more of her toast, her heart running too fast from being on constant alert. She wasn't going to mention Nancy Powell. At least, not yet. But she could try another tack.

"Did Charles ever have a sister?"

161

He blinked, clearly caught on the hop.

"I may be many things, but I'm no genealogist."

Leave it...

Her boss got to his feet, drained his cup and left a pound coin next to his saucer. "Time we said hello to Ms Salomon. And please, light of my life, no mention of my books or anything controversial. I need information, not approbation."

He treated her like an idiot. He wasn't going to get away with it that easily. "You've hardly mentioned anything about Charles to me. Why?"

"My dear Helen, you've quite enough on your plate already. But hopefully when we've seen the solicitor and then his flat, there might be more light than darkness."

With that quasi-solicitous tone, he was holding something back. A duplicitous enemy. She was certain of that now. Just then, his black coat seemed too big in the café doorway. His voice, exhorting her to hurry, too loud.

***

She followed him out into the anaemic sunshine. A world away from the mists and shadows trapped by those haunted Welsh hills. But here, *she* was the one trapped. By his agenda. His crap. However, as they walked on towards Hurst Crescent and the solicitor's house, she decided it was time for some sharing. Word for word she relayed the ghostly young woman's message that Jason had heard on his phone – not once but twice. Her recent strange dream of that young woman's face and how Gwenno Davies had, only last night, tried to kill her.

26.

Saturday 12th October 1946 – 10 a.m.

For three days and nights, Peris Morgan's story clung to Lionel's every waking thought and, with an inspection due on 3rd November, threatened to derail his important preparations. The advance letter notifying him had only arrived at the school yesterday but it lay secreted in his desk drawer like some bad omen.

Just eighteen months into the post, his future there would surely depend on a good outcome. A future spent struggling to show that beyond the farming seasons' demands – lambing, shearing, tupping, mulching, sowing, harvesting – lay pools of knowledge waiting for his charges to drink. But supposing the 'Welsh Not' was abandoned? The curriculum he'd so carefully honed instead delivered in an ancient tongue he could never master?

As he slipped both arms into his coat sleeves, and wound a plaid scarf around his neck, Lionel sensed deep in his bones that wouldn't be his problem. That another year would see him gone. His borrowed cottage's iron door handle, fitting so solidly in his gloved hand, would be replaced by a more flimsy affair, attached to some ordinary door in some ordinary terraced house in some ordinary urban street. But not in Birmingham where too many memories lay. No, not there.

***

With its build date of 1872 set in a stone plaque above its porch, Troed y Rhiw was a modest, square-shaped villa adjoining another, rendered in the same dull grey pebble-dash, but enlivened by a cotoneaster bush, bright with berries that pressed against the side of the porch. The four dark windows reflected the even darker contours of Dinas Hill but what made Lionel pause by the bell, instead of pulling it, was the sound of piano music he recognised, tinkling osmotically through those sturdy walls.

Bach's Goldberg Variations – stately and profound.

He knew the young organist lived alone. That his parents had both passed on – his father, from a seizure the day after his son refused the call-up. His mother, from a slow-growing tumour of the brain. So Beynon 'The Shop' had told him not long after his arrival.

"She'd bring food down to the miners here. In the smelt it was. No thought for herself, had Buddug. No thought at all," he'd said. "A fine woman. Pity for her, mind."

Lionel pulled on the bell cord and waited for the music to subside; to at least continue until the end of the phrase, but no. There came a sudden stop, and Robert Price's bleached face appeared in the nearest window for a moment and was gone. That's it, thought Lionel, preparing to walk away. But then the door opened an inch or two and he was beckoned into a gloomy hallway.

"I thought it was someone else," explained the young man, leading the way into a back room, simply furnished but lined by bookshelves full of music books and sheet music, some new, some yellowed and worn. Photographs too, of various family members including one of young Gwilym smiling, astride a donkey. "I have to be careful about answering the door, especially after..." he took a poker to the small coal fire, jostled the more ashen lumps into the grate.

"After what?"

"The visitation last night." The young man gestured towards a nearby chair; but best to stand, thought Lionel. At least until he'd finished his story. "Edmund Pitt-Rose it was. And another man I'd never seen before in my life. Dressed up like farmers, they were. Even down to their boots, and worse."

"You mean weapons?"

Robert nodded. Fear still in those wide brown eyes, but Lionel's mind was too much on fire with Peris Morgan's extraordinary story to plunge straight in. This young man needed coaxing, not a stick.

"But why here? Why you? Because of your stance on the War?"

"Sit down, sir. Please. Let me take your coat, or can't you stay?"

"I can for as long as you need me to. You offered to help me. Now it's my turn."

That seemed to relax him, but instead of sitting where Lionel could see him, chose to stand behind his chair. In the old-fashioned mirror over the fireplace, Lionel, having unbuttoned his coat, saw that tense face close to tears.

"My crime is to be in love," the deserter began. "Yes, there have been other girls – while I was studying music in Cardiff – when I began giving recitals throughout Wales, but no-one like... like the one with dark eyes. The most beautiful, wonderful person on this earth. Margiad Joy."

"Edmund Pitt-Rose's daughter?"

Robert nodded.

"How old is she?"

"Seventeen. I met her by accident, back in April it was. She was in St.

164

Barnabas' graveyard putting daffodils on her mother's grave. I'd just finished a rehearsal for Easter Sunday's service, and there she was. Like a vision. But nervous, mind. Looking over her shoulder all the time as if she shouldn't be there. And guess what? There was Gwenno Davies, all togged up in riding gear, on her pony, lurking by the lych gate. Spying on us."

"Did you notice her carrying a gun?"

"What!" Those brown eyes doubled in size.

"She had one when she threatened me. Looked ready to use it, too."

"How dare she, the minx. But this is what we're up against."

He went over to the nearest set of bookshelves and extracted a bound copy of William Williams' hymns, opened it at the middle and removed a black and white photograph. "That's Margiad. Up on Pen Cerrigmwyn last month. She'd managed to escape her guards..." He passed it to Lionel whose fingertips immediately felt numb. That description was indeed apt. The tilt of her lovely, oval face, her dark hair lifted by the breeze. However, her smile seemed forced. Those eyes troubled.

"Are these so-called 'guards' Idris and Gwenno Davies?"

"Yes. And a governess too, I believe."

"Her name?"

"Margiad's not said. But sir, I swear to God it's not normal there. Do you understand what I'm saying? Every time her father's name comes up, she just freezes."

He moved closer. "She's in danger, sir. I know it, here in my heart."

"Does mention of The Order ring any bells?"

Robert frowned. "What do you mean, sir?"

"A small group of men at Heron House behaving like beasts yet who think they're above the law they're supposed to uphold. Your recent visitors no less."

The young man paled. His fine hands trembling. "Her father?"

"So I've been told..."

"Stop, Mr Hargreaves! I can't listen to any more. Are you implying Margiad's involved in this?"

"I was hoping you could tell me."

Lionel handed back the photograph and rubbed his fingertips together for warmth. He got up and, in the few steps he took to reach the young organist, his oath of secrecy to Peris Morgan dissolved like February's snowfall under a surprise winter sun.

"What I'm about to tell you, must stay between these four walls. You mention danger – a word not to be used lightly – but I believe you're right.

And that danger is what young Walter Jones witnessed and died for. Margiad being taken back to Heron House by car as if she was a prisoner. Screaming, she was. Struggling to get out. Although I've kept that story hidden for too long," Lionel laid a hand on Robert's sunken shoulder. "We must trust each other. If we can't, then I stop investigating now."

The organist turned to face him. The full intensity of his anguish almost unbearable. "I trust you, sir. But before you say any more, there's something else you should know. Margiad gave me some news the Thursday before Walter's funeral." He pressed the photograph to his chest, the weight of his hand creasing the back of it. "She's six months pregnant. And it's not mine. I swear on my dead parents' souls, it's not mine."

***

Lionel left Troed y Rhiw burdened further by the harrowing exchange in that room full of creative works by those writers and composers driven to right the world's wrongs through their craft. To show the oppressed and downhearted a higher meaning to this mortal coil.

Yet, as he crossed the strip of main road and headed up more directly this time, towards Cerrigmwyn Hill, he knew that if only he and Robert could find proof of Margiad Pitt-Rose's secret Hell, they could, together, release her and bring real justice to bear.

And twelve-year-old Betsan Griffiths would be a start.

27.

Sunday 5th April 2009 – 1 p.m.

Llyr's head was messed up, inside and out. Having to abandon his precious van was bad enough. He'd been turned away from that full-up Travel Lodge at Leigh Delamere too tired to think straight, never mind drive. No wonder he'd done a roll-over for all to see. But would The Order understand? He'd have to wait and find out. Whatever, it was too late to get replacement wheels organised. He still had another job to do.

After the roll-over, he'd kipped in some shitty barn till it had been safe to emerge, almost suffocated on the train from Reading, before the cattle-truck underground to Highbury & Islington and arriving here. A last look in the mirror over one of Camden tube station's stained urinals was enough to make him slap more cold water on to his hot newly-shaved jaw. Pull his beanie down as far as it would go.

London didn't agree with him. Never had. Not even when The Order had stumped up for the Euston studio flat two years ago. Nor when Charlie had treated him to a made-to-measure suit and striped tie from some posh Dorset school and whisked him off to the Pullman Club in his Bentley. Not even with dinner there costing two hundred quid a head.

Suddenly, he wasn't alone. Some coon – the only word of his mam's that he really liked – bulked out by a fluorescent safety jacket, was pressed up next to him. Too too big, like the cock he was holding as he pissed.

"Want some?" he said, shaking off the drops. "I'm clean. Got proof."

"Fuck off." And with that, Llyr elbowed him away and pulled open the door. Was that the click of a knife he heard behind him?

"No-one disses me, d'you hear?"

Too many steps up to Camden's daylight. Too many bodies and the guy right behind him. Llyr could tell by snatches of yellow flashing in the corner of his right eye. He'd got enough on his plate, what with his van and The Ginger bint snooping around with that waste of Irish skin. He was glad he'd put the frighteners on her, not that it seemed to be making any difference. And as for the leprechaun chatting up the cleaner outside Charlie's flat, he should have finished him off when he'd gone down that adit up Pen Cerrigmwyn last year. Come to think of it, his whole life had been one of botched jobs and missed chances. But perhaps at last, thanks to the chicken choker lying in the Royal Free Hospital's morgue, things would take a turn for the better. Soon, he hoped. Like this afternoon. But there was still that Hounslow nerd with the ear stud, gelled hair and crap jeans poking his nose in. Asking too many questions. Now came shouting, yelling, swearing. He pushed through the human tide like the scrum-half he'd once been at the special school until a solid, deep sting in his left calf slowed him down. Then the right leg, through denim to bone.

Shit...

Someone pulled him to the top step and placed him in front as Mr Yellow ran off into the crowd. "You bleed," observed a French-sounding voice. "You need attention." This guy in a sheepskin coat, pulled out his phone. Just then, Llyr saw his future caged in. This time by bars.

"I'm OK. I'm OK," he muttered.

Either the Frog was deaf or a serial do-gooder. Whatever, Llyr snatched that Samsung from his hand, squeezed out from behind him, and crept down the first alleyway he came to, aware of a deepening pain in both lower legs, and the soft, warm sensation of blood filling his boots.

***

He'd soon got shot of that mobile and his own giveaway beanie before finding an open doorway to what appeared to be a deserted pub. The Lamb & Whistle. Just the kind of quiet dark he needed. Christ, he was hurting, losing more blood. He must keep on his feet, get back to Wales to check out what he'd removed from Flynn's study. But first things first. From his lookout in that phone booth in Thornhill Road, he'd seen the Volvo turn into Fylde Street leading to Euston Road. He'd known then that the traitor and The Ginger were heading for Charlie's solicitor in Camden and wondered how he'd found out about the death. No matter he himself couldn't be there in person. He'd soon find out the result.

And then like a black flash, he realised that if he *did* collect big time, the pigs could be fingering him as a prime suspect if things looked suspicious. Had Michael Markham, and others in The Order, thought of that when they'd pushed him Charles' way two years ago? Perhaps that's why an urgent meeting had been arranged with him in Dulwich for tomorrow morning.

"I just cleaned up, ye sod!" A woman's voice reached him from beyond the faintly lit bar as he made for the Gents. "Where d'ye think yer goin'?"

She appeared from the gloom. As fat as his mam was thin, with a skirt split halfway up to her bare thighs. "Get out!"

He turned to face her, knowing that would do the trick. His smooth, glistening head, those round blue eyes. They'd worked in his favour at the special school and with the stiff due to be cut up in three days' time. The stiff he hoped would soon be helping him on his way.

Seconds later, in a back room with a brown linoleum floor and a plasma TV showing some old black and white flick, she cleaned him up, wrapped a makeshift bandage under each rolled-up denim hem and wiped out his boots.

"Fancy a beer?" she said, really meaning, 'd'you fancy *me*?'

"No, ta."

"Ye'll need stitches," she said, straightening up. Disappointment in her made-up eyes. "Got a phone?"

He nodded. His blood was too hot. He had to get out and back on the trail. The Order wanted nothing less. As for his van, although not taxed or insured, it could still lead to him. Attention neither he nor his paranoid bosses needed.

Two silhouettes were standing in the doorway. He could sniff pigs a mile off. Wondered what the dangerous Paddy had spilled about him in Tolpuddle Street.

Shoving past his Florence Nightingale into a cluttered kitchen area, he found an unlocked back door and, biting his lips to stop himself yelping in pain, limped out into a yard full of old beer barrels that led to another alleyway where at last he was on his own.

***

There they were. Paddy and cling-on. He'd guessed right. But at a cost. He'd had to keep stopping, feeling dizzy, sweating, his throat getting drier by the second. He'd only been to Camden twice, but his reward was to see the grey Volvo slip into the NCP car park – the kind of warren he'd always avoided. Too tight corners. Too many concrete pillars. Never mind the spying cameras.

He'd wait till the couple reappeared and the car was his. Trouble was, there were two exits. He'd have to concentrate. Normally his strong point. But not now, feeling as if barbed wire was biting into his legs – as if he was that weirdo hanging upside down from the Cross in what had once been his bedroom – and by the way some tossers passing by were eyeballing him.

It had better be worth his while.

Come on...

What were they up to? Having a grope? He wouldn't put it past that leprechaun who should never have set foot inside his house. Yes. Despite what Flynn had been putting about, Heron House was his now. He knew it. Why? Because the Charles Pitt-Rose he'd pleasured for too long, never broke his promises. Kept a roof over his mam and da's heads, hadn't he?

Kept the lid on.

The GPS tracker he'd attached to the Volvo outside Sandhurst Mansion, once the Philippina had gone, was still safely in place. Now, his last job – a clever bug in the form of a calculator – was too. In the glove box. The car alarm reset.

Hello...

Had The Ginger spotted him? No. He'd moved behind a pillar too quickly, breathing in deeply. He thought of his van all tipped over. How he should have dumped her on the A40 somewhere outside Llandovery and got himself out of the whole game. Now he, not those loaded twats from Dulwich and Dinas Powys, working in the shadows, was at risk.

Move...

Both were running on ahead of him. Well, sort of running, and then because God and time were on his side, came the welcome rumble of a bus drawing into the kerb behind. He'd been too wound up to notice either its named destination or any actual bus stop and, while it drew away with a deep sigh and its doors folded shut behind him, he turned to see the Irish con merchant's grey face grow smaller and smaller. He realised then he should have caught a cab. But would he have been allowed on board? More time wasted.

"Where to?" said the driver. An Asian with seriously bad skin.

Llyr hesitated.

"Back to Islington. Brockenhurst Rise." Parallel to Thornhill Road. Perfect. He'd be taking his third recce of the flat, just to make sure no trace of him remained. Unlike his rival, hoping to collect a key at 4 p.m., he still had his.

"Wrong direction, sir," said the driver. "This is for Waterloo."

"Jesus."

"Best get off next stop." The guy veered round a slow-moving white stretch limo. He then, like all six of his lower deck passengers, stared at the blood-sodden jeans. "You been in a fight?"

"Could say that. Goin' back to my mam's to get sorted out."

"Mam?" he sneered. "I never heard that word before. Anyway, you need fresh dressings right now. Stay standing, please. I don't want my seats messed up."

"Can you step on it?" said Llyr, wanting to put him in an oxygen tent. "I'm late."

His legs were weakening. What's more, the dot-head was ignoring him. He knew what his da would do in this situation. Hit him until he begged for mercy. But he wasn't like that pervert in any shape or form. Even Charlie who knew how riled up he could get. Charlie who liked his cock and ass seeing to in a very special way.

That thought made him push past the brood mare and her giant buggy getting on as he got off, almost falling on to the pavement as he did so.

"'Ere you! Where's your manners?" she screeched after him.

Llyr didn't bother to reply. He had more urgent things to do. Having composed himself, he stepped off the kerb and flagged down the first available cab.

He shouted out his destination into its nearside window, adding as a bribe to the doubtful cabbie, "you won't know I've been in it. Promise."

28

Sunday 5th April 2009 – 1.10 p.m.

With no news from London, and the atmosphere in Heron House as cold as winter, Jason made his way down to the pub, not so much for the chips there – he wasn't that hungry – but for company. With his still-damp jacket collar up against the drizzle, he kept glancing around. Glancing everywhere, in fact. Listening for the sound of oncoming wheels, and all the while harking back to that dark, shape-shifting kitchen. That nightmare...

A red kite hovered overhead, wings stroking the sky until the time was right to pounce on its prey. He wished his own life was that simple. He'd come here to write, for God's sake. To hit the big time, and now look. All that had been a con. Sucker was his middle name. In every sense.

He'd be asking Monty Flynn for a refund the moment he got back. And then what? Buy his ticket to Hounslow? To needy Colin? The thought of it made him quicken towards the sloping car park hosting a 4X4 he immediately recognised, and three cars he didn't. At least Gwilym Price would speak to him. Judy Withers too, if she was there.

He pushed open the pub door to the smell of dogs, dinner, and Radio 2 bringing news of more troops being sent from the UK to Helmand Province. For a few seconds, with Archie Tait's face clear in his mind, he imagined himself tooled up in army fatigues, climbing into a crowded chopper, lifting off into the blue. Into danger.

At least being of some use.

The farmer's distinctive black hat perched on a nearby coat rack, but neither the friendly blonde licensee nor her partner seemed to be around. Instead, a guy whom Jason guessed was in his sixties, and a probable parent of one of them, was chatting from behind the bar to a well-dressed couple with home counties accents. The words 'estate agents' reached his ears.

As for Gwilym Price, no sign either, until he stepped out of the Gents with a distracted look on his face.

"Mr Price. Hi, there. What can I get you?" Jason moved to make an order.

"Not stopping, diolch," said the farmer, whose head, Jason noticed, was completely bald save for a few strands of dry grey hair. "Too much goin' on, see. In me mind and everywhere."

"Can I help at all? I mean, I'm just stuck up there at the asylum waiting for news."

The older man hesitated, lifted his hat off the stand and crammed it down on his head. "I can tell you now I've got to know you. I want to live to see that bastard Llyr Davies behind bars. Carol wouldn't have died the way she did if he'd not..." he halted, swiping his coat sleeve across his watering eyes. "When he's finally banged up, mind, I'll visit him every day to remind him what rape can do to a woman of any age."

So it hadn't been cancer.

Jason wondered if this was the earlier 'form' DC Pritchard and Jane Harris had mentioned? All thoughts of a possible lunch and a drink or two vanished and, as the bulletin on troop deployment ended, he realised there were enough wars here at home. Less public, but still devastating for those affected.

Outside again, in that deathly still afternoon. Nothing much was visible through the soft rain, except the widower's grief, but beneath it, Jason sensed a toughness hard as those rocks dynamited from the mine shafts, now strewn about Cerrigmwyn Hill. "My light went out when she had her stroke," the man continued. "One minute she was there, getting the tea, the next..." He looked hard at Jason. "And to think she'd helped Gwenno Davies give birth to it. Some gratitude, that."

"Quite."

"Like I've told you, she'd been up there with the milk van when she heard the din. Being Carol, she didn't think twice about offering assistance, but that Idris pushed her away. Let slip his sister could manage labour on her own."

"Sister? You sure?"

"That I am."

Now he's said it.

"Was it his child? Pretty sick if so."

"Who knows? But folk talk. That Pitt-Rose monster had dropped dead the month before. There is a likeness with him, mind. Specially that mouth. The round shape of his eyes. Never told the police, did Carol. Frightened she was. But not me. Only when it was too late, mind. Still, she'd described her attacker down to every last detail, and I passed that on. Why my Bob got done on Wednesday. And other stuff off and on ever since she died."

"I want him caught too. His overturned Transit van was found in the early hours on the M4, but at least Helen's safe. She'd managed to leave a Tesco receipt with her name on in the cab to prove she'd been there earlier, then given him the slip before getting a taxi into London."

The faintest smile crept across those damaged lips. "I told you she had an old head on young shoulders. But there's something else." Gwilym Price opened his Nissan's passenger door and gestured for Jason to get in. "I heard through the grape-vine that human blood's been found on one of Betsan's smashed ornaments. Not hers, that's for sure. It's being checked with a saliva sample found on some half-eaten sweet on the driver's side of his van." He turned to Jason, his eyes on fire. "I keep asking myself how come that waster's still drawing breath?" He banged his bare fist on the steering wheel. "There is *no* justice."

He revved too hard and the vehicle, still in first gear, lurched forwards. Jason's knees slammed into the glove box and the wooden crates in the boot piled up in a heap. For a moment he wished he'd stayed in the pub.

"Sorry. You alright?" the farmer turned towards him.

"Yep." But he wasn't. That hurt. Here was the last place for his Woolies' knee pads to have come in handy.

"Those samples are also being tested in connection with a rape up near Abergwesyn few years back. A schoolgirl she was then. Walking home after a netball match."

"Five years ago," said Jason.

"How did you know?"

"The Fuzz mentioned him having form."

"I'll be taking his balls off if I get half a chance. I've still got the right gear from when I kept the pigs."

They reached Gwilym's new aluminium gate and perfectly stretched wire fencing, however, the farmer didn't move. As if Cysgod y Deri's plain square farmhouse, with its six plain windows, the swept yard and surrounding neat barns, weren't enough of a draw. "I'm off back to my schooldays now," he said suddenly, ignoring a fleet of rooks cruising by overhead. "Not that I went to school much. Nice man mind, the headmaster, Mr Hargreaves, but learning from books wasn't for me. Anyway, there was my mam. I had to help her out." He glanced upwards to where Golwg y Mwyn's one chimney was just visible. "I remember Betsan telling me about this quiz he'd organised. Spur of the moment thing it was, on Heron House mainly, though he tried disguising it. Just after one of his pupils suddenly collapsed and died in front of him. Walter Jones it was. Funny business that. Saw something he shouldn't have, was the gossip."

Jason recalled the boy's sad memorial in the churchyard. The pine cones' remains.

"Helen and I saw his grave yesterday."

"Well, not long afterwards, Mr Hargreaves disappeared," Gwilym continued.

174

"You mean walked out?"

"No, I don't."

The way he denied the question made Jason release his seat belt and pull his jacket closer around his body.

"I'd met him up by Heron House. Shown him where to see the heronries. That's what he wanted, but did I believe him? No. During the lunch hour it was, so he didn't have long to spare. I had to get home, but overheard that bastard of a judge having a real go at him for trespassing."

As Jason took in the rest of the story, and young Walter Jones' sudden death a few days before, he realised how big a part the house and its mysterious occupants seemed to have played in the lives of those outside its dank dark walls.

"Although Betsan won the prize, she wasn't happy answering his questions, but back then, ten pounds was ten pounds with no other money coming in." The farmer turned to him. "Poor dab."

"I did notice a quiz certificate on the mantelpiece, signed by a Mr Hargreaves," Jason said. "Dated Wednesday October 8th 1946."

"That's the one. She was never the same afterwards."

Just then, a muddy red *Post Brehninol* van arrived and, parked up behind him. A fat guy wearing a baseball cap the wrong way round, squeezed himself and his bag out into the open, waddled over to pass Gwilym his mail.

"Late enough, as usual," remarked the farmer. "Before you were born, my Carol used to deliver this lot on her horse. Up hill and down dale, it was. But still the post always arrived before eleven o'clock."

The man waddled off without a word while Gwilym left the assorted envelopes he'd been given unopened on top of the dash. One, Jason noticed, was from the police in Llandovery.

"About Betsan," he nudged him. "What happened next?"

"Never went back to school, that was for sure. In fact, she rarely left home till she attended College near Swansea. Her mam died shortly after that and left her enough to get Golwg y Mwyn done up."

"So her mother didn't walk out?"

"Who said that?"

"Doesn't matter."

Meanwhile, those old eyes that had battled against too much rain and wind, glazed over again. "And then there was my uncle Robert. Gave my da's brother too much grief, he did. His own mam, too. Sticking to his principles like that."

"Just a minute," Jason still dwelling on the dead woman's past. "To win that kind of prize, she must have known quite a bit. Stuff that this Mr Hargreaves had to find out, perhaps?"

"She did. But try getting her to say. All she ever admitted was that she and Gwenno had been friendly."

"But Helen said they fell out."

A nod. "And," the man who'd probably heard of more goings on in this quiet backwater than if he'd lived in Tower Hamlets, finally unclicked his seat belt. "She got too scared of the judge to keep going there, see. He'd interfered with her and the others. Know what I mean? A twelve-year-old."

"Did her mother know?"

"Never. If she had, she'd have gone over and killed them with her bare hands."

Silence. The drizzly mist still concealing everything over roof height. Not a living creature to be seen.

"Did Betsan ever mention anyone called Margiad?"

"Just the once, and once was enough. Sodom and Gomorrah was Heron House, and I'd like to think that if Robert had lived longer, he'd have used that conscience of his to land those criminals in jail and have the place burnt down. And don't tell me those Davieses didn't have a part to play. But no proof, see?"

"Who was she?"

That silence around them seemed to deepen.

"Charles' older sister. Daughter of the house."

So Margiad had spoken the truth…

Jason sucked in his breath. The mystery was, piece by piece, beginning to make sense, and he decided it was now time to share his news of the exile's death and how the loathed Llyr Davies might well have rights to a small fortune.

***

"You'd think such a small community as this would be in the know," Jason said once Gwilym had recovered his composure. "Especially back then."

"Don't you believe it. But there was Peris Morgan – bit of a one-off, mind – built like a brick shit-house if you get my meaning, who tried dragging the law up here to sort things out. But guess what?" That angry face turned to Jason while its owner's hand felt for his door handle. "We're talking untouchable. He ended up being shot."

Holed up with this relative stranger from that misty, wet world outside,

176

Jason felt the whole of his dead-end life welling inside his body – an empty vessel filling and filling until no space remained. Until it spilled over. First the ghostly phone calls, the odd happenings not only in his room, and then the sex in that kitchen.

"Yesterday evening, at Heron House, something truly sick and weird happened to me," he began in barely a whisper and, when the rush of words had ended, felt the farmer's arms inside their waxed sleeves, smother him in a prolonged hug. A shared foreboding and despair.

29.

Sunday 5th April 2009 – 1.15 p.m.

They were late for the solicitor, and the nervous Philippina wouldn't be hanging on for ever at Sandhurst Mansion. But then, Helen reasoned, she just might. As she trailed Mr Flynn, she realised nothing between herself and him could ever be the same. She also thought about her little car. Was it still intact? Was her room at Heron House as she'd left it, with her gear set out ready to start her mam's birthday painting?

Despite the welcome sun now fully out, and the shops offering up impossible luxuries, every step she took towards D. H. Salomon & Co. seemed to be taking her further away from what mattered most, into a twilight zone of shadows. The kind that lurked in Heron House's every corner where ancient cobwebs peppered with dead flies hung out of Gwenno Davies' reach.

"Just round here. It's a short cut," called the Irishman, taking a left into the narrow one-way Meadow Passage, home to a crush of 19th century houses, some whose ground floors doubled as up-market businesses, apparently still thriving despite the economic downturn. Tailors, exotic rugs, continental lighting and then number 81.

Coleridge Fine Art.

Helen peered through its bay-fronted window which, together with a discreet Visa sign, bore a shortlist of regular exhibitors. Some she'd heard of, others not. However, what held her gaze was a large framed oil of Glastonbury Tor, situated centre stage, whose colours made her gasp out loud. This was André Derain with knobs on. The reds and oranges visceral yet luminous. She'd been *meant* to be here to see it. Survived to be here.

Then came Mr Flynn's impatient voice. "What the Hell are you doing? Get moving!"

"Won't be a minute," she said, jotting down the gallery's name, fax and phone numbers. Each stroke of her biro seemed to represent a future unfolding. A future that, once she'd waved goodbye to Heron House, would become clearer.

She tucked her little notepad away and stared again at the painting. But as she stared at that strange mound of land, it began to soften. The vermilion, cadmium and chrome orange to fade. Pits and ridges were no longer of land but a distinct face. The one she'd dreamt of while in that van; distorted in terror. However, this was no dream. There were sound effects as well, so their screams met. Hers and hers. She reeled backwards, but someone with a shining bald head she recognised from the study at Heron House, caught her just in time. Hissed that same foul threat in her ear.

When she'd stopped screaming, she also realised that she'd seen those black leather gloves and duffle coat in the van, never mind smelt the same sweat and cheap aftershave. But this time, there'd been blood. His. Then her own, leaving her body with a vengeance.

***

"That man's been here again!" she yelled after Mr Flynn's black coat, as he strode away from her and the green mound of Primrose Hill. "I *know* it's Llyr Davies, but I managed to kick him away and call the police."

"You *what?*"

He'd spun round to glare at her as if she'd attacked him. "Look, I'm really losing patience with you. D'you realise the time? What's at stake here? I need certain vital information now. Not the cops on my back. It's actually a matter of life or death."

Her pumping heart seemed to freeze. And now her boss, more a stranger than ever, was running like some ragged black rook – running out of her life, perhaps? And for a small moment, she imagined it.

Her phone was ringing. She slapped it against her cheek. DCI Jobiah? Spooky weirdo? No. It was Jason's number and him sounding different. Nevertheless, she was relieved to hear his voice.

"Thank God," he said. "I've been worried sick. Specially since finding out more about Llyr Davies. The Fuzz here are trying to find his birth certificate, so it was clever of you to leave proof you'd been in his van. I don't mean to sound patronising."

Her neck began to redden. Then her cheeks.

"You're not. I'm knackered, that's all. We're on the way to this solicitor's in Camden to check out Charles Pitt-Rose's will. Talk about paranoia and secrets. Mr Flynn claims Pitt-Rose paid him to keep the Davieses under wraps. How about that?"

A roaring motorbike drowned his reply; then, as an open-topped tourist bus crawled by, she described the gallery's crazy painting and how her bald abductor, injured and on the loose, had caught up with her.

"Be careful, Helen. He could be a psycho."

"I'm doing my best, but Mr Flynn's pretending Llyr doesn't exist. Why?"

"Who knows. Even Gwenno's frightened of him. She let that slip this morning in front of Sergeant Rees. Strange episode, that. Even spoke fondly of Monty Flynn."

"That is odd."

"But there's something else. Margiad *is* a Pitt-Rose. She told me herself…"

"How?" A small flicker of jealousy touched Helen's heart. He'd sounded almost proud.

"Usual method. Orange are still baffled."

"So am I. When you say *is* a Pitt-Rose, you're implying she's still alive. If so, she must be in her late seventies, yet the images I've seen and the voice you've heard is of someone not even twenty."

"Can you have a spook who's still got a pulse? Still forever young?"

"I'm not into this stuff at all." Helen stared at the normal world passing by. But what was normal anyway? "Nor Mr Flynn. He slaps me down every time I mention her as well. Either he's frightened, or has genuinely never come across her. And look how those two nutters reacted when you spoke out."

"Well, Gwilym's just confirmed Margiad was, or is, Charles' older sister. Only this morning she referred to the house as Hell. Should I believe her or is she just after attention?"

Helen felt sick. That horrible stain on Jason's bedroom carpet seemed to be leaching into her own body, adding to her own bloody burden. She pressed her legs together to stop any excess from showing through her jeans; from making her look like a hospital case, like her attacker.

"I don't know what to believe any more. My boss is *such* a liar."

The man himself was now just a bobbing speck in the distance. A nasty little blot on the scene.

"What else has he got to hide, I wonder?" said Jason.

"Don't ask. And how about you? Is The Rat leaving you alone?" A pertinent question as any.

"I wish."

"What's that supposed to mean?"

She waited. Something was up. The silence was too long.

"You've no idea what happened here last night, and Helen," he paused, his voice breaking up, "I don't know where to start…"

***

That weak sun was suddenly too hot. The other pedestrians too close. Helen moved along to the cool iron railings bordering Primrose Hill's crowded green hump. She steadied herself and closed her eyes tight, tighter to shift that revolting, perverted scene Jason had just described. But easier said than done. This was now Technicolor plus grunts and groans. On maximum.

180

"Again, do it again…" came an older man's breathless voice, from where Helen couldn't tell. "Faster, faster…"

"I can't."

"You damned well will. Marky's next. Been hanging on long enough for you to put him out of his misery."

Marky?

Helen's eyes snapped open. For a moment she'd lost her bearings. What had that been all about? Some sick game or other? A dare?

"Are you OK?" A Chinese girl with black, spiky hair was offering her a half-finished bottle of Evian water. But it was a darker, thicker water that seemed to be sliding below her feet.

"Thanks, but I'm in a rush. Time of the month, that's all." And as Helen spoke, she felt a huge clot of blood leave her body and not only overload her already saturated pad, but trickle down inside the right leg of her jeans. Was there a public loo in sight? Course not.

Dammit.

In punishing mode, she wondered if, despite Jason's protestations, his former loathing for the old woman had been replaced by some kind of sick desire. No, she wouldn't be phoning him back or sending a text. She didn't want to know. Men were a mystery. Right now, Mr Flynn the biggest of all. With that revolting encounter still embedded in her mind, she actually walked past 72 Hurst Crescent and Mr Flynn hovering in the shadow of its colonnaded porch. "We're here!" he shouted at her. "What the Hell's up with you?"

Jason for a start…

The dark blue front door was already opening behind him. Helen paused. Took a breath big enough to blow up a party balloon, except this was no party. "Mr Flynn," she said in her hardest, shiniest voice. I'm giving you one month's notice as from today. And no, I don't want to discuss it. I've had enough."

"You can't!"

"Yes, I can."

A woman's face peered round the door. Plenty of slap, thought Helen ungenerously. And an expensive haircut. Was this the solicitor? It appeared so, with Mr Flynn working his tarnished charm on her, enough for that door to open further to let him in, then close.

"Wait!" Helen shouted.

Having reached the top step she pressed her palm on the cold bell sited next to an impressive brass plaque bearing Dee Salomon's name. The Pink

Suit almost reluctantly, it seemed, let her in, locked the front door behind her and left her to it. "Given what's been going on at Heron House, I've a right to be here," Helen called after her, but only the echoing hallway heard. "And please may I use the loo?"

"First left," came the answer.

Millionaires' Row, Helen had thought when first entering Hurst Crescent, and those first impressions were proved right. Inside this tall town house, steel, glass and the palest, smoothest wood had transformed the original Victorian shell. While under her scuffed trainers, that still bore traces of that crowded wheelie bin, lay the most awesome stone tiles she'd ever seen. Heffy's parents' hotel, lush as it was, didn't come close. There were white lilies, too. Real ones, fully opened, giving off that funereal smell that always made her sneeze. Like now. At least her jeans weren't ruined.

Afterwards, as she squeezed out a blob of something exotic from a hand wash dispenser on to her palms, they were still trembling.

"We're in here," called out Mr Flynn from a doorway lower down the hall. "I'm keeping it brief. Every second costs. "No comments from you. Understood?"

Helen nodded, sensing more than a physical distance between them now. He'd knowingly hooked her and Jason into a secret, dangerous world for his own purpose. The kudos of the Heron House address had come at a price. A very hidden price.

She stared at him as she took her place in the office overlooking a rectangular garden where not a blade of grass grew. Only palms and more palms whose spiky, brown-tipped leaves seemed to sum up her mood. She looked across at him again. A barefaced liar, yes. But above all a fool.

"By the way, someone's cleared out your study," Helen announced as Dee Salomon, who had so far ignored her, now looked up from an unopened dark-green box file. "Jason discovered it yesterday. I've not had time to tell you."

Mr Flynn's eagerly-clenched fists tightened.

"But I locked it. Are you serious?"

Before she could reply, the pink-suited woman was clicking open the file and her matching pink fingernails were pulling out a collection of papers bound by a thin, black ribbon.

"It was unlocked. And I am," Helen replied.

"Did you call the police?"

"Like I said, there's been no time."

With a cavernous sigh, he slumped back in his chair.

"Was anything incriminating or potentially damaging in there?" asked Ms Salomon.

Was his answer too quick?

"No. Of course not. Why should there be?"

"It should definitely be looked into. In my experience, theft can lead to other more serious activity. And I don't just mean blackmail." She glanced at her discreet gold watch. "As I explained earlier when you telephoned, as a settled tenant of the deceased, and modest beneficiary…"

"Modest?" he interrupted, sitting on the edge of his chair.

"… you are of course entitled to see me. However, my time is limited. I'm obliged to tell you that I've received six telephone calls already, enquiring after Mr Pitt-Rose's will."

Mr Flynn perked up. "Really? Who?"

"All anonymous. All male. Five on Friday morning and one in the evening while I was working late. I'll be asking the police for a trace. I won't tolerate harassment because that's what it was."

"Quite right." Yet he was frowning. Something was wrong.

"So, we'll make a start." She angled a beige sheet of paper towards him. "Mr Charles Pitt-Rose's last Will and Testament. Dated 10th March 2009, witnessed by my part-time colleague, Simon Catterall, and Ellie Peterson, my secretary."

"That's not even a month ago," interrupted Mr Flynn peering at it. "Any reason why?"

She paused. "Between ourselves, I confess I'd had the feeling something wasn't quite right when Mr Pitt-Rose last called in here. Agitated would best describe his state of mind. As if he was frightened. When I asked if he lived alone, he hesitated before saying yes. So should any Inquest verdict suggest suicide, I'll speak out against it. Why any hint of a secret enquiry is deeply worrying. Did you know the Justice Minister's proposal for such an abuse of liberty's just been dropped?"

Mr Flynn shook his head. He didn't look normal.

"Dodgy contacts. That's what DCI Jobiah at Islington police station implied earlier today," said Helen. "What did he mean?"

Her boss placed a forefinger over his lips. Gave her a death stare.

"That's for them to find out," said the solicitor. "But as I've said, I feel my client was living under some kind of malevolent cloud and I hope whatever or whoever it was, soon comes to light. And now the will." She returned to that green box file. "Given my time constraints, I'll keep to the point."

At this, Mr Flynn loosened his crumpled tie, fiddled with his cuff buttons

183

while Helen wondered if some mysterious group or other might have caused Charles Pitt-Rose's death and if they'd ever be unmasked. For example, many Welsh people claimed Wales was run by Masons, and according to her mam, her da had even tried joining his local Lodge but had been turned down.

Now Mr Flynn was perched forwards on his seat as far as he could go. His eyes solely on Dee Salomon's painted lips. Clearly, news of extreme importance was about to follow.

Helen was right.

"...being of sound mind, do hereby bequeath the sum of two hundred pounds to Mr Montague Flynn, c/o Heron House, Rhandirmwyn, Carmarthenshire, for supervising its affairs for the past three years..."

His fists immediately clenched again. Spittle bubbled in the corners of his mouth. "Is that all? Two hundred pounds?"

Dee Salomon, having glanced at him with the utmost disdain, kept reading.

"... and the rest of my estate passes to Miss Betsan Anwen Griffiths, spinster of Golwg y Mwyn, Rhandirmwyn, Carmarthenshire in grateful appreciation of her loyalty and care towards my sister Margiad Pitt-Rose of Heron House..."

My God. Margiad.

Just then, Helen's period ache intensified, bringing a release of blood that made her press her thighs tight together. The Irishman had slumped back in his chair. Now was her chance. "There you go. How can you not say sorry?"

A sneaky, sideways glance.

"*You'll* be the one saying sorry."

"Please, both of you," said Dee Salomon. "Let me continue ...during her prolonged times of trouble. Should Betsan Anwen Griffiths pre-decease the signatory, this estate will be dispersed amongst any of her remaining family." Her words seemed to well up and swirl around like a winter storm on Llyn Brianne reservoir, while Mr Flynn stayed wordless, grey.

"But poor Betsan's dead!" Helen cried. "Jason Robbins and I found her when Mr Flynn had left for London yesterday morning. She'd been murdered, and it looked like she'd been expecting someone. Hasn't anyone let you know?"

Before the shocked lawyer could reply, the Irishman broke in. All trace of that recent threat gone. Steel now so easily replaced by honey. "Helen here, did give me the terrible news. She was a wonderful person who never harmed a soul. A real treasure. Let's hope her killer's brought to justice."

The solicitor got up, filled three Styrofoam beakers from the water cooler in the corner, and passed them round. She then eyed Helen before jotting down this information. "This changes everything. She may or may not have known about her good fortune. She may or may not have any family left." She paused. "Her death is being investigated, of course?"

"Yes," said Helen. "But she's not the only one the police are interested in…"

"Let Ms Salomon finish," Mr Flynn butted in again, fidgeting with his nails and his reading glasses, suddenly looking twice his age.

Dee Salomon meanwhile, sipped from her beaker, still focussing on the first sheet of paper. "Two things," she continued. "Firstly, and irrespective of whether any of Betsan's family decides to keep the house or sell it on, the executor – myself – must ensure Idris and Gwenno Davies are removed from the property forthwith. They are to receive the sum of one thousand pounds sterling apiece to relocate out of the area." She glanced up, giving no space for any reaction. "Secondly, and this is a surprise, we have Llyr who is in fact named on his birth certificate as Edmund Pitt-Rose's second son, born on July 3rd 1967, shortly before his father's death. His mother, being Gwenno Davies, may well force him to contest this will." She fixed her gaze on Mr Flynn. "Especially if being evicted and with no other living connections to Heron House, she'd have a strong case for a Deed of Variation."

The air in that office seemed as thick as wool. Thick and sickly. Mr Flynn seemed about to keel over but gripped the arms of his chair in time.

"Llyr Davies, eh? Well, well," said Helen feeling liberated. "There's another one who's not supposed to exist. Whatever his name, he's a criminal on the run." How this possible inheritor to a fortune had been following her just minutes ago. "He tried abducting me last night," she said. "I nearly died, and this was his threat to me." When she'd finished, Mr Flynn was staring at his hands. Still in denial. And then she realised with a judder he might be protecting the thug. But, why?

"Where's proof it was him?" he said.

"Just you wait, and as for the mother, she's nuts, like her brother. You've said the same."

Dee Salomon's eyebrows had hit her fringe. "Have either or both ever been assessed, or indeed, sectioned?"

"No," said the Irishman having pulled himself together. "But they're a menace. Why C. P-R wants them out. By the way, do you have a copy of this Llyr's birth certificate? Did Edmund Pitt-Rose actually sign it?"

"He did, and a copy's on its way."

"Where's the original?"

Dee Salomon, for the first time, seemed uneasy. "It's already been requested by a third party. Confidential, I'm afraid."

"How much of the lease is left on the Sandhurst Mansion flat?" Flynn asked.

"That's also a private matter, I'm afraid."

"And I'm afraid I'm sorry."

He didn't look it, and as for The Pink Suit, Helen could tell she was weakening. Especially after the birth certificate grilling.

"*Entre nous*, Charles Pitt-Rose bought its freehold last year, which considerably adds value. Given the location, I'd say it's worth one and a half million pounds at least, plus what Oracle Shipping Services made when he sold the firm back in 1989. But he never returned to Heron House after 1945, and certainly never mentioned any half-brother to me. After his father's death, all maintenance work was done by Londoners. No-one local. That's how much he disliked the place."

Silence, in which the scene beyond the window seemed to drain of colour: the palms, the Mediterranean blue tubs, the orange gravel, even the promising spring sky. Helen tried imagining Gwenno and Edmund Pitt-Rose at it, but couldn't. This must be some huge mistake.

"Does Llyr Davies know he's Edmund Pitt-Rose's son?" Mr Flynn demanded. "If not, why not keep it that way?"

"It's my duty to inform him," she replied sternly. "I also need to find out who's Miss Griffiths' solicitor, and if DNA tests *do* prove he's a Pitt-Rose. I'd be legally bound, whatever his situation, to advise him of his rights. However, should he end up in prison, any assets could well be frozen."

"Could be?" Mr Flynn said.

"A legal black hole, I'm afraid. You being Irish, Mr Flynn, are probably aware of the situation regarding convicted terrorists."

He nodded, while Helen's low-down ache carried on biting with a vengeance. She visualised her old bedroom in Borth. Would this really be her next stop? The possibility of such a sad sign of defeat was looming large.

Dee Salomon was checking her watch again. Mr Flynn got up, gesturing for Helen to do the same. His greasy, tousled head even more out of order. "What about the money I get for keeping the Davieses until they go?"

"That agreement ended on March 31st last. Any provision of a roof for them will, from now on, be in conflict with the deceased's wishes. Mr Pitt-

Rose is clear on that."

Yet Helen knew The Rat and her brother would, when Llyr Pitt-Rose became aware of his new status, surely be staying put.

Just then, without warning, another's voice pushed its way through her rising fear. That of a man. Welsh. Urgent, breathless, like the young woman she'd heard earlier:

"Again. Do it again for St. Peter's sake! Faster, faster. I'm nearly there..."

"I can't."

"You damned well will. Marky's next. Been waiting long enough."

"Judge Markham's too big, daddy. He tears me. Makes me bleed..."

"He's used to that. Just pretend it's..."

"What's wrong?" Mr Flynn was staring at her.

Jason, that's what.

"Nothing." She then faced the solicitor. "But did Charles Pitt-Rose ever refer to a Judge Markham at all?"

She suddenly noticed a blue vein pulsing in her boss' neck.

"Why?"

"Or Marky?"

The Irishman, having produced his chequebook, was suddenly very busy digging around for a pen while Dee Salomon flicked through the rest of the document and stood up, smoothing down her skirt. "Miss...?" she faced her expectantly.

"Jenkins. Helen Myfanwy."

"Miss Jenkins, as this news is now in the public domain, I can say that Judge Philip Markham passed away yesterday morning. His cancer finally defeated him. Not only was he a credit to his profession, but his son's also very well thought of. Now then," she eyed Mr Flynn busy topping and tailing his cheque with a less than steady hand. "I really do need to be leaving here in five minutes."

"Did Charles ever indicate that Betsan might have had living relatives?" he asked, rather too quickly.

"No, and no-one so far has come forward. However, they'd need to be traced sooner rather than later." She placed the completed cheque in her neat pink handbag. "I'd also be interested to learn what happened to this older sister, Margiad. There's no sign of any Death Certificate and in the case of Betsan being the sole survivor, Margiad may herself be alive or have living issue. Now that *would* cause an interesting scenario."

187

30.

Saturday 12th October 1946 – 10.30 a.m.

Golwg y Mwyn, unlike Troed y Rhiw, faced the mid-morning sun. It comprised three modest rooms and a privy abutting into a once well-tended but now dying vegetable garden set against part of the hillside. Lionel closed the wooden back gate behind him, marvelling at the triumph of human toil over the slide and settlement of Ordovician rock that had shaped Cerrigmwyn Hill.

Nevertheless, these withered remains of potatoes, carrots, onions and swede still lay in shadow, seemed to echo the general air of sadness surrounding this humble cottage. Digging for Victory had clearly served mother and daughter well, but now within these weather-beaten walls the quietest but keenest girl in his class was hiding. He knocked on the back door with his fist, primed for disappointment. But, no. Mrs Griffiths, the large, once handsome woman appeared as if she'd been waiting for him. He'd only met her once before at the school's Summer Fayre, where her table full of home-made cakes had emptied in ten minutes.

"Betsan's not set foot outside since she came home for lunch after that quiz of yours," she confirmed his suspicions, eyeing him from her vantage point on the back door step with the look he'd seen so many times in this part of the world. Sharp, knowing. Her hands whitened by flour. "Never said why mind. Missed choir practice too, even though that Mr Price shouldn't be in Rhandirmwyn at all. Off her food, too." She stepped down, moved closer. "Did something happen at school? That why you're here?"

He stared past her into the kitchen where she'd clearly been busy baking bread. With a loaf now costing 4d, this made sense, and the smell of it brought a sudden hunger. "Mrs Griffiths, I do really need to speak to Betsan, for several reasons."

The bread maker's eyes narrowed.

"Those two Liverpool lads, is it? Dim they are, and nothing but trouble."

"No. Not them."

"Best come in. But she's barely said anything since this morning. And when Betsan goes quiet, that's it. Shall I take your coat?"

"I won't be stopping long, thank you."

***

The sun, pulled clear of its cloudy veil, filled the back parlour with an almost holy light, turning the twelve-year-old's hair the colour of his late mother's wedding ring. It also caught the many pretty porcelain pieces displayed along the mantelpiece and in matching alcoves either side of the fire. Perhaps they were heirlooms, thought Lionel. Carefully added to over the years. A possible source of cash too, should the widow and her only child ever need it.

As for Betsan, wearing a brown hand-knitted cardigan and a skirt, obviously cut down from one of a larger size, she sat cross-legged on a multi-coloured rag rug with a book of biblical stories on her lap, facing a freshly-lit coal fire. She didn't look up when her mother introduced him, instead stared fixedly at one particular page. Lionel inched closer to see it bore a dramatic image of St. Peter's unusual crucifixion – all pain and grief.

Her index finger continued circling the disciple's open mouth.

"Does that upset you?" he asked.

She nodded. "Sometimes it's all I think about. That and..." She clamped a hand over her mouth as if she'd said too much, but Lionel knew that with the right tone of voice and gentle persuasion, she might help him solve what had driven Walter Jones' young heart to stop beating. "You shouldn't have asked about things at Heron House in your quiz, sir." She glanced up at the door to the kitchen, now closed. Lowered her voice. "They're punishing me already."

He'd taken care not to mention that place by name. It was she who'd turned a general query into the very particular.

"They? What do you mean?"

The girl set her book aside, got to her feet and reached up to whisper in his ear.

When she'd finished, Lionel stepped back. If his most conscientious pupil was to be believed, then she, too, was in a very vulnerable situation. His cheeks began to redden, not from the modest fire, but the realisation that Walter Jones had inadvertently witnessed Margiad Pitt-Rose torn from her meeting with Robert Price and driven back to Hell. To The Order, as her father and his 'guests' called themselves.

"Her baby's due in the New Year," Betsan added. "But it's not Robert's. Oh, no. They've only done kissing. She's told me everything, see. Before that, she'd been losing blood. Too much blood. So a blessing and a curse, I suppose."

Lionel was no doctor, but he remembered his own mother's monthly problems. How in the end, she'd had her womb removed. "Every month?"

Betsan blushed. Glanced at the door, still whispering. "No, sir. Every time she did it."

189

She snatched at his coat sleeve. Her round, open face tense with fear. "Please help her, sir. Please help to hide her somewhere away from her father and those other men. That's what she wants. She told me last week. Please sir..."

Those wide blue eyes had begun to cry. Her mouth to tremble. He mustn't risk Mrs Griffiths hearing anything or bursting in without warning.

"I promise I'll do what I can. Tell her that, won't you?"

"Yes. And thank you, sir. But watch out for Idris and Gwenno. They're..." she hesitated, glancing around the room as if there was a chance of being overheard, "evil."

That last word stung him like a needle, coming as it did from such a normally mild-mannered girl.

"So why did you ever go there?"

"For company, sir. I'd no friends at school or in the village."

"Any sign of a young brother Charles?"

She then must have heard her mother hovering behind the door because she quickly picked up a porcelain figurine of a child holding a spaniel puppy and placed it in his open palm. "For you, sir. It'll bring you luck."

"No, you don't," came her mother's voice from behind him. "It's not hers to give. Besides, and the Lord knows I've tried to be civil, Mr Hargreaves; but you've caused enough trouble here, what with Walter going the way he did, and now my Betsan a changed girl."

Lionel returned the ornament and, having given her daughter a reassuring smile, squeezed past the broad-hipped Welsh woman, into the kitchen and outside.

***

No sooner had Lionel closed the back gate behind him, than he was aware of being followed. Of heavy breathing and the rub of boots against the stony ground. Without turning round, he quickened his pace. Memories of his impromptu visit to Heron House and that sharp-faced girl in riding clothes with a lethal-looking crop and gun, kept him moving, twisting off balance on loose stones, occasionally grabbing the nearest piece of fencing to steady himself.

"Stop, please, sir!" came the unfamiliar voice of a young woman, and Lionel half-turned to see the organist's photograph come to life. An awful, frightened life.

"I'm Margiad Pitt-Rose. From the prison up there. Take me with you. I've heard you're a good man. Carol and Betsan both said I could trust you."

Carol?

He stared at that stricken face dominated by a fresh bruise around her left eye, then at the pronounced swelling of her stomach under her coat. His shy pupil had been right. Margiad Pitt-Rose was unmistakably pregnant.

"Who's been hurting you?" he asked.

"All of them."

"The Order?"

She turned away. "Who told you that?"

"Never mind. Just give me names."

"I can't. Not ever. You've no idea what they could do to you."

A pause, filled by the sudden rush of rooks overhead flying towards the forestry.

"Walk in front," he suggested recklessly. "I'll shield you. But please, even fields have ears."

What on earth was he doing? He asked himself repeatedly as the track widened and the short cut down to the road appeared. He'd only the one bed; one of everything. And what if the baby arrived prematurely, like he himself had done?

'It's not too late to say 'no,' urged his censorious inner voice. 'This is madness.' And yet, Betsan's concern had been genuine. This young woman whose black, wavy hair was lifted from her shoulders by the rising breeze, whose moving shadow connected with his, had nowhere else to go.

***

"There's a back way into my cottage," he said, once they'd reached the road with thankfully no-one else in sight. "I'll show you." And within the minute, she was indoors, removing her coat and gloves and warming her blue-tipped fingers by his still-guarded fire. Lionel drew up the same chair that Peris Morgan had sat in and asked if she'd like a cup of tea. If she was hungry.

"You're very kind, Mr Hargreaves," she said, "but I'd rather you draw your curtains and make sure both your doors are bolted. Does that sound mad?"

"Of course not," and while he busied himself, realised with a rising sense of danger, that from now on, his previously ordered life wouldn't be the same. "You need to be safe. That's what Betsan said."

He detected an almost eager flicker in her lovely eyes.

"Did she say why?" She leant towards the fire's warmth, still spreading out her cold fingers. "Did she explain what I've had to bear since I became a woman?"

"Without too much detail, yes. But..."

"I've money," she interrupted, without turning round. "Been well paid for what I do. But it's dirty money, and Robert Price must never learn how I've earned it." She fixed those large dark eyes on his. "You didn't seem at all surprised when I said his name. Have you been speaking with him? Have you?"

Lionel paused. He imagined being a trapper faced with an angry, frightened bear. "I had to borrow some sheet music for school," he lied too easily. "But he did seem tense. Apparently, your father and another man he'd never seen before had warned him off."

"When?"

"Last night."

"May they burn in Hell," she whispered, then crossed herself. "And where's Charles when it matters? Precious, selfish Charles. My young, carefree brother." She transferred her gaze to the fire. Lionel noticed the heave of her thin shoulders, a tear drifting down her cheek.

Just then, came the click of his cottage's front gate latch and an urgent knock on the door. Margiad sprang to her feet and, with some difficulty, crouched down behind the armchair she'd been occupying. Lionel peered through a tiny gap in the closed curtains, his carotid artery banging in his neck. Curtains drawn like this halfway through the morning could only arouse more suspicion.

Carol was standing with her cob by the gate. But not the Carol he knew. His sigh of relief short-lived. She gestured him to join her. Her face tense. Her grip on Lucky's reins tight enough for him to toss his head up and down in protest. She handed over an envelope postmarked Carmarthen. Probably to do with his ever-encroaching inspection.

"Sorry I can't ask you in," he said to her, and meant it. "I'm afraid. I've got company."

"Oh?"

"They won't be long," he dissembled, aware of his sudden blush.

"Doesn't matter," she lowered her voice. "Listen, I had to tell you about yesterday. I'd just been delivering the mail up at Heron House. You won't believe it. No-one would."

"Believe what? That everything there's all sweetness and light?"

Carol frowned. "This is serious. For a start, I've proof that Glyn Prydderch our local constable is in cahoots with them up there. Standing next to that Pitt-Rose brute, he was bragging about his sexual prowess. How some time it would be fun to try a..." she hesitated. "A really young one... a virgin. Even another boy. It's disgusting. I wanted to wash my eyes and ears out after hearing it."

"Are you sure it was him?"

Lionel's precious class reappeared in his mind. Innocents, born at the wrong time, with fathers, uncles, even grandfathers ruined by war. And what about those like himself, in positions of trust? It was beyond horrible to believe her.

"Another boy? Are you sure?"

She nodded.

That clear, fragile sky seemed to darken as if a cold dusk had descended. Like a rock meeting river water, he stepped forwards then back. It was too soon to hold her close. To feel her rapid heartbeat connecting through his pullover, shirt and vest to his own. That would have to wait.

"Where was this?" he asked instead, as Lucky whinnied in impatience.

"By the pool. Having heard voices, I sneaked over there, wondering what was going on. And that's not all. There she was as well. Bold as brass, I'm telling you."

"Who d'you mean?"

Now it was her turn to blush. "Margiad, you know, pleasuring one of the other men. I could tell that's what she was doing by..." She stopped to compose herself. "Early thirties he was, like her father. Him and the constable were watching and enjoying it. Egging her on. Edmund Pitt-Rose's own daughter. Can you believe it? And she's pregnant. I wish I'd had my old camera. The prints would have been real proof."

Lionel didn't need her to spell it out. That noose he'd already felt round his throat was tightening with every second.

Carol looked up at him with pink, swollen eyes. "Never forget what old Peris Morgan said."

"How can I?"

Although he could have held her close all day and night, Lionel guided her out into the road. "And what you've just witnessed, well, it shows the old soldier wasn't making things up."

She faced him again. Her tone suddenly changed. "So why, if he'd warned you, is that trollop inside your cottage? Look at her, staring out at me. Bold as brass."

Trollop?

Lionel whipped round to see Margiad's face framed by each curtain. Her bruise now more black than blue.

"So, *she's* your company. The reason I wasn't invited in. You must be seeing her, too."

Lionel's neck began to burn.

"Don't be ridiculous, Carol. She's desperate. And I mean desperate."

"If you believe that, forgive me, you're a fool. She loves what she does up there. Everything. Even screaming when poor little Walter saw her. All put on for effect." Carol brushed the worst of the dirt from her knees then began to walk away. "Just don't come to me when the kitchen gets too hot. She'll bring you down, Lionel. She's bad luck."

Carol half turned his way and, although she'd stopped speaking, her lips still quivered. "Just when I thought you and I might become more than friends."

31.

Sunday 5th April 2009 – 4 p.m.

Jason jumped down from the Nissan, still dwelling on Helen's shock at his stop-start account of Gwenno Davies and the equally expert Margiad. He had to grab the nearest fence post for support as yet another bout of dizziness cocooned him. He wished to God he'd kept quiet about the whole sordid episode, but the cleaner was a loose cannon. Better his version of events reached Helen's ears first. But would she ever trust him again?

"You'll have a cup of tea?" suggested Gwilym Price who'd recovered his rifle and a battered copy of *Farmers' Weekly*.

"Brilliant. Thanks." Yet he walked towards that immaculate new gate as if his confession and Helen's bombshell about Monty Flynn and his writers' courses still weighed him down. The lying git. He'd be getting a refund the moment the Irishman stepped over Heron House's doorstep.

Gwilym Price unlocked the farm gate's padlock and pulled it open, but Jason held him back. "Please," he urged. "What I've just told you was just between us, OK? I don't want the 'pervert' word on my CV."

The other man's mouth stretched into a smile as he indicated the two tall chimneys poking through the distant foliage. "It's not you who's perverted. Remember that."

Once inside the farmhouse, he carried a spare chair into the spotless kitchen. A space devoid of any woman's touch, observed Jason, warming his butt against the old cream-coloured Aga. He noticed an empty dog basket and the pine Welsh dresser opposite, laden not with fancy plates and trinkets but photos, ranging from sepia to bright colour, of an attractive woman at various stages of her life. A woman whose useful years on earth had ended with Llyr Davies.

He left the Aga's warmth to study the pictures in close up. A typical land girl posing with a rake. Next, a postmistress astride her sturdy horse, and finally her marriage to Gwilym, ten years younger. Not that he looked it, with his brooding looks. Those serious Welsh eyes.

"Who's that?" Jason pointed at a smaller image of an equally serious young man who'd obviously moved before the camera's shutter had come down. His dark form had blurred; and was that St. Barnabas' Church's delicate bell tower lurking in the background? Something about him seemed familiar.

"That's uncle Robert," said the widower filling Jason's Cymru mug and its tea bag with boiling water. "A true non-conformist, like the church who paid him." He then passed Jason an already opened packet of chocolate digestives. "I've had this psychical research society wanting to pick my brains about him. Do some digging. But I told them to bugger off and leave things be." He set down his mug, picked up his and Jason's uneaten biscuits and returned them to the packet. "Robert often comes to me, you know. Whether I'm asleep or awake, makes no difference to him. He pulls at my arms, breathes his cold breath on my neck. Begs me to find her. His Margiad. Carol thought I was going doolally. Told me to get help. But it's not me that needs help. It's Robert."

A persistent tremor passed through Jason's body. His hands seemed sealed like ice to a rock around his mug.

"He sings that same William Williams hymn over and over like some old record: 'O'er those gloomy hills of darkness, look my soul be still, and gaze...'" Gwilym Price's singing voice was more like a death rattle.

"Why?"

"For consolation, I suppose. He'd heard she'd gone off to London to start a new life, you know the sort of thing. Like you coming all the way here. But deep in his heart he didn't believe a word of it. I remember him coming over one Sunday after church, just after the Headmaster had disappeared. Early November it was. 1946. I was only nine at the time, but I'd never seen a grown man cry like that. Nor since. Grieving for both of them he was. Carol had been upset too but I never probed too much."

"What did Robert do then?" Jason glanced out at the sombre sky beyond the window. At the rickety line of trees along the brow of the hill opposite. He tried recalling that Headmaster's name as the other man shrugged.

"We never found out. The Christmas Eve carol concert was the last time anyone heard him play the organ. Not long afterwards, Beynon 'The Shop,' who'd been in the congregation, recognised him trudging through the snow along the road to Llandovery. Suitcase and all. Sounds of a scuffle then, he said, but no proof, mind, except for a mess of footprints. "Good riddance, conchie," we'd heard people say, but for us – what was left of his family – him disappearing like that was nothing but a worry. My mam tried getting the police involved, but they just shrugged their shoulders." He looked at Jason. "Nothing's changed, has it?"

"Nope. And Helen's already seen his ghost twice up by the old lead workings. Including yesterday when we were together. He seemed to be waiting for something or someone. Dressed all in black."

"Margiad, like I said. Sure to be."

"But definitely no singing."

"Saves that for me, then."

Gwilym Price stood up. "Sixty-two years of unrest have passed since that Christmas. Too many of the living still draw breath who know the truth of what really happened to him and Margiad." He regarded Jason with a question clouding his old eyes. "Are you up for helping me get to the bottom of it all?"

For a panicked moment, Jason thought about Helen. The thriller he'd planned to write. 'Thriller' now a faint, feeble word for another time, another life.

"OK," Jason said.

"Whatever it takes?" The widower came over, clamped a hand on his shoulder. "Getting those freaks in the asylum to talk? And their son who shot all the herons?"

"Llyr?"

"Still in short trousers he was. All hushed up and I never found out till after Carol..." He paused to pick up his rifle and check the barrel. Jason gave it a wide berth. "We only gave Llyr work to keep him out of more trouble, but he got sent away, just like Margiad's young brother, Charles. So Betsan says. Poor sod *he* was. No wonder he's just topped himself."

"Is that what you really think?"

"What else, given his background?"

"Did you ever see him around the place?"

"Never. Nor Betsan nor Uncle Robert."

"If it *is* murder and he'd been left Heron House..."

"Answer my question," Gwilym said.

"You're on," Jason replied.

They shook hands on it, and once the determined rook-killer had locked up and accompanied him out into the thickening drizzle on to the track leading past Betsan's taped-up bungalow, towards the old mine, Jason added his own lengthening list of unexplained occurrences. Beginning with Margiad Pitt-Rose's invasive demands, and ending with those four portly men he'd glimpsed by the swimming pool.

***

The whine of saws and distant quad bikes accompanied them both up the hill via a different route Jason had taken with Helen, on to more boggy ground, bristling with fan-like reeds. Here, rough-woolled sheep scattered in fear. That dead ewe and lamb now all gone. He saw how the vast crescent of scrubby hillside darkened by pines, harboured nothing but dereliction.

Neither attempted to speak above the din of the forest's machinery and when, for a moment it ceased, came the tinkling sound of water, so pure, so calming, Jason stopped to listen. He also had the oddest sensation they were being watched and that somehow, his life, so far like a rudderless boat, was being guided to shore.

"There's something else I've not mentioned." Jason broke the silence, needing this relative stranger's take on things. "Helen told me Monty Flynn only advertised the writing course to get more company at Heron House. Scared of the Davieses apparently. So why hasn't he left? Doesn't make sense."

Silence.

Puzzled, he followed Gwilym Price up on to the now familiar sloping track, whose wet stones had become embedded in fudge-coloured pools of mud. Hard to avoid them at such a pace, as though his companion had suddenly found his second wind. A purpose.

"This where you saw him?" Gwilym asked without looking round. Still not answering that question about Monty Flynn.

"Robert?"

"Who else do I mean?" Gwilym then paused, turned his glazed eyes towards Jason. "Look, son, I'm sorry, I can't help you with that leprechaun. No-one has the faintest why he ever came here, or why he's hung on. As for his fellow inmates..." he lifted his rifle from his shoulder and took a pot shot at something small and black flying over a copse of straggly willows.

He missed.

"But with Charles Pitt-Rose gone, you wait. Heron House was his after his da died. Common knowledge, and when the shit hits the fan, that's when I'll act."

Gwilym Price parked himself on one of a line of stones forming the entrance to the old workings and, lifting the front brim of his hat off his forehead, pointed towards the spoil heaps, blue-grey in the drizzle. "You take yourself over there by that adit you mentioned. If you spot anything unusual, just tilt your head to the right so I can see. Understood? They say the camera never lies."

Gwilym pulled out a small digital job from inside his coat pocket and fiddled with the telescopic lens while, for the second time that day, Jason walked on, the same way he'd come with Helen, until the different levels of spoil and scree now faced him, littered with disconnected walls and random blocks of crumbling buildings. The adit's mean, black mouth still all too visible, but this time was jammed open with a length of timber. Someone else had been here and done that. But who? Why? For a moment, fear whispered to him as he repositioned himself to face the farmer.

Click.

"Stay there," shouted Gwilym. "Don't move!"

One minute, then two, three, four, seemed more like a week in the perpetual soft soak of drizzle. And then, just as Jason was about to desert his post, he noticed a movement alongside the derelict engine house's nearest corner. A moving shadow solidifying inch by inch into what he realised was the young man in black. This time however, he carried an oar dripping dark weeds. Not only that, but he was proceeding towards Jason over the ravaged ground with that oar now raised to attack.

No time to obey Gwilym's instructions. He must move. Quick.

"What's up?" barked his companion.

"I'm not staying to find out. Come on," Jason said.

But the farmer with his own agenda, held the digital camera steady as the oncoming figure came closer, closer. Two mouldy sockets instead of eyes. The mouth a bleached, puckered wound.

"Hurry!" yelled Jason. "For Chrissake!" Yet what was his problem? How could a mere mirage present any danger? But mirages didn't speak. Or did they?

Yes.

"This is *my* place. Lle fi," came a surprisingly strong, young man's voice. "You and Gwilym, are you listening?" he said. "Leave it be."

By now, the farmer had shifted from his perch, camera gone, rifle cocked, to face his accuser. "You're guarding Margiad, is it?" Gwilym began in a non-threatening tone. "You can tell me, Robert. We were always close, weren't we? You and your little nephew, Gwilym. Remember?"

However, the spectre remained motionless and silent; that loaded oar ready to strike. Jason's heart seemed to stop because water – brown, muddy water – was leaking from that now gaping mouth. Next came the gurgle of bubbles that were nothing to do with the nearby stream. Then a shot. And another, coming from a different direction, further away. The forestry, Jason assumed. Rooks, pigeons, whatever.

"C'mon!" Jason yelled again, then began to run, faster than he'd done in months, stumbling, slithering away from the eerie past. The farmer could take care of himself, he reasoned. At least he was armed. He'd given him every chance to leave, and then, just as Jason finally reached Heron House's open iron gates, saw a mud-lined, beaten-up dark blue Ford Escort parked on the drive.

Immediately, something about it felt wrong and with an ever-increasing sense of danger, he quickened his pace.

32.

Sunday 5th April 2009 – 4.15 p.m.

As soon as they'd left Hurst Crescent, Helen's latest enemy made a short phone call to someone she couldn't quite hear, then led her by the arm back to the car.

"You humiliated me back there," Mr Flynn snarled. "Any more of that and you'll regret it. Understood? That Jew must be laughing all the way to the bank. I'm still three hundred quid worse off and Llyr Pitt-Rose could be ruling the fucking roost."

So that's what it's all about?

Helen forgot to close her mouth as they swung into Parkway heading east for Islington, going way too fast. She'd never heard him swear so much. Her driver had been left a derisory amount while Llyr Pitt-Rose could legally lay claim to a fortune. Could this cuckoo, with prior knowledge of this will and his status as a Pitt-Rose, have killed the chief beneficiary rather than wait his turn?

"Surely it's more than a coincidence Aunty Betsan being dead too," she ventured. "'Specially as Foundation Face had just glossed over it and why she'd benefited."

"You've poked your nose in enough. Just leave it to the cops."

And then, with another lurch of her aching stomach, Helen realised that hadn't he too, been hoping for the big windfall? Why else set off for London pretty sharpish yesterday morning before she and Jason had found the poor woman? Why so gutted in Dee Salomon's office?

More traffic lights, office blocks and the revamped King's Cross giving way to residential streets and chestnut trees too severely pruned. Perhaps like those at Heron House, they'd also been diseased.

And then, like a sly, cold breeze, came the thought that if the angry man next to her had killed Charles Pitt-Rose, the thug might be next. Even herself...

"To be honest, Mr Flynn, I'm more bothered about what you're *still* not telling me."

His pale eyes swivelled her way. "*What?*"

"Surely you don't need me to spell it out. For a start, why did you behave so oddly when I mentioned Marky, then Judge Markham?"

***

After that, another silence grew like a solid mountain between them.

Every few seconds, she glanced in both the nearest wing mirror and her vanity mirror to check her injured assailant wasn't around. Disguises were easy. He could be anybody out there, she thought, until she recalled his bloodstained legs. The noticeable limp.

"And you were quite out of order to announce the theft from my study in front of the woman," the Irishman snapped, as he found an empty parking space at the end of Thornhill Avenue and hauled up the handbrake. "I was trying to stick to the will issue, which God knows is bad enough news."

"Had there been important material stored there that you couldn't tell anyone about?" She scrutinised his every move. The snatching down of his visor. Screwing up his eyes then closing them. "Did you have a computer?"

"Yes," he said.

"And Internet access?"

"That's my business. More to the point, how about the courtesy of telling me *when* the theft occurred."

"Last night some time," Helen said.

"You might have said. That was Sergeant Rees' first question when I phoned him back there."

How did he know? Neither she nor Jason had mentioned it.

She added, "I'd noticed from outside that your sash window was broken. Perhaps, if Gwenno Davies locked your study door after you'd gone, that's how her son got in. Or she gave him a key."

"Shut up about him, will you? And no-one can climb that ivy any more than the Matterhorn. I'd been in too much of a rush to get away to lock everything up properly." He sighed like someone auditioning for Hamlet. "What a gift. What a fucking gift. Now, I just want out."

She tried to ignore the noticeable drop in temperature that seemed to be surrounding them; the solid menstrual gush leaving her body. The kind that might have bled into that old carpet in Jason's top bedroom where God only knew what had happened. "So why bother with Sandhurst Mansion when we could both be getting back and on our way?"

Now he was gripping her thigh. Too tight, pinning her to the seat.

"I'll tell you when I'm ready."

***

As arranged, Mrs Pachela was waiting inside the porch of Sandhurst Mansion, obviously keen to get away. Her anxious eyes roamed up and down Thornhill Road as she extracted not only the required set of keys, but two pairs of surgical gloves from her handbag. "You don't want to leave prints here, do you?" she said to Mr Flynn. "The police can't keep away

202

from here at the moment."

"Clever idea." Mr Flynn took the items and handed over the bundle of notes.

"I meant to tell you I had a message on my phone at home, warning me not to get involved with you. He mentioned you by name. I was quite frightened," said Mrs Pachela.

"He?"

A panicky shrug. "I don't know. No number either."

"Look, London's full of oddballs. Is there a concierge around?"

"Used to be till Mr Pitt-Rose complained about his radio being too loud. A new one's starting tomorrow."

Now the chameleon was checking for evidence of CCTV cameras and whatever else might spoil his plan, and Helen noticed small red veins turning the whites of his eyes pink.

"Good. Now is there anything else I need to know about Charles before you go. Confidential, of course. Any boyfriend, girlfriend? Other cars in his garage's visitor slot?" Mr Flynn asked.

"Not that I can think of. But you ought to know the police and men in white space suits took away much things. His computer, books, notebooks, old, brown photographs... I hated dusting them. They made me shiver," said Mrs Pachela.

"What photographs?" Flynn said.

She paused, biting her lip. "Of somewhere he called Hades. This big house it was. Dark, covered in ivy, with people in fancy dress by the front door, and a strange iron bird stuck next to one of the chimneys. Oh, and there was a picture of a swimming pool, but you wouldn't want to swim in that."

"Why Hades?" asked Helen, scanning her surroundings for her stalker's bald head and black duffle coat.

"Missy, if only the dead could speak," said Mrs Pachela.

***

Mr Flynn led the way into the galley-style kitchen, lined by bright orange-laquered units and a smart Range-style cooker complete with an industrial-sized hood. A cork-backed notice board was bare save for several ragged holes, suggesting whatever had been on there had been hurriedly removed.

She sniffed. Something and nothing...

Llyr Pitt-Rose?

"You start this end. I'll go the other," Mr Flynn, butted into her thoughts. "Five minutes max."

"What are we looking for? You said you'd tell me."

"Proof Charles Pitt-Rose was of unsound mind. Remember his solicitor's observations? How agitated he'd seemed?"

Bastard.

Judging by the lack of booze and suitable glasses, the apartment's dead owner must have been teetotal. Anorexic as well, given the almost empty store cupboards. As Helen trawled each shelf, as instructed, she wondered again why exactly their owner's Inquest might be held in secret.

A sense of that same danger made her stop and listen for the slightest sound. Her skin prickling with anxiety. This was someone's private stuff and the tight gloves she wore made sure the embarrassing flush stayed on her face. As for their smell – they belonged to a hospital, not here.

She replaced half a packet of rock-hard penne next to a shrivelled tomato purée tube sporting a green fur collar under its cap. Dented tins of this and that; a slice of birthday cake complete with a blackened candle. Whose? She wondered. And how come such a well-off businessman had existed like this? By comparison, the pantry at Heron House was well-stocked.

"Eaten out, most likely." Mr Flynn had found more drawers to rifle through. His long fingers raking amongst replacement light bulbs, batteries, boxes of screws, rawlplugs and other man stuff. "That's what they do, isn't it? Busy city types with dough to spare?"

Was that a small resentment in his voice? After all, if his books had stayed published with more commissioned, he'd surely be up in London too, not holed up in the back of beyond?

"But no restaurant receipts so far." Helen now examined a packet soup dated November 2003. "I'm not so sure about your theory."

"Meaning?"

"He may have been the life and soul of the party in public but back here..."

"Spare me the psychobabble," Mr Flynn said. "Perhaps he was just a tight old git saving up for some last-minute dream."

"Paid you well enough, though," she retorted. "Only guessing."

"Well, don't."

***

While Helen'd just discovered a small, windowless bathroom, her ex-boss was striding from the kitchen into another room which seemed to double as a lounge and study. The noise of more drawers being opened and shut collided with the sudden peal of nearby church bells.

Either the police or another visitor had made sure nothing useful had been left. Here, a hard facecloth, there, a selection of Superdrug shower gels and a half-finished bottle of cough mixture. The plug hole stuffed with grey hairs.

She suddenly needed a window, anything for some air; and back in the kitchen, stared out over the communal garden hemmed in by high yellow-bricked walls. She wanted to run – bad period or not – to the nearest tube station and from there to Paddington. There were paintings to do. At least one to start with for her mam by Thursday. Then for the Coleridge Gallery. As for Jason, yes, she'd have to see him first.

"There'll be no hiding place. So don't get cocky. And if you squeal to anyone else, you'll end up in bin bags where no-one'll find you. Got it, bitch?"

With a cold sweat clinging to her skin, she realised that access to that garden was via a door in an adjoining lower storage area that Mr Flynn had overlooked.

Locked, but no sign of any key nor of a forced entry.

Meanwhile, still more banging sounds were coming from the lounge. He was in a strop. Excellent. She'd help make it worse in whatever way she could.

***

The bedroom, just the one, was a complete surprise. More like a vice den, all done out in purple wallpaper with blood-coloured devoré curtains drawn close, blotting out most of the daylight beyond. The faint smell lingering in the stale air reminded her of something she couldn't quite place and, with so little light, had to use her instinct and sense of touch to explore. In each corner, she could make out life-size bronze casts of lithe, naked athletes – all men – in the style of popular ancient Greek sculptors, while smaller contemporary figurines in shining steel, demonstrating the usual and not so usual homosexual positions with no detail spared, lined a shelf along the far wall. All this a world away from Betsan's pretty, porcelain collection.

Candles, too, from whose thick, twisted columns hung bulbous encrustations of surplus wax. She sniffed them and realised where she'd smelt incense before. On the top landing at Heron House by the Davieses' bedroom.

To her left, taking up most of the wall space, stood the biggest bed she'd ever seen. She ran her hand over its black leather headboard and matching bedspread, smooth and glossy as a wet runway, then moved towards a wide glass-fronted wardrobe reflecting her furtive form. Its parade of velvet jackets, silky suits and Ralph Lauren underwear, that had clearly been rifled through, hid nothing of interest.

Hurry.

A commode. Yes, but cleverly disguised as a normal chair. She lifted its black leather lid and caught her breath.

Stale pee. An inch of it.

Yuk.

Yet something intrigued her enough to make her lift up the inner polyurethane container by its handle and let her free hand roam the remaining space.

Yes...

Her fingers touched something lying at the bottom. She withdrew the intriguingly thin oblong, and soon realised it was some kind of book.

Quick.

Mr Flynn was shouting for her. Where could she hide whatever had been so enterprisingly hidden?

Her pants. They'd do, and within a few seconds she was back in the dead man's kitchen and making the right noises.

***

Helen joined the ratty Irishman in the lounge-cum-study, but stayed on the opposite side to him. Her discovery dug into her flesh. She thought he might at least ask if she'd found anything on the Davieses. But no. He was punishing her. Big surprise, especially after she'd suggested Jason get his money back tomorrow.

Now, in the Arctic silence and even more curious about the dead man's life, she clicked open an antique desk tucked inside a deep, arched alcove. Surely if its owner had killed himself, he'd have locked everything up beforehand?

There was even a key that worked. Normally, she'd have asked permission to use it, but nothing would ever be normal again. She was only being seen to co-operate so they could be on the M4 before dark then back at Heron House to pack her things for the next morning. That word 'encumbrances' if true, could well include her.

The room was losing light so Mr Flynn switched on an Art Deco desk lamp – its subdued glow casting him in ominous shadow as he pulled open drawer after drawer with renewed urgency. "Plenty of old rubbish about Oracle Services and cruises for gays." He slammed the latest one shut. "Someone must have been here already. And I don't just mean the police."

"I've just found this," she said, having already extracted a stiff, cream-coloured card whose pinked edge was worn soft with use. Better to share it than be found out later. She was hiding enough already.

PULLMAN CLUB
3-6, Friar Lane,
W1
020743921
Full Member – C E Pitt-Rose & EW †

But it was those two initials and the cross in the bottom right-hand corner that had caught her eye. "Ethan Woods by any chance?" she asked, her tired brain on overtime.

A pause.

"Could be anyone."

As I thought…

"And the cross?"

"A lot of clubs have their own symbols."

But there was more.

Underneath it, attached by what looked like the remains of old glue, was a small, square photograph of a boy staring out from over a too-big collar and tie. His fair hair neatly parted. His big eyes wary. No more than eight years old, she guessed. On the back was the handwritten name Nancy Powell and the cryptic comment – 'C. Our bachgen who will never come back'.

Helen slipped that down the side of her pants to join the diary, and took the card over to Mr Flynn. Surprise flickered in his washed-out eyes as he took it.

"If those initials *do* mean Ethan Woods, perhaps Charles Pitt-Rose didn't know he'd turn out to be a half-brother," she said.

He glanced over to the door leading to the hallway. He was on edge, big time.

"Are you thinking what I'm thinking?"

"I can't. The Pullman's one of London's most exclusive clubs. Why bring a yokel like him along, whatever the pedigree? Unless it signifies something else entirely."

At last.

"Gay?" ventured Helen.

A shrug that didn't quite convince. "No. A leech. A sly leech."

Helen blinked. This was a result.

"Shall I ring their number? Sound them out?" she said. "Might be someone there on a Sunday."

"No," he said too quickly. "There won't be. Just keep looking here. Get a result and I'll top up your pay."

The desk lamp flickered, then lost half its power. She suddenly felt the weight of darkness, of unwanted possibilities mounting up by the second. Mr Flynn was busy again. The silver-tongued lizard who'd lured her and Jason into Heron House for reasons not yet adequately explained. "I think you do know all about Margiad," she began, "and what went on at Heron House while she was alive." She watched him close the drawer he'd been investigating and make his way towards her. His white surgical gloves glistening despite the dull, syrupy light. "I also think you arranged to have your computer and everything taken. You weren't that bothered about losing it, were you? You must think I'm thick."

Now she'd done it.

He turned to face her. "That's outrageous."

"So was admitting there was no internet connection there when you had it. You couldn't have Jason and me prodding around, could you? So why advertise for us? I know plenty of people who'd like an answer. And as for your books. Another lie, is it? Let's be honest." Her flushed cheeks began to burn. The adversary was closer now, with not whisky on his breath but something else, rank and sour.

She was trapped with him in Charles Pitt-Rose's shadowy world where the nearest door was too far away. So, what had she got to lose? "Perhaps you and that Llyr bastard are best mates after all. Maybe Heron House was left to Betsan to finally get rid of *you* and the Davieses."

"Shut up."

"No, I won't. There's two more things. You must have gone near her place on Wednesday morning to have seen Gwilym Price's dead dog. I also noticed you weren't smelling of your usual whisky and your boots were really filthy. And how come you knew Betsan had been expecting someone on Saturday? Neither I nor Jason told you that. And I wonder why the cops there haven't so far contacted you?"

"I said, give it a rest."

She was about to answer back, but an all-too-familiar bald-headed figure was limping through that half-open door, bringing with him that old meat smell again. But before she could move, a pair of rubbery hands slapped her eyes shut, then tightened over her throat.

"Got her," Llyr said. "What now?"

"Yet another visit, eh? My, my, such devotion."

"Do I help out or not?"

Pause. The Irishman said yes.

"Then get yourself spruced up," Mr Flynn added. "Pronto. Michael Markham's fussy. You may not care about your life, but I do about mine."

33

Sunday 5th April 2009 – 4.40 p.m.

With his head too full of everything he'd just seen and heard on Cerrigmwyn Hill, Jason ran up Heron House's drive past the blue car and kept his fist on the doorbell. He was a coward in capital letters. Something alien to Dan Carver. Perhaps now he could make amends. "Come on... come on..." he swore at the unmoving door, before spotting Gwenno Davies peering out at him from the reception hall's front window.

"You wait," she mimed, relishing her control over him. "Scum."

That same bright pink lipstick she'd worn yesterday now swamped her mouth. Just one glimpse was enough to make his minimal stomach contents rise up to under his ribs. He glanced back at the unfamiliar car. Who had driven it here? And why no response to the doorbell?

He was just about to investigate on the swimming pool side of the house when a familiar voice called out. "You. Got something to show you."

Idris Davies.

Jason hesitated, then remembered how the man had admitted to fearing his own son. An Achilles heel that could pay him dividends. He pointed to the empty Escort. "Whose is that?"

"I said, got something to show you."

The army of gunmetal clouds that had delivered a steady drizzle all day, now got serious. A brisk, diagonal rain slanted over the scene, wetting yet again his leather jacket, blurring the gardener with his territory. But not the expression on his haggard face.

Shit-scared was the word.

He was gripping his giant besom for dear life as Jason moved up to him, preparing what he had to say. If he played his cards right, Idris Davies could be very useful indeed. "Is DC Prydderch around?"

"Sssh. Over here. Quick."

Jason followed him to the slippery outskirts of the once fine terrace. "I've just heard two shots coming from the forestry. Gwilym Price may be in danger." By the time Jason had finished his story, ghost and all, they were standing in an overgrown corner between a chimney base and the kitchen wall where budding nettles reached almost waist-high. Too much out of sight, out of mind, he thought, tempted to make a run for it.

"The cop's in there." Idris Davies raised his free arm to point at the pool whose black sludge overflowed its boundaries. "But I never did it. Honest to God, I wouldn't harm a fly. Ask Gwenno."

Jason stared at the mess of neglect in front of him. There were no bubbles, no obvious sign of footprints or any recent disturbance. Was this oddball, like Monty Flynn, allergic to the truth? Was the fat Fuzz really beneath all that lot? If so, it was too terrible to imagine.

"When?"

"Just before you turned up."

"What happened? Did he slip?"

"No. It was the maniac known as my son who pushed him. And," he bent forwards to place his dry, tobacco-scented lips by Jason's ear, "he's in that frigging car an' all, I'm telling you. Don't go near it. It's a trap, see."

"You're lying. He's in London." Careful not to mention Helen.

"He isn't."

Torn between giving the man a good shake-up and kneeing his bony butt, Jason moved towards the pool, half imagining those same black-suited men and their vivid red glasses of wine all over again. He wanted to check more closely for signs of a struggle, when a sudden poke between his shoulder blades made him topple forwards.

"What the Hell?"

Too late to steady himself. Too late for anything except to meet the thick, stinking night head-on. His cries for help rewarded by a harder, more purposeful shove, and a laugh. No, two laughs. One old, one younger, as his mouth filled up and slowly, with nothing to cling to, he began to sink.

***

"Get rid of those wheels now."

"Where?"

"Down the Towy. It's in full spate. Perfect."

Jason heard all this above the sloshing sound of his feet treading the sludge to keep afloat, but soon thoughts of Helen, his brother and his mother all too far away, took over. And that waiting room in Pinetree Road where this had begun.

Even though he could swim, he wouldn't last long.

Take a chance...

With every last ounce of effort, he found an edge. Felt solid concrete beneath his hands. He shook his head for the stuff to slip from his eyes, so he could glimpse through sticking eyelids how the land lay.

So far so good, except he was sick. And as for raising his dead weight upwards, forget it. Then, a female voice eked through the slime to reach his blocked-up ears.

211

"Try again, Jason... For my sake. Please... please..."

"Who's that? Helen?"

"No. Not her. *Me*. Margiad, remember? I need you to stay alive..."

Jesus...

The steady rain did its work. For once, he thanked it for clearing his hands so they could get a purchase.

"Now. Up you get," she urged in a sickly-sweet voice. "One, two, three..." Then came the strangest sensation as if someone was actually pushing him. Someone determined, possessing almost superhuman strength...

Hell, no.

An invisible weight was also trapping his fingers against the pool edge. Too heavy for them to move.

He screamed then imagined he could hear laughter before another prod connected with his forehead, and another. He squinted up into the kind of yellow-brown light he'd seen before, and shook his head again to clear his view. But that made no difference. Then came footsteps, voices. All men.

"Poke him again, Marky. Harder this time."

Marky? Where'd he heard that name before. Think...

"You try, Jimmy. He's a determined blighter alright."

"Who the Hell are you?" yelled Jason, before more black slime invaded his mouth. "Get off!"

Another thrust, this time just missing an eye, while that rigid pressure on his fingers ratched up until they were numb. With the next blow, he saw four pairs of black shoes. Four pairs of black-trousered legs. Blood red cummerbunds, bow ties, then faces. All smiling.

"Please don't die like my Robert," begged the one who'd called herself Margiad. "Like all the others..."

He didn't hear the rest. How could he, drifting away as her voice faded, to be replaced by what could only be described as the purest peace?

***

"Mr Robbins!" came another man's frantic shout. "I'm sorry, I'm sorry, d'you believe me? It's not my fault, d'you hear? Honest to God, I was made to do it. Look, grab hold of this."

From between gummed-up eyelids, Jason glimpsed Idris Davies running along the poolside towards him, wearing giant-sized Wellingtons. His besom's handle jutting out so it was just within reach. He held on tight until a cloud of doubt made him let go. But what choice did he have? This sod was all he'd got.

"I'm telling you, my son it is what shoved you in. I'm scared of him, see," the old man went on, "he makes me do things. Bad things what I'd never dream of. Gwenno, too."

But something wasn't right.

"You're lying. That wasn't Llyr with you just now. No way."

"On my dead mam's heart, it's true. Just grab the handle again."

Jason clung to it like he'd never clung to anything else before, as the gardener guided him through the fetid gunge towards what turned out to be hidden steps below the rusted handrails. However, the extra bulk accumulated on his body dragged him downwards, until his left foot felt the first step at the very bottom.

"Wrong way. Up you come."

"Wait. There's some kind of obstacle down here. Is it Prydderch by my feet?"

Idris Davies stopped. Crossed himself with his free hand. "No. I lied. Can't help it sometimes. Not my fault, see?"

Yet there was definitely something preventing Jason's right boot from finding a foothold. Whatever it was, felt long and bulky. Perhaps some old log or other.

A third desperate shove moved it away, leaving him free to climb then stumble on to the silt-covered tiles. Having spat out the black muck from his mouth and wiped the same from his nose and eyes, he realised that Idris Davies, unlikely rescuer, had gone. But someone else had taken his place. Not outside, but in his head, via his cold, clammy ears. "Now you listen to me," came that tense young woman's voice again. "Seeing as you've no intention of writing any of my story down, we'll try the other way."

"What other way?" When all he wanted was to strip out of his ruined gear, and get into the shower.

"I know why you're here. Do you want me to tell you or not?"

"Just leave me alone!"

He tried running but couldn't. Each boot weighed a ton. Instead, he let the thick, persistent rain batter his head, delivering most of the slime down his neck. Icing his bones.

***

No blue car and Heron House's front door wide open, but not invitingly so. A whiff of perfume he recognised, then the dead fire and the answerphone's green light flickering. No time to ditch his stinking boots or worry about the mess his every step was making. He had to reach it.

There was one message and, as he pressed PLAY, prayed Gwenno

Davies wasn't nearby.

"It's Miss Sandwich, remember me?"

Helen...

He could barely hear her. "I can't really talk," she began, almost lost among a background of running water. "But you mustn't worry, OK? Just hope that only you pick this up. Got some news. First off, that foul guy Llyr's been hanging around here big time, but I am in control..."

Thank you, Idris.

"Next, Idris Davies isn't his real da..."

"Jesus."

"MF and I have been to C. P-R's solicitor, then his Islington flat." She lowered her voice so he could barely hear it. "Pin your ears back and delete once I've finished. I'll also be wiping my phone..."

Other equally incredible news unfolded until a sudden silence in which he realised that without her, this big old house was just a decrepit shell. Meanwhile, a noxious, black puddle around his boots had spread to the Persian rug's fringed edge. Nothing he could do about it because all at once came an imperceptible darkening of the light from the still-open front door and the bedraggled, limping form of a man he barely recognised, staggering towards him.

34.

Monday 6th April 2009 – 7.50 a.m.

It was too early. Llyr could have done with at least another two hours' kip. As it was, too much had gone wrong.

"I never enquired after your finger," Llyr said to his rival once they were seated in the Volvo, parked near the B&B they'd shared overnight with The Ginger who'd just managed to give her employer the slip. "Been careless somewhere? Want to tell me about it?"

Paddy started the engine and pulled away from the gutter. "You upset my upholstery," he warned."You get the bill."

Llyr smiled despite feeling sick inside. The early sunshine warmed his face but made little difference to the rising tension between him and his driver since yesterday's meet-up at the gay's flat. While the trespassers had been busy, he'd managed to locate an internet café and, by removing the fake calculator's micro SD card, played back their revelations following the Hurst Crescent visit. No wonder he, Llyr, had lain in his single bed going over everything, making plans while watching the wall clock's hands nudge round until daylight.

"Never mind the upholstery," he said, "I'll soon be able to buy you a new car *and* the rest."

Paddy flicked on his right indicator too early before leaving Nantwich Grove, to follow signs for Sydenham. Immediately that welcome sun slipped behind a cloud. And another. "I need to concentrate," was all he said.

Llyr let it go, thinking what if the now-tagged Helen Jenkins was trotting off to the pigs at this very moment? Her carer would be punished for that and for his excursions with her, while the other mistake he'd encouraged from Hounslow into Heron House, took his score to six. His own so far, just one.

Michael Markham, The Order's paymaster, swinging singleton and property developer *extraordinaire* had summoned them to his crib in Dulwich for some explanations. Best play it safe, Llyr reminded himself. Even though, hand on heart, he'd done his best as Ethan Woods and not got the expected result, there was still a future. Also for Markham's da, the biggest shagger of all, who'd now reached the Great Whorehouse in the sky.

"Heard the latest?" he said to the Irishman. "Mr Markham senior's just passed on. Prostate, it was. Very nasty. I'm sure our boss'll welcome some company right now."

"You're taking the piss. And why *Mr* Markham all of a sudden? You always call him…"

"Give it a rest. OK?" The bug he'd used was indiscriminate. Every voice important.

"I read the group email midday Saturday," Llyr boasted. "You must have been on your way to the big smoke at the time. For your investigations."

"Is my computer and all the gear in the right place?" Paddy's bony knees pressed against the fabric of his black shiny trousers. Two sharp blows on them, thought Llyr, and he'd be in a squatter for life.

"No-one bosses me around. I had enough of that at Holmwood."

"Second time of asking. Is my gear in the right place?"

"Angred shaft. OK?" Geoffrey Powell's idea seeing you'd already been down there. In some interesting company, apparently." He glanced again at Flynn. Time for more pressure. "What about your memory sticks? I couldn't find them."

"With her phone." Paddy patted his coat's inner pocket. The unflattering sun on him once again. "She'd deleted everything on it, damn her. By the way, your threat to her like that wasn't very helpful."

"Mr Markham'll decide what's helpful and what isn't," said Llyr.

"He can get stuffed."

Llyr grinned. This was going well. Time therefore for more straight talking.

"Wait till he finds out what you and The Ginger did. You got a death wish?"

"If you'd not messed up on the M4 on Saturday night, I wouldn't have had to babysit for the rest of the bloody weekend. And bloody it's been, too."

Llyr looked at him. "What d'you mean?"

"Wimmin's problems. Fibroids, whatever. Damn nuisance. Slowed us down good and proper. She'd never mentioned it before. So no good blaming me."

"I never said a thing."

"Anyway, not everyone's fussy in the servicing department. Look at Margiad. Didn't stop her. That's what I'll say in my defence when the grilling starts," said Flynn.

That Welsh name took Llyr by surprise. Well, almost.

"Who's she?"

"Damn."

Llyr studied that pock-marked face. Holmwood had been full of fuck ups like him. He should know.

"A local pro with the same medical issues, but who knew the ropes. Knew when to open her legs and the rest. Get my meaning? A hard act to follow, but I seriously thought Miss Ginger could be licked into shape. That's all," said Flynn.

Licked into shape.

Llyr himself had done enough of that in his time for no purpose. Paddy was rabbiting on again. Digging his own grave. Every word a shovelful of earth.

"Whenever the camera showed her undressing or in the shower, I'd thought, yes. You'll do very nicely. Trouble is, I never bargained for that Robbins twat answering my advert. Fancying her. Protecting her."

"You should've got rid of her straight off. Mr Markham and Geoffrey Powell wanted *me* to choose the new talent. Not you. The Swansea Clubs were a much better idea than *The Lady*, for God's sake. Cardiff and Newport as well. I'd even have gone sniffing round the Rhondda if I'd had to."

Margiad's name had just uncoiled like a dark spring in the back of Llyr's mind.

"And talking of mistakes, remember Abergwesyn?" The Irishman gloated before suddenly stopping at traffic lights. "Let's see what happens there, eh?"

"Below the belt, that."

"Just up your street, then," said Flynn.

Llyr noticed a fly struggling inside the heating vent, pulled it free and let it go. Time was when he'd have watched it suffer. Picked off its wings. And here he was, like a kid again, metal-detecting for approval. Even from someone he despised.

"When you referred to me as 'a leech. A sly leech' at Charlie's flat, did you mean it?" Llyr asked.

Paddy lost concentration. Swerved into the kerb and out again. He'd not known about the bugs placed in each room. Nevertheless, in his usual cunning way, played along. "Course. Honesty's my middle name."

Llyr restrained himself from rearranging those unusual teeth, waiting for the big question. Up it came. Paddy coughed. No phlegm. Another tease, like the rest of him. "So what are your plans should Heron House fall into your lap?"

Talk the talk, boyo. I can lie too, you know…

"Going with the flow, of course. Once our boss has sorted any planning permissions and the refurbishments are done, we could be up and running by the summer. You'll see. Long live The Order!" He patted Flynn's nearest bony knee. Nothing too familiar, mind. He'd had enough of that. Getting the old queen in Sandhurst Mansion to play ball in the hope he'd leave everything to him in his will.

"Wednesday's post-mortem had better find you squeaky clean, then," Flynn said.

"What's that supposed to mean? You been squealing that I strung him up?"

"Never. You know me."

***

As the Volvo turned into familiar territory, Llyr felt his stomach drop as it always did when remembering being alone in Heron House's cellar with the one he'd thought was his da. Why afterwards, he'd gone out and shot the herons one by one, so the pervert would get the blame. But did anyone listen to this cry for help? He was the invisible kid. Kept in the dark in more ways than one, wondering why he looked so different from his molester. The man with the besom. The bully's hands and the rest.

He pulled out his cheap Nokia – his tenth so far – and found Michael Markham's number.

Langland Road was exactly as Llyr had remembered from his first recruitment visit two years ago, except now, unlike those chestnut trees he'd poisoned in Rhandirmwyn, the ones lining the road were beginning to bud. The boss would be ready and waiting. Best to warn him they were close. Ease in gradually.

"Just need reminding of the last leg, sir," said Llyr. "We're almost there."

"Count six white art deco houses with dark green railings to your left," said the posh voice after a sly chuckle. "Continue past the Trattoria and park well down St. Mary's Road. And I mean, well down."

Llyr lowered his voice. "Sir, I got the company you asked for."

"I've heard him. Whose car?"

"His. He's driving."

"Avoiding cameras I hope or the plate'll end up on the Met's recognition database. What we don't need. And remember, back door, if you don't mind. You cleaned up?"

"Yes, sir," Llyr lied. Markham would have to take him as he found him. Last night in Boyd's B&B had done him no favours. Camp beds for a start. One basin, one towel and stained bog between the three of them.

"And I'm sorry about your dad, sir," he added at the end.

An unappreciative silence.

Call ended.

Llyr checked his phone's inbox and with one click, dead lover boy's sweet, useless nothings were deleted for good.

***

Llyr, with the calculator bug safe in his duffle coat pocket, set off round the corner rehearsing his spiel, keeping an eye out for every kind of camera and other prying eyes. Although the blood on his cuts had dried, he'd botched washing his jeans and each leg still weighed a wet ton. Michael Markham wouldn't be best pleased. But all wasn't lost. Not yet.

"I'll do the talking," said the keen Irishman, catching up. "After all, I was first to get news of the will."

But he'd not had the call about Charlie.

***

Kitted out in a beige Pringle sweater and brown corduroy slacks, the tall, middle-aged paymaster, complete with a black armband and matching tie, bearing The Order's symbol of a discreet black cross, was already by his back door. Straightaway his eyes alighted on Paddy's index finger and its fresh plaster, then Llyr. All his efforts in that choking boudoir, the Bentley's back seat, his own sofa bed and wherever else, had been in vain. The Order had invested in Llyr big time. His room in Beulah, the Euston studio, the van, not to mention travelling expenses… Would he now have to pay it all back?

You twat, Charlie. Flynn, too.

"All I can say," began Markham in a fake reasonable voice that made Llyr's gut go walkabout, "it's a good job Miss Griffiths has no kin lurking amongst the sheep droppings, and that Geoffrey Powell helped acquire your original birth certificate from the old queen's solicitor. Could have well and truly scuppered our future plans otherwise." He gestured to Llyr to come nearer. "You obviously didn't pleasure your half-brother hard enough or enterprisingly enough. How else can this unexpected result be explained? Three out of ten for that. Nil for your appearance, except," his cool hand followed Llyr's shaved jaw line, "you're much better smooth."

The words half-brother had made Llyr's throat fill up. He gripped the door frame to steady himself.

"Mind you," his boss went on, "if he'd realised your true identity, he'd never have let you through the door and into his bed."

"I never was a bummer, OK?" Llyr protested, "I'm straight."

219

He recalled their first clinch after a meal at a French restaurant. Then the rest… "And you try taking the size of him. A wonder I didn't need stitches *and* new tonsils. Sir, you really should've picked someone else to do your dirty work."

Paddy was clearly still enjoying himself.

"Ah, but who else possessed such a beautiful body?" Markham's new acrylic teeth were too big for his mouth. "Such skill?" He bent closer to the jeans, sniffed then straightened up. "But you still stink to high Heaven. Who cut you?"

Llyr also noticed how stray grains of muesli had lodged in the man's trimmed beard.

"Anyone we should deal with?"

"Some ape after his crack," Paddy said, trying to sound cool. "Llyr's done well to get here. Fair play, as they say in Wales."

"I wasn't expecting a fan club, and I'm not taking your coats. Get in." Their host indicated a gloomy passageway lined with a range of expensive outdoor gear, leading into the less showy end of the house. "Even wisteria can't be trusted."

Just as in January for the New Year's planning meeting, an impressive array of golf bags and gleaming golf clubs stood at the ready. Llyr had never been tempted to pick one up. Shaved grass, like shaved balls, wasn't his scene. As for where Markham played, he thought it was somewhere near South Norwood. An overcrowded cesspit like the rest of London.

They were ushered into the oppressively beamed lounge whose subdued lighting reminded Llyr of the Pullman Club. Through the open door to the adjoining study, he spotted not only the man's Black Knights Templar gauntlets and triangular apron hanging up, but also his pc's screen's tracking map. A shivering blur. Rhandirmwyn was rubbish in that department with too many trees and everything. Not his fault. He'd done his best. So go easy, he told himself. He was a Pitt-Rose now and, with a decent lawyer and that original birth certificate safe in his, not Markham's, hands, he wouldn't ever have to come here again. Nor endure any more of Geoffrey Powell's unwelcome attentions.

For the first time, Llyr felt a shred of gratitude to his sexed-up old mother.

His boss meanwhile, had switched on a gigantic flat screen TV where news of more bombings in Iraq came rolling in on the dust. Where the silent, treacherous Paddy was suddenly too close behind him. "How about a picture show?" Flynn suggested, way too confidently. "See if our Mr

Robbins is behaving himself at last?"

"Take a pew both," said their host, ignoring Flynn, opening out the *Financial Times* and laying it down in a very obvious way on one of the black leather settees. Their seats dimpled by frequent use. "For you, Taffy," he said to Llyr. "Expensive leather needs protecting while we discuss your recent cock-ups – excuse the pun. I mean disastrous errors."

"Him and all, remember?" Llyr pointed to Paddy who cast him a Method School stare of pure hate.

"Yes. Him and all."

Paddy sat clicking his finger bones one by one, like he'd done at the B&B. Lank, uncombed hair all over the place. Markham stayed standing too close; those corduroy legs like two brown pillars ending in a scowl. No offer of a coffee or beer, mind. Not even a glass of frigging tap water. "Mistake number one," he focussed on Llyr. "Instead of contacting us for help, you abandoned our van on the M4. What a gift for the filth that was. We'll be pushed to keep them off your tail now. You realise that? Especially as you were foolishly uninsured, untaxed."

Paddy nodded.

"We agreed you keep Miss Ginger with you at all costs and bring her here first thing yesterday."

"Why did Paddy choose skirt with such a gob on her in the first place?" Llyr retaliated while Markham made for his study. "I wouldn't have."

The Irishman flicked up a finger. An indecent gesture.

"Where's she now?" the golfer addressed him on his way back into the lounge. "You never said, and my tracker's just lost her signal."

Paddy's eyebrows shifted upwards as he turned on Llyr. "Is *that* what you did while she was asleep? Why wasn't I told? Just like I had to discover by accident that the queer was dead..."

Markham cut him out.

"What exactly happened at Boyd's B&B?"

"He let her go, didn't he, sir?" Llyr said, seeing Paddy wince. "First thing this morning. Taking a leak he was, while I was still out of it. Couldn't keep up with her, could he? Too much whisky in his veins."

Markham came closer to the Irishman. His flecked eyes like an owl's before the strike. "Not only that, you've been taking her to all the wrong places, too. Tut, tut, Paddy. So what's to be done with you?"

Flynn was turning a promising shade of green.

"We don't do business unilaterally. What did you feed Jobiah?"

"Nothing."

"You were a traitor to even step through Tolpuddle Street's portals."

The Irishman shook his head as if in disbelief. "You used a tracker on me? That's a pretty cheap stunt."

"And an audio recorder. You can't blame us." Markham had had enough of him. Clear as day. "Were your prints taken? Your DNA? We can soon find out."

"As if. Anyway, it was her fault. She dragged me in to report about him over there for picking her up Saturday night. Was I supposed to chuck her in the Thames? You wanted her here. I had to keep her on board."

Nul points.

"And the chicken-choker's flat? Anything useful for us?"

"Her idea again, not mine."

"Very risky. Her phone please." Markham held out his hand. "And your memory sticks."

Paddy faltered, which wasn't like him.

"Forgot, didn't I? Too much on."

Markham laughed. The suddenness of it made Llyr blink. "Move. I've a tournament to get to, plus funeral arrangements to finalise. At least my pa didn't want any fuss. Cleaned up after himself too, if you get my meaning. Thoroughly I might add, unlike some not so very far away." Again, he glowered down at Paddy. "I hope you deleted his rash and ridiculous final email?"

"Course I did."

"When?"

Paddy was squirming. Llyr remembered flies and butterflies in their death throes at the sharp end of his mam's dressmaking pins.

"Soon as I got it."

"I said, when?"

"I'm thinking."

The lounge's stale air seemed to suddenly cool. This wasn't going well.

"While you're thinking, we'd also like the keys Mrs Pachela so kindly sold you."

Paddy quickly emptied his coat pocket and when the Pullman Club card accidentally fell out onto the leather, the golfer was on it. Trouble was, Flynn couldn't stop yapping. "Dee Salomon thought Charles was frightened," he continued ploughing his own dangerous furrow. "And should his post-mortem suggest suicide, she'd elaborate."

Markham pocketed the card.

"Also that any secret Inquest would be deeply worrying."

Llyr saw the look on the golfer's face. Knew *he'd* wanted to be Charles Pitt-Rose's killer all along, hoisting the major obstacle to its death from the Bentley's newly-valeted bonnet. It was only while turned towards Paddy to hint at him to belt up, that he noticed a certain picture hanging on the less well-lit wall behind him. Had it come all the way from Heron House or was it another reproduction? Whatever. Seeing that weird upside-down crucifixion had always scared him shitless. It still did, because this wasn't only a biblical scene, but also an instructional manual.

***

Markham, meanwhile, was still dealing with Paddy. "For someone entrusted to set up new operations for us, you've caused too many problems. I won't waste time spelling them out except the word 'treason' – and I don't use that lightly – again comes to mind."

The Irishman's green complexion had turned to white. "Jesus and Mary help me."

"They won't."

He tried to stand, but Markham pinned him down. Llyr wondered who'd have to sort it if Paddy dropped his gut.

"I've done my best," Flynn whined.

"With freckles? White eyelashes and gynae problems?"

Llyr let out a nervous laugh. He couldn't help it.

"And your other success story?" The golfer settled himself in the adjoining seat. Thighs touching. "Did you check with us first before littering the place with also-rans? Nosy also-rans at that?"

His target was now the colour of herons' blood. Pinkly pale especially around the gills, while the grandfather clock in the darkest furthest corner suddenly chimed eight-thirty, making Llyr jump out of his skin.

"What was I supposed to do while that pair of crusts were trying to kill me? Remember you had to get the old Doc up there and pay him to keep quiet after the Warfarin incident? I should have gone straight to A&E, but that was the last thing you lot wanted," Flynn sniffed. "I've not been right since. Still get the nosebleeds. See what I mean?"

"I most certainly do. But that's because you'd poked the old bird too often."

Llyr pressed a hand over his own mouth. Knowing was one thing. Hearing about it like this, another. From his trouser pocket Michael Markham whipped out an immaculate white handkerchief bordered by small, black crosses, and passed it over. He then picked up the remote that worked the smaller screen below the TV. The grainy snowstorm effect

223

faded to reveal instead a scene that made Llyr's eyes pop, and Paddy to gasp...

"What we've been waiting for," smiled the golfer, sharpening the focus to where a veiny old hand was working someone's cock into life against the backdrop of a double bed's padded headboard. The riding crop's tapered end was busy too. "You and Gwenno no less, Mr Flynn. Only last week. Clearly having too much fun. Just like Mr Robbins in the kitchen while you were away. But not for long. Only a few seconds unfortunately, till the film ran out."

Mr Flynn, now. Definitely not good news...

"It's against the law to have CCTV without everyone's permission," said Paddy.

"In our case, cameras are a necessity."

Llyr dared himself to watch. This could be him all over again, at the farm now below the reservoir and at Heron House. He turned away from the screen.

"In case you ask," Markham said to Llyr, "your mother and her brother are at this moment being dealt with. They've long overstayed their welcome. Let's say, an unfortunate accident is unfolding as we speak. I'm sorry, Llyr, but I'm sure you'll understand. They've had a good innings. Longer than most." Markham glanced at the grandfather clock's face and checked it against his own. "To every thing there is a season and a time to every purpose under Heaven."

Llyr wondered precisely what 'being dealt with' meant, but couldn't find it in his wrecked heart to care. Wondered too about the two grands' worth to relocate them.

"Think of a lovely reservoir opened in 1972 by Princess Alexandra," added Markham. "A very useful dumping ground indeed. Ed Rees was right about that."

The Llyn Brianne reservoir.

Deep as Hell, but not such a bad place to end up in. And so what if his Welsh mamgu and tadci's little farm also lay beneath its icy water? Best place, to be honest, strapped down for ever in their iron beds, unable to harm anyone any more. They'd raised both Gwenno and Idris to expose him to far worse than any smelting fumes they'd ingested. Stuff Llyr should never have seen. Was it any wonder he'd turned out the way he had? In and out of trouble like a terrier with too many rat holes. Except that right now, and before he got old himself, he'd reached the end of his tour of duty. If he played his cards right he could soon be sitting on a fortune. Not ruling the roost, like Paddy had said, choosing classy meat and even pink pants to make more dough. But a log cabin and thousands of grassy acres in Montana. Far, far away.

Soon Paddy's handkerchief matched the colour of the red cummerbund Llyr had been given to wear on special occasions. Michael Markham stood up, helped the nosebleed to his feet, then, having slapped out his own trouser creases, indicated the cloakroom. "But before you go and spoil my newly-cleaned washbasin, you both should hear some other news. Last Monday, we, meaning myself and Geoffrey, finally located some very important remains. Felt it was time for a spring clean, so to speak."

"Remains?" queried Paddy through the borrowed handkerchief.

"A whole skeleton, in fact, of Robert Price, a Welsh conchie. A nobody, who could have ruined a lot of careers including mine."

"Whereabouts?" Llyr asked while the Irishman made for the cloakroom.

A pause. But pride won over caution.

"Buried in a small cave off the River Towy. Below the road out of Rhandirmwyn." The way he pronounced the name of that village, made Llyr wince. Typical Saes who hadn't got a clue. "Lured there on Christmas Eve by the ever-loyal Margiad. A real daddy's girl. Oh, and we also have the headmaster's notebook. So kind of him to think of us as well."

Markham then joined the bleeder where, from the open door, Llyr heard tap water gushing into the sink. He tried jogging his own memory. Before he'd been sent to the special school, there'd been talk of a Robert Price having a pregnant lover. He could not remember any more.

"Who was this Margiad?" Llyr called out.

The cloakroom cold tap was turned off.

"Seeing as Heron House will soon be yours, best you know."

Llyr felt sick again. And thanks to his mam putting herself about, he'd also be Margiad's step-brother, with even less claim to Heron House should she still be alive somewhere with greedy great-grand kids.

As Llyr crept over to St. Peter and raised the frame's lower edge to see the handwritten name on the other side, he realised Charlie hadn't breathed a single word about her. His only sister.

And here was her name on the same print that had hung in his bedroom.

***

The cloakroom tap must have been turned off again. Llyr stood by the doorway filled by Markham's toned physique. The other man just a sniffing, snivelling shadow.

"Is Margiad dead, too?" Llyr queried. "If not, where's her grave?"

His boss back kicked the door to close it on him, but didn't quite succeed.

Llyr stayed put. Ears on alert. Just then, from somewhere a phone began ringing until its answering machine took over. Tempted to investigate, he stopped when raised voices reached him from the cloakroom. Markham sounding even meaner. "And as for the chief beneficiary, Mr Flynn, any problems with her?"

"No."

"If I'd known Charles was going to top himself when he did, we'd have waited a bit. But there we go. Had to be done. Specially since that cosy chat old Betsan had with you last Wednesday morning, threatening to spill her happy memories to the media." Markham's voice then sharpened. "And no-one saw you pop in on Saturday either to firm up that cosy lunch *à deux*?"

"Give me a break."

"Main thing is, did you tidy up afterwards? Leave no prints of any kind? All curtains left open as you'd said they normally were?"

"I'm telling you, there was no mess. She was easy, as if she wanted to go to Heaven and I was doing her a favour," Flynn said.

Another lie.

"I'm not talking mess. I'm talking smell. Chloroform."

"Not a trace."

"Is this the truth?"

The question was then repeated in such a way that Llyr's breakfast burger turned over. Before The Ginger and the Saes had shown up, he'd glimpsed the old girl's broken ornaments from her kitchen. The result of a rage usually so well hidden, like some of them at Holmwood. Honey on the tongue one minute. Poison the next.

"What d'you think I am?"

"I actually don't have the words, Mr Flynn."

But Markham was still playing games. "Did you clear away your place setting at her table?"

"Naturally."

"How can I believe you when you'd left such a shambles at our future base? Even the St. Peter print which Prydderch's just delivered here?"

"Who's been telling tales?"

"Guess. And a good job, too."

Llyr flinched.

"He's a bastard," gurgled Paddy.

"Well, that's accurate enough, but your track record doesn't exactly inspire confidence. And if you think we're refunding your session with Dee

Salomon, who incidentally declined to deal with our prompt calls on Friday morning, you've another thing coming. In fact, *you* owe us. And your pathetic little bequest."

Sounds of a scuffle. Of more water running. More commands. One that made Llyr swallow hard. "If you want to keep breathing, get rid of Robbins by the 7th. Deep in the forest, away from any felling. Understood? Plus irrefutable proof you've succeeded. We want to see four, used, six-inch nails. Nothing less, and no mistakes."

Just then, a high-pitched alarm sound issued from his study.

Tracker alert.

Markham stepped from the cloakroom, hands wet, face flushed, to take a look. "The Ginger's heading back to base. I've already made arrangements there and, by the way, if her mother calls her on the phone I've got, there'll be no reply."

Llyr picked up more gurgling and spluttering noises. More protests. Paddy certainly had stamina when he needed it, but Markham had a Glock 9 milli.

Suddenly, on the TV screen, came a larger than life image of his white Transit in some yard or other. All wound round with police tape while his old surname came over like a whisper on the breeze. "The police are warning the public that Llyr Davies, who also calls himself Ethan Woods, is highly dangerous, could be armed, and on no account to be approached."

The door to the rear lobby was still ajar. What did he owe the Irishman? Anybody? He'd failed in all departments and now was his chance. If he missed it, he'd be sampling a metal table next to his step-brother. He thought about his birth certificate with Edmund Pitt-Rose named on it as father. It would have been good to see it, but he could always get a copy. Having cleared his mobile's Address Book and Inbox, he dropped it together with the calculator and Charles Pitt-Rose's keys on to the nearest settee, then made his move.

35.

Now what?

Although Helen had managed to kick and bite her way out of that grungy B&B they'd all holed up in for the night, it was kneeing her betrayer in the balls that had finally seen him off. He'd then chased her with surprising speed along Nantwich Grove as its orange street lights had faded.

No point dwelling on how they'd all shared that so-called 'family' room on the first floor; how she'd forced herself to stay awake until she could flee both men, who were clearly operating under instruction. The younger thug had accused her and Flynn of knowing about the will, so he must have followed them to Hurst Crescent. Her instincts about him had been right. Wrong about the other. She must call the police and Jason, then hotfoot back to Heron House to collect her stuff.

Once and for all.

She wished she could have spoken to him directly while her captors had used what had passed for a bathroom. But perhaps he'd call her. Soon.

Her purse's innermost fold held £5.35 pence exactly. All in coins, their worth incompatible with their weight. At least she still had her Visa. But where was DCI Jobiah's card that she'd kept there, too?

Damn.

Her body was too full of bad blood, rising, falling, into her head, into her unchanged pad. She'd shelled out enough money to be by her boss' side and for what? The man from Crosskelly had betrayed her. The empty pork scratchings packet suddenly blown against her ankles, said it all. No wonder he'd been so eager to check out the will on a Sunday, then the flat. He had to outwit the cut-up roughneck.

Feeling invisible to the purposeful throng around her, she glanced up and down the busy street. Where were they both now?

***

Despite the morning rush hour's exhaust fumes, Helen could smell herself as old, dead meat. Her manky hair stuck to her head. Her imagination now working faster than her legs, letting in a deadly thread of paranoia that made her quicken. What if the grey Volvo should pass by? What if Flynn and his co-pilot had guns? London was full of them. And knives. What difference would one small 'pop' make in this crazy hubbub?

She must get away from this place while that little boy's photograph and his diary were still safe in her pants. While she still had a pulse. Jason's advice before he'd put the phone down. But first things first. She needed simply to stop and investigate properly what she'd discovered at the dead man's flat. Her toilet visits in the B&B had been listened in to. How sick was that? No way could she have studied the little book there or risked being heard turning its battered pages.

Soon the crowds and shops thinned out until she reached railings and a large open gate leading into a children's play area where the second bench along was thankfully unoccupied. She opened up her rucksack and withdrew a slender, dark green book which bore the embossed word *DIARY* along its leather spine. Although the tiny brass clasp yielded to her fingers, the even more minute key, attached by sellotape, wouldn't budge in the lock.

At last.

The lock finally clicked open and, with no-one else within snooping distance, she turned back the worn leather cover and its mottled end-paper and on the first thin page began to read:

This diary belongs to Charles Edmund Pitt-Rose
aged 8 years, 5 months, 10 days, 6 hours.
Dormitory 9. Weyborne School. Bridport. Dorset.
Great Britain. Europe. The World. Hemisphere. Stratosphere.
Hades.
PRIVATE & CONFIDENTIAL
Any other eyes that look,
Will be severely brought to book.

Hades was an odd addition from one so young. Or was it? Then she remembered what the Philippina had said. He'd also allegedly used it to describe Heron House.

Her breakfast Diet Coke began to churn around inside her as she began to read the first entry, dated Monday 12th September 1945, where, immediately, she spotted Betsan's name. But in what context was impossible to see as without warning, the breeze had suddenly become a dusty wind trying to turn the well-used pages for her.

"Stop!" she snapped, facing the other way so she could concentrate. However, the wind only strengthened, bringing a voice she now dreaded.

That could, if she let it, drive her insane.

"I can't, I can't. Surely that photograph you stole shows how frightened he was? My darling little brother who was forbidden to see me, his loving sister. His *only* sister. Never to come home, even for Christmas..."

Margiad Pitt-Rose.

"Yes, that's me and it's taken you long enough to find out. But then, why should you care? You're like all the living. Selfish, blinkered. What a waste of a life."

Helen secured her hood even tighter around her mess of hair to blot out the cruel monologue. To keep her head free for her own thoughts. Hadn't Jason experienced the same phenomenon with his *Evil Eyes* book? Yes. Except this time, the agenda was different.

"And when it mattered, nobody listened," Margiad persisted, "to him or me. And don't think he was the only one to suffer. There were two other young boys who'd strayed too far. Learnt too much about things that were private, so they were..."

"What?" Helen shivered, glimpsing ordinary people passing the open gates.

"Violated then thrown in the swimming pool. Where they almost drowned my Jason..."

My Jason?

I tried to save them, but was punished for it. You see, their cries had torn at my heart, my soul."

That once refreshing Coke was now acid in Helen's throat. Her pulse jumping and that wind still tossing the branches and scattering litter.

"When did this happen? And who's 'they?'"

"Hasn't my Jason told you?"

"No."

"He's had every opportunity."

Just then, a Chinese guy with his toddler son walked by hand in hand, heads bowed against the wind. This picture of normality made her vision blur. They stared briefly in her direction, probably suspecting a multi-personality disorder, before moving on.

" It was yesterday, in your present time," the voice went on. "Ask him."

"You're lying. You want to suck every last ounce out of me like you're doing with him. Or rather, you did to him. I'm supposed to forget about that? Am I?"

"He enjoyed it. Begged me for more, if you must know. I can still hear every word... Now," the tone hardened, "give me my dead brother's things."

"You're disgusting! Leave us alone!"

"Never."

An angry crack of breaking glass suddenly filled Helen's ears, followed by that same eerie scream she'd heard outside the art gallery. Not only was the diary being pulled from her grasp by a relentless force she'd never experienced before, but the horrible feeling of something moving beneath her clothes towards her pants.

She shrieked for help, unable to get up and run away, but at last managed to push the memoir between the bench and her thighs. Sealed tight, as the voice grew even more threatening. "Give me the diary. He's *my* baby brother, not yours."

"So what are you trying to hide? Who hanged him? Someone we know?"

A pause in which that sickly smell of roses met her nose.

"My Jason will have the answers. You're not worth it. I had a child, remember? Unborn, but still something you'll never, ever have…"

Helen shivered and couldn't stop. "Your father's, was it? Like Llyr?"

That breaking glass din returned. She covered her ears. Saw the play area's trees and shrubs swaying back and forth as if in a deadly dance.

"I've been protecting you and your hard heart, but no more. From now on, you're on your own, and if you think my Jason will be putting your interests before mine, you're wrong. You've had your chance, Helen Myfanwy Jenkins. So let's see how you get on."

***

With that wretched diary safely reburied in her now dirty pink rucksack, and a growing sense of foreboding enveloping her, Helen didn't hang about. Instead, dizzily turned left into Radlett Road, thinking about that baby. Had it been a lie for her benefit, or part of a terrible reality?

Whatever. She was now in competition for Jason with a ghost. A ghost, for God's sake. Time to make a call. Two calls in fact. She burrowed in her rucksack's usual places.

No mobile.

She'd still had it in Sandhurst Mansion and when she'd crept into the damp mean bed next to the bathroom in Nantwich Grove.

That was it.

Those two thieves must have struck when she'd gone in there.

Running now, into the wind, the swollen pad between her legs shifting out of place with each stride, but she didn't care. Too much else was at stake.

"Where's the nearest phone," she panted at a passing suit. His directions a blur as she ran on, dodging the multitude of shoppers and drifters, all the while sensing that other force holding her back.

At the welcome sight of a silver threesome outside Islington Post Office she let out a cry of relief, only to have the breath punched from her lungs from behind, between her shoulder blades. With no chance to fight back, she fell on to her outstretched hands. Her rucksack adrift, just beyond reach and soon snapped up by a figure she half-recognised. When she got to her feet, the man had gone. Her rucksack emptied of the diary lay a few paces on. No-one she asked had seen anything. No-one helped. And it wasn't until she'd flagged down the first taxi to come along, did she realise who her cowardly assailant had been.

36

Saturday 19th October 1946 – 10 a.m.

The horrifying Heron House jigsaw was slowly beginning to piece together, but with that important school inspection looming, there'd been little time for him and Robert to save Margiad and young Betsan from any more harm, or to try and bring Edmund Pitt-Rose and his cronies to justice.

If only plans and reality could be so easily melded together, mused Lionel, wiping up his breakfast dishes and returning them to the correct cupboard.

So here, he was on the filthiest of mornings, cocooned in Cwm Cottage with not only a gnawing guilty conscience, but also a small mountain of pupil files needing urgent attention. Whatever the outcome on Welsh language discussions taking place in Cardiff, and the implications for him should any nationalist swing intensify, he'd changed his mind. He would not be throwing in the towel.

Although a recent *Western Mail* article had warned of seismic shifts in the ethos of Welsh education, he must cling on and hope his reputation – despite Walter Jones' recent death – would hold sway.

Once in the lounge, he glanced at the chair Margiad had used, but from the moment she'd heard Carol calling her a trollop, she'd abandoned her brief refuge.

"Too easy for someone like Carol to judge," she'd declared, fastening her coat except for its lower buttons. "What does she know? Has she ever been in love? Has everything stacked against her?"

For once, Lionel hadn't any answer. Just a question.

"Forgive my asking, but whose child is it?"

Scorn had still lingered on her lovely face, like a cloud's shadow on a hill.

"Robert's, of course. Why?"

"And will you be keeping it? I mean, after the birth?"

"Only a man could ask that. Yes. She's my flesh and blood, isn't she? I want her. So does Robert. He'll make the best father."

"I'm sure he will, and I wish the three of you well."

"The best thing about being pregnant is I get no more bleeding. It's been terrible. It really has."

Lionel tried to hide his embarrassment at such unexpected candour. "Well that is good news. But who's hit you by your eye? It looks recent."

"Gwenno. And not the first time, either."

"I'm sorry."

"You've been very kind," she'd said, touching his arm with sudden affection. "Unlike some people round here. And I wish I'd been allowed to attend the kind of school you run, rather than put up with the obnoxious Miss Powell all these years." She'd then turned her beautiful eyes on his. Eyes that made the bruise beneath even more of an aberration. "If you see my Robert, please tell him we'll soon be together. For ever."

"I will. Just look after yourselves and the baby," he'd said, hearing the young organist's last words beating their way into his head. "And Cwm Cottage is here whenever you need it. But there's just one other matter."

"Yes?" At this, her troubled gaze had fixed on him so hard, he had to look away.

"Betsan told me that she's already been punished for befriending you. Did you know?"

"Punished? How?"

"Those men and Gwenno and Idris. They've been doing…"

"Stop! She's making it up. What nonsense, Mr Hargreaves. She really has too much imagination for her age."

"I don't think so. I find her remarkably mature and sensible."

Would he ever forget the piercing stare that followed? Her barely concealed anger? No. Never.

And then, without another word, she'd gone. Her slight, dark form merging with the sombre foliage that with each passing week, seemed to encroach upon the lane outside and steal what little daylight he had.

***

Back to work, still with that unpleasant memory bearing down on him, while his conscience about neglecting Betsan nagged his soul. Meanwhile, the once small mountain of files now resembled Everest. He must concentrate.

He opened the topmost file on Freddie McCarthy and Malcolm Biggs evacuated from Maghull four years ago, who'd only once graced his schoolroom with their cheeky wit and funny ways. A rush of panic filled his chest. How on earth could he manufacture a better attendance record for them both? After other young evacuees had returned home, those two had stayed on at Top Farm, on an old drovers' route to Llandewi Brefi.

He'd only met them once or twice during the summer, bumping around on two rough ponies, happy as Larry. A lost cause as far as schooling was concerned, but a pleasure to see their smiles.

Margiad Pitt-Rose, however, was another matter. Still disturbing his mind. How had she known the unborn baby was a girl, for a start? And why say she was Robert's child when he'd denied it? Like burrs stuck to his coat while out walking, the sense she was hiding something wouldn't leave him alone. He pushed the Liverpudlians' thin file beneath the rest, hoping it wouldn't be noticed. No, he'd neither made regular visits to Top Farm, and the couple who'd taken them in, nor alerted Bryn George who'd stopped calling before Lionel had arrived. But try as he might to focus on Freddie and Malcolm's two bright faces before they faded for ever, another's took precedence.

That of a solemn young organist drenched in grief.

***

Lionel heard rain fall down the chimney, sizzling into the fire, while the gutters shed their watery loads against the cottage walls with such ferocity, he missed the familiar voice calling through the letterbox. It came again. This time he heard it.

"Lionel? It's me. Carol. Quick!

Normally he'd have sprung from his seat, over-eager to see the one who'd already lit the smallest of flames in his heart. But nothing was normal now since he'd harboured the pregnant, seemingly traumatised, Margiad Pitt-Rose through whose core ran a spine of steel.

"Lionel! For God's sake!"

The moment he opened the front door, Carol pushed herself against him. She was wet through, her body moulding itself against his. But this was no prelude to passion. She was shivering so hard she could barely speak. "It's Peris Morgan! Poor man's been shot like a dog. You must come and see!"

"Is he dead?"

Her nod shook more drops from her unprotected head.

"Where?"

"By my door. I found him just after I'd finished my round." She looked up at him. "What's going on? Why? Why *my* place?"

Lionel's mind became a stew of all the things he should have done. Should be doing. So much had been expected of him since the day he'd been born. He could already see the words on his tombstone. "This is serious, Carol. You must either leave or hide yourself somewhere safe. It's a warning." And, as he spoke, seeing her pretty eyes glaze over with fear, realised he could be next.

***

What should have been a short hop to Hafod Lane leading from behind Nantybai towards the River Towy, took them forty minutes in the buffeting downpour. The fierce gale making proper conversation impossible. Even holding hands. So he battled on ahead of her until Myrtle Cottage appeared, bang beside the track without any visible boundary.

Carol caught up, then overtook him. "Are you ready?"

How could he ever be ready for death? Especially that of a dedicated guard who'd made it his business to give the village at least some sense of security. A man who, in turn, had warned him.

Through rain-spattered spectacles, Lionel studied at the front wall and its door set back under a plain porch, but nothing seemed amiss. Carol stopped short and they collided. She then clung to him again, pointing at the uncut verge that appeared to be undisturbed. "He's gone! Look, he was there. There!"

Lionel edged away to kneel down and stroke this grass with bare fingers. Where was the blood? The trampling? Footprints or hoof prints, even a spent cartridge, it didn't matter, and the word 'hallucination' did cross his mind. A young woman with an arduous job, up hill and down dale, might just have needed a hot, sweet cup of tea.

She looked down at him as if reading his thoughts. "Now you'll think I'm making it all up. You don't believe me, do you?"

"Of course I do. But we must alert his family. Call the police."

At this, Carol's wet face changed, as if the life in her too had faded.

"No, no, no. Can't you see? Peris came to see you, didn't he? To warn you about Heron House? Tell you things that went on there."

"Yes." Lionel stood up, swept the rain from his hair and shook out his soaking coat. As he did so, her cob whinnied from round the back. If only it could talk, thought Lionel, his pulse already working too hard.

"And didn't I catch Constable Prydderch laughing and joking with that Edmund Pitt-Rose as if they were best friends? Boasting how many times Margiad could... well, you know... I'm sorry I can't actually repeat what was said. What I'm getting at is I've been seen chatting to you."

"Who by?"

"That trollop. I know I shouldn't have used that word to describe her. I saw how it shocked you, but she's hardly run away from all that activity, has she? And with the police so thick with them, it could make everything worse all round. Do you understand, Lionel? Do you?"

He nodded, feeling suddenly hollow. It was possible that the tragic beautiful Margiad Pitt-Rose was a decoy.

***

He knew where the Home Guard's last, loyal servant lived with his son and

236

grandson Kyffin and, having seen Carol safely indoors and heard her lock the door, made his way past the colony of lead-workers' dwellings, the closed Stores, the grey, stone church and up towards Rhandirmwyn village.

Plas was as silent as his schoolroom. Silent as a tomb in fact. He registered its neat, box shape, the shining slate roof with its dead chimney that said 'no-one's home.' Even the old trap, usually stored in the lean-to, was missing. And as for the piebald pony used for harness, and for Kyffin to ride in the local show, that had apparently gone too.

He pulled on the bell-rope and waited for any signs of life. Only the deluge replied. That and the sense of a black net closing ever tighter. And where would it end? He thought of his job, akin to climbing Snowdon in bare feet. How he'd proved so many wrong, and now, despite the opted-out Lancashire lads, boasted the best attendance records in decades. But what of his mission for young Walter? For his poor, grieving mother? Perhaps here, now, he could begin to make amends.

Lionel stepped back from the porch, realising from the clang of iron on iron, the smell of burning bone, the smithy round the corner was busy. Once he'd telephoned Carmarthen's police from the box by the pub, he'd pay Robert Price another visit to ask more questions. As it was a Saturday, the organist might well be at home.

Mrs Griffiths too, with luck.

Five minutes later, in the misted-up glass box, his call to Carmarthen police station was answered. He duly dropped a sixpence into the slot and asked to speak urgently to a Police Constable Francis. He'd only met the amiable Welshman once when he'd visited the school to spell out the dangers of rifles, air guns and any other weapons brought back as souvenirs from the War. "Wait there, Mr Hargreaves," the officer said once Lionel's story ended. "One of my men can be with you in ten minutes by the back roads."

"Thank you. As I said, Miss Carr is very fearful. I don't think she should be involved in this at all."

"May not be as easy as that, sir. We'll talk again soon."

It seemed to Lionel that in those ten minutes, civilisations could have risen and fallen. Every second a drawn-out ordeal. He duly faced the door, periodically clearing away a patch in the condensation. Fifteen times, he counted, but on the sixteenth he sensed something was different. And sure enough, instead of rain slapping against the glass square, there was a face. Or at least the top half of a face with just its eyes visible.

Hard, dark eyes.

And then that same rain was hitting him as if the protecting door had been ripped away. Now ropes. Thick and rough. One for each of his hands. As a youngster in Solihull, he'd been taught to fight by Uncle Ernest, an amateur welterweight champion whose one *coup de grâce* to the head, could send you to hospital. But Lionel had seen him off every time; even kept his old boxing gloves behind the school's storeroom door. Just in case.

But this was different. Instead of some youthful adversary were four mature men who'd tightened his bonds so fast he could only kick out until, with two agonising cracks of bone, his knees gave way.

"Hold him Jimmy. For Chrissake." The one called Prydderch was losing control. "And you, Marky."

"Bloody help me, man."

Lionel could smell them. Drink and another childhood memory – this time of dentists – delivered up his nose, in his mouth, blurring the crash of his head against metal, but not the spreading redness before his splintered eyes.

Red then black.

"Transport ready?"

"Where to?"

"Nothing but the best, of course. As befits his station."

37.

Monday 6th April 2009 – 10.30 a.m.

Gwilym Price had snored all night once Jason had installed him in the attic room next door to his, separated by a thin partition wall. The farmer, who'd fallen heavily on the forestry track, in his haste to escape his suddenly violent dead uncle, had refused to sleep alone in Troed y Rhiw. He'd also turned down Jason's offer to drive him for a check-up at Llandovery's Cottage Hospital.

"Let's open that bugger instead," his fellow lodger had pointed to one of three untouched Glennfiddichs in the kitchen scullery. "If you don't mind."

Jason didn't mind. As for repeating Helen's bombshell about Llyr and Betsan, he must bide his time.

***

Parts of him still smelt dodgy after his dip in the pool and he had to assume, after his sixth attempt to get a response from Helen via the landline phone, that she wasn't interested in him any more. Had probably scrubbed his supportive messages. More than anything, he wanted her to get in touch.

If he thought about it, this was just another shite page in the book of his life, so why not get legless? The Davies pair had gone off somewhere or other and taken all the house keys. So, nothing to lose. With a makeshift deterrent of garden twine, wound round and round the front door's inner handle and lock, both lodgers had got stuck in.

Now he was paying for it.

While the farmer was brewing up downstairs, Jason, half-blind from sleep and the malt still swilling around his head, checked Helen's door.

Unlocked.

He started. Could have sworn it was secure yesterday, but one bleary-eyed scan of the cleared-out room told him all he needed to know. Even that weird crucifixion print had gone. It was as if she'd never been there. He opened the large, empty wardrobe then went over to the bed to sniff the topmost pillow.

Nothing.

He felt desolate.

***

Neither he nor his unlikely friend spoke as they downed two mugs of the treacly brew apiece and chewed on toasted crusts – all that had been left in the bread bin. The morning's biting chill that Gwilym swore would bring snow by nightfall, made him grip his warm mug all the tighter. The same mug Helen had given him that Friday evening. As for his body, it still felt embalmed by that freezing sludge.

"Her mobile phone may be kaput as well," he said, having swallowed the last piece of crust and pushed back his chair. "And I don't trust this landline any more. I'm going down the pub to call the Fuzz from there."

"They probably saw to her room," said the farmer. "Scare her off, see? And you'll be next if you're not wary. Best to deal with the Metropolitan police, like I've done. DCI Jobiah at Islington police station. Black, I could tell, and very helpful he was. Used my initiative, see." The old man looked at him with a certain knowledge in his eyes. The worst ink-blot bruise on his forehead leaking a little blood.

This was clearly no country bumpkin.

"You mean this lot are bent?"

"I couldn't tell you earlier. Have to be careful, you understand. Yes, Prydderch especially. His da too, *and* his da before him. It's *known*. D'you understand? Used to come up here regular for fun and games. God help anyone who asked questions or rocked the boat. Why I could barely be civil to him up at Betsan's on Saturday. Why my Carol confided in the school's headmaster what she'd seen while delivering the post. Used to be four of them including Edmund Pitt-Rose himself, Glyn Prydderch and two others she'd never seen before, doing things with the daughter. Depraved she called it."

Jason frowned. "His son made out he didn't know who Gwenno was when he showed up here on Saturday afternoon."

"There you go. All lies. As for the headmaster, after Carol told him about it all, he just vanished. The search went on for months, and till the day she died, she fretted it had all been her fault."

"Seems she was lucky to escape for so long. When did he disappear?"

"18th October 1946. A Saturday. Pelting down, so she said. The day she'd found the last of the village's Home Guard shot dead by her house. Peris Morgan. Salt of the earth he was. He'd disappeared into thin air as well."

"What did she do, then?"

"Tried to get people involved. But, except for Mr Hargreaves, they was scared. Me and my mam too, to be honest. And Carol, specially after her cob was poisoned. She was about to move away up north when we met at a barn dance at Ystrad Ffin. I wish we'd left while we'd had the chance."

"Then I'd never have met you."

Gwilym turned away, embarrassed.

"Thing is, she'd found this little notebook in the wood store behind the Headmaster's cottage. Seems he'd begun it after Peris had come calling. Doesn't take a genius to see they'd both been at risk. Young Betsan too; although Carol wouldn't say no more, only that the last entry before he vanished said Heron House was home to The Order, whatever that means." Gwilym licked his forefinger to gather up stray biscuit crumbs then licked it. "Betsan certainly never mentioned nothing to me."

Scared, like you, no doubt.

"Where's this notebook now?"

"Stolen from Carol's kitchen if you please. Someone keen to get hold of it, obviously. Mind you, looked as if Mr Hargreaves' place had been picked over, too."

Jason tried to concentrate on the rest of the story. Heron House had been the magnet for evil by top brass over a long period of time, but he hadn't finished yet. Helen was out there somewhere, and too many questions needed answers. Like where was Monty Flynn in all this? Where had the Davieses got to? And what might be next on the agenda?

It was then he spotted Gwenno's strange riding crop lying across an adjacent chair, half hidden by the waxed tablecloth's edge. He picked it up and for some reason, sniffed it. Definitely not leather.

"Look at this," he said. "What's it made of?"

Gwilym took one look then laughed. "Too early for smut, son."

Jason stared at him with exaggerated disappointment until his companion relented.

***

"Par for the course, I suppose," said Jason, once he knew. "No wonder she was always stroking it in that suggestive way." He returned the thing to the chair while the rook killer licked his knife and gathered up the crockery like the tidy widower he was.

"And as for her and the brother," Gwilym said, "I'll give you a clue. I knew they wouldn't last long once you and Miss Jenkins turned up. Risk of them singing, see? Spoiling the next party."

Next party?

The farmer ran water deliberately fast into the kitchen sink. The sound of it made Jason reach his room in ten seconds flat and cram his foul clothes from yesterday into his dad's suitcase. He then added *Evil Eyes* and his empty refill pad but, as he was about to bring down the lid and press the clasps into place, his strength seemed to melt and another's take over. He smelt the overpowering whiff of roses. That tinged sweetness Helen swore she'd experienced.

Margiad Pitt-Rose was back. Her voice like velvet while that full-lipped mouth slipped involuntarily into his mind. "I need you now, my Jason," she pleaded. "More than ever. You promised to write my story. You promised, but you seem to be forgetting me. I'm ready to start at the beginning when my sweetest little brother was sent away to school. When I was all alone..."

"I will. OK?" Jason stumbled. "Later, when I've got a few things sorted."

"I said now."

He swore under his breath, trying again to close his case, but all at once felt an invisible hand creeping round his side and on to the zip of his jeans. At the same time, that stain on the carpet by his feet seemed to brighten, to move and spread. The liverish odour rising up from it reminded him of when his mum had her monthlies and would accidentally leave her used sanitary towels in the bathroom.

"You loved what I did the last time, didn't you?" cooed his predator. "We could do it again, and again. Even daddy said I was the best in the whole wide world at giving pleasure to a man. The best! Me. Think of it. Coming from him, the most famous wonderful judge in the whole of Wales."

Daddy?

Jason grabbed the still-open suitcase under his arm and fled from the room, slamming its door as he went.

"Seen a ghost, bach?" enquired the farmer in the reception hall, cramming his black hat on his head. His rifle leaning on the fire screen.

"Helen's mum lives in Borth. I must get her number."

No tone.

A quick inspection outside under the purpling sky showed someone had been busy severing the telephone line. Just like at Golwg y Mwyn.

"Shift!" he yelled at Gwilym through the front door, before something else caught his eye. Something dark blue on the move, nudging towards him. The bumper rock hard against his calves, pushing, pushing...

The only way was up. On to the bonnet and over the side, the sudden blast of Gwilym's rifle making him blind, deaf save for his friend's warning roar at whoever was driving. "Stop or next time I blow your brains out!"

Jason rolled clear. Gravel in his hair, on his skin and down his neck. And there was the farmer poised for a second shot. The Escort's near-side rear tyre went down, but still it dragged itself in reverse before grinding away through the gates.

***

"That was Sergeant Rees," said the farmer afterwards, eyeing Jason with concern. "One of our local law enforcement officers. Shitting a brick he was. You alright?"

"Thanks to you, yes."

Jason straightened up. Still in one piece. Christ, the old man was brave. Archie'd have been proud of him.

"We could try catching up with the scumbag," said his saviour. "Really finish his morning off nicely."

But all Jason could think of was Margiad.

"Look," Jason said. "I've got to explore the Angred shaft. Trust me."

Gwilym hesitated. Not surprising considering his recent experience there. "We might meet my uncle again," he said. "I'm not sure…"

"Please come. If we find what I'm expecting, everything could fall into place. And you did ask me to help get to the bottom of things, didn't you?"

"You're right, bach, but in my case the spirit is often willing but the flesh too weak."

"Not any more," said Jason.

And on the way, shifting the weight of his battered suitcase from hand to hand as he went, Jason relayed to his astonished friend his adventure in the pool, ending with that strange, rigid object he'd felt lurking under his feet by its steps.

***

"What did you mean by 'the next party?'" Jason quizzed him once they'd paused for breath alongside a pile of rusted pipes on the forestry track. "That everything's going to start up again at Heron House?"

Gwilym nodded.

"Come on, boyo. Those pious old Devils, those judges, may still be alive. Their deeds like nuts that daren't be cracked. To what lengths did they go, or will their descendants go to keep it that way? Ask yourself. Specially if Heron House falls into their hands."

"You mentioned Mr Hargreaves the Headmaster," Jason blew warm air on to his blue fingers before he and Gwilym resumed walking. "He's really caught my imagination."

"A fine man, even though he spoke not a word of Welsh. I started attending school once he'd gone. Felt I owed him that much. That one day he'd come back and see how I'd made a go of my life after my mam died. Now look…"

243

Old, bitter tears glazed his eyes. Jason stopped, rested a hand on his arm.

"Do you have proof of him coming to harm?"

"No, but Carol did," Gwilym sniffed then wiped his nose with his coat cuff. "Something Idris Davies said to her when he was sweeping leaves into the pool, the way he did. Why I'd like to take my little coracle in there tomorrow. Do some serious fishing."

"And I need to tell you something," Jason began. "I've kept it back till now, but I know it'll be safe with you."

"Go on, then."

The faint sound of gunshot peppered the chilling stillness as Jason finally relayed Helen's news of Charles Pitt-Rose's will. When he'd finished, the farmer grew unsteady as if he was about to fall. Jason held him just in time, and together, without speaking, they moved as one up the ravaged hill.

***

Cold enough to break your bones. Break your heart. Jason, burdened not only by Gwilym's reaction to the inheritance story, but his own heavy suitcase, led the way up past Betsan's sad little place where the police cordon had slackened and tattered in the wind. Up towards the scree-strewn ridges and spoil tips of Nantymwyn's former lead mine.

With the other man's wheezy breath accompanying his own, it occurred to Jason how strange it had been to come here of all places to find a real mate. Albeit one old enough to be his granddad. Gwilym Price was solid. Rock solid. One day he'd pay him back. He then found himself wondering how the Sergeant would extricate himself from trying to maim him, if not worse. After all, it was only Gwilym's word that the driver of that dented Escort *had* been him. And how about that other man Idris Davies had been talking to by the pool? To his English ears, one Welsh voice was like another. He looked round to see the farmer stopped in his tracks.

"Can't go on no more," he panted. "Thinking about what you've just said about that scumbag Llyr. What if he killed Betsan? And why didn't she tell me about the will? She must have known about it before Saturday."

"Fear, I expect."

"DCI Jobiah never said nothing an' all."

"Perhaps he hadn't heard."

Gwilym glanced at Jason and then other pre-occupations resurfaced, together with dry, old tears. It was clear he was drowning in grief.

"I keep thinking about my Carol," he said, "after she'd seen that Lionel Hargreaves for the last time. He'd taken Margiad in apparently. Taken pity on her…"

His words seemed to float like ice flakes in that otherwise dense silence. Jason shivered under his ruined jacket. "Carol was convinced Margiad betrayed him and my uncle to her da and his cronies. Look how Robert was with me yesterday. He's still very angry, and he's right to be. He's stopping his lover and her unborn baby having a proper burial, that's what it is. Her and her *da's* baby." His whole body seemed to slump as if exhausted.

"You're having me on?"

"Am I? She loved her da over and above anything or anyone. No-one's going to tell me different. She *loved* him. Better get used to it, son. She'd do anything to protect him from the law. Betsan said the same. How she'd give herself bruises for effect. But who was Betsan? Just a kid at the time."

Jason glanced back at Golwg y Mwyn's little chimney.

"So what happened to Margiad and her baby?"

"No-one knows, but she must be round here somewhere, sure to be, as Robert's never been sighted nowhere else." Gwilym began to move again as Jason crept towards the Angred shaft's black opening, got down on his hands and knees to remove the various wooden planks and bricks that littered its access. Immediately, he smelt death. A rank, sour-sweetness eking up his nose, making his recent breakfast shift in his stomach. He could also hear water. Deep and dangerous. But to give up now wasn't on his agenda. As a kid he'd been glued to a TV series about a rural vet in Yorkshire. One episode where he helped a cow give birth had stayed in his mind; where his gloved hands had explored her innards until her calf's glistening back legs slipped safely into view. So here he was, his own expectations goading him on, because also within his grasp could lie a matter of life or death.

***

No matter that sharp stones and barbed wire remnants dug into Jason's knees. He must keep focussed. Keep going. As his numb fingers gradually cleared the entrance, he realised that beyond this opening – from where Monty Flynn boasted he'd once explored the cave beneath – lay no helpful ledge, no gradual easing into the shaft like any normal access for workers, but a sudden, vertiginous drop.

"Careful, man," shouted the farmer. "I'll fetch the car and a decent torch. Hang on."

"I'm OK. You just keep a lookout."

Jason meant for malevolent beings from this and another more distant world, all with their own agendas. And if Llyr Pitt-Rose *was* responsible for nicking the Irishman's gear and hiding it here, he must have used ropes. He might also be checking up on it.

Damn.

His once cosseted jacket had become a thick, icy skin as he slithered forwards on his front into the gaping darkness, willing his eyes to adjust to it before venturing any further. He felt the void below caress his chin, sending a thicker, more fetid stink into his nostrils. He blinked and blinked again, before his right hand landed on what he guessed might be some small animal's dried turd. But no. It was firmer than that. More solid.

He sucked in his breath as he drew the object out into the morning's gloomy light.

What on earth?

Whatever it was, was tiny. A dirty green bone, inlaid at both ends with what looked like brown moss. Whether human or not, he couldn't tell. But he had his phone and its handy camera which he regretted not using at Golwg y Mwyn.

Everything ready.

Click.

Nothing.

Click again.

Zilch. Just a blank, white screen. The same wherever he pointed it.

***

With both items in his jacket pocket, Jason returned to the opening, thinking about magnetic fields and why the camera had been such a dud. Also aware that should he need outside help, Cerrigmwyn Hill would prevent the rest of his phone from working.

Both arms now, dangling downwards, scouring the shaft's nearest, rubbly wall. There must be a ledge after all. Why? Because something unnaturally smooth and slippery lay under his fingertips. Just as he gained a better grip on what was clearly a package of some sort, he felt a weight lying along the whole length of his body. A dead, heavy weight, crushing him into the damp grass. All the while, that same rotting smell was enveloping him, creeping into his nostrils, his throat. Choking, choking...

"Gerroff!" he managed to scream, trying with all his hung-over strength to force away whoever had landed on him. "What the Hell are you doing?"

"Give me her bone," came a man's voice. Welsh. Determined.

"Her bone? Whose d'you mean?"

"I'm not asking twice. Time's running out."

Was this Robert Price again? Dead all these years?

Think... Think... There must be a prayer I can say.

Jason closed his eyes.

"Our Father which art in Heaven, hallowed be Thy name…"

"That won't stop me, Jason. Nothing will. You'll see. She wants you more than me. Like she wanted her father more than me. And I'll see your bones will lie with hers and his child's, unconsecrated, damned for ever in limbo unless…"

"Where? In this shaft?"

"The bone. Now."

No…

Then the pushing started. Inch by inch, as if Jason's own body was suddenly weak, weightless, colluding in his own end. He was back on those childhood marshes again with his puppy who'd run off and drowned; never to be seen again. He mustn't give in. 'Fight,' said Archie. And he did, until all at once came the strange sounds of a grizzly voice singing "O'er these gloomy hills of darkness, O be still my soul and gaze…"

Immediately, Jason felt that killing presence lift away. In its place came a sense of something extraordinary. Beyond description. Beyond reason. And once the hymn had ended, and his heart stopped trying to burst from his chest, he and Gwilym both sat facing the shaft in total silence. It was too soon to speak about what had happened. Perhaps even unlucky, so they didn't even try. Instead, both worked together to haul up the three bulky bin liners, using the trailer ropes still attached.

"Best get these shifted a.s.a.p," said Jason whose unsteady hands, returned the debris to the adit's entrance. "You never know who might be hanging around to reclaim them. I'll take the heavy stuff. Feels like a computer. Obviously important."

"I'll bring the Nissan up as close as I can. Then hide the stuff at my place."

***

"I swear Idris Davies and Sergeant Rees were planning to dump that Escort in the Towy," Jason said, once Gwilym rejoined him. "Just before I'd been pushed in the pool. 'Plenty of flow to carry it away,' he'd said. But why bother doing that?"

"Fools. The tide'll take it down Carmarthen way, where plenty will see it. Question is, man, who'll be inside it?"

While they loaded the bags into the 4X4's boot and covered them with an old rug, Jason suddenly realised important fingerprints might have been destroyed in the process. Perhaps too late now, he told himself, although an article he'd read claimed prints on plastic lasted the longest. Something to do with sweat. Having shared this reassuring nugget with his friend, they set off for Cysgod y Deri.

Once clear of the forestry and on a straight track, he showed Gwilym the bone. "Robert referred to it as hers, then her dad's child. Whatever, I had to hand it over to him or else be pushed down the shaft where she is. Robert hates her. Said she prefers me to him. This is getting weirder and weirder."

The farmer didn't reply instead his jaw tightened as he examined the tiny specimen. "It's a human metatarsal alright." He glanced sideways at Jason. The shadow from his black hat turning his bruises the same colour. "But not from an adult."

"What then?"

"Foetal, most likely. Are you thinking the same as me?"

"I'm thinking how you saved my life," Jason said.

"I meant that to keep it might bring bad luck." Yet nonetheless, the old man automatically slipped the little relic into his raincoat pocket.

Another silence while the 4X4 descended away from Heron House and joined the potholed track to the farm. Gwilym was speaking again. "Uncle Robert loved William Williams' hymns. I just took a chance with his favourite. There's no telling what might have happened otherwise."

"I'll never forget what you did."

"Wherever his remains are, Robert's at peace now. God rest his unhappy soul," said Gwilym.

"And Margiad? Could you do the same for her?" What he really meant was, get her off my case.

Gwilym Price suddenly crossed himself. A gesture that made Jason's blood turn even colder. "No bach. I'm sure she led the killers to him. Deliberately. I've just remembered Beynon 'The Shop' saying how he saw these four well-built men hanging around up the lane from St. Barnabas'. Christmas Eve it was, just after the carol service. Maybe the same criminals as tried pushing you under in the pool."

"We're talking ghosts, Gwilym. They came then vanished into thin air."

"These didn't. Snow'd been down a week. Thick it was. Everything muffled. Very handy. Perhaps Robert was going to the Towy and a boat. Why we both saw his spectre carrying that old oar. As for Margiad, it looked like she'd been waiting for him. But not in the way you might think."

"You mean a decoy?"

"That's my feeling. Beynon's, too. Beyond heartless I call it. I mean, look what she did to you..."

As if he could ever forget.

"So when and how did she and her baby die?"

"No-one knows. The adit was cleared just recently, for safety reasons, but nothing human was found. I made a point of asking."

Jason felt cold all over. Blew warm breath on his hands and moved his freezing toes around inside his boots. Cysgod y Deri's farm gate appeared ahead of them, but instead of feeling relief, he tensed up. He urgently needed an internet connection for research, plus a working phone to contact another CID unit. Preferably Islington. Until he discovered more, all this past misery would fester in limbo, polluting the present. And, as he unlocked the gate's massive padlock, worked out how quickly Monty Flynn's hard drive and his other material could be accessed.

***

Eleven-thirty and the morning almost over. With the enemy liable to show up at any moment and Helen off the radar, these were his priorities. But Gwilym was still back in that winter of 1946, haunted by too many unexplained disappearances. "Thing was," Gwilym continued once he'd parked and helped Jason unload the goods, "Beynon was sure these men you've just seen was up to no good, but when he tried getting the local police round, no-one bothered. He was making up fairy stories or been drinking, they said. Even when he started getting written threats, like Peris Morgan's son did, nothing was done."

Jason, however, was still preoccupied with his ever more pressing agenda. "Are you on broadband here? Do you go online?" Gwilym seemed genuinely puzzled. "What d'you mean, broadband and online?"

Dammit.

"Look, once we've checked this lot out, I need to get to that pub."

"After our ungodly session last night?" The old man smiled ten years off his grizzled, toothless face.

"For research on the internet and whatever else. Then once we've got to the bottom of all this, your uncle's remains may well be found and he'll be properly buried."

But Gwilym's smile hadn't lasted long. "I've lost my wife, my best dog. I've had my life; whereas yours is in front of you."

"Look, you're not stopping me." Then Jason remembered yesterday. "Those photos you took back on the forest track when Robert was advancing toward you. Did any come out?" The other man shook his head.

"I meant to say, but with everything else going on, I forgot. Like I do a lot these days. My camera's gone bust. Totally. And it was almost new. All my recent snaps have vanished but losing the last ones of Bob is the worst."

38

Monday 6th April 2009 – 11.45 a.m.

"The Detective Chief Inspector's not around till twelve," said the brightly lipsticked Desk Sergeant at Tolpuddle Street's police station, once Helen had given her only the briefest outline of her life since yesterday morning. Not a face she recognised from her previous visit with the man whose duplicity had almost destroyed her. "Do you want to wait?" asked the cop. "If so, can I get you a tea or coffee?"

"Yes I will, and no thanks." She still hurt. In fact, everything hurt, and not just her body. Eluned Jenkins, when she'd phoned a few minutes ago via a public call box, hadn't just gone mental, but into the stratosphere. Being called 'twpsin' for accepting a lift from a dangerous stranger and trusting the Irishman, when she shouldn't have, was the least of it. But hadn't she and mam also trusted her da?

"At least you're with the police," her mam had said once she'd calmed down. "Get them to arrest those two. Find out what's going on and why he got you involved. I can drive down tomorrow."

"No, don't worry. I'll be seeing you soon anyway."

"For my birthday? Like you said?"

Then, almost missing the familiar reprimand for not having studied medicine, or gone for a job with the Welsh Assembly, Helen had judged the time to be right. After a deep breath she'd said, "Yes. But just wondering if... God, I hate asking but there's no way I'm going back to Heron House... Can I come back to Borth? Won't be for long. Only till I'm on my feet again."

"Would you want your old bedroom?"

"If that's OK with you."

Silence, followed by a sniff. Then another. Could this tough, capable woman, who'd tried being both parents for the past five years, be crying? By the time Helen had replaced the receiver, she knew that despite bad memories nipping at her heart, all would be well. Except for two problems. Why was her period delivering such an unusual surge of blood, when usually by day two it had eased off? And what would happen to her and Jason now?

***

Sitting exactly where twenty-four hours ago, Helen and her traitor had waited, she added more items to her list for DCI Jobiah's attention. She'd already felt a rapport with him. Why she'd come back here.

But midday was too long in coming.

With five minutes to go before her appointment, she went over to the main desk before two veiled women could beat her to it. "I'm worried about my friend Jason Robbins," she began, aware of being overheard, "as every time I tried to phone him at Heron House, the landline's dead. I mean *dead*. Something's going on. I just know it is."

"You used the mobile that was later stolen?"

"Yes."

"And have you made contact with his?"

"I did, but all I got was :'This service is not available.' For texts as well."

"Contact his provider," suggested one of the women who'd not heard the full story. "They'll tell you what's the matter. It's free."

Helen gave her a weak smile and returned to her seat, but a growing powerlessness and isolation soon overcame her. She returned to the Desk Sergeant as the women were leaving.

"I realise you're based in London, but please get someone to go round to Heron House," she urged. So her voice was raised a few notches? Who cared? "I've got really bad vibes."

"Funny you should ask. DC Prydderch – from Llandovery Police Station – made contact with me last night. On his way to Heron House, he said. And he'll be in touch again soon."

Helen frowned. "*When* did he contact you? It's important."

"I'll check."

"Thanks."

The Sergeant was gone a few minutes.

"23.04 hours," she said, upon her return.

Helen's frown deepened. "From where?"

"His patch, I assumed. Why?"

"He could easily have made Islington by mid-morning today."

"I don't understand," the Sergeant really did look perplexed.

"I do."

Just then, DCI Jobiah appeared in the background, looking well pissed off. For half a second, Helen hesitated. Could she bear to risk being fingered for having been in Charles Pitt-Rose's flat, or run for it?

He glanced her way and immediately his expression changed for the better.

"I was told you were here again. Please," he indicated a plain door marked PRIVATE, "follow me. Your B&B owner's already been in touch

251

with us, and very helpful he's been, too. As has a Mr Gwilym Price with some useful names. Your friend Mr Robbins had told him you'd already met me. I just wish at the time, you'd been able to speak more frankly."

***

At twelve-thirty, Helen emerged from the Detective Chief Inspector's office feeling as if she'd undergone an exorcism. Halfway through their conversation, he'd summoned DC Purvis in to help take the inquiry forward. First would be a fresh and thorough probe into Betsan Griffiths' death and that of a leading circuit judge in Cardiff with interesting connections. Next, an address in Dulwich, then a certain DC Rhydian Prydderch who'd almost certainly assaulted and robbed her on the pavement that very morning.

Helen's phone, traced to a west Dulwich location, would be returned to her as soon as it was found. Meanwhile, she'd left the police Jason's and her mam's numbers, together with Colin's, and the name and address of the former governess at Heron House. All just in case. As for that small photograph of Charles Pitt-Rose still safely tucked against her hip, it would stay there till she'd left that vile Heron House behind.

"If you see anything of Mr Flynn or Llyr Pitt-Rose, tell us." DCI Jobiah patted her warmly on the shoulder. "Your conjectures about your boss – in fact, both men – are very useful indeed. We'll set you up with a new phone until you get sorted. Call us from Paddington before you board the train. We must know you're safe."

"Thank you. But could you also please check on Dee Salomon – she's Mr Pitt-Rose's solicitor in Hurst Crescent, Camden?" she'd added before picking up her rucksack. "I saw how Mr Flynn looked at her. She'd also had six anonymous phone calls hassling about her dead client's will. Someone also wanted Llyr Davies' original birth certificate. She said she'd be calling the police but..."

"Don't worry. We'll be in touch with her. Now please think, Helen. "Is or was there anything at Heron House to suggest what Charles Pitt-Rose might have been up against?"

"In what way?"

Her stomach rumbled long and loud as mentally, she trawled from the ground floor up those worn, shallow stairs to the first landing and her room. Then a sharp stab attacked her groin. And another, before she felt the biggest lurch of blood ever, begin to leak from her body.

Blood, pain. Think...

"Yes, there is."

252

Tolpuddle Street had paid upfront for a taxi plus woman driver to take her to Paddington and, once Helen reached the station's crowded concourse, she immediately used the bog-standard Nokia to touch base and say so far so good. She then chose a ham panini and a hot chocolate drink before finding a rare empty seat near the carriage's loo. A WPC at the police station had helpfully provided a fresh supply of night-time pads and suggested she see her GP about possible fibroids and anaemia. But Helen knew stress was her problem, and that a break at Heffy's hotel by the Irish Sea, her answer. Where tea would be at six every evening, shopping every Saturday morning, and Heffy – lovely, pregnant Heffy – would still be up for a laugh.

While the train finally drew away from the platform to the cacophany of too many ringtones and news of a serious earthquake in L'Aquila in Italy, London's western suburbs thinned to the almost rural, letting Margiad snake into her thoughts.

"I've been protecting you. But no more. From now on, you're on your own, and if you think Jason will be putting your interests over mine, you're wrong. You've had your chance, Helen Myfanwy Jenkins. So let's see how you get on..."

"I'm going to get on fine," she announced, causing her neighbour – an Indian guy in a suit – to sneak her a worried look. "So go away and pester someone else. You're nothing to do with me. I never knew you, and wouldn't want to know you. And as for Jason, who the Hell do you think you are?"

Once she'd finished her snack and tidied away its litter, she dug down her jeans into her pants and pulled out Charles Pitt-Rose's small photograph. At Art College, before beginning a portrait whether from life or a photograph such as this, she'd been trained to search for the subject's 'soul.' Her tutor – a Rembrandt fanatic – had shown the artist's last self-portraits as examples. Immediately, she'd realised he was right. And now in front of her, on a busy train taking her further and further away from where this once six-year-old now lay dead, she realised Charlie's early life had been shaped by suffering. Although his fair hair lay neatly combed and his shirt collar stood up crisp and white, his eyes – large, clear and piercing – seemed to haunt her heart.

Outside, while the first fat raindrops from the darkening sky hit the window glass, an unstoppable tear fell on to his young cheek. She tried wiping it away, but only succeeded in bleaching out even more of that pale skin. And why had the governess taken the photo in the first place? As a souvenir before he was sent away for the last time? Or for a less honourable reason?

***

More rain. What else?

She was a living wreck as she finally stepped from the Swansea-Shrewsbury link train at Llandovery station. She also felt like a stranger, as if this small market town whose shops were already closed, had changed. The short stay in that overloaded capital had clasped her to its amorphous spirit. The Coleridge Gallery was another lifetime away, but nevertheless still beckoning.

Helen scoured the car park for her car. Apart from a fruiterer's van and a few chained up bikes, there was nothing.

Damn. Damn.

Hadn't Jason offered to get hers locked? Perhaps he'd somehow driven her to Rhandirmwyn thinking he was being helpful. She couldn't go to the cop shop in case Prydderch had somehow got himself back from London, so now what? No umbrella, no shelter and drenched already. Stay calm, she told herself. Think. No way was she hitching again. Nor would she attempt to walk it. Her groin, compressed for all those hours on the train, was delivering a deep agonising pain. She thought of the local library where she'd met one of the staff while looking for cookery books. Ffion. That was her name and she had a car.

She'd just turned into the main High Street, when a blue Escort pulled up alongside. Despite the mad rain, the nearside passenger window was sliding downwards. Ignoring her instinct to keep moving, she looked in. Sergeant Rees, out of uniform. "Miss Jenkins. Can I help?" he asked. "You look all in."

"I am. My Suzuki's not over there where I left it." She indicated the station, aware of rainwater trickling down to her bra. "Do you know if she's been moved somewhere?"

"She?" he smiled.

"Please…"

"Mr Robbins took her up Heron House."

So she was right.

"When?"

"Now you're asking. Look, I'm off out to the cinema in Brecon, but can run you back to Rhandirmwyn if you like. Really no bother."

"Where's DC Prydderch?"

He blinked in surprise. "At home. Why you asking?"

254

Because he stole that diary.

"I'm used to seeing him around, that's all."

The Sergeant seemed to believe her. "Keeps dogs, he does. And dogs need walking. "Now, you ready? You're getting soaked."

She couldn't imagine Prydderch walking anywhere, yet he'd come at her quick enough back in Islington. "OK. Cheers." She edged towards the saloon whose dents above its sills and its wheels were caked in mud, aware that the passenger door had already been pushed open from inside, bringing with it a distinct whiff of poo. But, so what? She had to get back. She'd just taken hold of its handle when suddenly, her replacement phone sprang to life. So busy was she stepping back onto the wet pavement, she only grasped the first part of DCI Jobiah's call. "Helen? You back in Wales yet?"

"Yes. Why?"

"Some important news just in. No time to spell out the contents of Mr Pitt-Rose's diary except to say that if true, it's extremely revealing. There's more to his death than meets the eye, and a lot ties up with what you told me. Can't say more at this stage."

'There are suicides and suicides…'

"But you do need to know there's a perfect match between the sample of Mr Flynn's DNA taken here, and from one of Miss Griffiths' broken figurines."

My God.

She'd noticed his cut finger but as he'd been in his dressing gown, had thought nothing of it. Could he already have been over to the bungalow on Saturday morning and changed out of his clothes?

"We also found proof he'd visited her the previous Wednesday morning. But Helen, listen carefully," the DCI continued, as she suddenly remembered Mr Flynn's return to Heron House that lunchtime with not a trace of whisky on his breath. "Do not, I repeat, do not, be on your own with either him or DC Prydderch whose late night call to me actually came from the Mayflower Hotel in Islington. Understood?"

Sergeant Rees was conveniently flicking through his radio stations, until he looked up just as she was stuffing the phone away in her fleece pocket. "My film starts at eight," he reminded her. "Need to shift, see. Hop in."

39

Monday 6th April 2009 – 11 a.m.

That image of his randy mam seeing to the Irishman was still haunting Llyr's head as he dumped what he'd nicked from Sandhurst Mansion in an empty litter bin and limped away from the only chemist in miles. The hardest bit so far, finding somewhere to buy bandages for his wounds. The poshies who lived round here didn't seem to need anything except banks and, even then, most, like Michael Markham, were into offshore trading. As for Geoffrey Powell – Jimmy's greedy sprog down in Dinas Powys – who now ran the whole game; God, he hated him. Hated the lot of them, truth be told. And he, Llyr Pitt-Fucking-Rose had been the fall-guy. He'd failed with the gay and it had been *his* Transit picked up. Who else would it lead to, thanks to the Brecon dealership sticker still on the rear plate?

As for the dough he'd earned, it was safe in the Co-op Bank for the short-term. He wasn't that dumb. Not with the recession in full swing and whispers of plans to tax what lay hidden in 'safe' havens. Yes, he'd kept up with all that financial stuff despite nothing on paper to prove he'd got brain cells. Despite Geoffrey Powell's recent neck-grip warning not to put The Order at risk in any way.

But the worm had turned and now he was asking himself how had he got himself into this heap of manure? Wrong place, wrong time, wasn't it? Persuaded by Flynn he could make it big, just like another fool with an ear stud not a million miles away. Someone he had to see, before heading for Cardiff Airport.

Whatever Jason Robbins was, he didn't deserve to die like that poor disciple. But Gwilym Price did. The man had a downer on him from the day he'd showed up for work at Cysgod y Deri. Him and his frisky, older wife who'd actually helped deliver him. How cooky was that?

Reason enough to get cracking.

***

He made Victoria Coach Station in twenty minutes, but the National Express service had been delayed by Somali illegals found half dead inside the luggage holds of two earlier departures. Now, at five o'clock, the next bus to Swansea was due to leave at any moment with four seats spare. Lucky or what? He'd opted for road rather than rail. Slower but more secure.

Clutching his still-hot coffee carton with one hand, his Superdrug carrier bag, containing a coagulant spray plus box of tissues in the other, he chose the furthest free seat away from the door. Just in case.

No Flynn. Nor any of the other bastards. So far so good.

With the old crust in the next seat eyeballing him, he hunkered down as far as he could against the red velour, and took the first calming gulp of his coffee.

It had been a hairy morning alright, but he'd survived. Just.

***

As the coach revved up before manoeuvring out of its bay, Llyr spotted a queue of three men all past their prime – all white – in uncool clothes, standing by the driver's area, asking about toilet breaks, snacks and crap like that, when he'd paid to be over that Severn Bridge a.s.a.p.

Only when they'd sat down could he breathe again, and the whole shebang left the heaving city behind.

Sod this...

He'd not bargained for his neighbour asking if he'd been in a fight. His frigging e-fit had been on the News, hadn't it? Larger than life, thanks no doubt, to the gabbing schoolgirl at Abergwesyn and The Ginger he'd been ordered to deliver to her fate.

Instead of freaking out, he just told the old git he'd made one or two mistakes while living in Brixton; then, still clutching his coffee, closed his eyes and let the past snake into his thoughts.

Had there been any photos of him at Heron House? he wondered. Dream on. The Order had wanted him airbrushed out of sight, out of mind, and no-one went against them. Even his mam and the one he'd known as his da. People he'd not yet found the right words to describe. "Too much lead in their veins," they'd said at his first assessment interview at Holmwood. "Just like their parents. Poor dabs." But *he* was the 'poor dab' when his few toys had been taken away as well. The wooden-paged books showing colourful pictures of farm animals, nothing like what roamed around Rhandirmwyn.

Once at the special school, he'd done regular Bible Study but never seen the point of it, except that stuff from the Old Testament about Lot and his foxy scheming daughters. Mothers and sons, fathers and daughters. Nothing had changed since men and women had squatted in caves. So Geoffrey Powell spouted at The Order's three-monthly virtual conferences, to enthusiastic applause, especially from his old aunt in her care home, who'd been Charlie's governess. A woman he'd never wanted to see again in his life.

***

Llyr blinked himself awake. Someone had switched on the video too loud as 'Gladiator' sprung to life and one of the latecomers stood up to survey the coach before sitting down again. He drained his tepid coffee while slanting rain from the leaden clouds outside, blurred his view. He wondered how quickly he could exit the crap that had smothered him since his surname had taken a turn for the worse. How Montague Flynn, the man he'd just shafted, parachuted in to Heron House from the Emerald Isle, was the one he feared most.

***

"Membury Services," announced the ear-shattering tannoy over the video's din. "Twenty minutes for tea and a pee. Last stop before Cardiff and Swansea."

The aisle in front of him became jammed with bodies. Or more precisely, bums, and bags; one of which hit his left cheek. Normally, he'd have reacted, but not now. He had to get off this bus in west Wales with no strings attached.

"You goin' sometime before midnight, son?" said the crust next door, whose recent parp said he needed the break more than most.

"When it's calmed down, OK? Bit mad at the moment."

"I need the toot."

Llyr stood up, let him pass then sat down again. If only he still had his van with its comfortable cab. Now the uniformed driver was chivvying everyone off the bus and into the rain until just one other passenger remained. A man with brown hair and a creased trench-coat. One of the three who'd boarded late. The one who'd earlier stood up.

"Out please, you two," said the driver. "Me bladder's burstin."

Llyr hesitated. He'd planned to stop where he was.

Don't raise your profile.

So, reluctantly he passed them both and the litter-strewn seats until he reached the steps down. Trench-Coat's aftershave stung his nose. He didn't seem to have much sense of space either. On to tarmac spotted with rain. Llyr pulled up his donkey jacket around his ears and stepped up the pace even though his left leg was killing him. Over a mini zebra crossing, past an overflowing waste bin then towards revolving doors with pink balloons bobbing around on either side. Someone's having a party, he thought, remembering the years when he'd had none.

WELCOME

Just then, something harder than a finger was pushing him into the spinning glass doors. Then he realised a silencer was lodged in the small of his back.

"Take a left," said a man's voice before he could react. "No messing."

GENTS

Where three guys pissing into their pots were too busy to notice.

"This'll do," said the voice behind him. "Number four. My lucky number."

The metal was pressing closer now. Against bone.

Click.

The cubicle door was secured behind them. Normally, Llyr would have leapt on to the toilet seat and kick-boxed his way out of trouble. Not now though, with everything to lose. At least know who's going to take you out, he told himself, dropping his carrier bag. Turning round.

Flynn.

The one from Crosskelly who enjoyed old muff. Alive or dead. Even Betsan on Saturday morning after her knock-out drops. Llyr had known all this. He wasn't a dickhead. But all the same, he should have told Markham. Earned some Brownie points.

"I saw you at her bungalow," Llyr said. "What you did to her and her things. You turd. You nothing."

He was rewarded by the kind of smile you don't forget.

"There's gratitude."

"What for?"

"My keeping your real name out of lights. Even your mam's when I'd refused her offer of help that morning, I'd insisted your future was more important than..."

Llyr covered his ears. He never wanted to hear about her again. Or her brother. He wanted America.

"Just think, I'll have everything when you've gone," Flynn crooned. "I'm already a beneficiary, in a strong position. Or have you forgotten?"

"Rot in Hell."

The brown wig had slipped sideways, but those cold grey eyes were unchanged. As was the dark nosebleed filling each nostril, the ragged teeth behind that smile. But this time Michael Markham's blaster was in his enemy's hands. Its black eye on his.

***

259

Llyr was a kid again, back in his tadci and mamgu Davies' farm, being made to watch while his mam using that crop of hers, showed off her sexy skills on her da and her brother. Skills she'd passed on... And on... And for what? To hear the scream when they'd struck her for not trying hard enough. Yes, even the scream as his eyes disappeared and ice cold laughter began.

40.

Monday 6th April 2009 – 5.15 p.m.

With his dad's world-weary suitcase safe in Cysgod y Deri's spare bedroom wardrobe, Jason waved his old friend goodbye and stood in the downpour until the Nissan had rounded the bend past the pub and vanished out of sight.

Keen to reach Llandovery before six, to buy a new oar for the patched-up coracle his grandfather had once used on the Towy, Gwilym would only be an hour at the most. Then, under cover of dusk, they could both investigate the swimming pool.

Jason gathered up Monty Flynn's computer – now encased in a fresh bin liner – and entered the Fox and Feathers by its back door where Judy Withers was waiting, no questions asked. He'd made that plain when, having spoken to DCI Jobiah at Islington Police Station about his find, he'd phoned her from the farm.

She led him upstairs to a boxroom-cum-office overlooking the Doethie Valley. 'The Drop,' as Helen had called it. "How's your girlfriend, by the way?" she asked, opening the door. "She seemed quite pale on Saturday."

Jason fought the blush creeping up his neck.

"OK as far as I know. Still in London with her boss. Should be back here with him tomorrow."

"By the way, and it's no big deal, but he never came in the pub on Wednesday morning. Just that I'd told her Saturday had been his exception."

"Right." But he wasn't really listening. Just wanted to make a start.

"Hope to see her soon, anyway." Then, while the deluge hammered on the roof overhead, Judy showed him where the internet connection lay beneath the worktop. "Take your time," she added. "And if you want a coffee or something to eat, just shout."

"I can't thank you enough," he said. "I'll explain everything later."

"Good luck."

On his own, he soon had the Packard Bell up and running. The start-up buzz sending a charge of dangerous excitement to his heart.

Windows XP 2009. The same as Colin's. Something at least. Also the fact that the Irishman had conveniently left his password inside one of his many unused notebooks. PENDU. How weird was that? But even more weird was evidence there *had* been an internet connection at Heron House after all.

Flynn was no longhand writer like he'd said. *This* was his medium and to scroll through page after page of retained emails was proof. Proof too, of a sinister, secretive world only someone like author Max Byers could make up. Further searches showed that Monty Flynn hadn't written a word of fiction in his life.

***

Now, where to start? he asked himself. Last Saturday might be useful. It was. He found the latest email dated Saturday April 3rd at 08.00 hours:

To all,
Some news. My prostate's finally bidding me farewell. My bladder and colon too. Hardly surprising given the wear and tear. Days, not weeks they tell me, so rather than advise you in the traditional way, I hope this will suffice.

> *Ni fleurs, ni courronnes*, as they say in France. No death notice, no funeral, nor mourning. And MM will co-ordinate The Order's renaissance now that The Gay is dead. Please give our Cause all the support you can. Life is for living. The future's bright. HH will be back in our hands. We blazed a trail. Thanks for the memories,

Ever yours,
Philip Markham. (Marky) †

URGENT DELETE

The Order...

Jason stared at the screen. Those recipients' names had already fired arrows into his eyes, now it was the turn of those two ominous words: The Order. And was that strange cross its special symbol? If so, why? The missing Headmaster had been right. The stone was rolled back.

He wondered if Flynn had picked up this email before rushing off to London and forgotten to delete it. Or if the sender popped his clogs soon after to join his mates by the pool? If so, it seemed any raving weirdo could have eternal life. And what did 'back in our hands' mean? And who on earth was MM ?

Jason rescanned the list of email addresses. As he did so, the warm room became oddly cold. Detective Chief Inspector Jobiah must access all this as soon as possible but, first, he wanted Philip Markham's mugshot. And quick.

Dogpile came up trumps. Three clicks of the mouse and there he was. Circuit Judge for Penarth, Cardiff, plus a load of letters after his name, facing him in be-wigged splendour. But no fancy wool could disguise that overfed face. The boozer's strawberry nose. Those eyes. Edmund Pitt-Rose was the same, and Jimmy Powell. Pillars of justice, like the two police officers, without a smear to their revered names.

Jason felt unsteady in the office swivel chair. His forefinger trembled on the mouse as he scrolled to earlier mail. The more he peered into these hidden lives, the more his own situation became clear, beginning with that enticing notice in *The Lady*.

Flynn had jumped the gun, when the rest of The Order, as they call themselves, had suggested a few discreet yet adventurous women for the upgraded Heron House. That is, once Charles was out of the way and Llyr, aka Ethan Woods, his promised beneficiary, forced to comply.

But Charles hadn't quite read the script.

As for gays and lesbians, they'd be recruited in the New Year to add variety. After all, Gwenno Davies wouldn't be around. Nor Idris. No, judging by the minutes of recent virtual conferencing, anyone willing and skilled would be welcome. Even teens could be trained up, Flynn had argued. Plenty of them around in the sticks where other paid work didn't exist. The new set-up could be a nice little earner.

'*Then I won't say why you're really there.*'

Jason kept scrolling, but when Helen's name came up, his hand froze on the mouse. His throat too, as the words began to blur. With her colouring and temperament, she'd been another mistake for which the Irishman had been soundly reprimanded. Flynn, who for a while, had been her father substitute.

He felt soiled all over again. And ashamed to be even seeing this stuff. But worse, scared stiff that at any moment, Flynn and both Prydderch and Rees would show up at the pub. The Davieses too had every reason to be worried, wherever they were. Things were changing fast. Even Jason's breathing had speeded up. His mind on fire. No time for anything else except getting back to Heron House.

Beyond the pub window, an overloaded section of guttering had slipped its moorings and swung against the window. Above this noise came another. An almost inhuman voice, shrill and harsh. The last thing he needed right now.

Margiad. Dammit.

"You promised you'd write my story. You promised!" she cried. "Why can't we start now? Think of it, Jason. You and I, together, for however long it takes…"

You and I?

"Yes. I even put my name plate on my bedroom door specially for you to see," she went on. "And showed you my bedspread, my foul bloody carpet. For you to understand the truth about me. To seek justice. Please…"

"Truth? That's rich, given you knew all along why Helen and I had been brought to Heron House."

"I was teasing."

"Liar."

Something suddenly hit the window glass and fell out of sight. The light overhead flickered and his bones felt cold. She was speaking again as if he'd not said a word.

"I love prologues. Why not begin with one on that snowy Christmas Eve in 1946 with me waiting and waiting for my Robert. The only one who could help me escape danger. Think of it, Jason. Think of it…"

Her demands hogged his mind as the screen of emails faded to a pale yellow-brown mass; the same colour as Llandeilo and Heron House's pool. But this was no street scene, no silent gathering or attempt to drown him, but a young woman's face in close-up. Identical to what he'd seen in the kitchen, except that her left eye bore a dark purple bruise and that devouring mouth had opened in a shriek so loud and piercing, he stumbled from his chair. "Do it!"

"Shut up!" he yelled. "Shut the Hell up!"

"Do you want me to stop making her suffer? Your Helen?"

What?

"Begin now, or I'll see she never bears children, never…"

He slammed the door behind him, yelled down to Judy to call a DCI Jobiah at Islington Police Station to urgently look at the emails. He gave her the password then as she began dialling, pushed open the back door into a changed world where although the rain still fell like steel rods, a once picturesque backwater had suddenly become a War Zone.

***

Where on earth was Gwilym? An hour he'd said. If anyone was reliable, it was him. Jason turned off the main road and ran up the sodden track towards Heron House, his sweat mixed in with the rain. Last year's straggly brown ferns brushing his legs. This was surely where Helen would be heading, with or without Monty Flynn. So this was where he must be. Having dodged the turbulent mini-rivers flowing down towards his boots, he quickened his pace again once the two iron herons on top of the gates came into view. Now not just birds but a malign presence. The gates were open, but from one hung the kind of padlock Woolies had never seen reason to stock. Protection for a castle, or a prison?

All at once the grunt of a car's engine grew more distinct behind him. This was neither the Nissan, nor Helen's Suzuki – more like that bashed-up Escort from earlier. He wasn't going to hang around to find out. Instead, with a second wind filling his lungs, he followed the untrimmed boundary hedge until reaching the stile. From here, through the lifeless chestnuts, he realised he'd guessed correctly. The battered, blue Escort was creeping past the driveway's rose island and stopped out of sight along by the lock-ups. Its punctured tyre mended.

Had this same crock that had almost killed him taken Gwenno and Idris away?

And then the familiar thread of terror passed through his veins. Had someone else seen him and her at it in the kitchen? Someone bent on revenge? Had there been a hidden camera? If so, was Heron House under surveillance or was he going bonkers?

A man's voice. Welsh. Angry.

Prydderch?

The first choice. Jason scrambled over the slimy stile and slithered down to the pool's edge where the weather had erased the remains of his recent escape. He took cautious steps around its perimeter to the corner of the house and, with the saturated ivy camouflaging his body, craned forwards.

Helen!

He almost called out to her, but to do so could risk her life. She was gagged, soaked to the skin and cuffed to Sergeant Rees. Proud wearer of a jam-packed holster. She was also being manhandled indoors. Not only were the insides of her jeans' legs stained red, but twin trails of blood followed her struggling steps. No sign of her pink rucksack.

For a split second, she glanced his way. Her swollen eyes delivering a warning he didn't need. Archie Tait was right. His brave best mate was urging him to jump ship. Because he'd be next.

No way. He'd not come this far for nothing. He wished he had Gwilym's rifle. Something to scare the shit out of this creep who probably knew way too much about him and Helen from their statements for a start. He dug out his mobile to check recent events and by some miracle, a DC Purvis from Islington Police Station immediately came on the line. "A Ms Judy Withers has just made contact with our team," he began in what seemed like a faraway voice. "Why I'm calling. And DCI Jobiah plus a crack unit from Cardiff are already on their way to Rhandirmwyn by police helicopter."

"OK, but Sergeant Rees has just taken Helen into Heron House. He's armed. She's bleeding badly."

"You're not to take any unnecessary risks, Mr Robbins. Understand? Leave everything to us."

Sod that. I'll take every risk.

"Monty Flynn's armed too, and highly dangerous. Call us if you see him. Before going to London on Saturday, he killed Miss Griffiths, and just recently Llyr…"

Call ended.

***

Rage spiced by fear took Jason first to the Escort where he salvaged Helen's filthy pink rucksack from the boot, then to the back of the house where he knew a rotting door lay half buried by years of grassy neglect. He'd seen the gardener use it to sneak in and out. The oddball who'd tried to kill him then save him.

Ajar.

The rain followed him in.

Despite the large, dripping cellar's deepening gloom, he checked out the rucksack. What he found made his eyes sting. No money in her purse and a basic model Nokia, with nothing stored on it at all.

No time to waste.

He threaded his way towards a distant door through all kinds of discarded junk. Old, stiff bridles, fishing gear, rotting croquet mallets, but more usefully, broken window glass, all shapes and sizes. With each step, the smell of death reached his marrow.

He grabbed the piece to best fit his pocket and wrapped his unusable handkerchief around the end before slipping it deep out of sight. Then stopped to get his bearings. To listen. A repetitive banging noise coming, it seemed, from Nantymwyn Forest. Nothing like tree-felling, sawing or shooting. Now came footsteps overhead and the sagging ceiling groaned as they passed. Jason guessed he was under the kitchen and, if so, hadn't he once seen Idris Davies appear from the larder?

He climbed six stone steps to the door. Metal this time, with a section of

266

fly-clogged mesh set in the top. He could hear his heart. Rees was leaning over the Belfast sink, ducking his head under the tap for a drink. Helen still attached to him by handcuffs.

So near and yet so far. Her protests just a muffled blur. He mustn't blow it. The coward might panic. Reach for his gun.

"I want my rucksack now. And my purse," she mumbled.

"You won't be needing them. Upstairs we go," said the animal. "No need either to clear your mess. We'll be private up there, and no tricks either, not like those them two fuckers who wouldn't drown. 'Sides, there's someone we'd like you to meet."

"Wait till Jason Robbins finds out about me. And your bosses."

Hearing his name was the trigger.

He tested the metal door. It was almost too easy. With her rucksack snug against his back, he crept past shelves of boot polish, silver polish, old floor cloths and sagging cartons of Daz – everything except something edible – into the kitchen where he trawled its walls and ceiling for any sign of a hidden camera. No joy, and he couldn't hang around.

With his right hand feeling the cloth-bound edge of his makeshift weapon, Jason followed the blood up the stairs. They were going to the very top of the house.

***

She was screaming. Must have pulled off the gag. Jason soon reached that darker world of the second floor where a trail of gas and roses led to his room. Margiad's nameplate, luminous in the gloom, was back in place over the half-open door. A complete bunch of keys hanging from the keyhole.

He covered his nose, pushed his way in and almost passed out.

Chloroform.

This was no bedroom but a morgue, judging by what lay outstretched on the carpet. A man he barely recognised. Monty Flynn. Naked and yellowing just like St. Peter. His startled eyes scrolled upwards.

And then, with a jolt, Jason noticed the man was still breathing.

Jesus.

Nothing he could do. Helen was still handcuffed to Rees, standing in her own pulsing blood thicker than the adjoining darker stain. Her eyes red and swollen from the effects of the gas. She was priority.

While the Sergeant was busy checking Flynn's pulse, Jason charged. "Undo these," he kneed him in the groin, making the cop double up in agony. "Now!"

With his glass weapon hovering close by, those silky hands soon got busy on the cuffs and once unlocked, Helen collapsed into Jason's arms. Her blue fleece still wet, her whole body shaking, but his at last. The Fuzz tried to stand, but the sharp, glass point prodded him back. "What's going on?" shouted Jason, "Flynn's still alive."

"Leave him be or you'll be next for the cross."

"The cross?"

"Careless waste of skin, him."

Jason felt bile burn the back of his throat. "You sicko. You tried to top me as well with that car." He kicked again and felt better, but Helen was trying to reach her ex-boss. He pulled her away. "Let's go while we've a chance."

Together they somehow made it down to Flynn's empty study. Having slammed the door behind them, Jason heaved open the sash window opposite. Seconds later, Rees was advancing into the room like a crazed buffalo. His Glock's muzzle pointing their way.

"You first," Jason hissed to Helen. "I'll hold you. Come on! He might shoot."

"I can't. Look at how much blood I've lost. It's no good. I'll never make it. She's killing me. Maybe Betsan meant *her* when she said Gwenno's mouth wasn't the only one who'd done her harm."

"If you start writing it, I'll stop making her suffer. Your Helen. If not... If not..."

"Ssshh."

He didn't need to ask who she meant and, holding Helen tight, felt her lightness against him. Saw her lifeblood covering his boots as he lifted her out into the ivy's wet embrace and slammed the window shut behind him.

On their way through the ivy, Helen's 'Curse'-word crept into his mind like a death watch beetle emerging from a crack in some old piece of wood. He clung to her cold hands even more firmly as she managed to find footholds and made progress downwards. He wanted to tell her he'd never let her go. To say so much, but Sergeant Rees was very much alive and, judging by those continual banging sounds coming from behind the house, Prydderch was probably somewhere out there, too.

"Just tell that freak you'll write her sodding story," Helen begged. "Tell her you'll spend every minute of every day of your life doing it. That's what she wants, isn't it? Margiad Pitt-Rose and you, with me off the scene."

'Begin now, or I'll see she never bears children, never...'

***

Helen needed a hospital. Fast. Nothing else would do. How could he

268

explain to her how he'd not had time to appease that terrible voice? How Helen's possessions had all gone from her room? They could come later. If there was a later.

And then, while negotiating the last of the ivy's wet embrace, he spotted a pair of black cars parked side by side along near The Drop. A Porsche Boxster and a VW Passat. Two slugs glistening under the Devil's rain. That was when the first gunshot from above stirred up a gravel dervish, sending up grit into their eyes.

***

Rees was glaring down from the open window, hurling abuse and firing off target as Jason and Helen finally reached the ground and, with a last, desperate effort, reached the first car.

Not only was the Passat's alarm disabled but, by another miracle, its ignition key still lay in the lock. Both front tyres stood skewed away from the edge of land as if ready for a swift getaway. But, who owned it? And the Porsche? Surely the Fuzz hadn't done *that* much overtime? His phone was ready. He punched in 999. Would God grant him a third miracle? No.

In disgust, he chucked the piece of glass awa;y then, hidden by the Passat's far side, made Helen comfortable on its beige leather rear seat. The plaid rug he'd found in the boot staunched her blood loss as he started the engine and with a sinking heart felt the rear near tyre deflate.

"Fucking 999."

Out of the drive now, the car was listing badly, but still driveable as, with terror in her eyes, Helen relayed DCI Jobiah's latest message received in Llandovery. How the suddenly determined Sergeant Rees had driven here like a maniac and once they'd stopped, had fondled her breasts before adding his restraints.

"There's nothing to worry about any more," Jason lied to her, feeling ill. Neither he nor DCI Jobiah had warned her about Sergeant Rees. "Try and chill. Shut your eyes."

"I can't. I know Mr Flynn killed Betsan but I keep thinking of his horrible colour, his curled-up feet and what they'll do to him…"

"He betrayed you, remember?" Jason finally found the right wiper speed and reached back between the front seats to touch her hand. "Both of us. But we have to move on. Together." Through the rear view mirror, he saw her faint smile. He slipped into first gear and the car lurched in the direction of the drive. As it did so, the air inside seemed to cool to a sudden chill. His hands felt as cold as when he'd been digging around in that Angred shaft. He blew on his fingertips. Turned the car's heating to maximum.

"I thought you weren't interested in me," she announced. "Why I gave up trying to reach you. Your phone was dead every time."

"When?"

"Once I'd reached Bristol."

"That's weird."

Like Gwilym's camera stopped working.

"It's her again."

"Stop saying that."

"You must have thought I'd not forgiven you for that stunt in the kitchen."

A knot of grief and fear seemed to tighten beneath his belt. In just four days they'd not only been to Hell but upon reaching the still open iron gates, he knew they were unlikely ever to leave it.

He kept the VW in second gear along the downhill track, praying his driving skills were still OK. He'd not been behind a wheel for years – never needed to in London. The half-full tank would easily get them to Llandovery's Cottage Hospital, but what about the blown tyre, splat-splatting with every rotation of the wheel? Even more disturbing was that despite the blasting heater, the cold inside the car seemed to be getting worse.

"They took my best phone," she added, out of the blue. "While I was asleep."

He glanced round at her. "Who did? Where?"

And by the time they'd passed the pub where Flynn's computer was now under lock and key, he'd learnt more of her fraught weekend. Realised too, that his normally robust heart had slowed down. Would they both freeze to death in this luxury car? Why else was a growing crust of ice lining the windscreen? And where the Hell was that promised police helicopter?

With one hand he rubbed away just enough to see through the glass, then leant over to open the glove box. Beneath a packet of Murray mints, travel tissues, some loose cigarettes, lay a small, white envelope already torn open. The details on the front made him swerve too close to the overgrown verge.

R. D. Prydderch,
Hafod Wen
Cilycwm, Carms.

"What's the matter?" Helen mumbled.

"Nothing. We'll soon be there."

"It's so... o... cold."

"I'm doing my best. The heating's kaput."

He pulled out the enclosed invitation to Geoffrey Powell QC's address in Dinas Powys this coming Friday at 7 p.m. for a new members' meeting and investiture.

Investiture?

60 m.p.h was too fast but right now, not fast enough. If that flat tyre fragmented, they'd be toast. And then, to add to the chill, she relayed yesterday's frightening encounter with her enemy in the play park. The new threat; how he was now 'my Jason.'

***

"Where's my car?" Helen again, shivering, and this time, trying to sit up. "Sergeant Rees said you'd taken it to Heron House for me."

Toe rag.

"Look, you're priority at the moment, OK? We'll get it returned for you."

She lay back as if reassured, but her normally expressive face bore the colour and rigidity of chalk. Her eyes blankly staring his way. "Hurry," she urged him. "Can't you see what she's doing?"

Meanwhile, his hands had lost all feeling. Likewise his nose and lips. That ice now thicker than ever, harder to scrape away. His nails left angry, dark loops on the glass that too quickly reverted to white. Archie Tait hadn't come to him. But someone had. With a different purpose. To destroy.

"She won't. She can't," he said. "I love you, Helen Myfanwy Jenkins. From the moment I first saw you in your little black suit on the platform at Swansea Station."

"That's why she hates me."

"Not true." But he wished he could believe it.

"Tell my mam and Heffy, won't you? She's pregnant. Something I'll never be..."

"And your dad?" he interrupted, unable to hear the rest.

"Never mind him. Just start writing that story the way she wants it..."

"You mean now? How the Hell do I do that?"

"Just try."

Her voice faded as more sleety spray hit the suddenly malfunctioning wipers slowing down to match his pulse. The stench of early decay closing in as they entered a dripping holloway of still-bare trees where it took too long for him to find the headlights' switch.

He soon wished he hadn't, for the beam picked up something green and chrome butting out from the undergrowth way above the Towy Valley. A

Nissan Patrol's back end. The driver's door hanging open over the abyss.

Don't look. Keep going. Maybe it's not him after all and this is all just a dream...

***

Once through this eerie tunnel, the frozen road opened out to a world of frosted brown fields and hills as though photographed from a long-ago time. Jason's right heel met the floor, but in his frightened heart, knew everything was too late. The stricken tyre flapped away into the verge as *Paper Planes* eked from his jacket pocket. In his haste, he let the phone slip between his knees.

"Yo, bro," Colin was shouting against a heavy traffic background, the din of a chopper hovering overhead and the grating wheel hub. "How you doing?"

"Fine. Bit on the nippy side, that's all." Nevertheless, Jason's teeth juddered together as he retrieved the phone. His tongue too stiff for his mouth. His tears freezing against his cheek. But would Colin notice? No way. The one thing that *hadn't* changed.

"Me and Lisa fancied a change of scene for a few days," said the financial adviser. "We'll even have a crack at some writing. You never know. Might be me who pens the best seller. So, any spare beds up there? Double or single, no worries. We'll make do."

Jason glanced at his rear view mirror, but its crusty whiteness was keeping Helen invisible. "Sorry mate," he managed to say as the Passat began its own heaving dance from side to side of the narrow strip of tarmac to the other. Out of control now, and on to the far verge, tipping, tipping, beginning to fall.

"Why?"

"I wouldn't want to lose you as well."

41.

Friday 10th April 2009 – 12.15 p.m.

Bad Friday because Helen was sore and starving, with just the faintest whiff of hospital food making her nauseous. Good Friday because Jason whose farewell kiss was still hot on her cheek, had not only managed to keep the big VW from skidding off the icy road last Monday, but also, during three-night time vigils at the Cottage Hospital in company with her mam, he had written the first twelve pages of Margiad's story.

No title yet, but what mattered most was that as the snow outside had thickened, he'd recorded faithfully each word that sing-song voice had delivered. How when her loving mother Joy had died, her depraved father Edmund, and the other crazed incumbents of Heron House, made life for their two children a misery. Especially dear little Charles who'd been so much younger. How all she'd wanted was his happiness...

"Thank God," Helen had hugged him. "She'll leave us alone now, won't she?"

"Course." Then he'd repeated how he'd loved her and promised that while she was convalescing at home, would drop everything to keep the memoir going. How her close shave with death had been because he'd pushed Margiad aside.

'Look,' she'd said. 'We were in a no-win situation. I didn't co-operate either, remember?'

***

As if compensating for Jason's departure, Heffy Morris was on her second visit to Aberystwyth's Bronglais Hospital with two ripe mangoes, the latest copy of Hello! and hair whitened by snow. However, it didn't take long for Helen to realise something was seriously wrong with her best, very pregnant friend. There'd been none of her usual 'Hi Hellraiser' greeting followed by the mad clinch. No 'Poison' overdose either, and why were those normally lustrous eyes welling up? Her typical smile barely a flicker?

"What's the matter, Hef?" she asked, reaching out as her latest visitor perched herself on the edge of the hospital bed.

"I'm OK."

"And I may be stuck here like a turnip, but I'm not blind."

A pause in which Helen's nurse gave her a wave as she passed into the intensive care suite. A busy den of wires and tubes that had saved her life.

"Look, you can always have this when it pops out," Heffy patted her considerable bump. "I mean it. Neither my folks nor the father wants to know, and you and Jason would make brilliant parents. Better than just me. Specially since…"

"Since what?" Helen hadn't really taken in what she'd just heard. But saw mascara trickling down those flawless cheeks.

"You know…"

"I don't."

"God. Haven't they told you or your mam what that evil ghost has done?"

Helen turned to see Eluned Jenkins waiting by the door to the recovery ward. She held a fluffy toy dog in one hand and a bag containing clean nightdresses and other necessities in another. Something normal. Decent.

"Only that I've still got my ovaries. That I'm in with a chance of someday having a baby using my eggs."

Heffy leaned as far forwards as her tummy would allow, her familiar perfume bringing back memories of life before all the crap. Her zebra-striped coat looming large. "That's not true. They're stringing you along. I've just seen your notes. Jason, too."

Helen shook her head. Yet in retrospect, hadn't his reassurances about her partial hysterectomy seemed too quick? His smile not shifted that haunted look from his eyes?

'You're not worth it. I had a child, remember? Unborn, but still something you'll never, ever have…'

Suddenly the snowflakes beyond her third-floor window were too huge, merging too fast, imprisoning her all over again. Was nothing ever going to change? Even with him?

She tried to sit up. Big mistake.

"I told you, he's begun writing her story," Helen said, breathlessly.

"Not soon enough, it seems."

"What do you mean?"

Just then, her mam called out, in her extra loud primary school voice. "Hello, cariad. I've some good news to cheer you up."

Heffy glanced her way then back at Helen. Eased herself off the bed and stood up. "I'll text you, OK? Remember, ask to see your file."

Helen watched Heffy walk away past beds of much older people than both of them. People who'd perhaps got nowhere else to go. Heffy exchanged a quick greeting with her mam who was now on her way. A wide grin stuck on her face.

"I've just seen Dr. Fisher and he says you'll be home in a week. Isn't that great?" She stroked Helen's hair and handed over the toy whose small beaded eyes were Gwenno Davies all over again. "Let's hope the snow's gone by then."

"What are you staring at?"

"You don't seem very pleased."

"I'd like to see the Doctor. Now. And my notes."

"He's very busy."

But Helen took a deep breath, tore her saline drip from the back of her hand and, summoning all her depleted strength, pushed her way out of bed. Dizzy yet determined, she evaded her mam and, as if back on that wet track leading away from Heron House, followed the grey linoleum towards the Ward Sister's desk.

42

Friday 10th April 2009 – 10.10 p.m.

"Just get yourself inside, mate," Colin grinned with relief when Jason sheepishly showed up late on his snowed-up doorstep with their dad's battered suitcase between them, "and if I see another press pass, or have to pick up the phone to some twittering media prat, I'll turn violent."

The hug that followed lasted long enough for passers-by to stare and snigger. "You've lost weight," his bro said afterwards, leading him indoors. "Been worried about you, specially after what you said last Monday afternoon. Mum has too. Is what we've been hearing and reading all true?"

Jason nodded, keen to change the subject and not look at the various newspapers Colin had kept. "Where's Lisa?"

The bitter laugh that followed, caught him by surprise.

"I got her Dear John yesterday, didn't I? But more important, tell me all about your Helen. How's she coping?"

Now wasn't the time to share her latest devastating news. So Jason simply said, "fine so far."

"Great."

However, over beers and pizza in the now less-than-tidy kitchen, he relived the past five days of knife-edged vigils at two quite different Welsh hospitals and how, with Helen's release date confirmed, he'd finally navigated the slushy roads back to Hounslow. No, Eluned Jenkins wouldn't be suing the hospitals for sparing her daughter the worst news after her op. They'd not felt her to be strong enough either mentally or physically to take it. And hadn't he, too, been complicit?

"So what now, Jaz?" Colin had polished off the last of the Kronenbourgs and cleared away the plates. You're not still interested in writing, are you?"

This time the tone was encouraging. "Got you a new lamp and swivel chair, just in case. I also kept your Woolies souvenirs. You happy with that?"

***

A week later, at eight-thirty in the morning, with pen and pad again at the ready, Jason watched Colin wade through the drifted snow towards the gate, stopping halfway to wave up at him. One of the few conscientious commuters opting for what public transport there was. But guilt at this heroic effort didn't last long. He too had an important job to do and, with a fresh mug of coffee plus a hot-cross bun to hand, began reorganising his material. However, since Helen's radical hysterectomy, everything had changed. Gone were Margiad Pitt-Rose's mellifluous lies; the sense of his skin suddenly cooling and those summer roses' scent snaking up his nose. He was on quite a different path now.

Damn.

His phone's ringtone filled the room.

"Yes?"

"George Cooke here. Senior Commissioning Editor at Gemini Books. Am I speaking to Jason Robbins?"

"You are."

"Please spare me a moment, Jason. I've a certain proposition to make…"

***

He and Helen, now minor celebs, had this global publisher wanting a part historical, part contemporary supernatural thriller loosely based on his and Helen's experiences. £25,000 could be theirs, with one proviso. All names and locations must be changed.

Bollocks.

Anger made him screw up that first anodyne chapter from its moorings and toss it in his waste bin. Made him choose a thick black felt-tipped pen and scrub out his working title on the refill pad's pink cover. Having decided on *Cold Remains* instead of *To Love and Lose*, he wrote that instead and underlined it with his red Woolies' ballpoint. Red for blood.

This daring thriller for afterlife sceptics and suckers for the Establishment with himself, not Dan Carver, relentless digger after the truth, would be even more powerful than *Evil Eyes.* Unputdownable in fact, because his and Helen's 'evil eyes' had been real, and this was their revenge. In black and white.

Margiad Pitt-Rose's threats had materialised. Helen would never be able to bear their child as her uterus, fallopian tubes, ovaries and oviducts had all been excised. She'd been punished in the worst possible way.

And wasn't this where it had all begun?

WANT TO WRITE A BEST SELLER?

Spend Easter at Heron House in Carmarthenshire's beautiful Upper Towy Valley, and be inspired by top fiction writer Monty Flynn. All modern comforts. Cordon bleu cooking and internet access. Young writers particularly welcome. Reasonable rates. Regret no wheelchair access.

He flattened the badly-stained advert discovered, together with Gwilym's faded business card, while binning his ruined jeans. He glued it inside the cover. Next, he laid Heron House's two Yale keys on his diary. Important reminders to be handed in at some point.

The freak blizzard's muffled onslaught against the spare bedroom window, suddenly made him look up and worry how Colin was getting on. But neither this nor the fact he'd not slept properly for a fortnight would hold him back.

Cuttings.

Be ruthless, he told himself. Those from the *Times*, *Guardian* and *Big Issue,* Colin had saved were the best. However, their sombre reporting was at odds with the weirdly vivid photos of that hidden crucifixion in the forest. The foul swimming pool and its grim harvest – Lionel Hargreaves, Peris Morgan and two young, innocent boys who'd never made it back to Maghull.

After a scalding sip of his drink, Jason moved the various biographies and comments on the three dead judges, the cop, and their deluded sons, to the top of the pile. Also a grainy image of Monty Flynn as a kid in Crosskelly. Next, Llyr Pitt-Rose gripping a rugby ball while at his special school. Beneath this, two lines from his retired headmistress referred to her former pupil as seriously disturbed, but she believed that somewhere deep down, there'd been a conscience and a need to be loved.

Right.

Posthumously convicted of rape, and of abducting Helen, Llyr's prints had lingered on Flynn's stash in the Angred shaft and on various items at Sandhurst Mansion.

Jason then placed the wartime images of Gwenno and Idris Davies near the edge of his mother's old dressing table near his new Anglepoise lamp. Still no news of the old siblings or the blue Escort, and Gwenno's bunch of keys to every room in the house, left in Margiad's bedroom door, had also mysteriously disappeared. Unlike the two-tone Hillman Hunter.

Despite intense questioning, Sergeant Rees, like DC Prydderch – both under police guard at an undisclosed location – had clung to their Human Rights and stayed silent.

Rees, however, had been found in possession of Michael Markham's Glock, used by Flynn for target practice on Llyr's eyes. A cold, savage killing that kept Membury Services closed for a week. The ex-Sergeant denied any involvement.

Post-mortems, inquests, verdicts...

So-far unidentified fingerprints on the iron ceiling beam next to Charles Pitt-Rose's rope, had confused the police pathologist and delayed any inquest and funeral. As for Betsan, her chloroform overdose had brought a quick end. Her murderer not so. Flynn's heart only fading as paramedics had cut him down from the cross. The narrative verdict on Gwilym Price's death, had meant nothing. He'd been found crushed against his steering wheel on the Towy's frosted shore. His Nissan, like Helen's Ignis, complete with a Panther GPS tracker expertly placed by Llyr. These had been traced back to Royal & Select Master Michael Markham, still missing from his cleaned-out home since midday on Monday 6th April. Other inquests were due to be held next week, although a coroner for the pool's victims had yet to be appointed. Angred shaft had again yielded no more human remains, but Robert Price's well-preserved skeleton had been unearthed from beneath Judge Geoffrey Powell's extensive wine cellar. The man who twice had harassed Charles' solicitor, Dee Salomon.

Sketches.

His for now. Pulled from nightmares and memories, particularly of that unique face with its livid bruise and greedy mouth. Dead birds, and haunted scenes of Nantymwyn which, like Heron House, was sealed off from the crowds of voyeurs and ghost-hunters. Perhaps another publisher would use as many of these visuals as possible and, once Helen was active again, hopefully give her art career a shove.

Letters and other memorabilia.

Charles Pitt-Rose's record of misery, compounded by his schooldays and his lover Llyr's unusual sexual demands, was key. DC Jane Harris had let Jason read enough of it to realise too, how Margiad's once loyal friend Betsan who'd periodically kept in touch with him, had grown fearful of the traitorous heart, hidden beneath those beguiling looks. How whilst still a schoolgirl, the Davieses and Edmund Pitt-Rose, with Margiad and her governess watching, had raped Betsan to stop the girl telling Mrs Griffiths what was going on.

But it was the St. Peter's crucifixion that scared Betsan the most. A torture Margiad wanted used on anyone threatening the staus quo at Heron House. However, her father, being a keen fisherman, had preferred water. Charles had also learnt from Betsan how his jealous sister had engineered his early exit from home so she could have daddy all to herself. In later phone conversations, Betsan had confided how her crucifix had kept that destructive spirit at bay, urging Charles to wear one too. But as a staunch atheist, he'd refused. Had he regretted it? Who could say? Because once

Edmund Pitt-Rose and his associates had killed his heavily pregnant daughter, Margiad, on Christmas Eve in 1946 for being a risk to his career, she'd remorselessly targeted her brother's wavering guilt.

As for the diary itself, Jane Harris had promised that once the four criminal trials had ended, this could be released to help Jason's research. She too, had suggested using fictional names and places for his novel.

Why was everyone so fearful?

Another sip of coffee. A bite of bun to fortify himself as Jason opened what the intrepid postman had delivered earlier that morning. First, an impersonal notification from his former manager at Woolies that his redundancy payment would be in his bank account tomorrow. The sum a pleasant surprise. But his first question was what could he buy Helen to make up for her loss?

Next, a damp blue envelope redirected by Helen's mother from Borth. He switched on the lamp and pulled out a postcard of Aberystwyth's pier:

6a, Ael y Bryn, Aberystwyth.
14th April

Dear Jason, (or should I say Mr Robbins?)
The police have just called to see me and my nephew, which is how I discovered your address. I am not long for this earth and hope you all will forgive me my transgressions. As governess at Heron House, I could have changed much, but my flesh and spirit were too weak. The Devil's magnet drew me in to The Order's arms. Joy Pitt-Rose – a pure and devoted mother – must still be spinning in her grave. Mine will be the sea. I hope most sincerely that Miss Jenkins soon makes a full recovery.
With regrets
Nancy Mair Powell †

That sinister sign after her name made him blink, want to wrap his hands around her scheming throat. He slipped the letter inside the diary's front cover and opened the next envelope. Less damp, prepaid, from Carmarthen, and inside a small monochrome photo of a young Charles Pitt-Rose with a strange one-liner on the back from this so-called governess. Clipped to this, a yellow stick-on note:

I felt you should have this. The Cottage Hospital found it inside Helen's underwear

and passed it to the Coroner.
Thinking of you,
Jane Harris.

Forgetting to breathe, he placed the photo in his jeans' back pocket. Part of Helen. Part of him for the journey. He was about to bin the note when he noticed more writing on the other side:

P.S. I've also found a pre-war photo of Heron House exactly as you'd described it, with those three people standing at the front. They look so normal.

Why I've come back here...
Jason checked his watch. Sod the mid-morning counselling session and not just because of the weather. Like his binned pills, he didn't need it. As for the Radio 2 interview from the flat later on, he was definitely up for that.

Time therefore for the fresh start and, already fired up for chapter one, his writing became faster, more flowing as the prologue was born. Margiad Pitt-Rose, about to give birth to her father's child, was ruthlessly luring the clinging conchie to his death...

***

Just then, from the corner of his eye, he spotted something on the snowy windowsill outside and wondered if some rendering had fallen there. Or a piece of branch. He swivelled his chair round for a better view. Whatever it was, was black and imperceptibly moving.

A rook.

One he recognised by its very white throat. Unfazed by the bombarding snowflakes, this snow-topped creature stared at him with unsettling intensity. What the Hell was it doing here?

He was then distracted by a violent tearing sound and turned to see his completed prologue on the dressing table, being ripped apart by unseen hands.

No...

A ringtone broke the tense, cold silence. He hesitated until the caller's number showed up. Eluned Jenkins was hysterical, almost incoherent. He kept the phone a few inches from his ear. Felt the nearby icy radiator.

"Jason, is that you?"

Not for long.

"How's Helen? I meant to ring last thing..." Jason said.

"She's having a nice, warm bath. But why I'm calling is I've just heard from these solicitors in Brecon, a Mr Shelley it is. He'll be contacting you as well…"

"Me? What about?" He began to shiver.

"Look, Jason, I don't know where to start." She took a deep breath which didn't slow her down at all. "But first, for Helen's sake, I hope you're still writing that mad woman's story?"

"I'm on chapter three already," he lied.

"Good. Well, you know Miss Betsan Griffiths who was killed up by Nantymwyn two weeks ago? Well, apparently, on Thursday afternoon, this Margiad's spooky voice had got into her head, bragging how she'd helped her brother Charles hang himself down in London. Told him he was guilty of incest and should never have been born. How it was his duty to die for that and for not rescuing her when their daddy gassed her and his own unborn baby after promising to take care of them. 'So what's it to be, gay boy and pervert, who used his own half-brother Llyr to satisfy his lust?'" Eluned Jenkins' voice rose to a higher register. "'The rope or the cross? Just don't keep me waiting…'"

A breathy pause followed, in which Jason's cooling skin began to crawl.

"Can you believe it? In 2009?"

Silence.

"Jason? Are you still there?"

"Just about." But his teeth were chattering, as they'd done in that black saloon.

"Well, this Betsan couldn't tell anyone how or why, could she?" The primary school teacher continued in full spate. "Too scared, Mr Shelley said. Except Betsan had known for some time she was the dead man's main beneficiary. Anyway, once the solicitor had checked it out with the Met, and they confirmed Charles Pitt-Rose really had been found hanged, she drove straight over to Brecon and changed her will. In case her own heart stopped beating. I ask you… But not before she'd thrown away her crucifix and this thing stuck on her car's bumper."

"A GPS tracker? Like on Helen's?"

"That's it, but guess what? I've just found another one at the bottom of her rucksack before it went in the wash today. Smaller, mind. No bigger than a shirt button."

What?

He'd checked the thing through last Monday. The day he thought she'd died in the back of the VW.

Silence, in which the ominous black shape beyond the window glass

282

fluffed up its feathers before settling back into place. Helen was suddenly too far away, and her mother was talking again. "Not even the papers have got hold of this latest development. It's been kept really secret."

He eyed the strange visitor again. His circulation leaving his fingertips the colour of pale wax.

"And as for secrets, my Helen never said a thing about Miss Griffiths. Nor you, Jason. Not even when we were at the Cottage Hospital together."

"She'd only met Betsan a few times," he explained, trying to keep calm. "Me not at all."

At least, not alive.

"Anyway, what I'm getting round to saying is, she'd left her own small estate and the big bequest to Helen as she'd felt sorry for her. Tidy too, she'd said. No mention of what would have happened if my girl had died, mind..." Here, Eluned Jenkins' voice broke down, syllable by syllable, ending in a loud blowing of her nose. "So it's all yours if you want it," she said finally.

He noticed both Yale keys now oddly bright despite their distance from his Anglepoise lamp. "I don't quite understand."

"Heron House, of course. Helen won't go near it. And we all know why."

Why I've come back here. Or have you forgotten?

His body felt numb all over except for his gut in freefall. He got up unsteadily for a closer look at the window, but not until his freezing nose was almost touching the whitened glass, did his heart fully flip. For he realised that in the rook's open beak lay a small, green-stained bone bearing brown mossy tufts at each end. Identical to the specimen Gwilym had pocketed. Had this really brought his old friend such bad luck? That shocking end? If so, he, Jason, surely was to blame.

He gripped the inner windowsill, holding his breath, repulsed yet hypnotised as that malevolence, with an even more steely expression in its eyes, began to tap her baby bone against the glass.

Sparkling Books

Imaginations

David Stuart Davies, *Brothers in Blood*

Sally Spedding, *Malediction*

Luke Hollands, *Peregrine Harker and the Black Death*

Tony Bayliss, *Past Continuous*

Brian Conaghan, *The Boy Who Made it Rain*

Anna Cuffaro, *Gatwick Bear and the Secret Plans*

Nikki Dudley, *Ellipsis*

Alan Hamilton, *Two Unknown*

Amanda Sington-Williams, *The Eloquence of Desire*

Perspectives

David Kauders, *The Greatest Crash*

Daniele Cuffaro, *American Myths in Post-9/11 Music*

Revivals

Carlo Goldoni, *Il vero amico / The True Friend*

Gustave Le Bon, *Psychology of Crowds*

For full list of titles and more information visit:

www.sparklingbooks.com

Sparkling Books